Sam de Brito is a writer and journalist who stays out of trouble in Sydney, Australia.

SAM DE BRITO
THE LOST BOYS

PICADOR
Pan Macmillan Australia

First published 2008 in Picador by Pan Macmillan Australia Pty Limited
1 Market Street
Reprinted 2008
Copyright © Sam de Brito 2008

The moral right of the author has been asserted

All rights reserved. No part of this book may be reproduced or transmitted by any person or entity (including Google, Amazon or similar organisations), in any form or by any means, electronic or mechanical, including photocopying, recording, scanning or by any information storage and retrieval system, without prior permission in writing from the publisher.

National Library of Australia
Cataloguing-in-Publication data:

Brito, Sam de.
The lost boys/author, Sam de Brito.
Sydney: Pan Macmillan Australia, 2008.
ISBN 9780330423786 (pbk.)
A823.4

Typeset in 11/15 pt Sabon Roman by Post Pre-press Group, Brisbane
Printed in Australia by McPherson's Printing Group

This story is entirely fictional and no character described in this book is based upon or bears any resemblance to any real person, whether living or deceased, and any similarity is purely coincidental.

Every endeavour has been made to contact copyright holders to obtain the necessary permission for use of copyright material for this book. Any person who may have been inadvertently overlooked should contact the publisher.

Papers used by Pan Macmillan Australia Pty Ltd are natural, recyclable products made from wood grown in sustainable forests. The manufacturing processes conform to the environmental regulations of the country of origin.

For Marce

In the middle of the journey of our life
I found myself in a dark wood,
For I had lost the right path.

Dante, *The Divine Comedy*

CIGARETTES AND VENTOLIN

It's difficult coming to terms with the fact you have no talent, no discipline and no hope of achieving the ridiculous Panavision wet-dreams that constitute your ambition.

I am no one.

I walk down the street and nobody looks at me, no one could even tell I've been here. I clean up after myself, put my schooner back on the bar and then I'm gone, a brown-haired, brown-eyed guy you don't remember being in the car next to you at the lights. A shape. A frown maybe, because I have a tendency to frown nowadays, coming to terms as I am with having no talent, no discipline, no clue of how I'm gonna get through this life.

I guess I should start with a job but they all suck. I hate working for people because you spend so much time worrying about their bullshit. And when their bullshit actually starts to mean something to you (and it always does), that's when I quit. There's nothing more depressing than listening to some dude getting passionate about human resources or inventory tracking software. I mean, that's someone's life, but it's not mine.

Which leaves? A lot of spare time. I made a little money recently and I'm sipping that to its dread conclusion, but mostly I just sit around and try to work out what I'm meant to be doing. I take a lot of naps, smoke a few cigarettes and masturbate quite a bit. I've got a routine.

I've been awake about three minutes before I have my first ciggie. It's just after 8 am and I've tried to clutch the last wisps of sleep to my face, hold them around me for another few, sweet minutes of nothingness, but then I'm awake.

I look around me, get out of bed like I'm emerging from a tomb, shamble into the bathroom and piss. I know I should at least look outside and see what sort of day it is, consider movement, joy, life, something, but it's already too much and I fall back onto my stained sheets like I've been felled by a sniper's bullet and search for the essentials on the floor beside the bed.

Cigarette. Lighter. Ventolin.

I'm sorted.

The ashtray is filled with butts, dirty question marks, the only real indicator I have that time's passing. If you emptied the tray out while I was asleep I wouldn't know how long I'd been in bed. I spark up, hating myself for doing this again, for not even having the strength to get out of bed, but it's too much. The weight of everything I haven't done right in my life rears up behind me like the shadow of a cartoon villain. I don't want to think about it.

I smoke the ciggie, suck the bad nipple, roll the fumes around in my mouth, the benzene, the formaldehyde (mmm, embalming fluid), ammonia (yum, toilet cleaner), acetone (aaah, nail polish remover) and, of course, the nicotine, carbon monoxide, the dimethylnitrosamine, ethylmethylnitrosamine, and all the other members of the 'ine' family, the vinyl chloride, urethane, hydrogen cyanide, acrolein, acetaldehyde, indole, acetonitrile and nitrous acid.

I hate every one of them but not as much as I hate myself.

I smoke like I'm about to get on an approaching bus, almost desperate, seconds between each puff; draw, exhale, draw, exhale, until the nicotine's fingers tickle the back of my neck and my heartbeat kicks up. I'm trying to read a book, some shit by Tim Winton that people tell me is incredible, but I can't even focus on the words. The lines shift up and down as my asphyxiating brain sizzles for oxygen, so I pull the book closer. No good.

The ciggie's almost gone, almost time to sleep again. I suck the final three millimetres of saltpetre, take it all the way to the cork and stub out. I'm dizzy now, overcome by baccy spins, so I search for the Ventolin, hear it rattle in the covers, then clamp my lips to the good nipple. One puff, two puffs, three, I feel my seared lungs open a little wider and I roll onto my back, clasp my hands on my chest like a corpse in a coffin and go back to sleep, sleep, where this shit all goes away.

HAS NO EFFECT

I get off the bus at Kingsford Junction and my stepdad is waiting for me in his big green Mercedes with the personalised numberplates so I can go into the White Horse and score.
— How many? I ask, taking off my school tie.
— Can you get four?
— Yeah, that'll be sweet, I say and he gives me eighty dollars.
Shamus has been on the beers, but it's Friday, so that's not surprising. What's surprising is he's got eighty bucks. My mum keeps him on a pretty tight leash financially because when he gets too much spare cash he tends to . . . well, do what he's doing now. Shamus has got a playboy's head of dark curly hair and wears a lot of silver jewellery with business shirts open to his diaphragm. He reads the news on television, so he's worried if he scores himself, people might recognise him. The lesser of two evils is to send me instead.
— Don't tell your mother, he says and I slam the door.

I go in through the pub car park and into the back bar where the Maoris hang. It's pretty dark but I can see the three hundred pound shape that is Jimmy sitting near the pool table. A few of the other dealers nod encouragingly at me, but I beeline for Jimmy. He won't rip me off and his missus usually goes deep into her handbag for the fat deals, feeling for the buds inside the twists of silver foil.

– Here, boy, this is a big one, take this, she'll say.

If I'm lucky, they'll have Buddha sticks, still wrapped in cotton thread on a wooden skewer. Or maybe just some dirty purple sinsemilla heads encased in those foilies his missus has quivered in her purse. If there's hash around, Jimmy will have a dozen little brown blocks stuck to the wall, camouflaged against the wood panelling of the pub, which he'll peel off and hand me.

As soon as I get close, I know it's not on. Jimmy won't make eye contact and his missus is smiling, which she hasn't done since a bloke got hit by a ute in the roundabout outside the pub last year. So I'm told.

I have a quick look around and spot the white bloke at the bar with neat hair. I just keep moving and hope he doesn't twig I'm underage. I walk out and go the opposite way to Shamus's car. He knows something's up and drives to the other side of the roundabout and onto Bunnerong Road to pick me up.

– No go, there's a copper in there.

– Jesus fucking Christ, Ned, he says and looks through the rear-view mirror.

I try to peek over my shoulder but Shamus grabs me, his hairy arm trembling with strength.

– Don't fucking look back.

– Sorry.

– You never look back.

We blast down Bunnerong, passing my old school, Daceyville Public, then hook into Botany Road.

– Is it okay?

– I think so.

– Why you so worried?

– Jesus, Ned, this car is well known.

Shamus is convinced he's under surveillance. It may be that the New South Wales Police has the money to follow early morning newsreaders around town. Or Shamus could just be paranoid from all the dope he smokes. It's a hard call.

– We can go down the Coogee Bay, if you want?

– What about your other bloke?

– Chook? Yeah, I can try him but he's not doing foilies any more.

Shamus digs more notes out of his wallet.

– Get an ounce.

Having a stepdad who's a conspicuous consumer of marijuana has its pros and cons. On the upside, when he's throwing zeds at the ceiling, leaning-tower-of-ciggie-ash arcing out of his fist, you can always dip into his bag and filch a few sticky heads. On the downside, he does the same thing to me while I'm at footy training, which fucken sucks.

Shamus drops me down the road from Chook's place, which is on Anzac Parade.

– I don't wanna wait here in the car, he says.

– I'll walk home, alright?

– Be careful, sweetheart, he says and gives me a wet kiss on the forehead.

Chook's a Leb, and a psycho, but I've scored enough times from him down at the Bay that he lets me come to his house now. Still, he's a little surprised when I ask for a full ozzie.

– You better not be foiling this up and dealing on me, you little cunt, he says.

– Nah, we've all thrown in. It's cheaper this way, there's

eight of us.

Chook's wearing a 'Bula Fiji' singlet with Rabbitohs trackies and Dr Scholl's masseur sandals.

– These cunts know you're getting it from me?
– Na-ah. As if. I've said naught, I swear.

He closes the front door behind me.

– Two hundred.

I give him the cash.

– Wait here.

He flip-flops back down the corridor into the lounge room, says something and a chick with dyed blonde hair pokes her head around the door, then disappears. I hear Chook fart.

– Fuckin' pig, says a woman's voice.

Chook comes back, smiling. When he's halfway down the hall he throws the ozzie at me.

– You better not be lying to me, cunt. You steal my customers I'll punch your teeth so far down your throat you'll have to stick your toothbrush up your arse to clean them. Eh?

I wish he'd get some new lines.

I get outside and have a look at the ozzie. It's chocolate Buddha. In-fucken-sane. After selecting the choicest buds for myself, I take the gear home to Shamus, who's sitting on our green corduroy couch with Uncle Doug listening to Willie Nelson at brain damage volume.

Uncle Doug isn't really my uncle, he's my stepfather's best friend. He wears powder-blue safari suits and smokes Camel unfiltereds that give him an enormous, jungle cat cough that brings up quivering globs of brown-flecked phlegm. If he's very drunk, the phlegm stays on the suit. Doug and Shamus smoke a lot of dope, drink whenever possible and will ingest any chemical you put in front of them. They're a fearsome double team and extremely pleased with the ounce.

– Where do you get this stuff, you little cunt? says Doug, who takes immediate control of the ounce and I realise it must be his cash. He doles out more buds as reward and I stuff them into one of those small plastic canisters you put 35 mm film in.

When I get home about midnight from the Pigs, I find Shamus and Doug asleep in exactly the same position I'd left them. The coffee table is a mini Pompeii, scattered with ash and dope stems. Both of them are snoring feloniously, chins resting on their chests, chewed-up dope on their lips. The sandwich bag that held the Buddha is empty. They've gotten so stoned they've given up on smoking and eaten the rest of the buds out of the bag like they're Cheezels.

I make a sandwich in the kitchen then switch the telly over to *The Graham Kennedy Show*. Shamus stirs and starts to mumble.

– Has no effect, he says.

The next day, Shamus hits me with a wad of cash and sends me back up to Chook's place for anothery. Less than twenty-four hours after I bought the last ounce, here I am for an encore. As soon as I see Chook's face, I know I've made a mistake.

– I knew you were dealing, you little cunt, he says and grabs me by the throat and pins me in his hallway. Self-preservation seems a better idea than protecting the questionable celebrity of my stepfather.

– It's for me dad.

– What?

– The ounce was for me dad and he wants another one.

– He smoked that whole ounce last night? says Chook, suddenly impressed.

I nod and he lets me go.

– I want to meet this guy.

This is the way a lot of people respond to Shamus.

– Your old man's a wild bastard, he's a fucken legend, they'll smile, shaking their heads, then recount how he'd smoked, drunk or snorted them under the table before walking through a plate-glass window. I just smile and laugh as if I'm indulging a reckless child.

Everyone loves it when the circus comes to town. Just try living with the big top on your front lawn.

THE REGIS

We've moved downstairs and, though none of us will admit it, we're standing at a tall table closest to the TAB so Scorps can punt. It's a welcome-home drink for Chong and Grumble, who are living up the coast, and they've had enough of Tinseltown, the wanker cocktail bar upstairs. I'm through the euphoria of the first six schooners and the beer is sitting in my guts like alien spawn, expanding, scrabbling, drawing me into moroseness. I'm watching Scorps, the fat cunt, wondering where my mate went. He has to be in there, under the endomorph physique and the twenty kilos of beer fat; the dude who used to pull in at eight foot Ho'okipa and scare the shit out of tourists leading them down Haleakalā volcano at dawn as a mountain bike guide. He used to be fearless, Scorps, now he looks like he'd shatter if you touched him in the wrong spot.

He watches the TAB screens through an awkward exhalation of smoke, then waddles over to scratch out another pointless bet. I can't remember when he even took up the durries, but he looks like a teenager just getting started; he gulps at the smoke and exhales like it's a bite of Brussels sprout. Scorps always loved his drugs and beer but now he's taken up gambling and eating and the busters with equal relish. He's got the full set of bad habits. I hope he doesn't start fucking kids or beating his missus, but that wouldn't be Scorps's style – too much effort involved. At his core he's a supremely lazy human being. I reckon he'd shit his bed if someone would clean it up for him.

– Fuck, see this? he says to us, motioning with a paw full of TAB tickets. – This thing was fifty to one and it just got beat by a short half-head. I would have won two grand if it had gotten up.

He looks at us completely amazed by his punter's prescience.

Ever noticed that every cunt that gambling gets by the throat turns into the same bloke? They tell you about their near misses and big wins but never how much they're doing their arse.

– I got twenty on this one, Dave's Domain. That's for you, Grumble, says Scorps.

– Yeah, well, give us the fuckin' money if it wins, says Grumble.

When he's around us, Scorps bets on horses, dogs, trotters – whatever the fuck it happens to be – that are named after one of the boys. It rationalises his degeneracy, like he's only doing it for us. I want to punch him, knock some sense into the cunt, but it would just end with him giving me that beaten mongrel look that says, 'You're always hurting me; I understand and forgive you because you're my best friend.'

I drain my glass. Fuck this. That Pink Floyd song 'Time' floats into my head:

Every year is getting shorter,
Never seem to find the time,

*Plans that either come to naught
Or half a page of scribbled lines.*

I wish I hadn't listened to that album again. Ever since I got an iPod, I've been trawling back through old albums. Scorps and I used to listen to Pink Floyd stoned out of our gourds when we were sixteen and nod wisely at the deep lyrics. Now they're positively terrifying.

*And then one day you find,
Ten years have got behind you,
No one told you when to run,
You missed the starting gun.*

Some snaked-faced Bondi moll is hanging around the table. She's got greasy hair and's wearing trackie pants. Old school Bondi. Ground floor flat, couch on the lawn. Scorps takes her to one side and they chat about something, probably coke, then she circles back to our table, looking outraged.
– Where's me drink?
The boys look at her.
– Who the fuck are you? says Grumble.
– Who the fuck are you, mate? she replies.
He turns to face her, smiling, open.
– I'm David and I'm having a drink with my friends. Where are yours?
– Who took me drink? she says, rushing by Grumble as though he's trying to fuck her. Jesus.
Chong looks at Scorps for some explanation but I don't need one, I know what's going on. I need another drink.
– Whose shout is it? I ask but everyone's still wading through theirs.
We're gettin' old: the chins are dropping, the guts pressing

at our Quiksilver T-shirts like bubbles in custard; it's starting to happen. Where the fuck did we go? Who are these cunts? What happened to you, Chong? You disappeared up to Angourie with Grumble to get out of Bondi but I suspect the big move was so you two wouldn't get hassled about pulling cones all day. And you, Grumble? You seem on the verge of a rape or assault charge every time I see you. After twenty years I still can't work out what you're so pissed off about all the time. And Birdy? At least you're not as rooted in the gravity of our sad little universe but then, you're dealing with fucking the same sheila for the rest of your life. How's that working out for ya, sunshine? What a team. There's no Richard Bransons here. Fuck this.

I decide to get a tweeny and lean against the bar, studying the girls across the other side, wondering where she is, if she even exists. As a kid I used to play the 'Wonder Who I'll Marry?' game. I'd get all warm and gooey walking home from school just knowing she was out there, that the person I was meant to be with was living and breathing somewhere. Now the game's been downgraded to 'Wonder Who I'll Fuck Next?' I wish I could be a little more proactive in the precipitation of the act, but on nights like this it's as much as I can do to stay in the pub, let alone go talk to a woman. That's what porn and heartbreak will do to you.

– Four VBs and a Carlton, I say to the barmaid, ordering the round out of habit, not remembering until she's poured four of them that I'm just buying for myself. She's one of about ten thousand who seem to work at the Regis. They go through them at a rate of knots here and you never get to know any of the molls' names and they never get to know yours. Proactive, I think.

– What's your name? I ask her and she looks at me like I've farted.

– Why?

– I dunno. Someone once told me you should know the name of the barmaid at your local.

– I've never seen you here before.

She hands me the beers and I give her the cash.

– I've been coming here for fifteen years.

– I never seen you before, she says, like I'm trying to impress her with my credentials as a local.

That's the funny thing about this place, it's full of people who've been all over the world or nowhere. And the ones who have been all over the world are usually the cunts trying to sound like they've lived here for years, are old school Bondi, while the ones who are old school wish they could just get the fuck away from the place, afford a house up the coast on the point at Crescent. What did Simmo call it? The great coalface of fuckwits; the fly-by-nighters, who do their five years in Bondi, befriend a Roosters player, get a good coke dealer, meet some tight westie bitch who's moved here while she works a job in PR, they fall in love, she gets up the duff and then they have to buy a house in Condell Park and they're gone, their two-bedroom apartment snapped up by the next Gold Coast model or Sutherland carpenter with an eighty dollar haircut up to the big smoke to make a name for himself as a DJ/dealer/property developer.

Like this bloke. He's got a waxed chest, wearing a singlet, distressed jeans and white thongs, walking up to the bar like it's a *Big Brother* audition when he probably unclogs dunnies for a job. The Bondi tradie superstar.

– Hey, Rhea, he says to the barmaid. It looks as though it's taken him an hour to get his hair as messy as it is. The desired effect is meant to be 'I Don't Give A Fuck' but it's as rebellious as that intentionally ragged handwriting you see on menu boards at Starbucks; it's the comic sans serif of hairstyles.

– Dexter! Baby! she says and kisses him over the bar.

What happened to all the Kevins? I wonder. And the Keiths and Freds and Bobs? Now every cunt is called Dexter, or Dylan or Jed. I steeple the beers and take them back to the boys.

– Where's Scorps? I say.

Chong looks around. Birdy shrugs.

– I dunno.

– I think he pissed off with that thing, says Grumble.

I ring him, I don't know why.

– Where'd you go? I got you a beer.

– I told you I was sweet.

– What are you doing?

– I'm just cruising with a friend.

– A friend? Your friends are back here, mate, not some dirty fuckin' coke slut.

– Neddy.

– Mate, if you gonna let chicks fuck you for coke, at least go the hot ones.

– Mate, I gotta go.

– You're a fuckin' joke, you know that?

I stand at the table letting the boys' conversation wash over me, trying to work out why Scorps's disappearance bothers me so much. I want to believe it's because he's my mate and I wanna see him going forward, extracting joy and satisfaction from life, instead of heading into misery. I finish my beer, then go to the dunny and leave out of the back door without saying goodbye to anyone. I'm on Gould Street when I realise what's really bugging me. It's because I think Scorps is having more fun than me. Because part of me wants to lock myself in some dodgy apartment with a hard-faced scrag and snort the night away.

SCORPS

– Daisyville? Where's Daisyville?
 – No, it's Daceyville, it's spelt D-A-C-E-Y . . .
 – DAISYVILLE! Hey, this guy used to go to a school called DAISYVILLE.
 – No, it's . . .
 – Did youse have to pick daisies at lunchtime?
 – Nah . . .
 – Did you have to be a poofter to go there? laughs the little cunt. His name is Arnold but everyone calls him Scorps because he got bitten by a scorpion on an excursion to the goldfields last year. That little exchange was my third day in high school, Seaview Christian Brothers College.
 Today it's my fourth. As we sit in the hospital-grey classroom, the new smells bubble around me, the urinous groins, the stink of pies on breath, sweat, wet tennis balls in bags, the tang of our wooden desks and the backdraught of carrots and

other mashed shit leaking up from the industrial kitchen that feeds the brothers a canteen of Catholic carbs.

We're all settled and our new form master Mr Fraser – Cyril, to his mates – a lisping, frog-eyed faggot with a happy hand for the strap – is reading the roll when the door is kicked open. It's done carelessly, contemptuously, a gunslinger's entrance, but there's no Eastwood. Instead, it's a midget – or close enough – a tiny, spiky-haired testicle of a kid. He's wearing long sleeves for the first time in his life and they dangle a good two inches past his fingers.

– Master Arnold?

Or Scorps to his mates. He's an old-timer, he's been at the junior school since fifth grade. He's known to authorities.

– You do not enter a room in that manner, says Fraser.

Scorps says nothing. He knows the scoop. Anything you say may and will be used against you in the court of Lou Lou. Scorps's silence pumps up Fraser's temperature. The Frog's an alco – I can see that already from the liver spots on his face, the RSL suntan of burst capillaries spreading across his nose.

A murmur goes through the class. Scorps is getting to him. Lines are being drawn in the chalkdust and Fraser better hop, hop to it if he doesn't want his froggy throne threatened.

– Hold out your hand, he says.

Scorps does, shirt sleeve dangling. The class laughs. Fraser lashes out at him, smacking his bot-tom. That's how Fraser says it and the way he rolls the syllables in his mouth leaves me certain he's sucked a cock. Scorps rolls too, twisting his body and his bot-tom in a practised manoeuvre that takes the sting out of the Frogman's slap.

– Roll up your sleeves, Master Arnold.

Elvis's last shit was quicker than Scorps moves. Another whack. Another roll.

– Hurry up! hisses Fraser.

17

And then Scorps's palm is exposed. I can see a lightning bolt sketched in blue pen on the back of his hand as he stretches it towards Fraser, who holds it, then claws in his top drawer for Lou Lou. She emerges limp, like a piece of warm liquorice but nowhere near as sweet. I can just make out her surface; tread marks. She's a cross-section of a car tyre, a steel-belted radial, and the shiny, exposed ends of the metal are visible in the heavy black rubber as the Frog flexes it.

Her name is Lou Lou and we'll soon be acquainted.

Fraser swings and, at the last second, little Scorps pulls back his hand. Fraser just gets the tips of his fingers. It looks like nothing but it's even more painful. Poor cunt. He'll get another one for being a smartarse.

– Keep your hand still! howls the Frog.

Swack!

This time he connects and Scorps's face betrays him. He takes back his hand and squashes it in his armpit.

– The other one, says the Frog.

Frog versus Scorpion. The Frog's winning.

Scorps hands over his palm. There's evil in the little cunt's eyes now – Fraser Will Go Down – but there's glassiness there as well and the kid hates Fraser more for the tears than the pain in his hand.

SWACK!!

This one's even harder.

CLUBBY WANKERS

– Look at 'em, says Grumble as I paddle with him. – Motoring around like faggots, polluting the water, scaring cunts with their fuckin' inflatable homma craft.

We stroke hard to get under the next one. I shift my knee down, balance and duck under the wave as it breaks on me, peeling over my face. I open my eyes in time to see the clubbies just make the set, punching the rubber ducky through the breaking lip at forty degrees.

– Ooooh, almost, I say.

– How much would you love to see 'em flip that fuckin' thing? Get a propeller up those tight cossies of theirs?

It's such a beautiful day. I dunno what Grumble is so wound up about. Bondi's buildings are out in their pastel best – Ravesi's Corner, Cairo Mansions, Oceanic Mansions, Majestic Mansions, all the fuckin' mansions, the Empire.

– What fuckin' good do they do? Walk around all day,

wearing their stupid fuckin' hats, saving drowning fuckin' wogs and Jap tourists and as soon as the swell cleans up they stick the fuckin' flags right in front of the best spot on the beach.

– They're useless, I agree.

– I bet they suck each other off in their surf club, listening to Dave Matthews.

– Wendy Matthews, more like it, I say gingerly. I'm not that comfortable with Grumble, we're still feeling each other out as mates; it's only taken eight years so far.

– That'd be right. Fuckin' useless cunts, he says.

A mini set has squeaked past the bobbing pack camped on the peak and walls up nicely inside. Grumble sits up on his board, spins, takes two strokes and he's into it. I think about dropping in on him but don't.

– AYYYYYY! he screams at a few grommies inside and then he's up and winding down the line, squatting like he's taking a shit. He trims high as the wave sucks up on the inside and stalls, a sheet of clean green sealing him inside, before, just as quickly, he's out, hooting. He carves back, then winds again and explodes into the lip. WHACK! He doesn't land the floater and comes off in amongst the swimmers who are staring around confused, wiping water from their faces, searching for Grumble's fibreglass death machine. Some hairy-backed Leb, who looks like Gollum with bitch tits, is holding his forehead, a watery line of blood trickling out from under his hand.

– Sorry, mate, says Grumble, you alright?

The bloke nods, disorientated, as the clubbies look over. Grumble scrambles back on his G & S, paddles, duckdives, paddles. I take off on an inside one, nosedive and get spat out onto the bank like a sucked mango seed.

– Fuckin' Lebs. What was he doing there? says Grumble as we paddle.

– It's gettin' alright out here, eh?

– I got barrelled. You see me get barrelled?

– Nah, I say, but I did.

As we angle for the channel, I hear the clubbies on the megaphone on the sand.

– Will the surfer on the green board come in to shore and report to the lifesavers.

– Fuck off, says Grumble.

– Is that you?

– I was fuckin' two foot inside the flags for three seconds and the wankers pull out the megaphone. I know where they can shove that thing, he says, then more loudly, over his shoulder – And your fuckin' rescue boards and rubber duckies and stupid fuckin' condom hats!

– The surfer on the green board, please return to shore. You've been warned about surfing in the flagged area.

Now Grumble sits up on his board and turns, gives them the finger. With most other blokes this would be showboating for the crew. Grumble, however, is hoping they come after him so he can bite some cunt's ear off. He eyes the shoreline, a flap of torn neoprene on his faded wetsuit opening like a gash on his back. Chong paddles past, grinning.

– Carn, mate, do as they say. In you go.

– Fuck off, Chong. Did you see that barrel?

– Nuh, he says.

– Bullshit, Chong, you fuckin' saw it. How long was I in for?

– I saw naught.

We duckdive the next wave together, an elegant ballet, popping out the back and into calm water where Birdy is already waiting.

– How was that one? asks Birdy, who's looking even more Asian than Chong, his pink pommy eyes squinting in the offshore.

– He cleaned up some fat cunt in the flags, says Scorps, who's been paddling behind us.

As soon as Scorps says it, he regrets it.

– What? Fatter than you, Scorps? screams Grumble. His long black hair is matted against his neck like some sweaty chick who's just been gangbanged.

– Fuck off, says Scorps, who's been chubbin' up since he got back from Hawaii. Grumble arcs a perfect golly at him, landing it on Scorps's bottom lip. He flips backwards and ducks underwater like he's got acid on him. We laugh. Grumble slips off his board and flips it over to check for dings. There's an onion ring on the rail, near the tail.

– Fuck! Fuckin' Leb cunt, I've had this board two weeks. Fuck. Fuck. Fuck.

– You fuckin' grot, Grumble, says Scorps, wiping at his face still.

Grumble looks back to shore, where a mass of clubby wankers are gathered around Gollum, checking the gash over his eyebrow. One of the beachies has come over and is pointing towards the peak.

– Ah, Grumble, you in a bit of shit, are ya?

It's Kaspar, the horsehead cunt. He's paddled over with that stupid fuckin' Roger Ramjet chin of his.

– Not as much as you had on the end of your cock this morning, Buzz Lightyear.

– Yeah? Gettin' fuckin' cheeky are we, Grumble?

Kaspar paddles towards him but it's half-hearted. Grumble would fuckin' kill him. Or die trying. One of the clubbies on shore pulls out a two-way and puts it to his faggot mouth. Out the back, the two cunts in the rubber duckie natter away in whatever sad tongue the cocksuckers use to communicate and start to slowly motor towards the pack.

– Here we go, these cunts are comin' after ya, I say.

The clubbies are cruising slowly, checking the colour of the crew's boards. Grumble lies down on his and paddles straight at them swearing to himself.

SODOMY AND WHISPERS

My Uncle Truman was the first person in Australia to publish a picture of a woman's tits. He did it in his newspaper, the *Kings Cross Whisper*. The tits belonged to Karen Miller, twenty-two, of Blakehurst. They were quite nice tits, for the sixties – kinda pendulous and pale, with areolas like wholemeal pikelets – the kind of tits you'd see pop out of your auntie's one-piece when she got smashed by a set wave at Terrigal; not the congealed volleyballs with door-stopper nipples you see on porn stars nowadays. Not that I have anything against porn stars.

I've never met Karen Miller, probably never will, but her tits are still with me. At the time, they shocked Sydney's politicians, priests and assorted other shitheads so profoundly they clamoured for my uncle to be prosecuted and his smut rag shut down. They say there's no such thing as bad publicity – unless you're Michael Jackson or Gary Glitter – and if the politicians and priests and Rotarians had just closed their mouths, the

Whisper might have gone the way of so many other start-up newspapers: bankrupted by public indifference.

Instead, fuelled by the reams of outrage about Karen's norks, the *Whisper* went the other way. Suddenly, people who never would have heard about Karen's tits had to see them. She was ogled and poked and, more than likely, ejaculated over by thousands of readers during her month in the sun. And what's more, people paid for it. This led to my Uncle Truman's none-too-original but nonetheless powerful realisation that sex sells.

Karen's tits were promptly followed by Mindy's, then Rosalie's arse and Tanya's tanned tummy. Truman bought in shots from overseas, set up shoots for local girls and built the *Whisper* into a cum-caked cash cow. Within three years of the paper's debut on the streets of Sydney's bohemian red-light district, my uncle expanded his empire, establishing the first sex shop in Kings Cross – and, let me tell you, there was a lot more than Karen Miller's tits on sale inside.

As a kid I'd go over to my uncle's house in the Blue Mountains and his spare bedroom would be stacked head-high with XXX porn magazines, dildos in boxes, blow-up dolls, lube, edible undies and butt plugs. Sex was *everywhere*. One of my most powerful childhood memories is the smell of latex, drifting off the thousands of coloured condoms that used to infest his house. When I was seven, I even decided my new imaginary friend was Lonni, the gaping, blow-up doll that stood sentry in his makeshift storeroom. I'd run in and kiss her on the mouth every time I visited.

With the advent of the video cassette recorder, Truman's business really took off. Up until the seventies, watching porn was an unwieldy experience that required threading a 16 mm film into a projector and setting up your own screening room; not exactly conducive to squeezing out a quick wank. Then, along came video tape; first U-matic, then Betamax and finally, striding into the market like King Kong with an eight-foot erection, VHS.

My uncle quickly saw there was a quivering, slippery hole in the porn market and proceeded to fill it, buying dozens of VCRs and using them to duplicate adult films. Being the generous type, he shared the wealth and enlisted his sister Abigail – my mother – to run off the dupes for him from the spare bedroom of our house in Kingsford, in Sydney's south-east.

I'm proud to say I was the first kid at school to have a VCR at home. In fact, I was the first kid to have fifteen VCRs at home, all purring around the clock, running off copies of seventies classics like *The Devil in Mrs Jones* (a stunning performance by Georgina Spelvin) and *Insatiable* (starring the incomparable Marilyn Chambers).

After school some days, I'd walk into my mother's converted office and find Leonard, an ex-heroin-addict who worked for my uncle, sitting at an editing machine, cutting down hardcore German and Danish movies so they'd meet timid Aussie standards.

– AAAAWWWWWW, the busty Dawn Knudson would moan on screen as some hairy-chested kraut jammed his beef into her. Then, as he'd withdraw, ready to bang it in her arse, Leonard would hit pause, spin the dials on the U-matic editing machine and rewind.

– WWWWAAAAA, she'd regurgitate in slow-motion as the cock pulled out of her. Leonard would then snip out the offending shot and lay the new 'tasteful' edit down to a master tape. It was then primed to be duped and distributed to the Australian masturbating public, who our government deemed were still not ready to witness the joys of anal penetration.

Truth be told, it was only later in life I realised what was going on in that office. At the time, my sister Megan and I were policed vigorously. When Leonard realised I was lurking, he'd walk into the hallway laughing, shaking his head at my attempts to get a peek at Dawn's woolly gash, and escort me to another part of the house.

Nowadays, people talk about the porn industry like it's this creature that lurks at the edges of strip joints and nightclubs, ready to claw unsuspecting young girls into sin and drug use. Back then, however, my family was the porn industry in Sydney. There were literally hundreds of hardcore magazines and movies to be found around our house. You'd trip over a box in the garage and they'd spill out onto the stained concrete: chicks with dicks, interracial orgies, sodomised nurses and pornographic 'novels' with names like *Daddy's Little Girl* (contrived plot, but still a good read).

Once, when a side table in our lounge room got mashed by a staggering body during one of my parents' many drunken parties, a sealed box of Norwegian gay stroke mags was enlisted as a lamp stand. My stepfather's favourite bong was an anatomically correct vagina – you packed dope in the ovaries, put your mouth to the lips and sucked, the smoke flowing through the fallopian tubes and into his eager lungs. I'd find bottles of amyl nitrite in the bathroom after parties, semen on the covers of the doona in the spare room and random strands of anal beads curled in drawers like centipedes. Sex, everywhere.

THE BERGS

Scorps signs me in and the two of us clomp down the stairs, the ocean view rising to meet us like the horizon in the cockpit of a divebombing plane.
– What you want?
– Veebs, I say.
– They don't got it here.
– Carlton, then.

Apart from taking up ciggies full-time, gaining twenty kilos and gambling, switching from Victoria Bitter to Carlton has been the biggest development I've noticed with Scorps in the last five years. And that's only because the Icebergs serves it. He goes off, puffing on a cigarette that looks too small for his hand and is definitely too small for his fat head. I sit at one of the high tables and take in the waves. It's about three to four but messy and I feel the usual false step of guilt that I'm in the pub on a sunny day and not doing something healthy like hitting the lip of a lefthander.

Sunday nights at the Bergs have been heating up since they renovated the joint, so I've been saving myself. Actually, I just stay indoors from Friday to Sunday arvo and it's only mounting shame that drives me up here by mid-afternoon. The Icebergs swimmers are out of the pool by that time. They do their forty metre race about 10 am in winter and by midday there are fifty of them slamming schooners upstairs in the club.

Scorps has already had about four by the looks of him.

Halftime's at the bar when I prop for my shout.

– Neddy, where you been?

– Around.

– Fuck, mate, you need to get out in the sun, you look like you're made of toothpaste.

– I'm ageing gracefully, mate.

Halftime was our school captain and he's got one of those year-round tans you see in Bondi, usually on blokes going to fat who jog in Speedos on the soft sand. He's packed it on in recent years, probably because he drinks fifteen schooners, five nights a week. He's got Polish blue eyes and has no trouble with sheilas.

– Mate, I've found the secret. As long as you keep your pecs bigger than your gut, you're fine.

– If you wanna end up looking like Anna Nicole Smith, I say.

– If I had tits like her, I'd never leave the house, I wouldn't be able to leave myself alone.

– Sounds like my weekend so far.

– You been flogging yourself again, Neddy?

– I'm shocking. I'm gonna have to disconnect the electricity so my computer doesn't work.

– Then you'll just move on to the lingerie ads in the David Jones catalogue.

– True.
– I'll speak to you later, he says. – I won't shake your hand.

I give Scorps his beer and see he's latched onto Nudge, who looks far less pissed than he does. Birdy's also lobbed, looking sunburnt, with a couple of the Wynn brothers.

– Where's me beer? says Birdy when I hand Scorps his.
– I didn't know you were fuckin' here.
– Come on, mate, he says.
– I'll get 'em, says a Wynn. – Whattaya want?

He heads off to the bar as Scorps belches. It is, as ever, disagreeable, like something you'd hear out of Jabba the Hutt after he's eaten an eel.

– What's fuckin' wrong with you, mate? You're green, I say.
– I've been exercising.
– What? Your elbow? says Nudge and we chuckle.

Scorps doesn't know how to handle attacks from Nudge. He's not really in our group, he's a little too switched on and adjusted. Scorps gets whiny.

– Come on, Nudge, I'm just doing my bit to support the club.
– You've been doing more than your fair share by the looks of things.

Scorps's weight is an easy target nowadays, we all have a go at him, the fat cunt. We're standing in a big circle, some of us with our backs to the ocean, others with backs to the bar. Nudge sees her first.

– Hello.
– Happy days.

She's midtwenties, dyed blonde and aggressively made up. Her skirt's barely decent and her tits are shouting out of a mesh crop top.

– This is a family club, someone says.
– Is she working?
– The Cross is that way, darling, says Halftime.

She walks along the length of the bar looking for her friends, then back down the other end of the room where a few dozen lunchers are hooking into fish and chips and burgers. Blokes' heads follow her wherever she goes but she seems oblivious, anxious.

– She's dropped her gear, says Nudge.

Now her boyfriend appears down the stairs. He's in jeans and a cut-off T-shirt with trainers, heavily muscled, with an undercut hairstyle.

– Look at this dirty Leb, says Halftime, none too quietly.
– Ease up, I say.

Almost every guy in the bar turns to stare at the Leb and after a few seconds he notices, looks around, tries a smile and sees that's not gonna work. He spots his girl and they talk quietly in a corner. For a second I feel like I'm in Alabama, 1955. I don't like which side I'm on.

– Who let that filth in here? says Nudge.
– Dirty little drug-dealing cunt.

There's murmurs all over the bar.

– How do you know he's a drug dealer? I say.
– Have a look at him and his sheila, Neddy.
– He's a grub.

I shake my head.

– Fuck, I might see what he's got, says Scorps and we laugh.
– Are you listening to yourselves? I say.
– Ned, would you want that shit coming over to your place?
– What? Just cos he's a Leb?
– He'd fuckin' rape your dog, says Scorps.

– You're an idiot, I say, and Scorps shapes to belch again. I'm standing directly opposite him as he opens his mouth but this time he fountains a perfect line of pink vomit at me. It looks like a long length of salmon-coloured fabric being pulled from his lips. It lands square in the middle of my T-shirt, a cartoonish splash of colour. Bits get the boys either side of me.
– What the fuck was that?
– What have you been eating?
Birdy has to lean against a table, he's laughing so hard.

ROCKET FUEL

Scorps is in the shower skolling the rocket fuel. He's got even less pubes than me, which is excellent, and his cock is tiny – well, tinier than mine. While my parents were out, we went through the bar and poured an inch off all the bottles into an empty Nescafé jar. It ended up a dark brown colour and reeks.

– Fucken hurry up, I say to him, pulling back the shower curtain that's spotted with mould. He's trying to skol it but he keeps dry-heaving on the taste.

– That's fucken wrong.

Long lines of salty mucus are pouring out of his mouth.

– Don't spew, don't waste it.

He dry-heaves again, the faggot. I cackle and turn the taps on in the basin to make more noise.

– Come on, you homma, don't get your fucken grovel all over the jar.

Scorps goes again and manages to keep it down. His eyes are

watering and he gives me that helpless look he gets when he's been hit by six set waves or is about to spew. It's great being a teenager; the only things we have to worry about on a daily basis are when those pubes are gonna grow and how to avoid getting strapped by Mr Fraser for not doing our homework. The fucken faggot.

I get into the shower as Scorps steps out, his cock a piece of boiled macaroni. For him, the worst is over. He's got the filth down his guts and has managed not to hurl. I wipe away his drool from the lip of the jar and start to chug, gulping it, ignoring the burning in my mouth, my throat, then my stomach. People drink this shit for fun? I heave once but stay on until I see the bottom of the jar drain clear of the brown liquid.

Done.

I heave again and Scorps laughs. He's already feeling it, giggling like a fucken little girl as he dries himself in the tiny yellow bathroom of our house. Shamus bangs on the door and tells us dinner is ready and I sing out we're coming.

– Yeah, bullshit, some Abo will be coming in your arse tonight, says Scorps. Homosexual jokes and racist humour are a sensation at the moment. If you can combine both, even better.

We bail out of the dunny and into my room where I put on a pair of salmon-pink pants, an aqua-coloured Penguin shirt, a canary yellow jumper and light grey leather shoes. I look hell. Scorps is a little more conservative – he doesn't have the eye like me – and has opted for a pair of aqua pants, a yellow Penguin shirt and a pink jumper with white tasselled loafers.

– We look like fucken boyfriend and girlfriend, I say.
– You're the chick then, suck me off.

I grab him in a headlock and flip him across my room, taking out my bookshelf. It's far more violent than I intend but I'm pissed by now. Scorps sits up and all six volumes of *The*

Chronicles of Thomas Covenant fall from the mangled shelves and hit him in the head. I laugh. He gets sulky because I can bash him.

At dinner we're ridiculously talkative and my olds, despite their own drinking careers, somehow don't suss that Scorps and I are para. He's blithering on to my mum about how his dog Legend will lick water out of his mouth. I remind him that dogs lick their arses and cags, so really he's actually sucking his dog's bum and testicles. My mum tells me to pull up.

Scorps pats Winston, our old English sheepdog, who's sitting under the table chewing a lamb shank. Winston has a white fringe of fur that covers his eyes like he's Doris Day. It's a mystery to me how he doesn't run into things. I watch Scorps slowly pull back the fringe revealing the buttons of Winston's bloodshot albino eyes.

– I wouldn't do that, says my sister Megan.

Winston growls an evil low warning.

– Full on, says Scorps and pulls his hand back. Winston immediately calms and lies back down. A moment later, we all sniff the air.

– Is that you? Scorps says to my sister.

I know the smell.

– It's the dog.

– You scared him, he farted, says Megan.

Scorps is impressed.

– That's the dog?

– Yes, we're going to enter him in a competition, says my mum.

35

BOILER

– Chong's chick's gonna be there, says Grumble.
 – Have you met her yet, Neddy? asks Scorps.
 – Chong's got a chick? Is she a gook? I say.
 – Nah, she's an Aussie. An Aussie slut, says Grumble. – Kasp used to fuck her.

I'm impressed. If Kaspar used to fuck her, she must be half alright.
 – Fair dinkum? Is she a good sort?
 – She's a boiler, she's thirty-seven.
 – Nothing wrong with that, I say. I've been fucking a boiler myself. Sally. She's an artist but she's only thirty-six. And I haven't told these cunts.
 – Grumble tried to root her as well, didn't you, Grumble?
Grumble just laughs his impossibly sleazy laugh.
 – What's she like, Grumble?
 – She's alright. I was blind.

– Where at?
– The Cauldron.
– The dirty Cauldron. That says it all.
– Fuck, Chong must be over the moon. He's never had a girlfriend before.
– And she's a white woman, says Scorps.

Chong lives in Council Street, at the top of Bondi Road, with his mum. She's in Korea buying ten thousand pairs of Teenage Mutant Ninja Turtles underpants or a container-load of battery-operated rice cookers. Import, export. Their apartment block is one of those staggeringly ugly jobs that went up all over Bondi in the sixties that make you wonder how many council members were on the take. It looks like the architect was pissed when he drew up the plans. He got to a certain point and said, 'Fuck it, that'll do.'

Grumble buzzes and we wait. The intercom opens at the other end like a lid coming off an empty paint tin.
– Hello? Who is it? says Chong. Such a polite boy.
– It's us, Chong, you fuckin' pig dick, yells Grumble.
– Let us in, I say.
– Fuck off, you dickheads, says Chong.
Then he buzzes us in.

Chong opens his apartment door with a face of complete resignation. He knows how much shit he's about to cop but he's gonna let it wash over him, like a sweet spring shower.
– Chong.
– Pigsy.
– Boys.

I go straight for his groin and pinch the head of his penis. He slaps my hand away and we walk in. Kaspar is already on the couch cooking a baccy. Next to him is an angular blonde whose best years are behind her. Chong stands very straight, rubs his open palms together and indicates the chick.

– Boys, I'd like you to meet Andrea. Andrea, this is the boys.

We wait for more but Chong's not huge on intros.

– Come on, Chong, we've got names, says Scorps and we do it ourselves.

Grumble hugs Andrea warmly and I can just see the scene at the Cauldron, him and Kasp double-teaming the boiler at 4 am, shakin' on the speed. I don't know how Chong handles knowing that she's had the Hun's big horse cock in her mouth. I wonder what her angle is. She was obviously a stunner in her day, but she's pushing forty now and, like most Aussie chicks, has seen her fair share of sun. She's got a western suburbs via Cronulla beach-girl twang, the voice of the pea-brained Aussie. It strikes me as incongruous she's open-minded enough to root a gook. Her eyes are almost Asian themselves, slittish, watchful. She wants us to like her. We'll see.

Maybe it's just the sex, I think as I go to the fridge and help myself to the water jug.

– Is this that barley water shit, Chong? I yell out.

– Yeah.

– Fuck that.

I put it back and go to the tap. Chong's got about twenty years of rooting built up in him. He's a big cunt, handsome enough, got a good body, nice skin. He's bound to be eager to please after a decade in the wilderness wanking over white women. Maybe Andrea's the female equivalent of all those fat expat Aussies in safari suits you see with unenthused Asian chicks?

– So what have you got, Kasp? asks Grumble.

– Hash oil, answers Chong.

– Full on?

Scorps reaches for a small glass vial filled with black liquid that's sitting on the camphorwood chest the Chongs use as a coffee table. Kaspar snatches it up and Scorps nearly knocks over the bong.

– Now, now, Mr Scorps, says Kaspar.

Andrea laughs. It doesn't make me warm to her.

– Give us a look, Kasp.

Grumble goes for the mull bowl and Kaspar grabs that as well, tucking it up to his chin like a modest old lady pulling the sheets to her neck in bed.

– Hang on, Grumble.

– Pack me up, you fuckin' homma.

– Now, boys. You've just gotten here. We've got an order in place.

– Give me a look at the hash oil, says Scorps.

Kaspar motions. He's got all the time in the world.

– Just wait.

– For what?

– For the Kaspar Show, I say.

Kaspar smiles at me like I'm a toddler.

– Yes, Ned, I know it's difficult when we're not talking about you.

Andrea just watches as we pass the bong around.

– You don't smoke, Andrea? I ask.

– Not really, not any more, she says. – When I used to live in Indonesia we smoked so much and the stuff there, it really had a kick, let me tell you, but the stuff you get here, it's full of chemicals, it's not like what we used to get when I lived in Indo.

Fuck, I guess she wants me to ask her about Indonesia, but I can't be bothered. I'm pretty ripped, so all I can manage is – Yeah?

– Oh, yeah. Once we had this bag of heads, it was like this big.

She makes the shape of it with her hands. Big bag. I nod. She's got a story to tell. We let her tell it.

– And we smoked joint after joint after joint. No one smokes cones in Indo. And we must have smoked like half of this bag and we were so off our faces we could barely talk.

She starts laughing at the memory. Chong smiles. I wonder if I'm missing something.

– And then we all had these incredible banana smoothies and the next thing I know it's morning. All of us fell asleep, just like that. We were so off our faces.

She laughs again. I wait, then realise that's the story.

Fuck me, chicks really need to go to storytelling school. The first thing they need to learn is it has to have a point of difference: a funny ending, some sort of killer twist. A joke or line. A piece of wisdom. All the boys are thinking the same thing, then Chong laughs; a slight chuckle.

– Yeah, it happens like that, eh?

ALESSANDRA

I wake, still energised by alcohol, and roll over to find her staring at me.

Here we go again, I think.

I had a ball all night at a barbie and met her as the fun was fading. We came back to my parents' place to scuffle under the bed sheets until the birds told us it was time to try sleep. I ate her out for three hours because I didn't have a condom and every time I looked up from the job she just gave me a half-smile that said she wasn't gonna come in thirty hours.

I do the good-morning stuff and try to recapture some of my drunken attraction to her, but it's plain that she's plain and only the great god of Vic Bitter can once again transform her into the sex kitten she was four hours ago.

– I'll call you, I yell at her cab as it pisses off up the street and leaves me to my scrambled head and coffee. Then I remember. It's Grand Final Day. Beer, the Boys, BBQ chicken. I dress quickly and stop off at the corner store to get a pie and Gatorade for brekkie. A cabbie's getting on as well.

– Wanna take me to Double Bay?

He gives me a nod through his pie and we head up the hill.

The game is well into the first half when she walks in. They're from the apartment upstairs. About twenty-five of us are drinking and screaming at the television when a self-conscious hush comes over the boys. I'm talking to Scorps.

– Have a look at that, I say, and he follows my gaze.

– Looks like more than one game is gonna be played today.

Guru sees us checking the girls out.

– Who's that in the blue with the cast on her arm? I ask.

– Ahhhh, she lives next door, mate, she's got big hands, says Guru.

– How'd she break her arm?

– Dunno, I reckon they're fuckin' lezzos. Go and ask them, Neddy.

I walk towards them, watching the girl in electric blue, and I'll be goddamned if I'm not hearing music in my head. It's the first track from Ministry's second album and I can feel my heartbeat speed up to meet the grinding guitar and I actually stop to check Scorps hasn't slyly cranked the stereo in the corner.

Nup, the music's all me, and as I stride across the patio I have the weirdest feeling I'm walking downhill. When I get to the girls, the lady in blue has already been buttonholed by a big guy with a shaved head. Her less attractive friend stands beside her, smiling relentlessly.

– Hey, how ya doin'?

– Awww, good. How are you goin'? she beams.

– I'm finer than frog's hair, I say. – Listen, I wanted to ask you something. Are you and your friend lesbians?

Smiley bursts into surprised laughter and turns to blue babe.

– Alex, did ya hear that? He just asked me if we were lesbians? And she laughs again.

Alex turns indiscernibly, curling her top lip, and looks at me sideways with huge blue feline eyes. She says nothing.

It's like a trip or an E or the flu. You're standing there and everything's fine, you're tappin' your thigh wondering if it's ever gonna come on, and then like the softest breath from the smallest child you feel it pricking on the back of your neck or at the tips of your fingers, then the base of your calves. A sniffle, a sneeze and the breeze becomes a steady stream, a heady scream, a pulse, a dawn, a lawn growin' in your lap and slap!

Perhaps I underestimated this? Miss?

DISCO

I am completely pissed now, having had two twist-tops on the walk up to school from Charing Cross where we met the rest of the boys. There are two groups of us, really. There's me and Scorps and Birdy, then there's the other guys like Grumble and Kaspar, Chong, Joe Gold, Larry, Suggs and Maggot. They're taller and hairier and can bash us.

Kaspar has two blonde chicks with him none of us have ever seen before. How he has managed to meet, talk to and convince them to hang out with him is incomprehensible to me. I am so awed, it doesn't even approach jealousy. The guy's a fucken astronaut. He's got really good hair, Kasp, and if you like blokes who are tall and have blue eyes and a chiselled, almost equine face, then you'd have to say he's good-looking, the cunt. One of the chicks he's with is named Tara. She's a sort and Kaspar knows it. He's smoking a skinny joint with the chicks and Maggot and Grumble are hassling him for a bit.

– Come on, fuck your sisters off, Hun, pass the joint, says Grumble.

Some of the boys call Kasp 'the Hun' because his dad's German. I don't cos he'd bash me.

– Yeah, yeah, yeah, says Kasp. He couldn't be more relaxed if he was in a hot tub with a geisha pressing blackheads in his back.

– I'm just gonna walk up the road here with my friends Tara and Tasha, ain't that right, girls?

They're giggling like they'd pash him on the spot. Dickhead.

– And we might stop off and watch *your* sister getting lengthed in the bushes, says Kasp. Grumble fakes to punch him in the head and Kasp flinches. Scorps and I just sip our twisties and keep a look-out for teachers.

When we get to the school hall, Mr Jeffries is prowling, smiling, giving us a nod here and there, studiously avoiding extended looks at the arriving girls' arses. It must be tough being a teacher. All that young moot. It's everywhere and it'd have to be hard to know where to look. The whole place is seething with possibility, but it's kind of like being in a French supermarket for me: I look but don't really understand, because I HAVE NEVER EVEN KISSED A GIRL. There's no way I'm telling anybody this, I know what they've got in store for Disco, poor cunt.

Disco is chubby and brainy and his skin is so white we ask him if he's been soaking in Omo. He has an amazing amalgam of Cheezel-orange ear wax, dog brown hair that falls down his face like a tent flap, and goggles for glasses which make his eyes look like onions rolling around in a martini glass. If you can convince Disco to talk to you and that you're not gonna flog him, you find he has a throaty, kinda pompous voice, like he's channelling an English university professor.

He's a bit of a sad case, Disco. He's got some kind of weird foot deformity and has to wear this high-heeled play-boot to school. When he walks, he swings his hip around and it looks like he's disco dancing. Any time anything goes wrong at school, like a window gets broken, something gets grafittied, a sly comment is made at assembly, the teachers will ask who did it and the whole form will rise up in unison. – Dis-co. DIS-CO, we'll say in this kind of singsong voice all one hundred and sixty of us have perfected, which sounds like we're imploring the baddest-arse in the form to turn himself in to the law. School boy irony.

Anyhow, Disco's mum is very protective of the poor fat fuck. She buys him breakfast every morning at this café down the road at Charing Cross and *cuts up his bacon* for him while we're standing around the corner smoking cigarettes. Then, sometimes, she walks him all the way to the gates *holding his hand*. I mean, what is she thinking? Fuck, parents are dumb. Why doesn't she just paint a target on the poor stumbling prick's chest?

Most mornings, Grumble will run up behind Disco as he walks to school from Charo and pick him up by the waist, his arms waving around like that robot in *Lost in Space*. Grumble will then dump him in the bushes, which is weird and kind of dislocating because Disco carries himself with the bearing of that English university professor. Seeing him back-slammed into some old moll's roses is just all wrong, like watching an authoritative prisoner-of-war try to maintain his dignity while being hosed down by an ill-bred Nazi tormentor.

Anyway, someone has told the boys Disco has never kissed a girl, so Grumble has promised his sister, Francine, we'll give her twenty bucks if she pashes him. Francine's blonde, suntanned, a surfer – the last sort of chick who'd ever give Disco a second look usually – so when she busts a move on him later in the night the poor cunt doesn't know what do. There's no way Francine is letting that lobster escape, so despite Disco's food-cluttered braces, ridiculously stilted attempts at conversation and cranking stiffy, she pashes him. Then makes an excuse to get away.

Disco, well, he's dazed. He doesn't know what to think. He's in love. He goes back to his Lapidary Club mates, who're hanging at the back of the hall, eyes glittering with admiration. Disco is stoked. He's waving his hands around like a Hasidic diamond merchant, snatching looks over his shoulder for another glimpse of Francine until he spots Grumble and Joe Gold cacking themselves near the smoke machine. Grumble walks straight up to him, arced like a guard dog.

– You pash me fucken sister?

Disco is horrified.

– Well. Well, actually she pashed me, David.

Poor Disco is on the verge of shitting himself. He's past green but just at the edges of his fear is this tiny shimmer of a swagger, like he's saying to himself, 'Fucken oath I pashed your sister and I might be coming over to your place to play chess soon.' Grumble doesn't waste time.

– We paid her, you dumb cunt. Look.

Francine's in another corner watching with her friends. She turns and waves the twenty.

Disco goes home about ten minutes later.

ASTRAL TRAVEL

About 10.30 am, I wake again.

It's beautiful outside. I can hear kids screaming in Bronte Park, the whistle of those annoying Vortex footballs and touch-playing goobers shouting commands to each other like they're on the front lines at the Somme.

Too much.

I eat. Some toast. Vegemite and butter and a coffee as my computer boots up and I check my emails. I'm hung over from last night but it's a cheap headache. I drank like a madman for three hours, pounded the beers into me like it was still six o'clock closing and was in bed by eight-thirty. Emails, mainly to do with porn, dick pills or university degrees stream into Outlook. I sit down and bang out a few sentences of a screenplay or a novel or whatever I'm working on and then re-read them and am swept by sadness; how mediocre what I've written is, how endless the path to completing something of substance seems. I think about writing some more but it's a weak baby seal of a thought and the rest of me lopes over to club it, splattering the snow with the blood and cranial fluid of reality.

You're a fucking loser, mate.

I need something, anything to make me feel better, even if it's only for a few minutes.

I click on the Explorer symbol. The page isn't bookmarked but as soon as I type the first letters in the address bar, the link's there complete. Maybe it's http://www.1stmovieclub.net or http://www.video-post.com or http://www.hardcorejunky.net. The page loads and dozens of thumbnailed images appear, mainly of beautiful young women on their knees gripping improbably huge cocks and stuffing them into their mouths, semen creeping from the corners of their lips like tomato sauce after you've scarfed a hot dog. Others are backed up to unseen hulks, cunts gaping, arseholes ready, impossibly long legs, suntanned, smooth, open.

A sigh of possibility goes through me that one day I can be with one of these girls. But how? I'd have to be rich or successful or at least fit and muscly. So I beat myself up about being none of those and revert to the job at hand. So to speak.

It may take me minutes or hours to find the sequence of images that possess the right anatomical hot buttons to get me off. My cock will be hard and I'll stroke it every now and again then as I click open windows, sometimes thirty, forty, fifty at once, methodically snapping them closed when the featured woman doesn't meet with my approval: too ugly, too old, too fat, too hard, too slutty, or too dark. I mean, the picture's too dark. That can be very frustrating. I'll find a beautiful girl, being jammed full of man meat, and the vision will be shit or there won't be any sound or she's just not in the correct position to do the job for me.

I guess I'm pretty fussy when it comes to my fantasies but they're my fantasies. What I do need is for the woman to be quite young – not kiddie porn age, that does absolutely nothing for me – but in her early twenties or late teens. On the flip side, she can also be quite well preserved and in her forties. What both kinds of women will have in common is an incredible rig and look like the type of girl *who would never fuck me in real life*. That's what really does it. What's even better is if they bear a striking resemblance to someone who has rejected me in the past.

I like to start with the legs. I've always been a leg man. There's a certain type of woman who has thighs that don't touch when they stand up straight. If they had their back to sunlight, you'd see a silhouette under their vagina, between their legs, which resembles the top of a bishop in a chess set. The legs are tapered at the top of the thighs like a frankfurter that's been cinched shut. They're long, almost mantis-like, with coltish thin ankles and well-formed calves. There's nothing worse than underdeveloped calves on a woman.

I'm also not a big fan of belly fat, so I like a firm stomach, honey skin and a great set of tits. I'm a big fan of sillies. Yes, you can tell they're fake, but who cares? What I actually like most about fakies is what it says about the woman: that she's prepared to mutilate her body to please the opposite sex. This can only bode well for how things will go down once you get into the bedroom.

I also like to get the setting and clothing right. I love those movies where you'll see some demure blonde in a neat suit walk into an office where there's seven guys with ponytails fixing a coffee machine. They'll turn to her and point and she'll show them her labia. Before you know it, they've stuck everything, bar the coffee machine, inside her and are standing around, cocks flaccid, her semen-splattered mouth gaping like a blind baby sparrow waiting for a bug. That sort of stuff just makes me believe in a better world.

Now I right-click the movie and save it into a folder in my tax files, labelled '95'. I dunno why I called it 95 but I think it had something to do with camouflage. I figured if it was just some boring number then people wouldn't be inclined to investigate. Click on it and woaaah . . . I think I got up to about two thousand movies in there at one stage (before the purge). Man, anything you want you can find in old 95. Blondes, brunettes, blow jobs, female, female and male, MMF, MMMF, MMMMMMMF. I dig those.

So away I go. I prefer to use saliva as a lubricant because it's readily available and easy to clean up, unlike creams which tend to hang around all day giving you a filmy feel on the old todger. Sometimes, I'll edit a bunch of smaller clips together to give me a bit of lead-in time – some cinematic context to the gangbang – or other times, if the clip is particularly good, I'll just repeat it over and over.

Now, I've read about prisoners or yogis who can astral travel out of their body but, let me tell you, I can travel into other blokes' schlongs. Give me a half-lit room and a laptop and I'm in the San Fernando Valley waving twelve inches of man beef over some suntanned, siliconed, g-stringed, stoink starlet who's aching for my love mud.

Usually I don't go for duration, because the longer you're in this position, the greater the chance of a girlfriend or flatmate walking in and, well, you know, it could be a little confusing for both of us. Once the deed's done, I like to mop up with a used pair of boxer shorts, which I ferret back into the dirty wash basket, careful not to be detected, and then I sit back and ride out the guilt.

Damn.

Another wank.

Do I have a problem?

I should stop doing this.

Does it make me a weirdo?

All that sort of stuff.

Then I'm back at the computer. That's when the real trouble starts because now I've had the wank, there's really nothing to distract me from confronting I have no talent, no discipline, no hope etc. So I type a few more sentences (notice I say sentences, not paragraphs or pages – it's that bad) and I'll remember I have some dishes to wash, or some boxer shorts to launder or an old hair dryer that I could rewire.

I dunno who said writers love writing but I hate it. It sucks. If my kid ever says they want to be a writer, I'm taking them straight out and tattooing INVESTMENT BANKER on their forehead and locking them in a room with every back copy I can find of the *Financial Review*. Writing is the hardest thing I've ever done. Especially when you have no discipline and no hope of achieving the ridiculous Panavision wet-dreams that constitute your ambition.

So what are those ambitions? Putting it simply, it's to have never-ending threesomes with twin eighteen-year-old models.

Pretty shallow, eh?

Man, I wish I wanted to feed the poor or save harp seals or something noble but threesomes with twin eighteen-year-old models just seems like a whole lot more fun.

Am I selfish? I'd say that's a safe bet.

Am I superficial? Guilty.

Do I give a fuck what you think of me? Now here's the giggle, the real pain in the arse. Yes, I do. I want you to think I'm a good person and, more than that, a worthwhile person. So this is what I'd tell you if you asked me what my ambition was.

– I want to teach people with my writing that it's okay to be themselves.

Pathetic, eh? But really, it's secondary to the whole threesome thing.

Then again, if you got me when I'm a bit pissed and maudlin at the pub, I'd pull out the 'teaching people' line. That's the difficulty, because a lot of the time I am pissed and maudlin so that line doesn't feel like bullshit, it feels like me, until I zap onto the Net and start cruising and see some dude being smothered by teen vagina and say to myself, 'Ah, now that's what life's really all about.'

Around this time (11.30 am) it'll all get too much for me and my thoughts will turn to bed.

Sleep. Where I am king of all teen models.

I'll have a cigarette lying on my futon and then off to the Land of Zeds.

HUNGRY LIKE THE WOLF

The St Brigit's dance has gained mythical significance amongst my mates.

Joe Gold, Kaspar, Suggs and Grumble have been going for a while and claim to have pashed and even fingered girls, but that's par for the course for those guys. I'm still waiting for my pubes to grow and don't have a clue how you'd even talk to a chick, let alone jam one in them. Thank God for twist-tops.

Before the dance, all the boys met up and we convinced a passing tradie to go into the bottlo and get us a case of Toohey's Country Special because it tastes shit and is therefore cheap. Two dozen 225ml bottles split amongst six of us gives us four each. We drink them quickly and hilariously as we admire each other's Penguin shirts, except Joe Gold who's got one with a little horse and polo player. Fancy. We're hyped on the joy of being out and about and alive with it all ahead of us.

– Did ya hear about that chick, Imogen, from Brigidine? says the Buccaneer. He's a fat cunt with terrible acne and super-tight curly hair. He is without a doubt the ugliest boy in our form, but he's strong and can bash me.

– They're all fucken molls at Brigidine, says Birdy, sagely.
– As if you'd know.
– Zif I wouldn't.
– Yeah, well, shut up both of youse, I'm telling a story.
– Fucken tell it.
– So this chick, Imogen, some bloke from Marcellan is rooting her around the back of the church there, except he's para. He's doing her doggie and as he's about to blow he spews all over her back.
– AWWW. FUCK OFF!
– FULL ON!!?
– THAT'S FILTHY!

The Buccaneer always has great stories. He's the male equivalent of a fat chick with a good personality.

– Yeah, shut up, shut up. So she freaks out and starts crying an' shit an' she runs off but this cunt's so blind, he just lies in his spew and goes to sleep.
– AWWW, that's fucken FEK.
– Fucken groveller.

The Buccaneer's loving this. His ackers are glowin' on his face like Christmas lights.

– But then, when he wakes up, he feels something on his chest, eh? This chick, she's made a little nest on his chest with toilet paper and inside there's this fucken huge, sloppy loggy. SHE'S SHIT ON HIM!
– AWWWWWWW, we scream.
– How good's that?

By the time we polish off our beers and arrive at the church hall, things are well under way. I know absolutely none of the females present – going to an all boys' school is not the best way to establish a network of girlfriends – so I just stand with Birdy and Scorps near one of the walls and pretend not to be as drunk as I feel.

A tall blonde with a squarish jaw and blue eyes keeps walking by our group, looking us up and down. She knows Birdy and says hello and then . . .

She. Talks. To. Me.

– You go to Seaview?

– Yeah.

– Do you know Luke Lawrence?

Of course I know Larry. He's the toughest cunt in our form. His arms are thicker than my legs. I've spoken eighteen words to him in four years.

– Yeah.

– Aw, cool, I know him too.

Her name is Maddie and she looks pretty much like what she is – the daughter of a boofy Maroubra copper – but all I'm seeing is blonde hair, blue eyes, blonde hair, blue eyes. She's Elle Macpherson, as far as I'm concerned.

– You wanna dance? she says and I just about pass out.

We're both terrible and Scorps and Birdy are laughing at me, but they haven't got a chick and I have. Sucked in, you dregs. Then I remember what they did to Disco at the last dance and I look around for Joe Gold and Grumble but they're nowhere to be seen. Still, I'm heaps suss.

The first song we get is 'Hungry like the Wolf' by Duran Duran and we're both breaking out some hand rolls and side to side stepping. I even do a head shake during 'Billie Jean' and I know all the words to UB40's 'Red Red Wine'. I can tell she's impressed. We're both getting a bit sweaty and the Moby Disc DJ is sensing a change of pace.

Then something unbelievable happens.

To this day, I don't understand why a dance organised by a Catholic school – which, I think it's safe to say, isn't in the business of teenage sex – would let DJs play slow songs. You'd just beat it into the DJ, wouldn't you? – Four four tempo, you cunt, nothing slower than three four or you don't get paid.

I mean, you bung on 'Sweet Dreams are Made of This' by the Eurythmics, what do you think is going to happen? You have to pull in closer to your partner and even a glacially slow mover like me will get around to grabbing the chick's hand. I can't really tell if Maddie wants me to kiss her but, by the time I even consider it as a possibility, the song is over.

The DJ, however, must be bucking for an orgy. He follows up with 'Reunited' by Peaches and Herb then, incredibly, astoundingly, 'True' by Spandau Ballet.

Even I can't fuck this up.

By the time Tony Hadley is getting through his second lot of 'Ah Ah Ah Ah Ah' Maddie is in my arms, her lips feel for mine and it's like I've slipped *inside* her. My tongue is like an otter released into the wild as I slide into the hot silk of her mouth and the music buzzes around us. Fuck me, I knew this was meant to be good, but I feel like I'm swimming in hot Milo, it's like Maddie has fairy lights strung through her hair and life hasn't even existed before this moment. This was the feeling I've been searching for, the reason I'd sensed for plodding around this fucken dirt circle. I don't want to open my eyes, don't want to dare break the mood, but I can't help thinking about Disco. What if this is a rort? What if the cunts have set me up?

I creak my peepers apart and see Scorps and Birdy winking at me through the red haze of the disco lights. Both of them have no concept of a poker face. If I was being scammed they'd be cacking themselves laughing, so I return to Maddie's neck and mouth.

The thing about kissing is, even though I've never done it

before, I'm good at it. I'm gentle and responsive and I use my tongue judiciously, not like an archaeologist's pick trying to mine Maddie's chocolate Moove-fed fillings. She senses my skill because she doesn't leave my side for the next few hours, blinking up at me every time we break for breath and she SMILES.

She's far more experienced, a pash princess from the dark streets of Maroubra Beach, but she humours me this night and as I run my hands over the stretch fabric of her fluoro yellow tube skirt, it's like melting into dark chocolate, like we've become a marbled confection and if we cooled we couldn't help but stay that way forever.

'Burning Down the House' by Talking Heads kicks in and we move over towards the wall to continue kissing and I even brush Maddie's arse a couple of times before a nun materialises to separate us. What's even more surprising is Maddie seems really happy to have kissed me and wants me to call her.

– I have to go, my mum's picking me up, she says.

And then she's gone, her blonde locks bouncing away – my princess, my goddess, me love. I've got a stiffy you could punch holes in leather with. I FUCKEN PASHED A CHICK.

My joy lasts exactly fifteen seconds before the Buccaneer sidles up beside me and snorts in his mock villain voice.

– You know that's Larry's girlfriend, don't ya?
– Luke Lawrence?
– He's gonna bash you. You're fucked.

THE KASPAR SHOW

The only reason I see Kaspar now is because he's dealing. Even then, the small snatches that I see of the guy are like walking into a never-ending commercial for Kasp. He never leaves you in any doubt as to how good he is. He's always ridden the biggest waves, fucked the hottest chicks and definitely has the longest schlong in any room he walks into. But I'm in dire need of reflection and have decided a good smoke is what is called for, so I've trailed down to the Hun cunt's beachfront apartment on Campbell Parade to get some sticky green stuff to help focus my mind on job hunting.

Kasp's girlfriend is there when I arrive. Penny's that sort of exuberant blonde with a strained smile who seems to know everybody better than they know her. Every time I meet her I'm confused by the warmth of her welcome. She runs her own promotions company in between merciless binges on the Devil's dandruff, so I'm guessing her interest in me, as she drags on her second Marlboro, is chemically enhanced.

– What are you doing with yourself at the moment, Ned?

– Trying to write, doing a bit of work in a café.

I'm always trying to write but I never seem to get anywhere. At the moment, I'm working on a screenplay like the rest of Bondi.

– You ever done any promotions work? she asks but, before I can answer, the Hun is back with a block of compressed heads the size of a snack box of Kentucky Fried Chicken.

– Okay. How much money you giving me today, Edward? says Kaspar.

I look at the block. It's easily a pound.

– You got enough there, mate?

– Enough for you, Mr Jelli, he says, exhaling his Stuyvie.

– Honey, says Penny, frowning. – Will you not interrupt me? I was having a conversation with Ned.

– Yeah, yeah, yeah, says Kasp. – Well, I'm trying to do some business and you're interrupting that.

Penny frowns again, looking like she might stab the guy, so I jump in with my order.

– Just a fifty, mate.

– Just a fifty, he mimics.

Kaspar's the sort of bloke who can take eighteen minutes to make a Vegemite sandwich. First he'll wipe down every surface in the kitchen, open the windows so the air quality is just right, sit the butter in the sun so that it reaches the requisite consistency, then spend a year or two finding the right knife in his kitchen drawer. Now he needs to find a plate and make sure it's dust and smudge free and he'll make a big deal out of checking its cleanliness before laying it on the benchtop like it's one of the fuckin' Dead Sea Scrolls. Then he'll bring out the bread, select his slices and retie the bag, smooth the wrinkles out of it and replace it in the cupboard.

He does this when you're in a hurry, when you've just nicked up to his place for some buds and have a cab waiting downstairs, knowing full well you have to watch him. It's the Kaspar Show and he enjoys the fact that all eyes are on him because, well, he's the star. Tonight, I don't get the Vegemite sandwich routine but bringing out the block of dope is another variation. It has to be unpacked and sniffed and fondled and rewrapped. The whole production is designed to show me that Kasp is a heavy hitter, that he doesn't really have to worry about selling fifty-buck bags to shitheads like me, but he's doing me a favour because he's a top bloke.

– So what have you been up to, mate? I ask him.

– Aw, mate, been really busy. Got so much on, eh?

Yeah, I can tell from nineteen cooked baccies in your ashtray and the bong on your coffee table.

– Yeah? So what are you doing?

Kasp glances up at me to check I'm watching the Kaspar Show, then returns his attention to measuring up my fifty.

– Mate, can't say too much. I'm working on something with the rugby league but they've asked me to keep it dark. He gives me this information like it's caused him pain.

– Don't be silly, honey, it's not that big a deal, says Penny. – He's doin' some MC-ing for the rugby league at their games.

Kasp looks at her with infinite patience, then shakes his head.

– Yeah, that I'm making as much money after six months in the business as you are after six years, he says.

The Kaspar Show then takes a break as the two of them batter each other with character assessments, and I notice the domestic disharmony has caused Kasp to distractedly flip some buds into his mull bowl. He's gonna punch a few. Things are looking up.

As he grinds away, Penny returns her focus to me.

– So, as I was saying before Mr-Know-It-All interrupted, have you ever done any promotions work?
– Not really. What have you got to do?
– Well, you know I run a promotions company? she says.
– Yes.
– Every Thursday, Friday and Saturday night, I run teams of girls and guys through venues to promote Marlboro.
– The cigarette brand?

POOR SIMPLE CUNT

I can think of nothing else for the rest of the weekend. Luke Lawrence's just not someone I want to piss off. He's the best fighter in our form and even guys like Joe Gold and Grumble keep him on side. Last week, down the back of school, he fought the biggest guy in our form, Santos, this humungous wog cunt with braces on his teeth like Jaws in the *The Spy Who Loved Me*. I've never seen a fight like that in person. They were fully punching each other in the head, and every time Larry landed one on Santos, his braces would slice through his lip until the poor bastard looked like he'd headbutted a pincushion.

When I arrive at school, I know someone – probably the Buccaneer, the fat cunt – has already found Larry and paid him out, told him that Ned Jelli was pashing his girlfriend at the dance. It's only a matter of time. After recess, I'm heading back up the stairwell to Geography, when I feel hands on the back of my shirt. I'm spun with such force the world blurs, then I'm hurled backwards into the black bricks. Fully winded. Larry has his fist bunched in my shirt, lodging his objection under my chin.

– You fucken crackin' onto my chick were you, ya wog cunt?

Larry doesn't much like wogs cunts. I never considered myself a wog cunt in primary school because there'd been so many other wog cunts at Daceyville. I didn't hear any of the various racial taunts of the day – slap-head (Asian), dirty Abo (Aboriginal), greasy wog (anyone brown who wasn't an Abo), filthy Lebo (Lebanese), big nosed kipper (Jew) – until I arrived at Seaview Christian Brothers College and I became a wog cunt. My mother's maiden name was Black. My stepdad's name is Kinsella. They are about as woggie as the Reschs beer Shamus drinks and the cheese and beetroot sandwiches my mum makes me take to school. We are an Anglo family, yet I've been saddled with my real dad's name – Jelli – and I am, therefore, a wog cunt.

– Nah, mate, nah, I say to Larry.
– Don't fucken call me mate, you wog cunt.
– Sorry, Larry, sorry, I didn't know she was your chick.

Students are gathering around us and, yet, beneath the terror moisturising my bowels, there's just a hint of Disco-like pride. I've kissed Luke Lawrence's girlfriend and even fifteen year old boys know that puts me in the same ballpark as him. Maybe I'm not sitting in the front row with Larry and his cool friends, but on the weird sliding scale of male–female attraction, I'm just up the aisle. Maybe Larry senses this, maybe he sees it in my eyes, because he cocks one of his rugby league fists at my face.

– 'IT 'IM LARRY! I can hear someone shouting. It's the Buccaneer. The cunt did put me in. Now he's spruiking from the background, taking the piss, dropping the 'h' off all his words, mocking Larry's blue-collar origins. Larry's from Malabar, while the Buccaneer is from Dover Heights, and although they're both at the same school and their parents probably have very similar bank accounts, Malabar is lower down the social scale according to eastern suburbs snobbery.

– 'IT 'IM LARRY! 'IT 'IM LARRY!

I look at Larry and accept my fate. He pulls his fist back further, then punches. I flinch, but he pulls up inches from my face and bursts out laughing.

– Only joking, mate, she's not really my girlfriend.

– Eh?

– Nah, mate, you're right. I just pashed her a few weeks ago. Fingered her too.

He jams the finger in my face but I swerve.

– Okay.

– You shit yourself. You should have seen your face. You poor simple cunt.

And then he walks off. As Larry passes the Buccaneer, he gives the prick a short right in the guts.

– You fucken fat smartarse.

KISS KISS

The book's the bait.

I go upstairs to have a piss at Guru's, leaving the boys howling at the big screen over some obscure call from the ref, and see Alex (Alessandra to her friends) walk into her apartment and follow her. I am drunk, so I don't even feel the hook in my mouth. It's like some sick, silk thread has led me here over geography and emotions and years, winding through people and jobs and airports and takeaway food stores. I don't even see I'm being reeled in like the dumbest, dullest, blindest mullet, up a monofilament of fate until I'm flappin' away on Alex's kitchen floor.

We swap platitudes for a few minutes as she makes herself a cup of tea and it's obvious to the audience in my head we have only nothing in common until I see *Kiss Kiss* by Roald Dahl on her coffee table. A book! Now that's something I know about. Reflections, wry observations, the way a good story can transport you, take you to places, times far, far . . .

She is blinking at me like a lioness.

– I'm gibbering, aren't I?

She pops out a few blandishments about Dahl and I sit on the floor listening up at her like she's an archangel.

– Can I kiss you?

– That wouldn't be a good idea.

I don't.

But I carry the book down to the boys, holding it above my head like a Trophy of Further Contact. I know I'll have to see her to give the book back. She knows it too because inside the cover is her name and phone number.

The big guy with the shaved head looks at me, then turns away.

The next evening I drive my mum's car up the hill to her apartment block, park in the dark under an old Moreton Bay fig, then get out and sit on a crumbling brick fence watching Alessandra's high window, the curtains flapping around the shadows. I sit there and wonder what it would be like to laze on that sill with her and watch the traffic chuckling down the hill.

The courtyard where we met is still clogged with spent kegs and broken lawn furniture Guru hasn't gotten around to moving. I sit there and think about that moment when she walked downstairs, and I shiver like I've drunk something icy I thought would be hot.

TOP TEN PER CENT

I'm surprised when Larry calls me to tell me he's getting married to his girlfriend. I've seen him a few times recently when we've gone to the gym together and he said they'd been arguing.
– She's a fuckin' punish sometimes. Nasty.
– Whattaya mean?
– Just nasty. She's been at me for months to move in with her, so I do. Now she's pissed off all her fat troll mates are getting married, so we've got to fuckin' do it as well.
– So marry her.
– You're fuckin' kiddin', aren't ya? She's got massives.

Meaning massive issues. Don't we all. Larry eventually caved. Not such an unusual move; you've heard the story. Fighting continuously with your girl? Move in with her. Arguments continue unabated? Marry her. Blues push your hand towards the carving knife? Have a kid. It's an age-old recipe for tragedy repeated the world over. It's why TV stations and breweries stay in business.

67

After Larry proposed, they moved back in with his mum, Maisie, so they could save for a deposit. Things got tense. Maisie tended to do most of the domestic chores, like making the bed. The girlfriend – sorry, *fiancée* – didn't approve, feeling it was an invasion of their sacred ground, their place of sex. She made Larry promise he'd make the bed and wouldn't allow Maisie into the room to clean.

– Fine, he said.

Larry tends to get on it on a Sunday. When the fiancée hadn't organised a lunch with her friends or a picnic or shopping at the markets or some crap like that, he'd be straight down the Clovelly Hotel, bash twelve schooners into himself, maybe a biccy or some rack, and wake very dusty for work Monday morning. The fiancée would already be hosing herself down with hairspray, squeezed into a lacy g-string that looked like it was doing an appendectomy on her. One morning she shouts, 'Remember to make the bed!' as Larry drags himself into the shower and stands whimpering under the jet.

Time is tight. Some mad wog is complaining about the drainage on his balcony. Larry has to get into work early to deal with it, so the bed, well, it slips to the bottom of his list of priorities. When the fiancée gets home, she knows straightaway. The sheets are drawn with hospital precision; something Larry isn't capable of after twelve hours sleep, let alone twelve beers. When he shuffles in from work ready for a few quiet billies and a couple of hours in front of Fox Sports, she's growling.

– Your fuckin' mum made the bed.
– So what?
– I don't want her in here.
– You're a punish, you know what?
– I don't want that bitch in here.

That's about all Maisie heard hovering in the hall. She appeared at the door like a Viking warrior queen, words her weapons. Glancing blows were exchanged. Larry backed his mum. Wedding's off.

We'd see the fiancée from time to time up at the gym as she proceeded to gorge her way through her depression over the failed nuptials.

– Is that her? I'd say as I sat up from the bench press.
– Have a look at it. What's she been eating?
– Her fuckin' whole family, by the looks of it.
– Did I dodge a bullet or what?
I suppose.

It's Larry's turn on the bench press and he gets down to it pretty seriously, the heavy gold chain around his neck dancing on his pecs as he exhales. He's in excellent shape for thirty-five and, at the moment, so am I. I've been swimming and throwing up most of the high fat shit I eat when I'm depressed, so I'm looking pretty good.

– Pretty cut there, mate, says Larry as we do arms later on.
– Yeah, I'm going alright.
– Look at us and look at the sheilas our age, they're just awful. They've lost it, it's over.
– And most of the blokes. Look at Scorps.
– Fat cunts. But we're still rooting twenty year olds and we barely look thirty.
– On a good day.
– We're on fire, we're the top ten per cent, mate.

By the looks of things, most of the top ten per cent are up at Healthlands Gym at the moment, groaning, straining, lurching between the racks of free weights like they're about to lock hands around the neck of a bison and wrestle it into submission. A big sunburnt bouncer with a crocodile-face, a sure sign he's been on the roids, pulls up his singlet in front of the mirror and stares at his abs. He looks happy with what he sees.

THE MOUNTAINS

It's a long drive up to the Blue Mountains when you've got no seat to sit on. My mum and Shamus have just bought one of those Californian Mini Mokes and while they look pretty comfortable up front, there's nothing but bare metal for us to slide around on up the back. At least there's no seatbelts to worry about.

It's raining, so we've put the roof on the car and zipped up the flaps which act as the doors. It doesn't stop the rain dribbling in. It's so fucken hot and Shamus is smoking Chesterfield Filtereds, my mum's on the Peter Stuyvesants, and this rich blend of international smoking pleasure is funnelling back onto my sister Megan and me. We're sitting on pillows, Megan reading some dumb *Secret Seven* book which no doubt will give her car sickness.

Shamus finishes his beer and shifts into third as we climb off the expressway at Emu Plains and into the damp green of the foothills. He pushes the can through his door flap and lets it go. I don't hear it hit the bitumen behind us but watch it cartwheel through the scratched plastic that is the Moke's rear window.

– Shamus, says my mother.
– Birds will eat it, he says.
– It's a fucking aluminium can, Shamus.
– Sorry, darling.
– Don't litter in front of the kids.
– Sorry, darling.

As we climb up through Springwood, Woodford, Lawson, the rain disperses and the sound of cicadas increases like static, until we reach Wentworth Falls (elevation 867 m). I like it up here. It's quiet and there's plenty of space and trees. You've got room to think.

Shamus blats up a final stretch of road, passing a hundred feet of white picket fence, before we reach the gate to my Uncle Truman's place. He hooks a left, going too fast, puts the Moke sideways a little and expertly rights it, shuffling the wheel between his hands like a race car driver. He chuckles.

– Shamus, says my mother.
– Keep some tar under it, Shamus says, then spins us up the crushed granite driveway.

We climb out of the Moke, pushing aside the flaps like we're climbing out of a tent.

– Hel-lo, says my mum to the open door, all happy to see her big brother.

There's no answer, just the wind keening through the big verandahs and gargantuan pine trees that surround the house, the distant winding of a minibike and the occasional rolling carol of a magpie. I help Shamus unload our bags that are stacked in the back seat between Megan and me to stop us punching each other. I can hear the sound of Holst's *The Planets* trickling out of the house and down the valley into the bushland views.

There's a layer of mist hanging above the massive pines and it's cold and damp.

– They must be in the garden, says my mum.

I run around the corner and look down the hill to where my uncle has his epic veggie patch. There's a sprinkler going on the apple cucumbers but no Truman. I run up the stairs to the kitchen door and there I see him kissing my Aunt Sandra in front of the stove while a huge earthenware pot of steak and kidney bubbles in front of them. They giggle. My Aunt Sandra looks a lot like the other women in our family. She's dark-haired, with big tits and a little overweight. Truman's also chubby, wearing a terry-towelling hat and a brown balled sports shirt with Stubbies. He looks like a grogged-up garden gnome.

– Hello, me darling, he says and kisses me on top of the head.

– Hello, Ned, says Sandra.

– Where's Flynn and Bailey? I ask.

Megan and my little cousin Sass try to follow us up to the barn but we tell them to piss off.

– Only boys allowed, I say.

– Why?

– Because we said so.

– Why?

– Just rack off, will youse, says Bailey and hurls a pine cone at Megan's feet.

– STOP IT!

– THEN PISS OFF!

I throw another pine cone and the two girls huddle behind a stack of bricks that my uncle's been going to make a duck pond with for five years. The bricks are covered in moss and lichen, which drops off in blobs every time we hit them with another pine cone. The chicks are fucked, their cones barely make it to Flynn and Bailey and me. They quickly run out of ammo behind their barricade, and when Megan darts out to grab another pine cone, I hit her on the hand and she starts crying and pisses off like I told her to in the beginning.

Flynn, Bailey and I then climb a ladder to the top floor of the barn to show me the shit they've ripped off from a house down the valley.

– You guys are gonna get so busted, I say, taking in the new velvet couches, chairs, antique coffee table and cut-glass decanter set.

– No one will find out, says Flynn.

– What if your mum and dad come up here?

– They never come up here.

It looks like they've gutted one of the Bronte sisters' parlours and relocated it to their shitty barn. It's pretty dark up here, but there's random shards of light coming through the corrugated iron roof, where we hacked into it with an axe last time I visited.

– How'd you get this stuff up here? I say.

– With the pulley, says Bailey.

– We tied a rope around the couches and then Webster and Forrester helped us pull 'em up.

The backs of the two couches have nasty rope burns on them – the least of their problems considering the rain dripping through the roof onto the cushions.

– What else you get?

Bailey walks over to a liquor cabinet like he's Lord Byron and swings open the doors. There must be a dozen bottles of spirits.

– Fuck off. Have you had any?

– Yeah, not heaps. We're waiting until Mum and Dad go down to Sydney.

– You want some?

– What's it taste like?
– It's all pretty shit.
– It burns your throat.
– They're better when you mix it with Coke.
– You gotta any Coke?
– Nah.
I take one of the bottles – Chivas Regal.
– What's this?
– Scotch.
I crack the lid and sniff it.
– Aw, that smells shithouse.
– Have a skol, says Bailey.
I do and immediately gag.
– Got any magazines? I ask.
– Yeah.
– Where are they?

Flynn pulls a box out from under the couch. It's filled with hardcore Danish porn but there must have been something wrong with the printing press. All the skin tones are out. The women look orange, their hair white.

– Have a look at that one, says Flynn.
– Yeah, that's a good one, says Bailey.

NIGHT-TIME BARRELS

Kaspar bought the chicken and it almost made it down the escarpment.

The six of us blaze down to Werong just after dawn, Birdy and Grumble each driving their shitboxes, our boards jammed into the back of both cars like Vita-Weat biscuits. As we get onto the straight, scrub-rimmed roads inside the national park, Chong produces the mull bowl, pulls one, then passes the billy to Grumble, who bends like he's trying to give himself headies, one elbow high in the air as he jams the lighter into the cone, Chong holding the steering wheel from the passenger seat.

– Car coming, I say from the back.

Grumble sucks the last of the glowing dope through the cone and ejects a plume of smoke like he's a tea kettle screaming on a stove. A Commodore with a bullbar screams by on the other side of the road, buffeting us.

– Lick me, says Grumble and passes the billy back to Chong,

gears down and chases after Birdy, who's about a hundred metres in front of us in his yellow Sigma. Grumble hurtles past and we chuck brown-eyes and wave the bong at them. Kaspar, who's in the passenger seat, just nods, then leans over to pull his own billy, shaking his head to whatever tunes they're playing.

We get to Stanwell and the hang-gliders are already out, tracing elegant circles in the thermals, enormous technicolour eagles searching for nonexistent prey.

– Would you ever do that? I say.

– Nuh, says Chong, chuckling in a voice that says he wouldn't even consider it.

We pull up at the Werong car park and look down the coast. The swell is pushing in from the south and the green of the bush seems to run to the very edge of the water. The air is cool and we're all psyching because the walk down to the beach is always epic. Underneath my anticipation, there's just the tiniest bubble of anxiety I always get from surfing.

– What the fuck is that, Kasp? I hear Scorps say and turn to see Kaspar unloading a hurricane lantern and a camping stove.

– Yeah, yeah, you boys can grovel around with your tinned spaghetti, I'll be pan-frying some fresh snapper.

– You're gonna carry all that down the mountain, you fuckin' homma? asks Grumble.

– No, Mr Chong's helping me, so he can have some snapper as well. Ain't that right, Chong?

– Yeah, I'll carry something. I don't care.

We look at Chong like he's just done the Nazi salute.

– You're fucked, Chong, says Grumble.

– I'll carry something if you want, Kasp, says Birdy and the rest of us – me, Grumble and Scorps – just shake our heads.

– You bum boy, Birdy. You guys all gonna sleep in the same tent, smell each other's farts? I say.

– Four man tent, got a rain fly, carbon fibre tent poles, vents, says Kaspar.

– Yeah, I'll go with you, Kasp, says Birdy.

– What about you, Chong?

– Yeah, I'll go with Kasp.

– What about your tent then, Chong?

– You guys can have it.

– Sweet, fuck youse, I say.

Scorps shakes his head, dispirited.

– You ever been in Chong's tent before?

The track down the mountain to the beach is about two kilometres and it's slippery because of the rain. I've stupidly worn my new Vans and after a hundred metres they're got tide marks of orange mud up their sides where I've sunk into the clay. Ahead of me, I can see Kasp carrying his Esky, and banging on the side of it, a roast chook in a white plastic bag he got from the chicken shop in Rose Bay before we left.

Bump, bump, bump, goes the chook against the Esky in time with Kaspar's steps.

I've only got a small bag, some cans of baked beans, a loaf of bread and my board. I'm clagging from the walk already and have a puff on my Vento.

– I don't want to even think about the walk back, I say.

– Shut up, says Grumble.

He's always grumpy on the walk down. He gollies at a huge orbweaver spread-eagled in silk to the left of the track. The glob hits it perfectly in the abdomen, and as the spider tries to scurry away, the mucus holds it fast. Caught in Grumble's web.

All of us have got the same amount of stuff to carry, except

Kasp, who's got his tent, an Esky, lamp, a grill and an air mattress, which he's split amongst his bum chums Chong and Birdy. The path is tricky when you're carrying things. What looks like straight rock turns out to be crumbling sandstone and as soon as you make contact, it squirts from underneath you like a knob of cunji.

Surprisingly, Birdy, who's gibbon-like in his athleticism, is the first to go down. The tail of his board cracks into a rock because he's held the hurricane lamp he's carrying up off the ground to save it from smashing.

– You could have broken your back with that little manoeuvre, Birdy, I say.

– Good boy, Birdy, you'll get pancakes in the morning, says Kasp.

– Pancakes?

– Yeaaaah, says Birdy and grins.

Fuckin' sickening.

A light mist of rain is falling by the time we make it down the side of the mountain and onto the flat before the beach. The vegetation to our left has been groomed along the contours of the escarpment by eons of wind, like Farrah Fawcett's blow-waved flicks. The swell is messy, three to four foot.

– It's shit.

– Who cares, I'm out there, says Birdy, always the keenest.

– You're gonna help put up the tent first, says Kasp and for the first time Birdy realises the infernal side to his deal.

– We'll get a few for you out there, says Scorps.

– Ah, it's shit anyway, says Birdy.

We head down the grassy slope, the easiest part of the walk. Because we've got less shit to carry, Grumble, Scorps and I power down, leaving Kaspar and his two catamites behind. Chong is keen to get down there as well and takes the steps a bit too quickly. He loses his footing and grabs at Kasp for balance, tearing the roast chicken out of the bag. It tumbles down about ten metres of hill, shedding skin, part of a wing, regurgitating its famous rosemary stuffing, until it hits the flat, caked in mud, and rolls to a stop at Grumble's feet.

– Chong, you fuckin' idiot, screams Kaspar.

– Chong.

– Cho-ng, we mimic Kasp, who's scrambling down the steps to rescue his chook.

– Leave it alone, Grumble, he screams.

Grumble bends to examine the fallen fowl, pinching the remaining wing between his thumb and forefinger.

– Hello, dirty bird, he says and giggles.

– Fuckin' leave it alone!

– That's gonna taste hell, Kasp.

– I'd be stoked carrying that all the way down here.

– You miss flying, don't you, dirty bird? says Grumble.

He stands straight again, giggling to himself as Kaspar nears.

– Fuckin' don't, Grumble!

Grumble takes three steps backwards, then two to the side, lining the chicken up round-the-corner style.

– GRUMBLE!

BAM! Grumble boots the thing fifteen feet through the air, into the side of some bushwalking fruit's tent.

Werong is a nudist beach, so you have to be on guard for fags and kiddie fiddlers. As is the case with nudist beaches all over the world, only fat fuckin' weirdos ever get their gear off down here. You could wait thirty years to see a skinny chick, and as soon as she came close it'd end up being some Winnie-Red-cured, Wollongong boiler with legs like sticks of cabanossi. The first thing I spot when I poke my head out of the tent is the orange arse-fuzz of some sixty year old creep who's washing plates in the creek near us.

– Fair dinkum, I say.

– What?

– There's some old poof out here showing me his arse.

– FUCK OFF, screams Grumble through the tent and the bloke turns around. I duck back in the flaps and see Scorps has got his arse out as well. He farts and his ring puckers like an old lady blowing a kiss.

– I'm in hell, I say.

It's been a shit night. It rained and Chong's tent leaks. Grumble did smoked oyster farts all night, then Scorps did baked bean farts, and it was only when I did one as well that I realised that because we've all been eating smoked oysters and baked beans, our farts smell the same. So the times I thought I was enjoying my own aroma, I'd been inhaling these other cunts' gases.

– Fuck this, I say and scramble out to find Kaspar turning over a flapjack on his gas stove, a bowl of pancake mix beside him.

– Eh, I say and he nods like he's expecting me to ask him for breakfast.

Birdy jogs up from the beach with Chong.

– Seen the waves? asks Birdy.

– Nah.

– It's cleaned up.

– It's goin' off.

We're stepping into our freezing cold wetsuits when Birdy drops it on us.

– Tell 'em, Chong.

– Not now.

– Tell us what?

– Mr Chong has got Andrea up the duff, haven't you, Mr Chong? says Kasp.
– Full on?
– Yeah.
– Whattaya going to do?
– I don't know, he says.
– You're a fuckin' idiot, Chong.
– You knew that was her game, she was fuckin' tryin' to trap ya.
– Those night-time barrels got ya, Chong, says Kasp.
– Were you using a dom? I betchya weren't, I say.
– None of you cunts use 'em.
– Yeah, but we haven't got a thirty-eight year old sea hag preggas, have we? says Kasp. – Debbie gives me all the night-time barrels I want but I make sure me little spermies skoff on the pill.
– Was Andrea on the pill?
– She said she was.
– I bet she did, like she says she loves that corkscrew dick of yours, eh, Chong?

Chong is snookered. Blinded by the old velvet mousetrap, he didn't even feel the crosshairs settle on his back.

– Have you asked her whether she wants to have an abortion, Chong? asks Birdy.
– Nah, not after the last one.
– What? You've got her pregnant before?
– Yeah, last year.
– Aw, mate, you were warned, Chong, I say.
– At least she's a good cook, eh? he says, trying to sound hopeful.
– Yeah, well, you'll only be eatin' at home from now on, Chong boy.

Scorps gives Birdy a playful hit across the head.
– Don't use all me wax.

RAGING RAJAH

It's just after dinner on a Tuesday night when Shamus says he's going to visit Uncle Doug.
– What for? asks my mum.
– He needs a hand with some curtains.
– Don't bullshit me, Shamus.

Things are tense at the moment. My mum set up a Cabcharge account for her business at the beginning of the year and she's gotten a docket back from the company for $419. It took about a week for the story to trickle down to us kids, but what happened is, Shamus and Doug decided they wanted to watch the sunrise in the Blue Mountains and took a taxi to Katoomba. Round trip of four and a half hours. There's been a lot of door slamming.

– He wants to have them up before Sherie gets back from her sister's place, says Shamus.
– You're going to smoke dope. Since when does fucking

Doug Moran put up curtains?

Shamus couldn't look more offended.

– Darling, he bought them on the weekend. He tried to put them up by himself on Sunday and nearly broke his neck coming off a ladder.

I'm sure someone, somewhere in the world has spoken a bigger load of shit today but Shamus is winning the race in this hemisphere with the curtains story. My sister Megan and I are watching *Neighbours*, sprawled on the floor in front of the telly.

– Can I come? I say.

I'm working on my own pot addiction and can sense a hot joint in the sunset. One thing I'll say about Shamus, it's always a case of the more the merrier.

– There. Ned will come with me, says Shamus.

He knows I can drive the Merc home if he gets too pissed. My mum's not snowed.

– If you get that boy stoned I'll fucking kill you, Shamus.

– Abigail, he says and she goes into the bedroom and slams the door.

– Can I drive? I say.

Doug lives in East Sydney which is barely fashionable. His local hotel is called the Tradesman's Arms and all along the street are brothels of differing quality and price range. The Tradesman's is well acquainted with Doug, who's known to walk up from his place completely naked to order a schooner, stand on a table and sing his anthem: – I've been SUCKED! I've been FUCKED! And I'm HAPPY! For this reason a pair of underpants (cream-coloured Y-fronts) is kept near the beer taps so Doug can be made decent and the ugliness of a forced ejection won't be necessary. He's already hacking up globs of chestnut phlegm in between tokes of a big tea-coloured joint when we arrive at his house.

– Come here, you little cunt, he splatters, gives me a horse kiss on the right temple, then presses the number into my hand. I look to Shamus.

– Don't tell your mother.

Two joints later I'm finding it hard to talk and Doug remembers he has a bag of coke in his bedside table. I've never done cocaine before. Even Doug hesitates when passing the rolled note to me, sensing he's stepping over some kind of boundary, blurred as it is by hooch and Reschs.

– Don't tell your mother, you little cunt, he says and I stoop to conquer.

Truth be told, it's shit coke, but my virgin synapses meet the rush of endorphins like the Amazon jungle does a bulldozer. I start yabbering like a chimp and within five minutes have a hard-on you can crack fleas on. I'm not really sure how the conversation turns to sex, but soon Shamus and Doug are questioning me about my status. When they discover my virginity is intact, the decision is made.

– We'll get you a root, you little cunt. You want your cock sucked? says Doug.

I most certainly do.

Five minutes later we're standing outside a brothel on Liverpool Street as Doug negotiates with a woman he seems to know. She's wearing a pair of stockings under a tight leopard-skin leotard. Flo has a great pair of legs for her age and a face that is utterly pornographic. She leads me into the amber light of the terrace and what would normally be the lounge room. A bed is pushed against one wall, a tasselled lamp glowing warmly as she takes off her leotard and rolls off her stockings, revealing a bush of greying pubes that looks both exhausted and enticing. I take off my clothes and my cock bounces out of my underpants like a diving board delivering a fat man into a public pool.

– My, don't we have a Raging Rajah? she says.

As I slide into the warm tapioca of my first cunt, everything becomes a little fuzzy.

So this is what all the fuss is about? I think as I move in and out of the sweet heat. Leaning down to kiss Flo, she shakes her head and tells me 'No'. I promptly ejaculate and that's when I hear sniggering from the window facing the street. Doug and Shamus are peering in from under the blinds, sharing a joint and a schooner.

THAT THING

I call Alessandra and she doesn't ring back. I can't sleep that night. I actually get stomach cramps and check the answer machine about fifteen times in the wee hours. The nausea. Jesus. Do you need to know about the sweated phone calls, the unreturned messages, the fury of ego and disbelief I whip up in myself waiting for some kind of response from this girl?

She stands away from the phone receiver rolling her eyes at this new threshold of desire I pour down the line at her. She's used to the avid attentions of men but I take it to another level, soak her with thoughts and assumptions and compliments and strange transparent need. She's stepped from the movie in my head.

Finally she agrees to a cup of coffee, the ubiquitous, non-threatening, no strings attached, test-the-water date. Of course she says she has to be somewhere in an hour. I pick her up in my mum's bubble-mobile and she says I drive a girl's car and I love her for saying that. As she sashays in front of me towards the café, that love hardens watching her marble thighs and sculpted arse, the hard tug of her stomach under her sweater. I sit next to her and lay my usual 'I'm a dreamer, visionary, romantic' bullshit on her and she blinks at me slowly as if to say, 'Is that it?'

– What do you believe in? I squeeze.

– I believe in me, she says.

I charge back in with my prepared speech, barely registering her words.

– I believe in laughter and love and the ocean and the purity of music and . . .

More blinking.

She's like someone who comes to a nightclub determined not to dance, no matter how funky fruity the tracks fall around her. She isn't gonna dance because she doesn't like the club; it's in the wrong part of town and the people throwing the bash are not from the right set. Dancing would legitimise this place, these people, and draw her world one degree closer to theirs. To me.

She doesn't want coffee. I order beer and remember from the barbecue that she didn't drink alcohol then, either.

– I try not to depend on anything, she says. – If I like something too much I try to do without it.

– Doesn't sound like a whole lot of fun.

– Fun is what you make it. I don't need to get drunk to have fun.

I feel like I've drunk ten cups of coffee. I can feel the pulse in my biceps. My stomach is snatching at the air in front of me as I watch the lazy roll of her clear cat blues sweep across me then over my shoulder to the footpath outside.

I must have her.

I feel like I've picked up a new video game and don't know which buttons do what. I reach for my beer and remember I've just put it down. I take a sip and find the last mouthful still there. I talk and the words are from yesterday.

I love her now.

– I just want to have that thing, I say, that thing when you walk into a room and you see her and she smiles and you know exactly what she's thinking.

Alessandra scratches the skin under her cast and gazes some more over my shoulder and I wonder if someone has set up a TV behind me. I lean back in my seat and knock my boots under the table trying to loosen the reins, feel the horse under me.

Don't freak her out, I tell myself. I smile, feeling the throb in my arms. Just be cool and she'll fall into your hands like a ripe mango.

– I have to go back now, she says.

This wasn't in the script. She's standing and before I know it I'm paying the waiter and following her bum back out the door. In the car I feel the weather change inside me. I fumble over things that maybe we could do sometime and she shrugs around the world, letting double meanings pass by, ambiguities stay cloudy, until I start swinging at the fog, pull on the handbrake outside her house and let my cards scatter on the ground around me.

– What I'm trying to say is, I could fall heavily for a girl like you.

She looks at me like I've dribbled on myself.

– Do you think we should become involved? I say, switching to faux formality, going for the gag. She says she can't imagine that at the moment.

– At the moment, does that mean maybe later? I drool.

– It means I don't want to be with anybody.

– But maybe later?

She's getting out of the car.

– Do you want to do something next week?
– Maybe.
– Should I call you?
– If you want to. I have to go.
– Look, am I wasting my time?
– It's your time. Rome wasn't built in a day.
– What does that mean?
– I have to go.

LINDY CHAMBERLAIN

My stepfather is beating my mother.
    He's drunk and he thinks my mum's been fucking some guy named T-Bone. Even if she has been (would you sleep with someone called T-Bone?), it's kinda rich coming from Shamus. A couple of months ago I was going through our bookcase, a huge wall of novels, pulling out authors like Steinbeck, Graham Greene, Burroughs, when I opened up *Fear and Loathing on the Campaign Trail* by Hunter S. Thompson. Out flipped a letter.
    It was from some woman in Darwin, who Shamus has been having an affair with. Shamus has been up in the Northern Territory reporting on the Lindy Chamberlain case. Lindy is this Seventh Day Adventist chick who was camping next to Ayers Rock with her husband when she claims a dingo ran into her tent and fucked off with her baby.
    It's the biggest story of the year as far as the media are concerned and maybe the biggest story of the decade. Everywhere you go,

people are talking about it, discussing Lindy's guilt.

Shamus and Doug have been in Darwin covering the trial. They've been gone for months at a time and it would appear Shamus has been doing more than just filing grabs for the midday news. Even I know they've been having fun. When Shamus came home last time, I heard him tell a story how Doug had been naked, rolling around Alice Springs in a shopping trolley singing 'Onward Christian Soldiers'. Then he fell out his motel window onto a cactus and had to be taken to hospital for prickle removal. Doug loves getting his cock out.

I dunno if the affair is still going but the letter was ardent. I don't know who put the letter in the book either, but when I showed it to my mum, she slapped me really hard across the face and told me I was never to read other people's letters again. Rightio.

So maybe Shamus is feeling guilty?

There's a smashing of glass and I hear my mum scream really loudly. Megan has come into my bedroom and she's crying.

– He's killing Mummy.

I'm trying not to cry, but I'm real scared. I've never heard my mum's voice sound so panicked. I dunno what's going on in there but all I can hear is the dull thud of someone being punched over and over again in the body. It's a brutal sound. Everything goes real quiet and all I can hear is my mummy crying really hard. Then there's a scuffling sound and the punching starts again. My mum is screaming but she's getting weak.

– Do something, Neddy, he's killing her.

I don't know what to do, but Megan is so scared, she's hysterical. She's got snot dribbling down her face and whenever I move she clings to my pyjamas, shaking. The beating starts again and with each blow Megan flinches until she starts jumping up and down, screaming and crying.

– He's killing her!

*

The house is dark as you walk slowly towards your parents' bedroom. All you can see is a sickly dribble of light under the door and the sound of your mother sobbing. Huge elliptical breaths. Pain past fear. You lay your hand on the cold doorknob, rusted metal showing through the white chipped paint, you twist and push it open.

The sour reek of your mother's shit hits you before your eyes can grade through darkness and lamplight, then you see her twisted in the bed sheets, slumped against the wall, hand running sentry around her body as she tries to hide the dark mush smeared on the mattress. She cries angrily that you've seen her like this, but as she moves to drive you out, the pain returns and you see the huge angry bruises on her white body where the streaked shit allows.

She kicks out with her feet for you to leave and only then do you see Shamus sitting on the darkest edge of the bed, head dead in his hands, not caring who sees his creation. You stand there until she screams you from the room, and you unravel through the house as your tiny sister shivers, terrified beside you in her nightie, and then you're in the slap of the night, your bike under you, creaking up the black slink of the road until the lights of the junction and the payphone stand out for your hug.

You call the only person you can think of.

HOTEL BONDI

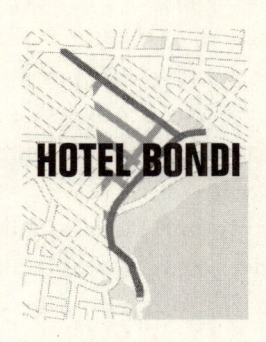

Fuck, I'm pissed.

I wanna go home, but I'm so fuckin' toey. I haven't had a root in months and as I look around at all the beautiful soft things in smooth fabric, I wonder what do you have to do to be with *that*? I guess talking to them would help but I'm feeling kind of chubby at the moment and the fifteen schooners I've had in the last six hours probably haven't helped my definition or articulation. I feel fat and white and unhealthy, but maybe, if I kinda give off that air of unattainability, one of these chicks at the bar will come across.

I'm trying not to look at them too long, just sweep a casual glance over at them, but they seem pretty engrossed. They look like backpackers, which wouldn't be unusual at the Hotel Bondi at 3 am; it's full of the cunts. One of the girls has a bit of a pinched face, from undereating and too much exercise, but that's how I like them. I can see the muscles move under her skin when she lifts her drink to her thin lips. She's the one, so I move across to get in her eyeline, lean back against one of the pillars and try to act casual.

It's a fucking travesty what they've done to this pub. It used to be a real shithole, but everyone knew where they stood. Literally. When you went to the bar, your feet peeled off the carpet, each step sucking like you were walking on melting bitumen. Back then, the tourists and backpackers hadn't completely taken over the joint, then they reno-ed the place and now it looks like a Swedish brothel – or what I imagine one would look like – all blond wood and chrome and the smell of English tourist arse sweat.

What is it about chrome? Does anyone like it apart from pub owners, drug dealers and interior designers? I've never met a person who's walked into a pub after it's been gutted and they've stepped back and said, 'My, I like all the chrome.' It's ugly and unforgiving. Every time you touch a surface, you leave a mark like a snail. I'm starting to lose my balance because I have one leg cocked, heel to the wall. I'm just about to reach out and grab the chrome banister when the lemon-sucker, the thin-faced backpacker, gives me a quick look.

Here we go, I think and get that squirrelly feeling in my stomach that rises up every time I realise something is completely up to me – not to fate, luck or someone else. That edge of reality you reach when you know this is your situation to fuck up or fuck, as the case may be.

I'm just about to walk over to her when Scorps appears.

– You wanna get some rack?

I'm kind of relieved because now I have an excuse for not talking to the girls and I can maintain the image in my head of being this smouldering, unattainable loner.

– From where?

– My guy. In the Jungo.

– How much?

– Two fifths.

– Since when is a gram two hundred and fifty bucks?

– Since he got the best shit.

– That's bullshit, it's just the same as all the other crap, he just tells you it's better and charges you an extra fuckin' fifty bucks.

– So let's call your dealer then, says Scorps, knowing full well I don't have one.

– Fine. Get it.

– Cash me up.

– I'll cash you up later.

In the time this takes, a gangly dude, wearing what looks like a tea-cosy over his curly hair, has moved on the three backpackers and seems to know them. It's enough to derail me. My posture gets pouty and I sip faster on my beer as Scorps goes off to make his rendezvous with the coke bandit. Coming up the ramp that allows wheelchair-bound alcos equal access to the Bondi's overpriced drinks, is Mr Boom. He's absolutely slaughtered and I watch fascinated as he grips his schooner in front of him like a man climbing a pole, sloshing the contents left and right as he staggers through the crowd.

On the promenade, in front of the Bondi Pavilion, there's a bronze statue of a lifesaver pounding into the surf, the sprays of water frozen forever as he plunges forward to rescue a drowning swimmer. It's the image most of Australia and the world have of this beach. A more realistic rendering of Bondi would be Mr Boom, lurching, eyes barely open, his schooner spilling a stream of amber fluid.

The true miracle is Mr Boom has even made it into the pub. He's been barred that many times for ordering drinks and walking off without paying, starting fights, fondling girls, shitting himself, you name it, that he's the one face emblazoned on the baboon brains of the fifteen or so security gorillas that prowl the early morning crowds. They usually just shake their heads as Mr Boom goes into his spiel.

– Where you from, mate? Hurstville? I've lived here me whole fuckin' life, eh? And you're telling me I can't come into me own pub?

Mr Boom is a damaged solar probe in the icy black of deep space. Years ago he was one of the hottest surfers in Bondi, a chocolate brown marvel in the water, but he'd be hard-pressed to have gotten out there in the last six months. The hard-drinking, hard-smoking lifestyle of his early years followed the greater trends of Bondi and he was suddenly downing five, six, ten pills a night, frying whatever circuits had escaped the hydro and the binging.

I've met the guy four hundred times but he still doesn't remember my name. I don't think he remembers the name of anybody he met after 1986. Still, he knows my face and knows I'm good for a schooner.

– Heeeeey, maaate, he says. – How ya goin'?

– Yeah, good, Boom.

The strongest link he has to me is through Scorps, so his next question is as inevitable as a runny shit after a night on the grog.

– Where's Scorps, he with you?

– Yeah, he's here, mate, he's just making a call.

– Tell him to say hello, will ya?

– Yeah, mate, he should be back in a minute.

– How's ya sister? he asks and I can't help smiling. The cunt is like a stroke victim and I doubt he's even hit thirty-five yet. Every significant memory and attachment comes from his teenage years, when he'd had a drunken pash with my sister Megan.

– Yeah, she's good, mate, she just had another baby.

– Yeah? He smiles, and for a second I see the Mr Boom Megan was attracted to. The cocky, smiling surfer pops his head above the tide of warm beer and unfulfilled expectations and for a moment he seems to forget his life has amounted to nothing.

Then it comes.

– Hey, you couldn't buy us a beer, could ya? he says, gulping his almost full schooie down to half. He's an optimist, Mr Boom. And a decent judge of character.

– Yeah, no worries, mate, I say and go to the bar, leaving him with some hairy-lipped sheila he's hooked into, happy not to have to torture myself with his attempts at interest in my life.

It's amazing the people who turn up at the Hotel Bondi at 3 am, and for every person who asks 'What the fuck are you doing here?' you have the stock reply – 'Same thing as you'. It's a great leveller, and for anyone my age to be trawling around the place at this time of the morning, there's an assumed pathos that immediately transforms into an esprit de corps, a brotherhood, when you see acquaintances roaming the crowds of pink pommies looking for a warm hole to crawl into and forget about yourself for a while.

In one corner, working two Japanese girls, are the Simmo brothers, a proven double act at this time of the morning. Both of the guys' innate shyness seems to drain away, replaced by a VB swagger that's seen both of them wake up with far more sheilas than their sober personas would suggest. Coming through the glass doors at the front of the pub are Grumble and Chong, doing their best to walk straight as one of the bouncers trails behind them, sniffing their vapour trail, awake to Grumble's antisocial aura, waiting for him to slip up. They stop when they see the line at the bar, insulted by the wait. The bouncer turns his head towards some loud laughter, just in time for Grumble to reach over to an empty table and skol a half-empty bourbon and Coke begging to be spiked.

– Date rape drugs gladly accepted, he belches at Chong.

There isn't a harder gig in Bondi than being a gook and having to work a surfers' pub, so the influx of tourists has been a good thing for Chong's sex life since Andrea died. To his credit he's a dumb workhorse prop when it comes to sheilas. He just hits it up, ruck after ruck, and gets smashed with elbows and sneers, bent back into incredible positions of refusal and rejection, but he just keeps running the ball. Aussie chicks don't want a bar of Asian guys, and even some of the most polite, well-brought-up girls I know still shiver at the thought of the Yellow Man touching them.

Chong should stand a better chance with all the Jap tourists who now infest Bondi. Or so you'd think. The problem is, any Japanese who are loose enough to be out and drinking at 3 am usually haven't travelled all this way to fuck a Korean, and it's the blonde Aussie boys who slide into their bedtime barrels. In the surf, local grommies, too young to have seen Chong's head in the line-up before, will burn him mercilessly, dropping in on him because they think he's some clueless slap-head tourist out in Sydney for six months to spend his industrialist father's money. Chong, of course, takes it as a personal obligation to do a reo off the offending grom's head.

– Don't drop in on me again, you heckling little cunt, he'll say in a perfect eastern suburbs drawl as he paddles by.

Chong and Grumble are an odd couple but they have one thing in common – they love the thax. Be it a putty grill of some rough Turkish hash, sticky, chemical-choked bikie hydro, north coast bush weed they've grown on their place at Angourie, sly sinsemilla or hash oil from out of an Afghani's arsehole, Chong and Grumble will be punching when all others have fallen by the wayside. Both are ripped shitless as they look around for the boys. They see me and meamble over.

– You look so hot, says Grumble and groans sexually.

– Awww, so do you, slip it in, I say.

The fag talk is a hold-over from high school. As far as I know, none of us has fucked a bloke, though I've come close. It provides a nice base conversation for our interactions, like chicken stock for a recipe.

– Shut up, you fuckin' faggots, says Chong.

– Fuck off, Chong, says Grumble, why don't you show us your pig dick and we'll shut up.

– Fuck off, Grumble.

That's about as witty at it gets at this time of the morning. I have to chuckle at the pig dick comment. In high school, we passed a bestiality porn mag around class and were stunned into silence by a particularly pert German blonde fellating a nonplussed pig in front of a Bavarian backdrop. The bizarre thing about the pig's dick was it was a flesh corkscrew. Google it. It's 'veird'. Being racist young deadshits and keen to humiliate our Korean mate, we of course posited that this was why we'd never seen Chong's cock. He had a pig dick. It stuck. We're all thirty-five years old now, by the way.

I'm just starting to get worried that Scorps, the sly cunt, has scarpered with the okie doke, when he appears through the front doors wearing that Hindu cow expression he gets after scoring drugs. For me it's girls. For Chong and Grumble it's buds. Scorps, well, he couldn't be happier than when he has a sweaty gram in his pocket ready for consumption. What's strange is that any bloke who does as much coke as Scorps, you'd expect him to be skinny as a drool of pelican shit, but he seems to put on weight if someone whispers the word barbecue.

I don't have to say anything to him about keeping the coke dark from Grumble and Chong.

– Boys.

Scorps makes some small talk then heads for the brasco, me

following at a safe distance. We're all mates, but at 3 am I'm not ready to get convivial with my half of the gram, and by the silence Scorps demonstrated, neither is he. He's already found a stall and after I hiss his name, Aladdin's door opens and I'm inside, already getting that jazz in my stomach, the same one I'd had when the backpacker glanced at me, but this one's a touch different because I know it will be requited. Like a trip to a brothel, a trip to the dunnies with Scorps is bound to get a result. We're not there to head butt spiders.

– What's it like?
– He says it's insane.
– Ever known a dealer to say different?
– Hold the door.

Scorps goes to work.

In this world, they say you're lucky if you can do just one thing really well. For some of us it's playing the flute or making vegetable curries, for Scorps it's chopping coke. He's a maestro and can reduce even the gluggiest, chunkiest bag of Ajax into something inhalable in the most trying of circumstances. Selecting his Icebergs membership card, Scorps sets about chopping, crushing, apportioning, then lining up two fat tangents of moral degeneracy, snorting his with a shake of his head, like a horse whinnying, then handing me the note.

– You know you get can get hepatitis from sharing notes?
– Then fuckin' use one of your own, he says.
– Fuck, just give it here, I say and whooska, she's gone.

Both of us soon have that thick-throated contentment that lasts about two minutes.

– Give me the bag, I say.
– Why do you get to keep the bag?
– Cos you're a fuckin' fiend and I don't trust you.
– You're worse than me.
– Gimme the fuckin' bag, Scorps.

For some bizarre reason, considering the fact I'm three times as untrustworthy with drugs, especially rack, Scorps caves in to me in these situations.

– Don't fuckin' sly dog me.

– Maa-ate, I say, giving the word the intonation that suggests 'as if I'd do that'.

Back amongst the backpacker scum, I break away from the boys, deciding that the hundred and twenty-five dollars worth of self-confidence I've just purchased is not gonna be wasted talking to my fuckwit mates about their questionable sex lives. I'm a big-game hunter, and I begin prowling the caverns of the Bondi looking for my prey. I'm standing near the gaming room, sizing up a tiny brunette and her red-headed friend when I hear a female voice.

– Oi, it says, and I cop a jab in the ribs.

It's my cousin, Alice, by far the most attractive of my female relatives, looking tanned and firm in a green Balinese dress with a high collar. She's as pissed as me, having been at the races all day. I suggest a line and she's up for it.

I actually don't like what cocaine does to me. Whatever physical restraint I can exercise over my libido is cast aside by the rush of endorphins, my cock becomes a heat-seeking tube steak and I can rationalise almost any perversity under its influence. Maybe that's not fair on the drug, because the perversity has to be there to start with, but when I'm sober and straight it's a little easier to keep them where they belong – as thoughts, fantasies. I can keep the creep at the back of his cave.

With cocaine, that all gets thrown out the window. The Buddhists say it's impossible to live a good life if you're using any kind of intoxicant on a regular basis, be it alcohol, cocaine or LSD. Why? Because it's hard enough controlling your impulses when you're sober – but when you break down your levels of resistance with things like grog and rack, it's almost impossible.

You end up fucking your best mate's wife, crashing your car, beating your dog, and the creep moves to the front of the cave and starts throwing rocks at passers-by.

I know all this shit – I understand it on a fundamental level – but let me tell you this: life is more fun when you drink and rack up and smoke dope. Maybe not every day, but going to any bar, club, barbecue or social gathering with average humans is pretty hard to get through when you're drinking mineral water and they're chugging bourbon. We've all done stupid things drunk; with cocaine, it just gets multiplied and I find myself taking incredible risks just to get my cock inside something wet.

Like Alice.

Walking to the bathroom, I watch her smooth arse in front of me, her swimmer's legs flexing and relaxing with each step. She's by far the most attractive of my female relatives, did I mention that? All the times I've masturbated over her come swimming into my head.

Fuck, she's my cousin, I think and the taboo makes it even more arousing. I go into the women's bathroom with her and close the cubicle behind me.

If I was going to list the horniest places on earth to be with a woman, a toilet stall has to rank way up there, just behind a waterbed and just in front of a hot tub. You *know* something's going to happen. Right?

As I rack up amateurishly, I ask her what's been going on in her life.

– Any boys?

– Nah, she says, watching the size of the lines I'm chopping.

– Here ya go, I say and pass her the same note Scorps and I used. That's three of us with hep C, I think as she bends deliciously to stroke the powder into her face. She hands me the note and I do mine, then we stand there in the cubicle, grinding, luxuriating in the rush for a few seconds.

– How's that feel?

– Hmm, good. Stings a bit.

I can't help myself.

– You know, Al, I've always found you attractive, I say.

– Yeah? she replies. Alice has never been too big on conversation.

– Not just in a cousin way. Like physically.

– Yeah? she says, again, her face going concave with disgust. She's already reaching for the stall door latch.

– See you out there, she says.

I stand there for a second then walk out and look into the mirror.

– Did I just try to fuck my cousin? I say aloud.

RUSTLERS OR HUSTLERS?

The crew stand like display jewellery at the front of the pub in the light leaching through the doors. The girls are shivering in their midriffs while Kaspar, our supervisor, chats like an old mate to the manager. I pick over the sticky carpet through the stale cumulus of ciggie smoke, holding the brim of my cowboy hat, and grin. Jade throws up her arms and pulls me into a hug, while Wendy and Lulu flash me the street smiles they never use after the shift begins.

Behind me I can feel the collective sigh of the early drinkers in the bar. Old men and young guys acting like old men, getting pissed at four on a sunny afternoon. Any of them would have given up their last beer for the hug I was getting. After heavy seconds dwelling on the girls' arses they drag their elbows back around to the TV sets that are continuously televising some landslide tragedy down in Thredbo.

Kaspar breaks away from the manager, who looks like he's

been nudged awake. The Kaspar Show can have that effect.

– We all here? he asks.

– What does it look like, hardhead?

– Now, now, Mr Jelli, he smiles at me. – Just remember who's paying you.

– Your girlfriend. Not you.

– Can you two grow up?

– Yeah, yeah, yeah, says Kasp before holding up a commanding hand.

– Have you smartarses stocked?

We walk outside to Kasp's dog-cock-red summer-fun four-wheel drive. He opens the back hatch and pulls out a huge box full of cigarette cartons.

– More reds for me, says Lulu.

– And blues, I say.

Lulu and Wendy break open the cartons and stack loose packets in their satchels while Jade brushes out her long blonde hair. Kaspar stands with his leg cocked on the bumper bar. The ciggies, stacked according to milligram strength, in gleaming, crisp cellophane, look good enough to eat.

We walk back into the dank, public bar of the Pigs, the opening door stirring the crypt-like air for the first time in a century, and heads turn out of habit to look at us. The pissheads ignore me, sneering slightly at my cowboy hat until behind me, like a VB dawn, the girls emerge in their cowgirl outfits. The grog frogs relax and attempt casual poses.

As normal, I pair off with Lulu. Wendy is with Jade, while Kaspar folds himself up to the taps to wage his perpetual war against the barmaids. I give Lulu a little slap around her bare waist.

– You wanna do the talking?

– I'm shitty, you do it.

– What's wrong?
– Just boy bullshit.
– You should dump that fucker.
– He's such a damn baby.
– Here we go.

We're at a table of four guys with bad haircuts and short-sleeved 'going-out' shirts and I don't even have to look at their shoes to know they're all wearing buckled black motorcycle boots or RM Williams.

– How're ya doin', boys?

They barely acknowledge me, fixed on Lulu's stomach and cleavage as she smiles tightly at the space above their heads.

– That good, eh? I say.

They look at me like I'm an overpriced shit sandwich.

– Aren't ya gonna ask us why we're wearing silly hats? I say.

The leader, a doofus with a decent glow on, ignores me and engages Lulu.

– Yeah, alright. Whattaya selling, sweetheart?

– We're selling these.

Lulu does her best *Price Is Right* hand-sweep over the cigarettes.

– For just five dollars a packet, she says. – But for you, tonight, it'll only be five dollars.

– I've just given up, says the doof.

I point to the TV, where rescue workers are stretchering a mashed skier out of the disaster area.

– I bet five or six people who are buried under all that gave up ciggies in the last month, and look where it got them? The table laughs nervously.

– I don't smoke, says another guy when Lulu looks at him.

– That's okay, we've got one and two milligram packets here to start you off.

The table laughs again and everyone shakes their heads.

– Bloody disgusting what you're doing, promoting cancer.

– Oh well, we've all got to die sometime, don't we, mate? I say.

– Bloody disgusting, you should be ashamed of yourself.

I point at the guy's half-sucked schooner.

– Somehow, mate, I don't think you get up the barmaid every time you order a beer.

– You seen those ads on telly? He counters. – What smoking does to your arteries? That shit they squeeze out of it?

– Yes I have. It's actually creamed corn but, heh, that's advertising. Have you ever seen what cirrhosis of the liver looks like or alcohol-induced brain damage?

– It doesn't give you cancer, says the doofus.

– Look, mate, overpopulation is the greatest problem facing the world today. We're just doing our bit to winnow out the weeds.

– Then why aren't you selling those things in China? he says.

When we get to the last venue, Kasp loosens up like he always does and lingers in the car park at the Coogee Bay Hotel. As the girls go in to do the beergarden, he gives me the nod.

– Neddy, he says and I hang back as he rolls one in the darkness near a panel van.

– Did you see that chick in the white pants? I say to him.

– Ye-ah, she wanted to jump on, brother.

– You're fuckin' kiddin' yourself.

– She was gyrating on my knee, Edward. I felt like I was feeding a horse.

A Samoan security dude appears around the corner and I freeze. Kasp is not fussed – he's a student of human movement.

– Ahhh, now we see Captain Black Shirt.

– Ayyy, says the security guard, smiling shyly.

– Where were you when we needed ya in the back bar?

– Come on, Kaspar, I can't be following youse around all night.

– You follow this 'round, says Kasp and holds up the joint.

– That's different, ay?

Kaspar sparks it up and hoovers hard on the goodness. I follow, of course, then security gets his go and sucks on the joint like he's trying to siphon petrol out of a station wagon.

– Ease up there, Samoa! says Kasp and I laugh as security's two-way starts to sing about things I don't have to care about.

– Gotta go, boys. Thank you, he says and nods.

I'm ripped, feeling the music from the beergarden in my biceps, happy to not be in an office, an unloved orifice, a dream that I can't wake from. I stretch my legs, happy, soft and runny inside.

– Pretty fun night, eh? I say.

– You did a good job, Edward, he says and though Kaspar is five months younger than me, the slap on the knee he gives me feels paternal and I glow inside.

DRIFTWOOD

Scorps and I are going for flathead, tossing lazy lines into the evening harbour at Rose Bay where they're building the new cop station. I look at the old black trees tumbling down to the sand and the contented rocking of the moored yachts and suck in the cool air, wondering what part of this Alessandra doesn't want.

– Mate, you've got it bad, he says.
– Can you tell?
– Look at you, you look like someone's told you Santa Claus fingered your arse as a child.
– I just can't stop thinking about her. Everywhere I go I'm wondering what she'd think of this person or that view and it's killing me.
– If she's making you this unhappy and you've never even been with her, maybe that's telling you something.
– Maybe.

We sit in the dark roots of a fig tree and he stuffs sticky hydge into rolling papers and passes it to me to spark up.

– My grandmother says, 'What is for you will not go by you.'
– Yeah, yeah, what will be will be.
– Clichés are clichés for a reason, mate.
– Well, I've got a good handle on one of them, I know why they call it heartache.

Through the sheer volume of my attempts at conversation, Alessandra is beginning to fall into a small comfort zone with me. Tiny insecurities are being thrown up from her past like driftwood from a whirlpool. She is letting me in a little, she is taking my calls, but it's the time in between that is killing me. I drag myself around the landscape of my life like someone has replaced my blood with urine. An opaque static clouds me as I dig around in myself wondering what is wrong with me, why she doesn't want me.

The knots, the clots, the sick current of anxiety that my stomach floats on as I walk in my front door and see the vicious blink of my answering machine light. The cruel rewind and then the moment of tainted hope as the first syllable of the caller is heard and a wave of bleakness breaks across my chest and I hate Birdy for his voice, for taking up the precious space she should be occupying.

Finally, I manoeuvre her out again. An almost real date. A drink.

I dress and breathe and tell myself to keep it simple as I ready myself. I don't organise a thing. I put on my most comfortable clothes, the scuffed squared-toed boots, and just am. She lifts into the bubble car like the star from the previews, ready for her first big scene. Her eyes flutter over me like a marksman and my chest crawls with nightlife.

Ad-libbing has its pitfalls. Every bar I suggest she knocks down. She's new to Sydney but she's done the high spots with other courters. She's agreed to this date but it's clear she wants to get something out of it, go someplace new, at least have a story to tell her friends.

We settle on BB's, a wine bar in the arse of Bondi that I know she's never breathed life into before. As I sit with my beer, looking at the chipped paint of the table, the tacky tile mosaic on the bar and the quiet swell of the guitarist in the corner, I know my new minimalist script is working and Alessandra knows it too.

She's talking about her flatmate.

– He's always got to be seen in the right place in the right clothes and he doesn't seem to realise a guy can look great in just a T-shirt and jeans.

She smiles at my T-shirt and jeans.

DANGER WANKS

I've got my hand in my pocket in Maths class, working my cock.

I've torn a hole through the lining earlier in the day, in anticipation of Miss Bootsakakis's pelt. She's our maths teacher, Greek, and as hairy as a newborn grizzly, with Elvis sideburns, barrel legs and calves like loaves of Schickenhoff bread. She shaves her legs but if you get close when she's reaching for the top of the blackboard, her skirt shifts up and you can see where the hair begins at top of her knees. Like the rough just off a golf green.

She's gloriously hairy, wildly unattractive but, because she's the only female teacher in our form, she's become the focus of more sexual energy than Bo Derek, Lynda Carter and Ginger from *Gilligan's Island*.

Christ, she's almost shaggy, and the density and blackness of her cunt hairs is one of the hottest topics in the quadrangle at the moment. We talk about how it would smell on hot days, how the sweat would drip off it like an inverted mohawk, how the pinkness would push through the hair like a tiny newborn joey wandering from the pouch.

Jeez, I'm toey.

Anyway, it's third period and Miss Bootsakakis (why don't you call me Maria, Ned?) is working that chalk like it's one of her hairy nipples. She's grinding it into the blackboard, crumbling dust onto the black of her pantyhose and patent leather shoes. I've sat myself in the back right-hand corner of the room and I'm casually trying to lick some spit onto my fingers, then get it into my pocket and onto my cock.

I can't believe how hard I am. I can't believe I'm even attempting this, but danger wanks have become something of a specialty amongst our group of late. Birdy was boasting he'd managed to bang one out in the Grace Bros car park about a month ago while he was waiting for his mum. The Buccaneer says he's squeezed one off in the shed at the Black Rat's place while he was staying over. I've even had a quickie up the back of an empty 359 after footy training, but I'm not ready to own up to that just yet.

The thing with danger wanks is you can't admit to them too soon or it comes off as creepy. Only once you've put a respectable amount of time between yourself and the act can you admit to it, and then only in certain circumstances. You can't come to school one day and announce you've spanked yourself in the change rooms at General Pants. You have to wait until the conversation emerges – as it inevitably does about once a week – and then casually tell the group you've managed to get one off in Maths class while everyone cacks themselves laughing.

So here I am, stroking away, but not stroking too hard otherwise it will look suss. I have my legs crossed and am sitting on my right hip, trying to give myself some cover as I imagine taking Miss Bootsakakis from behind. First I'd roll that shiny dress of hers up around her waist and shimmy those pantyhose down, let that fur get some air.

– Hmmmm, I moan to myself and Disco looks across at me.

Jesus. I freeze, thinking I've been sprung. I don't dare move a muscle, but I can feel his eyes on me. Slowly, I turn to look at him and grimace, suggesting I have a stomach ache, and he drags his onion eyes back to the sequence Maria is chalking out. I wait a few deadly seconds, squeezing Oscar to keep the blood in him, before I resume.

Oh yeah, there you go, I think, before reaching up to my mouth for another dollop of saliva.

Yeah, yeah.

Miss Bootsakakis's ankles are thicker than most necks. When she plants herself in front of you, you imagine it would take a government rezoning to move her. I slip it back in her, the pelt between her legs dripping as I work it in and out, in and out, then she reaches behind her and takes hold of my cock. She looks over her shoulder at me, winks and moves my angry purple head into her arsehole. I close my eyes. The ecstasy.

– Come up here and do this one, she says.

You want me to do that one, do you? You dirty bitch.

– Ned, come up here and do this one.

I'll come up there. I'll fucken blow my whole load up there.

Oh yeah, oh yeah, I was going to come, I was going to COME!

– NED JELLI!

Fuck! What? I open my eyes. Miss Bootsakakis is staring at me. As is the class.

– Come up here to the blackboard and do this problem for me.

Huh?

I've got a handful of stiff cock pressing against my trousers like 6' 4" in a board bag. Stand up? Not happening.

– No, miss.

– Excuse me?

Miss Bootsakakis isn't one to put up with shit from any of us. She's been called a wog, a wookie and a wolfmother behind her back. She's grown a thick skin but she knows there is only one way to get respect in a classroom: unbridled arse-kicking. She comes towards me like she's Mick Cronin jogging in to toe-bash a Grand Final conversion.

– I feel sick, miss.

And then she's on me, dragging me upright by the ear. I try to turn to the wall and pull my hand out.

– What have you got in your pocket?

– Nothing, miss.

– Don't you lie to me, what have you got in your pocket, show me?

– Nothing, miss. There's nothing in there.

So she spins me around and thrusts her hand into my trousers, straight through the hole and onto my now deflating penis, glazed with semen.

– Oh my God.

Strangely, I smile.

– Go see the nurse, she says.

KATJA

I wake up with the jarring realisation that another day has escaped me and I have no talent, no discipline and no hope of attaining my ambitions.

It'll be midafternoon by now, so I'll eat. Actually, I'll overeat. I'll start with something easy – cereal or baked beans on toast – then move on to another charming culinary marvel I perfected when I was ten years old and had to make dinner when my parents were out on the drink: spaghetti with tomato sauce and cheese. Just boil up the pasta, squirt ketchup on it and add shredded cheese. Voila!

I eat like I smoke – desperately, like someone's going to slap the bowl out of my hands at any moment. I shovel the macaroni into my mouth while I watch something, anything, on TV that might hold my attention. I would try to read but I am unable. After a sentence, a paragraph, my attention wavers because I cannot relate to any of the emotions being described. Love, hate, anger, pity, compassion, they don't penetrate the dull mucus that surrounds me.

Maybe there'll be a football match on and I'll try to watch but it will be extremely difficult.

How do they do it? I ask myself. How do they commit themselves to train, to excellence, to achieving?

It must be fantastic actually being great at something, being able to walk around and have people nod at you and say, 'That's Ned Jelli, the football player, he's amazing on the wing'. And then I watch the gorillas collide for another few tackles and my awe will be replaced by frustration: that I can't even match some brain-dead twenty-three year old when it comes to commitment, that I can't even focus on one aspect of my life long enough to get fit, or get rich, or complete a fuckin' sonnet.

Anything.

Overwhelmed by how pathetic I am, I'll return to the computer for another trawl through the sluts of cyberspace. I'll go through the girls I've already downloaded and find them strangely lacking, so I'll step out into the wide-open web to find new cunt, fresh cunt, cunt I've never seen before.

If Internet porn has taught me one thing, it's that you shouldn't kid yourself about the search for the perfect woman. A lot of guys say, 'Yeah, she'd be perfect if her arse was a bit smaller or her tits were a bit bigger or she was just . . . something that she's not'. On the Net, even your most freewheeling fantasies can be tracked down and flogged over if you have the time and bandwidth. And what you'll find is that the perfect woman one day, the one who sent your cock harder than pig iron, who had your thighs shaking in expectation, the perfect princess you couldn't actually believe had her perfect arse in the air, opening her perfect, bleached pink arsehole to receive some deep-veined throbber, is somehow not so perfect today.

You've moved on to the brunette with the bigger tits or the redhead with the sluttier expression or you'll be sick of suntans altogether and now be morbidly attracted to pale girls with heavy drooping tits, or black chicks whose shaved cunts look like a suburban lawn after it's been passed over by a bushfire. It won't be the perfect princess who gets you hard any more. No, you'll want a tighter arse, greener grass, and if these are the demands you place on your fantasy, how the fuck can a normal woman, with pimples on her bum and crow's feet and a muffin top of fat sneaking over the waist of her just-short-of-fashionable jeans, ever hope to compete?

So you know what? Accept what you have and enjoy it because the fantasy is going to fade. The mistress or the whore or the perky little twenty-two year old that works next door – you'll get bored with her. You'll get bored with her just as quickly as you got bored of Silvia Saint or Seka or Sophie Evans or Katja. Every beautiful woman you see on the street, or on the Net, someone, somewhere is bored of fucking her.

I'm on allinternal.com now, a site that features heavy anal sex, with the penises ejaculating inside the girls, instead of on their tits or face. People go on and on about the objectification of women in porn, but it's hard to see how it plays out in reality. At least you see women's heads and their bodies and maybe even a facial expression here and there. Take a look at most frames of porn, at pictures, movies, cartoons: the man has been reduced to cock alone. That's all he has to offer the process. His todger. Not a face or a personality. Not even a body. Just a cock. Still, it's nice work if you can get it.

I'm enjoying Katja Kassin's career at the moment because in every one of her porn shoots she looks just a bit disgusted with herself. I hate it when the girls are as dominant as the men, tugging cocks like they're shaking bottles of champagne on a Formula 1 dais. I need my fantasies to be compliant, yes, eager, of course, but just a little distressed, like they can't believe they've been reduced to this disgusting act, like they're just a little humiliated by the fact their parents or their friends from school might see them. Yes, that's what I like, just a bit disgusted, you whore, you're disgusted, you're disgusting and then I'm done and I'm disgusted. I'm disgusting.

Is this my second wank today, my third?

What's wrong with me?

This is fucked.

What sort of life is this for a thirty-five year old man?

It's a sunny Saturday and I haven't even seen daylight. There's people outside actually enjoying their lives, doing something and being someone. What sort of loser am I?

And then I'm in bed again, smoking another cigarette, my lungs already aching from the hot smoke. I wheeze, inhale the fumes, exhale, inhale some more, stub the cigarette, suck on my Ventolin and sleep. Forget this place, forget this world where you're a fucking cypher.

INDIANA DRINK MACHINE

At that moment I get punched in the stomach, taking all the breath out of me. It's Indiana Drink Machine. He's one of the brothers, one of the few who still wear a full cassock. He used to be the boxing master, thus his method of greeting the students. The only time we see him out of his cassock is when he does the rounds of the dozen or so vending machines that he refills with cans. Then he puts on a slouch hat and army vest with twenty-seven pockets filled with screwdrivers and WD 40, giving him the appearance of Indiana Jones in *Raiders of the Lost Ark*.

– Master Jelli, he says to me.

– Brother, how you doing?

– Coping, coping, Master Jelli, he says, then presses one of his meaty hands around my bicep and gives it a squeeze.

– You're getting very big, Master Jelli. Are you working out in the gymnasium?

– I'm doing a bit, Brother, with Larry.

Larry, who's sitting with Kaspar about ten feet away, rolls his eyes as if to say, 'Don't bring me into it'. They both know what's coming.

– Why don't you come up to my room at the beginning of lunchtime and we'll see how big you really are?

– Okay, Brother.

He glides off looking like a Dalek. Larry grins at me, the fuckwit.

Indiana's at the entrance to the brothers' quarters waiting for me. He slaps me hard in the middle of my back and steers me inside. It's dim and quiet in the hall, like you'd imagine the back rooms of the Vatican would be. There's an ancient brother, also in a cassock, installed in a wheelchair up one end of the corridor muttering to himself. I don't know what his name is but we see him sometimes on the top balcony, where they stick the veggie brothers to get some sun as though they're pot plants. The poor cunt's skin is purple around his eyes and when he looks at me he licks lips like pork crackling. Indy doesn't even acknowledge the drooling fuck.

– Come, come, he says and pushes me in through the door of his bedroom.

It's neat and clean as you'd expect, with boxing trophies crowding most of the shelves and a huge rendering of the Virgin Mary over the bed. Which makes sense – our school is known as Our Lady's Mount, though we swap it around to Mounting Our Lady.

– Cross yourself, please, Ned.

I kneel before Our Lady and do the sign of the cross.

– Now, take your shirt off, says the Drink Machine.

I've been through this a few times before, as has Larry and Kaspar and Halftime, who's the golden boy of the swimming team and doesn't have to play footy, so he brings on oranges for the First XV at half-time, the Polish poof. We've discussed the Drink Machine situation and the ramifications but we also understand it gives us a bit of prestige, a bit of leeway that plenty of the other boys don't get. We're not idiots but you don't fuck with Indiana Drink Machine. He has a voodoo power over most of the other brothers and teachers in the school – he's *revered* and he's a tough cunt who can break your jaw despite the fact he wears a dress.

Indy waddles over to his desk drawer where he takes out a Polaroid camera.

– Now stand here, in the light.

He grabs me like he's wrestling a cow and I feel the power in his arms. He's got to be seventy-five, eighty years old and he'd pop me like a grape if he wanted to. I stand in the light and try to adopt a pose that looks somewhat less than enthusiastic, but Indy's on to me.

– Stand up straight, boy.

I give him a constipated smile as he squeezes off a couple of shots. He puts them on his bed to develop and reaches into his drawer for a tape measure. This is the hard part.

– Come here, boy.

Indy knows as well as I do that he has to give his deep weirdness some semblance of credibility. It comes in the form of a well-thumbed exercise book and the tape measure. He tells us, and himself, that he's measuring our vitals to track our progress for football or swimming, to see how well we're developing in the weights room.

The argument might hold some sort of water if I was a star rugby player, but I'm struggling to hold down a spot in the 16Ds and my devotion to anything physical, be it surfing, skateboarding or showering, is because it's perceived as cool and gives me an identity which girls are comfortable rubbing up against.

Fuck, here we go, I think.

Indy also smells quite horrific. I don't know what goes on under that cassock, but in summer it smells like a groin casserole. The good brother also seems to have very little comprehension of oral hygiene because his teeth look like children's fingernails after they've been clawing through a flowerbed. His breath is treacherous and falls on top of you like a wet dog.

– Arm first, he says.

I hold out my bicep and Indy runs the cool fabric of the tape measure around it, giving me far more of a rub than I would have thought necessary.

– Chest.

For this one, he steps behind me as I hold my arms out like I'm being crucified. And maybe I am, but I don't think it's a centurion's spear that's poking my bot-tom as Indy presses his stomach against me. He loops the tape around my pecs, noting the measurement in pencil in his exercise book.

– Thigh.

I hold my leg up for him, but he's not having it.

– Don't be stupid, boy, I can't get a measurement through your trousers. Take off your pants.

This is the one that gets us all. The four of us who've been invited into the fat fuck's weird little wank club don't tell too many people about what goes on in Indy's room, but we're forthcoming with each other. We all dread the thigh measurement.

Indy likes to sit on the bed for this one. As I face him, he dips his head into my groin to get the measurement. There's only one thought going through my mind as he fusses around down there, his breath rising up like an ogre's exhalations: Please don't touch my penis, please don't touch my penis, please don't touch my penis, I say to myself.

Indy grunts and gets his face a little closer to my groin. If I had even half the hard-on I had with Miss Bootsakakis it would be jabbing him in the eye. The thought of him nudging down

my underdaks (lime green today), then popping my cock in that mottled mouth, is almost too much to bear. I see I have a pee dot the size of a five cent piece darkening my undies but he says nothing, just kneads my thigh, cinches the tape measure, then slaps me on the arse when he's finished.
 – Excellent, he says.

When I get back down to the quadrangle, Larry and Halftime give me the look.
 – Pictures?
 – Yep.
 – He do the thigh?
 – Yeah.
 – I fucken hate that.
Scorps, who's sitting with them, looks a bit hangdog.
 – What's wrong with you? I say.
 – Why don't priests find me attractive?

DOUBLES

– So, Kaspar has just gotten back from Indo and he's doing the stroll from his place, down to south end, says Scorps.

We're up the Regis. Me, Birdy, Chong, Grumble and Scorps, who's in storytelling mode.

– There's nought surf, so he's taking the mal just to get wet. There's heads everywhere, all the boys asking how the waves were in Nias, did he get on the choof, has he seen Debbie yet?

– Ahhh, is this about Debbie, is it? says Grumble.

– Shut up, Grumble, Ned and Birdy haven't heard yet.

I belch and talk through the Veebs gas.

– Heard what?

– What I'm just about to tell you, ya fuckin' hardhead.

I belch again and hand him the cue.

– It's your shot, CNN.

– Fuck!

He's pissed off because he wants to finish the story. Chong's always helpful.

– I'll take your shot.

He grabs for the cue, but Scorps yanks it back.

– Fuck off, Chong. What are we on?

– You're on bigs, I say.

I've gotten my eye in and have sunk four off the break. I have to take advantage of that tiny window between the first and second schooies when the alcohol's doing just enough to slow your pulse and iron out the agitation of the day, but not enough to cloud your judgement. Scorps bends, adjusts and works one of his balls down the cushion and into the hole.

– So? I say.

– So he's walking and he sees Mr Boom and he's like 'Have you spoken to Debbie?' And by now he's starting to suss that something's up.

– Didn't she pick him up from the airport? says Birdy.

– Nup. It was toooo er-leeee, says Scorps imitating a whiny chick's voice. Debbie's a good sort but she sounds like a dolphin.

– Have your fuckin' shot, I say.

He bends again and doubles another big into the middle pocket.

– Yeh-heh-ess, says Birdy, who's his partner. Now Scorps lines up a length of the table shot and I know before he hits it he's gonna miss. He's fucked at distance shots, plays them too hard. He slams the ball and it shimmies out of the hole.

– Fuck.

– Come on, Grumble, I say.

– Fuck, says Scorps again. He sits on the stool, shaking his head at the injustice of it.

– Finish your story, mate, says Birdy.

– Yeah. So he paddles out the back and it's shit but there's still a few of the boys there and they ask him the same thing, 'Have you seen Debbie yet?'

– She's pregnant?

– Nah, but Kasp is starting to freak a bit. All these guys saying, 'Have you spoken to your chick?' So when he gets home he calls her. She's meant to be coming over to his place after she finishes work and he asks her what the story is, but she says she can't talk while she's at work and hangs up on him. He calls her back and her mobile is switched off and then she doesn't turn up at his place, so he goes over to hers and she's blind. He asks her what's going on and she says she couldn't help it, but she slept with someone while he was away.

– Who?

– Some guy, she says he wouldn't know him. So Kaspar freaks and he goes home and punches about eighty cones and goes up the Hotel Bondi and he sees Mr Boom again, except Boom is blind now too and he's saying, 'I'm sorry, mate, I'm sorry, mate'. Kaspar gives him one in the head, then starts bashing him cos he thinks it's Mr Boom that's been fucking Debbie and they both get thrown out.

– Was it Boom? I say.

– Yeah but Boom is yelling at him, 'Why you fuckin' bashing me? What about the rest of the cunts?'

– There's more than one?

I look at Chong, who's listening to the story with a dim grimace. Kaspar and him are good mates, so he's protective.

– Fuck, just take your shots, you cunts.

– How many blokes did she root? I ask Scorps.

– Eight, he says, enunciating the word like he's pulling hot cheese off a pizza with his teeth.

– Fuck off, laughs Birdy.

– Eight? He was only gone for six weeks.

– Who are they?

– All the Bondi boys . . .
– Full on?
– Did you know about this, Chong? I ask.
– I dunno if it was eight, he says.
– Bullshit, Chong, I asked you and you said it was.
– Yeah, well, we shouldn't be fuckin' laughing about it.
– Fuck off, Chong, if it was one of us, he'd be up here giving it to us.

Birdy is still staggered.
– Eight?
– Yeah, and after one of the boardriders' presos, Gooch and Col two-outed her on the roof of the Diggers she was so coked up.

That strikes a blow even with me. Gooch is a dirty cunt. Imagine knowing that bloke had been up your girl. It's enough to make you spew.
– That's fucked, I say.
It's Grumble's shot. He swishes by me.
– I'm just fuckin' spewing she didn't root me, he says.

ELLE MACPHERSON'S SHIT

I've got my arms hanging over the railing, like I'm in one of those old-fashioned stocks they used to set up in the town square to lock criminals in. I'm sitting on the promenade at Maroubra Beach watching my boardies dry in the incredible heat.

It's the school holidays and I've finally managed to buy a cool pair of Billabongs after several fucked attempts with brands like Hot Tuna, Salt Water and Mango. One leg is pink, the other blue, with the colours reversed on the rear of the shorts. They're hell. Larry's still in the surf, but I've gotten out because I've got a rash on my stomach and it's stinging heaps. I feel the sun dim behind me and turn to see Birdy.
– You wanna tax some plants? he says.
– Where?
– Pagewood.
– How many?
– Fucken heaps, mate.

Birdy is wearing a pair of Quiksilver boardies with large, different coloured polka dots on them. They're last year's design and far cooler than mine. They're just a bit shorter than the tan marks from his wetsuit and a line of white skin pokes out from under them every time he moves. We wait until a few of the other boys get out of the water.

– You sure? asks Cookie. He's a little Abo mate of Larry's who rides a kneeboard but we don't hold that against him.

– Ye-aaah, says Birdy, staggered we'd even question his credentials. – I looked over the fence. The guy's got 'em growing next to his shed.

We all catch the bus up there from the beach. Me, Birdy, Larry and Cookie. The house is near Snape Park and has a high aluminium fence. We go around the back to a little alley and see a big chrome chopper tilted to one side, parked.

– He's a bikie? I say.

– Nah, he just rides a bike, says Birdy. – I've seen him.

– Pretty serious fucken bike, says Larry and we gather around the thing. It looks like it's been smeared in honey. It drips with power.

– Dog.

We turn. Cookie's already looking over the fence. A professional. We join him and see what he's talking about. A big black German Shepherd sits on the back steps beside a scuffed kid's Green Machine.

– Fuck that.

– Where's the plants?

– Round here, says Birdy.

He moves along to the end of the fence where an aluminium garden shed is wedged in the corner. There's half a metre between the shed and fence and it's stuffed with about a dozen mature dope plants.

– Fuck off.

– Bullshit.

Larry and I are impressed. We've being doing a bit of growing ourselves and know how hard it is to get good plants in the shit sandy soil around here. This guy's a genius considering how little sunlight the plants are receiving. Cookie leaps the fence and pads onto the grass like a tomcat. The dog stands from its nest at the door and walks towards him growling. Cookie wrenches a metal star picket out of the guy's flower garden and slices it through the air with a whomp. The dog looks at Cookie for a few seconds, weighing its options, then sits back down.

Fuck it, it thinks.

We immediately jump the fence and start heaving at the plants. They're huge and don't want to come out of the ground, but we're persistent and they finally tear out of the soil, trailing huge clumps of dirt. We're laughing, throwing them over the fence into the laneway where Birdy's found a box from a television set and is stuffing them inside. There's pounds and pounds of dope. We have to bend the stems and snap them to get them inside and then we're running up the alley. We get to Botany Road and hail a cab and jump inside with the box, leaves poking out everywhere.

– Maroubra Road, says Cookie.

The cabbie doesn't know what to think of us, and after a minute the smell of fresh dope fills the car. We wind down the windows, laughing, until we get to Cookie's place and drag our thieving arses inside. We pull the dope apart on his mum's kitchen table, separating the leaf and heads, and piss off the stems. Larry has fired up the oven and we lay some of the best bits on a baking tray, then shove it inside to dry. We divide the rest of the thax into four piles and stuff it into plastic shopping bags.

An hour later we're stoned as chooks, back on the promenade, arms slung over the railing, watching the lefts break into the dunny bowl at North Maroubra.

– Would you eat a piece of shit to fuck Elle Macpherson? asks Birdy.

– Yep, says Larry, not even hesitating.

If I've been given any sort of natural talent, it's that of the gross description.

– Nah, nah, I say to them. – It's not just a piece of shit. It's long, like a breakfast sausage, and you have to bite into it and it's like Plasticine, so you get smears of shit on your front teeth.

The boys cringe appreciatively.

– And there's a hair in it that comes out in strands as you take a bit off, I say.

Larry pretends to dry heave.

– And passion fruit seeds that you have to split with your teeth, he says.

– And a toenail and peanut sticking out the side. That's why you sometimes have painful shits, I say. – It's a peanut scraping your intestine lining.

– You're a fucken disgusting cunt, aren't you? says Larry, smiling.

We all agree we would eat the shit but only if it was Elle's shit.

SOON

Now I'm floating in a swimming pool with her on the twenty-fifth floor of a delightful apartment complex in The Rocks, looking down on the city like a pharaoh. My guts feel like the elastic in a golf ball after you've peeled off the cover, and I know if you touch me in just the right place I'll unravel in convulsions of joy and form a puddle of sheer bliss at her feet.

Guru was right. She does have big hands. Mannish and certain. Big everything. Ceramic thighs, a stomach shiny like Charles Foster Kane's missing sled, an arse you could break your fingertip on, and that murderous amber hair. Alessandra rises out of the heated pool like the Lady of the Lake, stubborn steam clinging to the tight Lycra of her one-piece, the blue waterproof cast dripping danger as she walks like a lazy princess to the sauna.

Thank god I've been working out, I think as I follow her out of the water, slowly, taking my sweet time.

Stay casual, I remind myself. Aloof.

I walk to the floor-to-ceiling window and press my hot wet hair against the winter glass, beaded with rain, and stare down at the grey harbour like the city is moving in my heart.

This is all I ever want.

Today she has brought a 'friend' with her, Arna, and, like litmus in the presence of an undeniable chemical reaction, he is turning green. Arna sees that Alessandra is warming to my new feigned indifference and the tiny hidden hope he'd kept sheltered behind his platonic pretence has flattened and drowned in the pool where his Kentucky Fried Chicken physique is coagulating on the surface. I look at Arna's flabby boobs prowing the water and thank god again for push-ups.

Something is happening here.

I'm almost too scared to acknowledge it in case I jinx myself, but something is definitely happening. I open the sauna door and don't even look at Alex as I sit on the chalky wood bench and the heat tackles me into stillness. Then, my fuckin' blessed god, she's pouring water on my chest and I feel like a stone in a stream, she's looking at my body and for a hot second I am perfect; a slick, steamed crustacean.

– You do me, she says and hands me the ladle and stretches back on the bench like a gymnast. My hands feel crystalline as I scoop up the holy water and pour it in a laser stream through the heat and mist onto her eaves.

You know how those bullet trains that ride on a magnetic current feel.

You're a goddamn bullet man.

You wanna print up T-shirts.

It's happening.

She's dried off now and Arna's dried up, gone off back to his two-seater car and bra. Her damp hair is pulled back in a livid ponytail and she's humbling the street in the most beautiful pair of navy blue corduroy pants you've ever seen in your life, buying a packet of Tic Tacs, and you feel like someone's following you with Batman's searchlight.

How can walking across the road with one girl seem like the Superbowl?

Where is all that fucking cheering coming from?

You look around you and every hair on your body feels like a tugging fishing line, a point of exit for the hot, hungry happiness hissin' sin inside. When you ask if she wants to meet some of *your* friends, she wrinkles up her lip and nods that gorgeous motherfucking ponytail that you wanna write an epic poem about.

Sitting down to drink that night it's with a savage energy, a New Year's flush, and Scorps and Birdy smile at me because they're happy I'm happy. The schooners are sweating droplets of ice water and, as the sun sets over the beach, I watch the steady pulse of the swell scatter the diehards still in the line-up. I feel the tight, muscled brisket of my stomach and the light seasoning of my sunburnt neck and the beer is like an anointment, the boys my loyal companions. The Icebergs' salt-hazed windows are the lens of my wild, royal eye and all is good because the hot slug of her interest sits in the back of my stomach, a warm place during conversation. I lean into it like a homeless guy around a fire in a trashcan . . . she'll be here soon.

GETTING OUT ALIVE

It's funny how things work out.

Birdy was the punish in our group when we were growing up, always needing to blow his own horn, bullshitting us about things he'd done, places he'd gone and chicks he was meant to have rooted, arguing about money, always arguing about money. And then something happened. While the rest of us tried to make our own rules, Birdy followed the time-worn path of our parents. He got a job, saved for a mortgage, got over it when his heart was broken and met another girl. While the rest of us groped along the monkey bars of love, grasping from one relationship to the next, Birdy just settled in for the ride. He matured, he accepted his faults and laughed about them. He grew bigger than himself. And now he's getting married.

It's nothing too flash, just a group of friends and family gathered around the rotunda in Grant Park at South Coogee. We're all there. Scorps looking swollen, Grumble pissed off and ready to smash someone, Larry weighted down by gold chains, looking like he's just come off the door at a Lakemba nightclub, Kaspar in a skivvy, wondering why he doesn't have his own TV show, Chong, Zen as ever and, me, scoping the crowd for the next chick I'm gonna waste five months of my life with.

– You get him a present? asks Scorps.

– Whatta you reckon?

– Can I go in with youse?

– Fuck, there's already four of us, we might as well have got him a pack of chewy each.

– You want some? he says and offers me a mangled finger of Extra.

– Don't be a dickhead. He's one of your best mates. Fuckin' make an effort.

He thinks about this, chewing.

– What'd you get?

– Some vase thing.

– Sweet. I'll give you fifty. Can I write on the card?

The ceremony is pretty simple, with a dash of theatrics thanks to Birdy's stagehand workmates. There's a blast of music, a puff of smoke, then a bloke in an Elvis costume appears and grabs the microphone. I don't have to tell you what he says next.

– Thang you very much, thang you very much.

– Who's this fuckin' kook? says Grumble.

– It's the celebrant, dickhead.

The ceremony is loose. Birdy's best man is his brother, the maid of honour is Laney's little girl, Karma, and we all sit on the grass in a little terraced amphitheatre sweating in our suits.

– Is it free piss at the reception? asks Scorps as Laney glides in from behind a screen of bottlebrush.

– I think so.

– Fuckin' wanna be, the pommy cunt.

The couple stand either side of Elvis, who's glinting in the sun like he's emerged from a chrysalis.

– Do you, Aaron, take Laney to be your lawfully wedded wife? If you do, say, 'Uh-huh'.

Birdy smiles.

– Uh huh, he says and the crowd laughs.

All I can think is, at least one of us has got out alive.

DEAD BABY

Fuck knows how Mr Wang got this excursion past the brothers, but he did. Even though we're a Catholic school, the administration is bound by some law to teach a nondenominational religious class for all the Jews, Hindus, Moozies and Satanists in our form. That's where Mr Wang, our resident Chinese radical and atheist, comes in.

Guru and Hump reckon Wang used to be a nuclear researcher in Beijing, then defected here while he was attending some conference and claimed diplomatic immunity. Knowing Hump and Guru, that's total bullshit, but Wang is a brilliant scientist, and if you gave him enough time, I reckon he could prove to the Pope that God is just vibrating molecules.

Anyway, to fit in with the curriculum, Wang's come up with a course he's called 'Death and Dying'. It's meant to be a scientific look at the hereafter and a comparison of what different religions think happens to you once you're planted. Wang wants to strip away the myths so, somehow, he's arranged for our form to visit Glebe Morgue and see an autopsy. Not on film, not photographs – a fair dinkum, slice-the-fucker-up-with-a-circular-saw autopsy.

Who wouldn't want to pull cones to watch that shit?

Today almost didn't happen because Disco's mum heard about the trip and kicked up a stink. She approached Indiana Drink Machine at the bus stop last week, suggesting her son's gentle nature might not be able to withstand the sight of real dead people. There was talk of canning the whole excursion, then Grumble and Joe Gold threatened Disco with violence and, unbelievably, he went home and stuck it up his mum, told her to stop interfering and she dropped off and here we are. Warms your heart, don't it? Could be a coming of age story starring a Culkin brother.

As an entrée, we've come over to the stumbling fat fuck's place, because he lives opposite school. Actually, Grumble told Disco we were coming over and he had no say in it. His bedroom is in the front of the house, in the sunroom, and you can look out his window straight into the headmaster's office. We know his mum works as a brain surgeon or some shit and won't be home. Right now there's fifteen of us in his room, punching on. It's classic, because we can open the curtains and see straight across Birrell Street and watch Indy walking up and down, scanning for life forms.

About twenty years ago, Indiana Drink Machine had a skin cancer removed from his forehead and it left this fist-sized circular indentation in his head. It looks like a little radar dish. Couple that with the fact the cunt rolls around in his cassock like a black-clad robot, and he doesn't seem quite of this world sometimes. Indy is the enforcer of the brothers. He knows every rat hole and alleyway around here. He's hard to beat. You'll jig the last two periods, piss off after lunch and take the back streets down to the Jungo. You'll be well clear of the school, home and hosed, then turn a corner and there will be Indy.

Meep, meep, meep, meep. The cunt's got you.

Worse still, he does random breath tests to see if you've been durrying up. If you've already been caught smoking, forget it. Every time he sees you, he'll stop you to smell your breath. I reckon chewing gum sales around here have tripled since the introduction of RBT.

Suggs is on the jar now, sucking it down like it's a chocolate milkshake . . . only smoky! Suggs is a fucken machine on the choof, the red-headed freak. He packs, lights, pulls and exhales like he's scratching his armpit. I look outside again and Indy is still watching the street. It's like he senses a disturbance – he knows something's up but he can't quite penetrate the bricks of Disco's house. He starts across the street towards us and I fling the curtain shut.

– He's coming!

Poor Disco, he's shitting himself we're gonna get sprung. On the scale of silence, a room full of sixteen year old schoolboys ripped to the gills on Henrietta Street hydro is not real high.

– Exterminate, exterminate, squeaks Birdy and we're gone for a good twenty seconds, squirting out those tight, girlish giggles only stoned teenage boys can seem to manage. I peek through the curtains again and FUCK ME. The cunt is right outside Disco's bedroom, still as an Easter Island statue, staring like a sniper down the street towards the ocean.

– Shhhhhhh, he's right outside.

We duck down, like that will help. I think there's actually seventeen of us in the room. Kaspar starts it off.

– Meep, he says.

Then Grumble.

– Meep. Meep

We're imitating the noise Indy's scanner would make if it actually existed. It's almost the funniest thing I've heard in my life.

– Mem, mem, mem, MEEP, says Birdy.

Foilie loses it, tries not to laugh then projectile snots out his nose. It lands on Scorps's hand. He looks at it, horrified, then wipes it across Disco's face. The room collapses on itself but we all know we're pretty safe. If there is a flaw in Indy's design it's that he's half deaf and wears a hearing aid. We could actually be playing oom-pah music in Disco's bedroom and the cunt wouldn't twig.

After about a minute of rolling up and down the street, the Drink Machine returns to his post outside the school. In ones and twos we go out Disco's back door, over fences, through the back lane, across Seaview Park and appear from different spots up and down the street. Indy breath-tests Grumble, but he's on the Juicy Fruits so he's sweet.

By the time we get to the morgue, I'm almost straight enough to talk again. We could be in the foyer of a public library except for our tour guide. He's a pasty-looking dude in his thirties wearing a hairnet, who looks kinda like Kiefer Sutherland outta that movie about the vampires but with acne. He's deeply disappointed we're an all-boys school. He's got that look about him that would have you questioning your decision to choose him as a piano teacher or scout leader.

– What you're seeing today is the end of the line, says Kiefer, switching to a hard-arse, I've-stared-death-in-the-face persona.

– How's this wanker? says Larry to me softly.

– 'Scuse me? says Kiefer, getting on his toes to look up the back. – We're gonna need to keep it quiet, please. This is not a playground you're entering.

– It's a House of Death, says Birdy in a Vincent Price voice, loud enough for everyone to hear. We piss ourselves. Kiefer points at him.

– You, you son, you're the sort of person who'll end up in here one day if you're not careful.

– What the fuck does that mean, Kiefer? I say softly. More laughter. Mr Wang makes little shushing noises but mainly just smiles. He looks more stoned than we are. I reckon he's laughing like a cunt inside that he's even got a bunch of private school kids this far.

Kiefer sees he's not getting anywhere being the tough guy, so he switches to being our mate.

– You guys are pretty lucky to have a teacher like Mr Wang, he says.

Wang grins a bit more. I'm sure he's ripped. Maybe he's Thai?

– Thanks to your teacher's efforts lobbying the New South Wales health department, you are the first group of high school children in the State's history to enter this building.

Fuck. Didn't know that. We exchange looks. Cool.

– Up until now, the only people who've been allowed past this point – he motions to a white sliding door behind him – have been health department officials, police officers and medical staff. He bangs on a little more about regulations and not touching the bodies and blah, blah, blah, and then the door opens and we're in.

First stop is kind of like a staging area with silver gurneys, a concrete floor and drains. In one corner are a bunch of heavy blue plastic bags – fuck, they're body bags – and they're covered in blood. A murmur goes through our group. Disco, who's near me, makes a soft sigh, like he's peeing himself. Kiefer's enjoying this. He's in his element.

– This is where we clean up the bodies that come into the morgue. Those bags you see in the corner, they contained the bodies of three teenagers and an older man who were killed in a light-aircraft accident yesterday.

Fuck off. This is heavy.

– The gentleman who was flying the plane is believed to have been under the influence of marijuana (Kiefer pronounces it mara-jee-wana, the dickhead) when he experienced engine trouble. Maybe he would have been able to deal with the problem if he hadn't been smoking mara-jee-wana, maybe not. But what you're about to see is the consequence of his decision and it cost three young men their lives.

We're all starting to realise where we actually are. I have never seen a dead body before. None of us have, except Grumble, who says he saw his dad dead when he was ten. Birdy says the cunt hung himself and that's when he had to go live with his grandparents. Anyway, Kiefer doesn't have to call for quiet any more. He's got our full stoned attention.

– If it's the last thing I do, it'll be to stop kids like you taking drugs, he says.

Rightio.

Kiefer swings open another door and we're hit with the smell of antiseptic. It's quiet as a tomb – because, because, fuuuuck OOOOFF . . . OH, MY GOD.

The room is huge and tiled and lined with more stainless-steel gurneys. There's bodies everywhere, all naked, all not moving. Dozens of them. It's not like in the movies or the cop shows where they're all in their own little drawers; they're out in the open – the whole room is refrigerated.

Most of the people are really old men and women, frozen in their sleep by the looks of it. Their ancient vaginas and penises are on show like dried flowers; some of them have their false teeth popping out, all of them you've seen at the shops counting out change. It's incredible to see old people without their clothes on.

The very first corpse to our right is a guy, he must be early twenties. He looks like he was a body builder or something – a fit cunt, with an almost perfect physique, but now it's criss-crossed with enormous purple stitch marks. Not the stitches you get in hospital, industrial size stitches, no-nonsense jobbies that aren't expected to heal nicely. He looks like Frankenstein's monster.

– This is the gentleman who was flying the plane, says Kiefer. He's slurring with power, taking in our shocked faces as we stare at the stiffs. Next to the body builder are the other kids from the plane, similarly torn apart and sewn together. There's unnatural bulges and bruises all over them. One of the guys is my age and looks like someone's tried to stuff a chair inside his body. I hear Disco make another whimper and move over to him.

– You alright? You wanna go outside? He nods his head and I move him out into the corridor.

– Just don't fucken pass out and ruin it for the rest of us, okay?

Disco nods but he's struggling. He sits down and stares out into the bright sunshine coming through the front doors from Parramatta Road. When I get back, Kiefer is standing next to a headless male body.

– This genius thought it would be a giggle to stick his head under a train.

We gather around. The guy's spine is sticking out of his neck like the bone in a leg of lamb. Kiefer looks like he's got an erection under those hospital pants of his. He bends over the corpse, pointing at the neck with his pencil.

– One of the interesting features of decapitation by locomotive is the way the extreme pressure of the train wheels seals the blood vessels shut.

We all lean in. Fuck me. Sure enough, all the arteries, sticking out of the guy's neck like big purple worms, have been pressed closed like the end of a tube of toothpaste. On the gurney, between the dead guy's feet, is a large, blue plastic bag. It's the only body that has a bag like that.

– What's this? asks Birdy, always a nosy cunt.

Kiefer smiles.

– Whattaya think it is?

He smiles again.

– Awww, it's his head, says Scorps.

Kiefer picks it up and hefts it.

– The average human head weighs about twelve kilos, which is pretty heavy. Wanna try?

I don't know about you, but a good *Pink Panther* cartoon or special effects movie can freak me out heavily when I'm stoned. Walking down the street can wig me out if the buds are good enough. Standing in line in a morgue, ripped to the tits, so I can hold some bloke's head in a bag, has to rank up there as one of my better spin-outs.

Kiefer hasn't finished, though. He walks to the end of the room and unzips another bag so he can show us the freshly exhumed corpse of a murder victim. It looks like a side of beef. The arms and head are gone, with just the torso remaining. Kiefer, like all blokes who spend too much time in rooms by themselves, goes a bit far and starts sniffing the body to freak us out. Then there's a cry from the back of the room.

– FILTH! It's Birdy, standing over a scraggy-looking blonde chick. A junkie who's OD'd. She's cordoned off from the rest of the bodies by a little chain that has a sign on it saying *HIV possible*. The class pushes towards the woman and as I turn to follow I see a flash of skin in the far corner of the room. A tiny shape, flour white and crumpled on its own gurney. It's a baby, a girl, not more than six months old. She looks like she's been tossed in the corner like a doll. She isn't laid out like the rest.

She looks discarded, forgotten, cold. I want to put a blanket over her.
 – Cot death.
 Kiefer is beside me. He looks at the kid and picks her up, straightens her out, makes her look a little more comfortable. I like him a bit more for that.

SMIDGEN BLAZING HEARTS

She's wearing a loose skirt with a red rose print and floats next to me like a young queen. Something has definitely changed. Alessandra seems to breathe beside me for the first time, the snarl has smoothed from her face and her laughter, like bubbles in hot water, seems a premonition of some unstoppable sweet fission. She doesn't jump when our pinkies brush as we walk, there's a felt on the ground between us and the air's hung with half-finished sentences. She swings around as she walks like a grown-up Judy Garland on the yellow brick road, smiling, humming tunes, blowing my mind with every ripple that runs through her long legs.

I feel weak with expectation, yet I dare not let the thought in. We cross the street and walk into the deep green of Cooper Park and the moist night closes behind us like theatre black. The leaves are thick on the path, and over the whisper of the night I can hear the clap of my soles overlapping the clack of her heels, the two sounds breaking rhythm until slowly, like summer cicadas, they slide into syncopation and our footsteps are a single bass line amongst the grey luminescence of the trees.

A children's birthday party is going on in a soft cul-de-sac of the park and the little boys and girls have lit hundreds of tiny candles in the velvet undergrowth. In the damp silt of the creekbed they've laid more tiny lights along the dark artery of water like supplicants' torches gathered at a holy river. We walk into this child's dream and I hear her breath stop as the smidgen blazing hearts wrap around us. Children run between the trees laughing and crying out for missing friends and somewhere deep in the dark a transistor radio pours a soft stream of violin into the woods.

Your pinkies touch again and you slow her amongst an extended family of slender pale gum trees. You lean against the smooth waist of a she-tree and she gazes up through the leaves into the midnight blue of the southern sky and when she looks back at you her eyes shine with something ancient. Her rose skirt hugs the soft touch of the tree as she leans into the night and you know this is forever.

She makes you feel the soil from which you've broken, makes you feel your mother's great grandfather and his grandmother before, and the certainty that, once, they too had seen those eyes, they too had felt this moment, the absolute forest-clearing purity of having someone beautiful want you, if even for a night, a kiss, a glass of water and just like that you reach for her.

She comes with you and you move your cheek against hers, barely touching, the follicles of your skins alive as they intertwine, a microscopic Velcro moment, the charge of each other filling the tiny void as you slowly brush faces, mouths at the diagonal, completely aware, until you brush noses, then lips, barely touching, her breath sweet from the tomatoes in the salad, her lips still alive in the creases with balsamic, you taste each other's exhalations, wanting her breath inside you, wanting to seal your mouth over hers and take in nothing but Alessandra.

And you kiss as the trees sigh and the moon ties itself to your memories and the children hum with exhaustion at their mothers' legs.

MISS HELENA vs SEKA

It's a school day and I'm sick and thick with a cold and my mum is meant to be out of the house most of the day. Shamus is at work or working at getting pissed and my sister, no doubt, is busy throwing up her sandwiches at school. That just leaves me, a tub of vitamin E cream, a room full of video recorders and the big box of porn tapes hidden in the top cupboard of my parents' closet.

I have no idea I'm heading for greatness that morning as I watch Miss Helena on *Romper Room* and feel the now familiar tugging at my flannelette pajamas.

Why not? I think. I'm sick. I need to look after myself. Orgasms are supposed to be good for you.

I slip into the dunny to collect the vitamin E, creeping across our white shag carpet, listening for clanking in the kitchen. I have the TV set up at the foot of my bed where Miss Helena, the criminally sexy kids' show host, is now pole-dancing for me.

She's blonde, blue-eyed and her red lipstick burns like syphilitic genitalia as she holds a mirror frame up to her face, speaking to camera. I make my posture decidedly casual so if my mum walks in it'll look like I'm just slouching under the covers.

– Romper, stomper, bomper boo, says Miss Helena and I settle in.

– Tell me, tell me, tell me, do. Magic mirror, tell me today, have all my friends been good at play?

– Oh no, Miss Helena, I've been bad, I say.

She gazes back at me, the lustful bitch.

– I can see Brad, she says.

– That's right, Miss Helena, I say, stroking.

– And Kimberley and Kylie.

– Yeah, we're all here, come join us.

– And Benjamin and Daniel.

– One big party.

– And Tamsin and Ned.

I harden even more. She's never mentioned me by name before.

– You can see me, can you, Miss Helena?

– Yes, I can see you, Ned.

She smiles at me. I flick back the covers. Risky, but I need the room.

– And what are you gonna do, Miss Helena?

She's staring out of the Trinitron at my cock. Did she just lick her lips?

– Do me, Mr Do Bee, she says.

I almost hit myself in the face with my sprog.

Television is a minefield. F Troop with Wrangler Jane, *Petticoat Junction* with Betty Jo, Billie Jo and Bobbie Jo, even Princess Susan in *Battle of the Planets* is enough to give me a fat on a good day. Or a bad day. Whatever.

There's only so much wanking a bloke can do over G-rated TV shows, however. For a real attempt at the record, I have to reach for the hard stuff. So I wait. Eventually my mum gathers up her handbag and keys and slams the front door, the rooster screech of the Ford Falcon starter motor a sure sign she's on her way. She backs into Lancaster Crescent, wrestles the steering, thunders off towards Eastgardens and I am King of Porn.

The box sits innocently enough at the top of the cupboard. Could just be holding some old newspapers or shoes. Maybe a satchel. Flip it open, however, and there you have it. Great Googily Moogily! I'm talking the golden age of Colour Climax films, *Swedish Erotica* numbers 1 through 23. *The Devil in Miss Jones.* Herschel Savage, Joey Silvera, Bunny Bleu and Seka.

Oh, Seka.

There's no VCR in my bedroom, so I set up shop in my mother's office, the dozen Betamaxes and U-matics humming away. I rip my daks off and sit on her desk, a couple of AGC Finance warning letters sticking to my slightly damp arse. And away I go.

Every time I follow the same routine: stroke it, reach for the stars, explode, clean up, eject the tape, ferret back the instruments of my shame to their rightful resting spots: Vitamin E cream to the bathroom, roll of toilet paper back on the dispenser, *Swedish Erotica 9* back in the box. Then I lie in bed swamped by guilt and disgust for about fifteen minutes before Alex Wileman chugging lemonade in the Mello Yello ad sets me off again.

Five wanks before lunchtime, nine by 3 pm. My penis looks like a tiger prawn it's so red raw. After the fourth wank the poor guy isn't capable of producing semen any more. He spasms, dry heaves but spits out nothing – an exhausted worm gasping for breath.

Have mercy on me, he's saying, but I'm showing him who's boss.

You wanna get me worked up? I'll give it back to you in spades, Oscar.

With half an hour before my sister arrives home from school, I make my move on my personal best wank record. Number eleven. Never been done before. Never been attempted, for all I know. I need someone dependable, someone I know will get me across the line.

There's actually never any doubt in my mind – Seka has to be my dance partner. Her pose on the front of *Free and Foxy* – white panties, garter and stockings, hips switched to one side, hands cupping each of her breasts – quite possibly defines femininity more comprehensively than any other image in my life. She is an angel. Perfect in every way. And she takes it up the arse.

This time I apply extra cream, ignoring the pain of my grated spanner, and stroke towards glory. It takes a long time but Seka is a champion: that rosebud cunt, those bell cup tits, that brown skin. I concentrate, thighs tensed like an Olympic long jumper, speed up my rhythm and, and, AND, ANNNNNND, YES!

Reach for the stars, explode, clean up, eject the tape . . . umm . . . eject the tape? The VCR stirs, whirs but won't spit out *Free and Foxy*. Seka is trapped inside. I turn the machine off at the power. I turn it on. Seka's a prisoner.

– What the fuck is wrong with this thing? I say out loud.

Fifteen video machines in the house and I choose the dud. I pick it up. I hit it. I shake the fucken thing upside down (not easy with a U-matic) but Seka is entombed. All I can see is the spine of the tape staring out at me – *Free and Foxy* – my guilt exposed for all to witness. This is bad.

– This is very, very bad, I say to myself.

I ferret back the instruments of my shame to their rightful resting spots – vitamin E cream to the bathroom, roll of toilet paper back on the dispenser – then wonder what the fuck I am going to do about *Free and Foxy*.

I go to the kitchen and look for tools. I'll pull the VCR apart. I'll gut a thousand dollar machine before I leave that tape in there. As I search for a screwdriver, my hand touches a familiar handle – the soldering iron my stepdad uses for electrical repairs. Then it comes to me. Simple.

Back in my mum's office, I plug in the iron and let it heat up. Then, like a laser cutting tool in *Thunderbirds,* I use it to carve open the spine of the video tape, following the edge of the label until it falls out and into my hand. Sorry, Seka.

Inside the soon to be eviscerated cassette, I can see the twin spools of magnetic tape. I haul it out in giant double handfuls. Tape arcs around me like a gymnast's ribbon before pooling on the floor: ten feet, then a hundred, three hundred feet.

Where the fuck is it all coming from?

That's when I hear the Ford Falcon motoring up the street. I heave at the tape like a lifesaver reeling in a relative. The cogs in the cassette squeal and still the tape comes. Five hundred feet, seven fifty, a thousand. For fuck's sake!

My mother's feet scuffle on the sandstone path outside the office window. My Uncle Truman laid that path. It's beautiful, rough hewn, but deadly at night. There's ripples and ridges on the stone that can trip you up and send you sprawling, chin stripped to the bone if you're not careful. I pray my mother's high heels find an edge and she falls over. Instead I hear the front door open.

Heave, man, heave!

Groceries are dumped in the kitchen.

Like your life depends on it, man! HEAVE! The tape is singing in the air around me. I'm a human scribble. Footsteps sound on the floorboards outside my room.

– Ned?

Fuck.

She's seen I'm not in my bed, sees the office door closed.

– Ned?

Two thousand feet of magnetic tape is festooned around my ankles. The door opens. I smile.

– A tape got stuck.

My mum's trying to process the scene.

– What tape?

– Just a TV show.

– What have you done?

She looks at the soldering iron, then peers in at the melted video cassette.

– I was trying to get it out.

She reaches around the back of the machine and presses the, until then, unknown release button. The machine gulps and pops out *Free and Foxy*. Unfortunately, I'd forgotten about the side label. Seka's holding a purple cock like it's the rung of a ladder.

ISLAND CULTURE

My asthma is playing up because I've been punching a tonne of cones lately. All I have to do is run for a taxi and I'm wheezing like the Elephant Man. I'm off to visit some of the boys at their new apartment in Bondi Junction, so I stop at the chemist on Anzac Parade to buy myself an asthma gun.

    The government, ever concerned about my welfare, has brought in this new system for asthmatics where you have to carry a little blue card around with you. The chemist writes down on the card the date you last bought yourself a dose of Salbutamol, otherwise known to its fans as Ventolin, so you can be 'monitored'. The way it's meant to work, some bald cunt, with dish plates of sweat soaking through his lab coat, is supposed to take three minutes out from typing up four hundred prescriptions for suppositories, answering phones, watching for shoplifters and ringing through orders for Panadol, so he can question me about my lungs.

I park my car, Hank the Tank, and go in. There's four old fucks waiting for their pills, so the chemist, a pudgy guy with an egg-in-the-nest bald patch like a Franciscan monk, has to eventually stop what he's doing to come talk to me. I hand over the card and he looks me up and down. I'm already ripped and the overhead fluorescent lights have the place lit up like a torture chamber. I feel like I'm on Mars and the chemist seems to know my story before I even open my mouth.

– How often are you using your Ventolin (you little, stoned fuck)?

– Maybe once a day (maybe fuckin' twelve times a day).

– It says here you bought an inhaler two weeks ago (you lying shit).

– Yeah, I left it in my mate's car when we went surfing down the coast (and pulled forty-five cones in eighteen hours).

– Are you taking a preventative?

– Yeah, Flixotide (which ran out nine months ago).

– This card's full, you have to buy a new one (up yours).

– How much is that (you fat cunt)?

– Four dollars fifty (all for me, baby).

– I don't have four fifty. I've only got enough for the Ventolin (and a bag of goodness).

– Well, I can't serve you then. It's the law. You have to have a card.

– So why don't you just give it to me, what's the four fifty for?

– It's to cover administrative costs (or that's what the Pharmacists' Association told the government when they pushed this horseshit through Parliament.)

– What? For you to ask me three (fuckin') questions? That's not bad money, is it?

– There's other paperwork involved (which I never do).

– So what if I have an asthma attack right here in front of you? You wouldn't give me a Ventolin?

– That's a different situation (but I wouldn't mind watching you asphyxiate, smartarse).
– Well, I can't breathe.
I start wheezing.
– Yes you can.
– No I can't. I can't breathe.

I start bunging it on and an old lady who's waiting for her shopping bag of pills looks distressed. I can see the pharmacist doesn't really give a shit either way and I'm resigning myself to having to pay for the asthma card, when there's a drumbeat of running footsteps and two guys explode into the chemist. One is a massive Tongan, who's wearing a Mambo singlet, the veins in his shoulders as thick as green beans. He has a foot in plaster and is using a crutch to take a swing at the guy he's chasing, who's using the shelving to keep some distance between him and island culture. That guy is my cousin.

– Bailey, I say, and he looks at me and breathes a sigh of relief.
– Edward, you gotta help me.
– You fuckin' stay out of this, says the Tongan.
– Get out of my store! yells the pharmacist.
– He's gonna bash me, mate, says Bailey.
– Get out of here or I'll call the police.
– Good. Fuckin' call them!
– Bailey, what's going on?
– You gotta help me, Edward. This bloke thinks I owe him money.
– I don't fuckin' think anything, you swindling little cunt. Giss me fuckin' cash.
– I wish I could help you out, Manoa, but it's got nothing to do with me.

I step toward the guy and he shapes to hit me.
– Mate, why don't you just settle down?

– I'll fuckin' knock you out, cunt, he says in a slow, low voice, like steam coming out of a sewer grate. I back off and go around into the vitamin section to get close to Bailey. The Tongan keeps trying to zip around the aisles and grab him, but he's on crutches and Bailey's quick.

– What do you want me to do?

– Have you got a car, Edward?

– Outside.

– Alright, he says quietly. – Wind the passenger side window down and just drive past slowly and I'll run and jump in and then just fuckin' take off.

– What if he gets you?

– His foot's fucked. Just go, please, Edward.

I go outside and start up Hank. The only problem is Anzac Parade is one way, split by a grass verge, and I'm already in front of the chemist. It's a busy street so I can't reverse back. I have to go around the block. I floor it, hoping my little cousin won't be mashed into the haircare products by the time I make the loop. I pull into the traffic stream and wind down the window, slowing to about 10 kays an hour as I pass the chemist. Pissed-off drivers give me the horn, the finger and the shits as they sound off behind me.

– COME ON! I yell and Bailey darts from behind his shelf, the geriatrics clustered in one corner watching him as if it was an armed rob. Manoa is hot on his trail, but his foot is giving him plenty of trouble. He can only hop and Bailey soon outdistances him. He runs alongside the HQ then leaps headfirst through the passenger window and pulls his legs in. I speed up, then corner into Botany Street.

– What the fuck was that about, Bailey?

He's giggling.

– Aw, he reckons I ripped him off on some car stereos.

– Some car stereos?

– Yeah. He says I didn't give him his fair share of the whack.
 – Did you?
 – Probably not.
 – Have you got a Ventolin?

CARTOONING

Larry has some bush weed he's surgically snipped from the plants he's growing under his mum's nose out the back of his house at Malabar, while I've got a film canister of goodness I've lifted from Shamus's latest ounce. We're in a half-constructed housing commission semi in Daceyville and our breath is hoffing into steam in the early morning air. We've gotten in the habit of meeting half an hour earlier than our bus leaves for school, so we can pull a few. Larry's mulling up a bit of his buds with a bit of mine as we discuss plants.

– I just can't tell in time, I say.

– The males get this tiny little white flower down near where the branches come out from the main stem, he says.

Larry's explaining the importance of separating the males and females before they fertilise each other and send the dope to seed.

– I know, mate, but by the time I suss it, it's too late to

move them.

– You gotta look every day. Go out and pull the branches down and check.

He's grinding the buds into a fine powder between his index finger and thumb. Too fine for my liking.

– Don't fucken mull it too much or it'll suck through the cone.

– Fuck off, I know what I'm doing. Smell that.

He holds his fingers, smudged with resin, up to my nose. The odour is heavy and sweet and immediately sends my bowels running with anticipation. We'll be ripped off our tits before 8 am. He packs up the metallic red hash pipe, fills it to the brim, pats it down, then lights it with a tiny circular flick of the wrist. The granules of dope glow red, sitting up out of the cone like zombies rising from the grave. Larry draws slowly, so as not to drag the mixture in through the hole of the cone, then covers the top of it with the lighter and passes it to me.

I suck it in, feeling the hot, sweet smoke hit my lungs like an old friend, and pass it back. Another suck from Larry and it's gone, the dregs zipping down the plughole and hitting his tongue like coals into water.

– Fuck, he spits and wipes his mouth on the blue and gold end of his school tie.

Walking out into the quiet streets, we smile at each other, both of us in the golden dawn of our dope smoking. The air is cool and frost is crunching on the grass like cornflakes, the pinks and greens of the weatherboard houses look like the backdrop of a Fritz Freling animation.

– I'm cartooning, I say.

– Me too. Fuck, I'm ripped.

The THC, the Tetrahydrocannabinol, the active chemical in marijuana, has hit the sweet meat of our sixteen year old brains like salt onto a slug. We're children rolling in the cosy, creeping warmth of our bedrooms, unaware it's a house fire licking under the floorboards. I hoff another cloud of steam into the air and for a second it's a genie's face, smiling before me.

– Fuck, I'm ripped.

Larry is a good four inches shorter than me, but he's wider, set low to the ground, with a league player's flat nose. He has a wisping fringe of blond hair that makes him look like a dashing pit bull and doesn't augur well for him in the baldness stakes. His arms are muscled and tanned and he walks with a square-shouldered confidence that announces his fighting prowess to anybody smart enough to pick it. He's my mate now, but I'm never in any doubt as to the pecking order of our relationship. Larry can punch shit out of me and I know it and he knows it. Larry can punch shit out of anybody.

We get to the bus stop and Birdy's already there. He lives in Matraville, so he gets a different bus to Kingsford. He's on to us immediately.

– You guys have been mullin' up.

– So?

– Fucken blow me out, you cunts.

This is exactly why Birdy didn't get an invite to our little powwow.

– Fuck off, Birdy, you fucken scab, I say.

He shapes up to me, gives me a playful slap in the face and dances around, his blond flicks bobbing like a candle flame.

– I'm getting a pound on the weekend, he says, I'll pay you back.

– Of course you are, Birdy, says Larry. – Pound of butter.

Birdy's always getting a pound on the weekend. None of us have ever even seen a pound.

– What would you know, Lawrence?

– I know you're not getting a pound on the weekend. You know how much that costs?

– Yeah, mate. Two grand we're getting it for. My cousin's bringing it down from Mullumbimby.

– Is this the same cousin who surfed Wedding Cake Island at twenty-five foot? I ask.

– I said twenty foot.

– On a five-ten twinny?

– It's true! I was there.

– Yeah, we know, you pulled into a ten foot barrel going backdoor towards the rocks.

Larry and I both cack ourselves. Any figure Birdy quotes we just halve it. The cunt's pathological. Birdy kicks my Rip Curl bag across the footpath and onto Gardeners Road. It opens up and spills my geography folder and an orange. I run and grab my stuff before it gets cleaned up by the traffic, then peg the orange at Birdy as hard as I can. He's expecting it, so he swerves and it flies by and hits some Year 8 chicks from St Clare's, splatters over their school shoes.

SYLLABLES

Alessandra takes my hand and her grip is thick and hard and dominant and though we don't talk about the kiss, I can feel her on my lips like sea spray. We walk back to her apartment and the stairway up to her building seems forged from a sandstone fairytale, the surfaces damp with secrets and whispers.

It's hard sex, with rough edges, like two different languages trying to sing the same anthem. She jerks around in bed and rides me like an inanimate appendage until finally she's asleep and I watch those same mythical curtains roll around with the night's dead breath and then I'm asleep, walking up a dark wet road into a stormy sunrise and she's waiting for me. I hold her and we kiss and tears come to my eyes and my soul seems to shiver with the cold touch of the spirits I'm giving life to.

I wake and for a second the realisation I've been dreaming sweeps me with loneliness and loss until I feel the weight of her hand on my chest and turn to see her, a rare feline divinity, proud, thick lips crushed into the pillow, body flowing into the sheets, her grace draped over my smile. The Age of Alessandra breaks above the landscape of my chest.

Al-ess-an-dra.

Four syllables to sing.

I look at her and feel like crying and laughing at once, my grin nearly flips my lips over my earlobes. I lie there in her sheets feeling every crease against my back, the bright talk of the birds metres away in the branches at her window, that window, our window, and then she wakes and just stares at me with those calm cat blues, winks and leans over to kiss me.

TIME TRAVEL

I hate football training. I don't get the point. Run, push-ups, run, kick the ball, run, hill sprints, sit-ups, run some more. Can't I just sit and watch?

I'm not very good at footy. I don't seem to have much hand–eye coordination and tend to drop passes at crucial times. My mates call me 'unco' but I just like to think of it as uninterested. They love football. They love rugby league, they love rugby union. They know who's playing who, when and where and Jesus . . . I get exhausted just talking about it.

Come Saturdays, when we have to play football or get detention if we don't, I get a jittery feeling in my guts. I know I'm gonna get trodden on, pushed to the ground, shoulder charged or head slammed. I just don't see the fun in getting hurt. And football training, it's just preparing to get hurt, like doing a test run for slamming your cock in a car door.

– On the ground and give me six inches, says our coach.

He's a former Seaview boy, the son of one of the teachers. He volunteers his time. He wants us to lie on our backs and hold our legs straight out in the air, so our feet are six inches off the ground.

– Hold 'em, Jelli, he says. He can see I'm fading. I mean, doesn't this cunt have something else to do with his Wednesday afternoons? If I was twenty-five years old, I'd be at the pub, or fucking my girlfriend, or shooting wildlife.

– HOLD THEM! he screams at me. Really. What does he give a fuck for? How can you attach your self-esteem to a bunch of teenagers running around a park? We're the 16Ds, for fuck's sake. It's not like any of us are going to break into the Australian schoolboys' squad if we do another lap around Seaview Park.

– Okay, down, says the coach. – Rest for a second.

The more I think about this, the more it bothers me. What normal twenty-five year old guy wants to hang around with teenage boys and see them sweat?

– You reckon he fucks kids? I say to Scorps, who's still breathing heavily from our run.

– For sure.

– Alright, I want you all to sprint to the top of the hill, to the water tower and back, says Coach.

I look up at the blue daylight-savings sky while I've still got breath. I've perfected a technique I call Short Time Travel. I feel the grass under my back and think about the bus ride home, when my legs will be warm inside my tracksuit pants and I can go back to reading *Fear and Loathing in Las Vegas*. I really concentrate on it, thinking about when the pain of running and tackling will be over. That time *has* to come, it's not like I'm gonna die in the next three hours. So I think about that moment, draw it to me.

– GET UP, JELLI! screams the coach.

My team's already ten paces up the hill. I stand and run. Fuck, I hate this.

When I get home it's dark. I push through the overhanging bushes that shroud our front gate and walk into the side garden to find it ablaze with light. Our front doors are a matched pair, wood and glass. As I open one, the other vibrates as my side catches. It's warped from getting rained on. The vibrating door is like an alarm telling you when someone gets home. In seconds my mother has appeared, red eyed, holding a tissue.
    – I want you to go into your bedroom and pack some clothes, darling.
    – Why? What's wrong?
    – Your Aunt Sandra's had a heart attack, she's dead.
    Only bad things happen quickly.

Sandra had made shepherd's pie for my cousins and, as they were all sitting down to eat, she grabbed her chest and fell forward into the mashed potato. Flynn and Bailey and Sass thought it was a joke, but my Uncle Truman knew all about Sandra's weak heart. He'd spent his married life worrying if the other shoe would ever fall with his beloved wife and that night it came rushing down. After the ambulance left, she was choppered to Westmead Hospital but died in the air.
    Truman called his three kids into his bedroom and held them.
    – Mum's gone.
    Just like that.

We drive up to the mountains that night and all the rellies are there, my cousin Alice, my Uncle Matt and Aunt Anne. There isn't much we can do except stand on the edge of the whirlpool, while the adults sip their cans and glasses of iced white. Flynn,

Bailey and Sass look like little shuffling lobotomies with pink eyes and noses. I sit down and think forward to the time when they'll be happy again, just like I did at football training, except I know this will be months down the track, maybe years.

Maybe never.

PROL

The Triple M Tower at Bondi Junction is swaying from side to side. Alright, not swaying so much as it has a blur of movement each side, like it's vibrating.

– I'm fuckin' tripping out, I say to Grumble, who laughs.

– Yeah, that's why they call it trippin', dipshit, and he hits me over the back of the head. Cunt.

Scorps, Chong and Birdy are with us and we're walking down from my flat to find things to freak out on. I got the trips from Arroyo, at work, after a mate of his sent them over in the post from the US. The trips were tiny little blotters of white paper with a Superman cartoon printed on the front. The edges were serrated like a postage stamp, but the whole thing was smaller than the nail on your little finger.

– And that's gonna hammer me? I said to Arroyo when we sussed them in the dunnies.

– Trust me, Neddy, you'll be licking the wallpaper on

half of one of these, he said.

So of course we all had a full.

First we sit around the flat listening to Led Zeppelin and Pink Floyd and whatever other musical clichés we can drag from our record collections. Chong and Grumble have brought their guitars and are playing along with whatever songs they recognise, both of them bent over the blond wood of their instruments like they're defusing nuclear bombs. The seriousness of the moment disappears when one of them fucks up a riff and they smile at each other because they both know how tough that section is.

Birdy is mulling up a second batch of dirty hash ones for us, holding out a B & H Special Filter like it's a tiny parakeet perch. He's running the lighter underneath the ciggie, back and forth until the paper browns, then cracks open in spots, the tobacco sufficiently dry for our discerning tastes. When you mull, you need the baccy to be a bit crisper than if you just break open a cigarette cold. Especially if you're having a putty grill, cooking up the hash ones.

Birdy opens the contents of two cigarettes into the mull bowl, splitting the ciggies down the middle like he's peeling tiny bananas. He gives the baccy a quick grind then starts on the putty. This week, it's blond hash and he's telling everyone who'll listen it's from a huge bust that's been in the papers.

– You see that doctor that got sprung last week? says Birdy.
– The wog bloke?
– Micos?
– This is that stuff.

Dr Nick Micos and his mates had been pinged bringing more than a tonne of blond Afghani hash into the country and had panicked, dumping most of it out at Malabar tip. When the news got out, crazed dope smokers descended on the dump from miles around, searching for the THC El Dorado.

– That's bullshit, Birdy, the coppers got all of that stuff, I say.

I've just started as a copy boy at a newspaper. I read the front pages.

– Yeah, I know, fuckwit, who do you think this came from?

– Rightio, Birdy, associating with corrupt coppers, are we, bad boy?

– Fuck off, Ned.

For the moment, we're happy to let Birdy's bullshit ride. He rips a small nugget off the larger block that he's been flashing like a gangster's bank roll for the last three days. Next he pushes the hash into the groove of one of his house keys, sparks the Bic under it and gives it a quick roasting with the heart of the flame, careful not to send it to charcoal. After a second, the hash catches alight and he quickly blows it out, sucks in the trailing smoke, then drops the smouldering glob into the bowl where he attacks it with thumb and forefinger. He kneads through the blobby bits, breaks up any clumps and starts packing them up.

I'm already ripped when the acid starts to trickle into my brain like rain water under a screen door. Zeppelin's 'Over the Hills and Far Away' is on the boom box and suddenly I begin to feel rather than see my friends. I look over at Birdy and his eyes are shining with exactly the same juice that's surging up my spine. The sun is just setting through the window behind us and the easy light lies on us like dew, our arm hairs sparkling, the fuzz on the backs of our necks glowing like baby halos. In that instant the world shrinks to the size of the five people in the room but grows larger than anything I've inhaled before.

– I'm tripping, I say to Scorps and he's more my brother than ever before.

We catch the bus. We don't really know where we're going but the journey is all that matters, the moment is ours, we are the moment. We get on at Bondi Junction and sit up the back, each taking a bench seat for ourself. We're scattered around the bus, anonymous, like armed air marshals on a commercial flight, hidden from the civilians who fill the seats next to and around us. I'm upholstered in warm felt. I'm baking in my own skin. I look across the aisle at Grumble and he makes a low growl.

– Prol, he says and the forty-something woman next to him shifts uncomfortably.

I laugh because it's such a fuckin' ridiculous thing to say, yet such a perfect sound for how we feel. Prol. It falls out of your mouth like drool, sounds vaguely sexual and can be extended or contracted, however much effort you'd like to expend.

– Pra-larl, I reply and the guy in the business suit next to me turns to stare.

– Pra-la-la-la-laaaaaaal, replies Chong. He's about three seats back and getting adventurous.

I am shaking with laughter. I am a castanet. The guy in the suit is still staring.

– PRAAAAAAAAAAAAAAAAAAAAAAAAAAAAAAL, says Scorps two rows in front of me. It's loud, plaintive, a magnificent release. Four or five passengers tense and turn towards the sudden increase in volume.

I may well die on this bus. The light is celestial; the tyres feel like they're made of tofu, sucking up the sounds and vibrations of the road. I have to lever breath into myself in between sprays of aching laughter.

– Praaal, offers Birdy. It's a delicate but confident sound, a nice counterpoint to Scorps's intensity. I look over my shoulder at him and his eyes are gleaming. The young girl next to him seems to understand and is smiling into her book.

– PROOOWL, counters Grumble. It sounds like a sleepy lion on the savanna. It's reckless in its magnitude but delivered with consummate skill. The woman next to him gets up and squeezes past some standing commuters to move down the front of the bus. No one takes her seat.

It's hard to explain how funny this is to us. Each of our growls might as well be autobiographies, for all the information they hold about our personalities, current mood and willingness to push the boundaries of convention. The other people on the bus are looking at us like we're insane, but they are outside the bubble, they don't, can't and probably never will understand this moment or their own moment because the acid has dissolved doors inside us that cannot be closed again. It's broken the banks of the river inside the five of us, formed tributaries, connections and understandings we can't ignore. Wouldn't want to.

We know something that you don't, is what we're all thinking.

We're feeling something that you're not.

We're at the centre of something impossible to explain, yet simple to enunciate.

Prol.

HOW TO SEND YOUR SISTER CRAZY

I am punching my sister and it feels good. She is crying – screaming, actually – but that's not going to do her any good because Shamus and my mum have gone out for lunch and I'm 'looking after her'. I am angry and I don't really know why. I feel empty and I need to fill it up with something and as I watch Megan play with her dolls, singing to herself, seemingly carefree and content, I get angry she's so happy. So I get on my knees next to her and punch her hard in the stomach. She looks at me shocked, wondering why I would do something so awful and violent and unnecessary, and cries.

I scream at her that I've had enough of her shit and I go to the coffin and I take out some rope. The coffin is really just a long wooden storage box that runs down the side of the bar in our dining room. It has a hinged lid and a child, even a small adult, can lie down full stretch in it, close the top and find out what it would be like to be buried alive. I've done it often.

Other than that, we use it to store blankets and other stuff, like rope.

I take the rope and I make a noose, which I learnt how to do from one of the guys at Scouts. Then I fling the noose over a beam of an unfinished pagoda in our garden and I scream to my sister that I'm going to hang myself. Despite the fact I have just beaten her into tears, she comes outside and sees me standing on a chair, noose around my neck, ready to end it all. Megan is ten years old and has flaky blonde hair and an expression of innocence that quietens me.

– Get down off the chair, please, Neddy, PLEASE!

She's screaming, truly terrified by what I am doing. I can see the incredible impact it's having on her, almost feel it tearing through her brain, stretching into her future. I can see the scars rolling out in front of her, into her adulthood. The enormity of my evil feels incredible. I feel like God. I stand a little straighter and make to kick the chair from under me.

– PLEASE! she screams hysterically and hugs my legs, trying to stop me from falling. I can feel her whole body shaking with fear that her big brother is going to kill himself.

Primal chemicals are coughing out of my core, pouring out of my brain, surging, real. I've got no intention of killing myself but she doesn't know that. It's method acting.

Eventually I relent, and stand and hug her.

– I'm sorry, I'm sorry, it's going to be alright, I say, stroking that downy hair of hers. I can feel her warm tears spilling through the shoulder of my school shirt as she cries. Her breathing slowly returns to normal and I pull her back from me, grin at her and she forces a tiny smile.

Then I punch her again. And again and again.

She runs back into the house and tries to lock herself in the bathroom but I'm too strong for her. Her screams and tears are almost maniacal as I prise my way into the bathroom and continue to punch, eventually driving her into the bath where she hits her head on the taps and sobs until I leave her.

When she appears about ten minutes later, I again go to hug her and she flinches involuntarily. Like a beaten animal, it takes me much, much longer to get her to trust me this time, but I've got fuck all else to do. Eventually I settle her down and she stops crying. I gather her doona off her bed and get the big cushions off the green divan and set her up in a little snuggly nest in front of *Simon Townsend's Wonder World*. I make her promise not to tell my mum and Shamus and, gulping air, still crying a little, she nods agreement. I even make her a drink.

As she settles into watching television, sucking her thumb, rubbing her nose and mouth with the soft edge of her pyjamas, I give her another hug and tell her I love her. Then I punch her again. And again. I have never heard anything like the screams she makes.

I wonder for a second if I can actually send her crazy.

THE RATS

I dislike rugby union almost as much as I dislike the Roosters.

The Waratahs are playing tonight and somehow I've found myself up at the Rat House with Scorps and some of his investment banker mates. Most of them are wearing dress shoes and business shirts tucked into pressed jeans. If you asked them, they'd call themselves risk takers because they punt millions on the movements of indices and what other guys who also iron their jeans are doing on the other side of the planet. Funny world we live in.

The bankers are cheering the Waratahs but my mind's wandered to the barmaid. She's young and I'm turned on by her, simply because of her youth. She's quite attractive but not in the way I usually like. It's her youth, the fact she's a good deal younger than me, that's getting me jazzed.

– When did we start getting turned on by younger chicks? I ask Scorps.

– Always.
– No. When we were twenty-two we didn't look at twelve year olds and go 'Fuck, I'd like to jam it in her.'
– Speak for yourself.
– I'm serious.
– I dunno, mate, he says, then stands quickly.
– GO, YOU BLACK CUNT!!! he screams at the TV as one of the Waratahs' wingers chips over the top and chases. The ball is caught by the opposition full-back, who calmly reefs it into touch.
– Another line-out. Fancy that, I say.
– You just don't understand it, mate.
– I played the game at school. How don't I understand it?
– It's technical.
– It's boring as shit. All they do is fuckin' kick it back and forth. It's forcings back between millionaires.
Scorps belches and rests his schooner on his gut, where it leaves a wet smile on his shirt.
– Think about it, I say. At some point we became dirty old men. When was that?
– I've always been a dirty old man, my body's just caught up to my mind, he says.
– I used to be totally turned on by older women. When I was twenty, the horniest thing I could imagine was a sexy thirty-five year old.
– Still is.
– Not as sexy as that, I say and nod at the barmaid. She's wearing black bike shorts which are just starting to pill around the inside curves of her arse.
– True, says Scorps.
My phone vibrates in my pants, like a third party's penis, and I pull it out. It's my cousin Bailey.
– Hello, mate, I say.

– Edward, how you doing? He always uses my full name for some reason. When he speaks, he sounds like he's exhaling smoke.
– Just having a few beers, mate, what about you?
– Oh, I'm just hanging out. Not a lot.
– I'm at North Bondi RSL. You wanna come up?

Bailey doesn't make these phone calls for no reason, but then again, if there is a reason, he may not know it himself. He's one of the most subconsciously honest people I know, despite the fact he's committed more crimes than anybody I've ever met. While his body and his conscious mind seek dodginess and the fast buck, some part of him knows what he's doing is wrong, so he lays down the breadcrumbs to secure his capture. It's not a good psychological dynamic for a criminal.

When he arrives, I see he's already well pissed. It's half-time, and Scorps and two of the bankers are arguing about interest rates. I get a headache when these blokes talk about this shit, more so when I hear Scorps trying to sound authoritative. I break into the conversation.

– What it comes down to is you're guessing, I say.
– Nah, mate, it's informed decision-making.
– Which is how you lost me ten grand last year?
Scorps always looks hurt when I bring this up.
– If I could give you back the money, Ned, I would.
– Nothing stoppin' you.
Scorps's mates are a bit surprised by the sudden hostility, so he explains.
– I put Neddy into some tech shares last year, he margin lent five grand US and they went bad and he ended up getting burned.

I can see I'm embarrassing Scorps, but something pushes me on. I'm sick of listening to the cunt bang on about the millions of dollars he's got 'under management' when he hits me up for a loan every three weeks so he can punt it away at the Icebergs.

– You're the poorest investment banker I've ever met, mate.

The bankers chuckle uncomfortably.

– Fuck off, Neddy.

It's said softly, sincerely. Still I probe the wound.

– What sort of car do you drive, mate? I say to one of the bankers, a tall South African Jew.

– Umm, a BMW, he says.

– And what about you, mate?

– An Audi.

– I've got a Valiant. 1971. And what about you, Scorps, what do you drive?

– Mate, I don't need a car, it's a waste of money.

– But you did have one, didn't you? A Camira, wasn't it?

– You're a fuckin' dickhead, you know that?

– What's wrong?

– You say some fuckin' stupid things sometimes.

He walks off to the bar and I call after him – I prefer to call it informed decision-making.

There's silence before the bankers smile at the newcomer, cousin Bailey.

– So, Bailey, is it?

– Yeah, mate.

– Who do you work for, Bailey?

– I work at Union Carbide.

– The chemical company?

– Yeah.

– Are you a chemist?

Bailey smiles.

– I do shutdown chemical cleaning. I get inside the vats and scrub them.

The bankers are impressed.

– That must be very dangerous?

– It's not too good for your lungs, but they give you breathers to wear.

Bailey can't help smiling and the smile says, 'These blokes are wankers. Are they really your friends?' Bailey and I should have more in common than just a party every year to open Christmas presents, but it hasn't turned out that way.

– I think the chemicals Bailey needs to worry about aren't at Union Carbide, I say.

– Speaking of which, Edward, you wanna smoke one?

He holds a hand up like he's caught a fly, but I know the only thing buzzing in there is a sticky bud of hydro.

The money market declines to joins us, which I'm happy about, because this is probably the time Bailey will reveal what he wants to talk about. We go up the hill to my car, the Val, and I pop the doors and we climb in the front. Bailey's seat collapses when he leans back.

– Fuck me, he says, but I'm already reaching around to prop a milk crate between his and the bench seat in the back.

– It's rooted, I say.

– I thought the car was moving, he says and his billy goat giggle has an edge of hysteria to it.

– You wanna roll it? he says.

– Sure.

I pull my street directory out of the glovebox to mull on.

– So what have you been up to, Edward? he says.

– Not a lot, mate, been trying to write.

– How's that going?

– I been trying to write for ten years. Same shit always happens.

– What's that, Edward? he says, sipping the schooner he's brought with him.

– I end up writing about my mates and chicks I've rooted.

– What's wrong with that? Sounds good to me.
– Who wants to read that shit?
– I would.
– You're my cousin, you have to.
– I dunno. Sounds like you're on to a good thing there.
– What about you, Bailey, what have you been doing?
– Not a lot, Edward, just workin', trying to pay off my debts.
– From the prang?
– Yeah, it's pretty tough, though, I'm thinking I might have to go bankrupt.

Bailey has been a consistent car wrecker his entire life. When we were kids, we went out bush for holidays and our parents let us drive the Moke around in a paddock. There was nothing to hit, just long grass to put the car sideways on and a huge bonfire of dead wood a farmer had stacked in the centre of the field. We'd lapped the pyre in huge ellipses, like we were at Daytona, until Bailey, aged eleven, convinced us to let him drive.

– It'll be sweet, he said.

As soon as he got behind the wheel, I knew we'd made a mistake. Bailey triple-shifted like a good Blue Mountains car thief should, then thrashed through the gears like a kid used to driving cars he didn't own. He threw the Moke sideways around the first corner, took the next at a higher speed any of us had managed all day, then overcorrected on the next bend, fishtailed and ploughed into the wood pile.

The first car Bailey owned himself, he totalled, but he was smart enough to leg it from the scene, then report it stolen. After that, he got done for DUI and lost his licence. That didn't stop him driving and when he arrived at our house for lunch one Sunday piloting a Falcon station wagon, none of the family thought it was their business to tell him to park it and catch a cab home.

Five hours later he buried the Falcon into a fig tree a block from our place and ran off again, only to return when he remembered he'd left his mobile phone in the door of the car. The police were already at the scene and arrested him on the spot.

Because he didn't have a licence, Bailey was banned from driving for five years, which he endured with the quiet grace of a man who knows he's gotten away with plenty of other shit. So for the next five years, he rode his push bike twenty kilometres to and from work for his 5 am starts at Union Carbide.

Finally, the big day ticked around and the New South Wales government allowed him back behind the wheel. Bailey promptly bought himself the biggest, baddest four-wheel drive on the market.

– I knew I shouldn't have been driving, he says, sipping his beer.

– So why did you, mate? I don't get it.

– I had to be at work the next day and I was at Maroubra and if I left me car there, it would have been, fuck, sixty bucks in cabs there and back.

– So you drove.

– Yeah.

– Drunk.

– Blind. I could barely see the road.

Or the Commodore sedan he slammed into when it ran a red. It wasn't actually Bailey's fault, but that didn't matter. He took out two parked cars and some traffic lights and when he tried to stagger away into Centennial Park, outraged drivers tackled him and held him down until the jacks arrived.

– Edward, I'm just lucky I didn't go to jail, he says as I hand him the unlit joint. He offers it back to me, but I refuse and he sparks it up.

– You're lucky you didn't kill yourself or someone else.

– That too, he says exhaling the sweetness.

– I don't get it, Bailey. I've been driving longer than you and I'm pretty sure I drink as much as you do, but that shit doesn't happen to me.

I take a couple of hits and pass the number back to him.

– I know, he says through the smoke.

Bailey's bowed his head and, after a few seconds, I realise he's crying. I haven't seen Bailey cry in fifteen years, since his dad Truman's funeral. I let him go and just watch the traffic fizz by on Campbell Parade. After a while I grab his knee, give it a squeeze.

– Why'd he have to go?

– I reckon you got to stop asking yourself that, Bailey.

– But he just left us, he didn't give a shit.

– He didn't do it on purpose, mate.

– Then what was it?

– He was drunk. It was an accident. You should understand that.

The tears are squirting out of Bailey, like they do from faces unaccustomed to crying. The joint's been forgotten in his left hand as he wipes his face with his right.

– I think about it every day, Ned, every day I think how it'd be different if he was around.

– Mate, you gotta start moving past this.

– I hate myself, Ned. Do you know that?

– No you don't, mate.

– Yeah, I do. I hate myself.

THE NEW LIFE

We walk out of Alessandra's apartment and it's one of those white, bright summer mornings that feel like the beginning of a road movie. There's still a sweat of night on the leaves and the air holds a last tang of chill, when she takes my hand and we cross through the traffic coursing over the hill at Double Bay. I feel like someone has screamed 'Action!' and all of a sudden I'm the leading man and the very centre of the universe has shifted axis and now lies with Alessandra and me.

    She's dressed in a canary yellow linen dress and I'm thinking how few women can get away with that colour, but between the wood-smoked butter of her skin, the angry amber of her hair and the supernatural blue of her eyes, it's a tone picked from God's palette for his one love. BMWs with slumped rich fucks upholstered in pinstripe ease by her and the looks aren't lecherous or salivating but truly astonished; like these men, too, are amazed she's walking the earth near them and not trussed in some silver screen dream. The BMW boys hoe through her attributes and then by default look at me and I feel the envy of these other men and it projects clear as a thought bubble above their heads.

– Who is this cunt, what's she doing with him? He's a lucky bastard.

I am a lucky bastard.

We sit on upturned milk crates outside Coluzzi's and sip too-hot coffees from tiny scratched glasses and I feel the eyes of others on me. She's just that kind of beautiful that she has to be someone and she's talking just a little bit above discreet, her eyes exploding with the sheer joy of being her and everyone who looks at me is thinkin' it.

You lucky bastard.

The sun is brighter, the air is fresher, bread is crunchier, every song on the radio is speaking to me about her, her, her and I wonder whether it's possible Jeff Buckley wrote his whole album about Alex.

The next day she drives her little blue car from her house to mine and, knowing I'll be in bed, sticks her keys in my letterbox and walks to work so I can drive it for the day. When I wake, there's a message blinking on the machine telling me to get up and enjoy the day in that ridiculously enthusiastic voice of hers and Jesus! What's it been? Forty hours since our first kiss and I have a whole different vocabulary.

There's the old favourites 'Alex says' and 'Alex did' and then there's 'Alex and I', 'Alex wants to' and 'I should tell Alex'. I talk to my mum in the kitchen and she's watching me like I'm born-again, happy for me, not judging my new faith, just wary of my fervour.

It's the simple things that transport me. Getting a video from the store with her is like shopping in Paris, visiting the supermarket an exquisite sojourn. Every aisle I turn down is a runway of promise with her electric hand next to mine, the rough cobble of her corduroy pants under my palm as I, incredibly, cup her arse while the hot light of her eyes ploughs the shelves for teriyaki sauce. There's a constant charge around her and I'm junked on it, jonesing, emptying my pockets to buy more. Everyone feels it and she knows the right compliment for each situation, whether it's the check-out guy, the baker or her landlord, they're all glazed by her charm and warmth and enthusiasm.

I feel like someone or something has finally descended from the heavens to acknowledge the brilliance, the deserving goodness I've always known was inside me, and the reward is, well . . . her name is Alessandra.

I'm calling old friends and acquaintances to hook up with them so I can drag Alex along like a shiny new manbag, to say 'See, I'm better than you, look at what I've got', and though she ignores it at first, Alex can feel the trophy cabinet going up around her, the stench of Brasso and the dead weight of the pedestal pooling at her feet.

THE CREEP IN HIS CAVE

And then it's 6 pm.
    It's easier to get up now, because the day is almost gone. I have no more choices. I don't feel guilty about the buzz of activity outside in the park because all the real people are winding down, heading home to grab a DVD, maybe have dinner somewhere, a pizza. No battles are won at night. No one starts anything after dark. I am just like them. I'm just hanging out at home – chillin'. There's still football on the TV, there's always football on somewhere. A whole planetful of men kid themselves they're not just wasting time until they die with one football code or another. Three billion men distract themselves from the uselessness, the utter passivity of their lives, through football – because they back this team or that.
    – Where you off to?
    – I'm going to the footy.
    Of course you are.
    There's a big game tonight: the Roosters are playing Brisbane

and some of the boys are getting together to watch it. None of the boys get together to watch my team play – the Rabbitohs – it's always the Roosters. Every week a new must-see game, so we can follow the joy and the despair of a bunch of morons-with-managers we don't know and never will.

My mobile rings. I know I won't answer even before I see who it is. It's Scorps and he's wondering why I don't return his calls, why I don't want to drink with the boys, but I can't because I am so ashamed. Ashamed of how many days I am wasting just like this one. Ashamed of how many hours I spend thinking about nothing but me. Ashamed I'm even breathing the same air as Alexander the Great, Caesar, Shakespeare, Henry Miller, Ted Bundy.

At least they did something with their lives. At least they had a go.

For a moment I consider being a serial killer. The sex with my victims appeals to me but it does seem like a lot of effort: the planning, the getting to know the schedules of the women, the keeping one step in front of the police. I don't think I'm cut out for it, and again I'm crushed by despair that even a piece of human garbage like Ted Bundy had more get-up-and-go than me. Good luck to you, Ted.

So I let my phone ring out and then I order a pizza and some more pasta – carbonara dripping with cream and ham and fat because I know full well it won't stay in my guts. The pizza guy taking the order doesn't have to ask for my address. I'm a regular. A regular loser who spends his Saturday night by himself, hiding from the world, hiding from himself, in his hermetically sealed safety bubble.

I phone for my food, I get my groceries home-delivered via the Net, I pay my bills electronically, I even get my sex through broadband. I am an island. I can't be touched. Everything is as I want it and I am so sad I can barely look at the television without the tears coming.

The wait for the pizza takes four to five centuries. I can feel every second scrape past me, every moment of my life that I will never have back. I concentrate on the football and marvel at the excitement, the rapture in the commentators' voices, and I think how good it would be to be so enthusiastic about your job and that, maybe, I could be a commentator. But then I realise all these guys, they played for Australia or they won a Grand Final by the time they were thirty and I'm well past that. There must be so many other former players and coaches trying to get those jobs, and even though these guys are just talking about football, they are also far, far more successful than me and I hate myself, I am no one, and I look at the clock and only three minutes have passed.

This is agony. How long can this last?

And then the pizza girl's at the door. She's young, a surfer, and in the past we've discussed the waves. She must be seventeen. She's got that effortless skin, the fertile flesh of a teenager, and I can't even imagine what it would be like to touch her. She looks sunburnt.

– You get out there for one today? she asks and I almost laugh.

– Nah, mate, not today, had to work, I lie.

– It was pretty good. Be alright tomorrow.

She sees my new surfboard propped against the wall behind me – another question mark in my life.

– How's that one go? she says and I can barely tell her. I've ridden it twice and I feel like a fraud even having this conversation with her. I am one of those guys I used to hate. The wanker with more money than skill, who keeps his brand new surfboard bolted to the top of his car because it's never gonna move from there.

– Yeah, pretty zippy. Good in small stuff, I say to her and hand her thirty-five bucks. I don't want my change, I don't want anything from her except for her to walk away so I can close my door and not be reminded that there are people out there with lives, with energy, who don't sleep all day and wank when they're not sleeping and eat a family-sized pizza and pasta by themselves on a Saturday night.

Every time I go to the door, I try to give the impression there's someone else inside my apartment, a neat, happy, blonde girlfriend, who's making the salads in the kitchen. A few times I've even said out loud 'I'll get it' to the television, to give the impression I am not the freak that I am, the creep in his cave.

The pizza girl's happy with the tip. She nods.

– See you out there, eh?

– Yeah, mate.

And she's barely reached the stairs before I have the door closed, the pasta into a dish and I'm slurping up the rich sauce, feeling the fat and the heat on the back of my throat, a good sensation, a happy sensation, something positive for this second, for as long as it takes me to get this shit down my gullet.

Next is the pizza and I chew through it like it's a chore. The food is good but I am not hungry now. I am not even particularly enjoying this. It's a tiny positive charge in the humming negativity of the room and I know I'll feel awful when I'm finished. I can feel my stomach stretching with every bite. I can feel my revulsion growing with every mouthful, my disgust, my shame. I am just a pudgy guy sitting in his flat, stuffing his face. Every breath I take now is laboured from all the food in my body. I know there is only one thing to do and that's to throw the shit up.

I lean over my dirty toilet bowl, face inches from the shit stains and piss splatters I couldn't even imagine having the energy to remove, and I stick my fingers down my throat. It takes a few tries to move the food up my gut. My body is arguing with me. It's good food, there's nothing wrong with it. My stomach has no need to bring it up, it clamps shut on me. But I'm persistent and slowly I can feel the reverse tide building, tearing up my oesophagus.

The first lump is almost dry but again I bring more up. The pizza, the pasta, then the cereal from this afternoon. It all floats below me. I fill the bowl and then put my hand in it. Fistfuls of the stuff, pounds of food and now it's gone, wasted, but it won't end up as fat on me and, for a moment, for the first time in the day, I feel like I've achieved something.

I spit and see the blood in my mucus and know the damage this must be doing. What am I? Bulimic? A chronic masturbator? Lazy? A smoker? It's too much. I wash my face and rinse my mouth and turn off the lights, the TV, like there's an air-raid siren going outside.

And then I'm in bed.

Maybe it's seven, maybe it's seven-thirty, but I'm going to sleep, I'm going to escape this bullshit. I light up the smoke and it's disgusting, but then so am I. I smoke it deep, right to the butt, and then stub it out. In the dark, the afterburn of the ciggie tip glows in front of me like the Devil's red eyes. I hate this. I hate me. Tomorrow it will be different. Tomorrow I will stop smoking. I'll go for a run and a surf and buy some vegies.

I suck on my Ventolin, my twentieth puff of the day, and I drift off to sleep, the sleep of someone who's already slept for eight hours during the day, and I know that I'm only going to repeat this freak show tomorrow.

CUDADAWEDS

I can barely understand this wog bastard. Mr Pizzoni's about nine hundred years old and he smells like an old boot filled with crushed garlic that's been wrapped in a sweaty pair of underpants and smeared in motor oil.
– Yawannamedacudadawedsaswell? he says.
Fuck, I don't know. What did he say?
He's a nice enough bloke, Mr Pizzoni. He comes around every couple of weeks and cuts the grass for my parents and does a good job. The guy's got hands the size of the A to K phone book and looks like he could rip a jacaranda out of the ground like he was plucking parsley. It wouldn't even enter his comprehension to do a job half-heartedly. You need the lawn cut? He'll edge around the trees, the paths, sweep up the leaves, bag the clippings, tweezer the bindis out of the grass if you ask him. The guy's like a plague of locusts. Trees scream when he enters the postcode. He's smiling at me.

– Sorry? Could you say that again, Mr Pizzoni?

– Youwannamedacudalladosewedsonafens?

I smile back at him, still no clue what he's saying.

– Eyescudalladosewedsonafens? Ovadair.

He points at the back fence, where my mother's growing dope plants, about twenty of them, all four foot tall. She used to tell me they were tomato plants, but the arse fell out of that story about the time I turned twelve. Last month she and Shamus had to cut the tops off the plants because they were getting taller than the fence. Maybe that's why the fucken things never seem to grow any tomatoes, eh, Mum?

Mr Pizzoni's waiting for my answer.

Fuck, I give up.

– Yeah, yeah, sure, Mr Pizzoni.

My mum's up the shops and Shamus is at work. They've left me thirty dollars to pay Mr Pizzoni, but I just want the cunt to hurry up and go because it's cracking midday and my next-door neighbour's put her banana chair outside in the garden. I know this because there's a knothole in the side fence and if I squint through it I can see straight into the yard.

I hear Mr Pizzoni's mower start up out the back, so I go to the side fence with my binoculars and press them to the hole. I've discovered that if I look through the binos, it magnifies the slither of yard beyond anything my naked peepers can manage. It takes me a second to process what I'm seeing but, when I do, I have to step back, compose myself, then resume perving.

Our neighbour is an opera singer. He's got to be in his late thirties, but his missus is midtwenties and loves to sunbake. Today she's spread out facing my knothole, top off, legs open towards me. It's much, much more than I could have hoped for. With the binoculars I can see everything. I might as well have my head between her legs. I spot two stray pubes loitering out the side of her bikini bottom, and when I focus on her tits

I can see almost every pore of her nipples. The little bumps of flesh look like piles of tiny brown stones piled on top of one another.

Mr Pizzoni's mower has struck something solid. I hear the blades clash and the motor slows, coughing through the heavy grass, then winds up to top speed before chomping into serious business again and almost stalling. At least I know where he is. I inch down the side of our house and peer into my sister's bedroom. She's transcribing the words to some Spandau Ballet song from a cassette using Shamus's reporter's tape recorder. She hits play and the band craps on about GOLD! and being indestructible.

She knows those lyrics back to front but she's doing a comparison of the words from their latest album and a live concert the fucken fruits did in Belgium that was shown on *Sounds* with Donnie Sutherland last weekend. I think my sister may be retarded. At least she's occupied.

I go back to my knothole and slowly open my boardies, carefully parting the Velcro fly so as not to make too much noise. With one hand I put the binos to the knothole, focus in on that juicy cunt, and with the other hand I get to work on Oscar.

Man, you can see the curls of her pubes pressing against the white fabric of her cossie and her cunt lips are just visible. When she bends over to straighten out her towel it looks like . . . What does Larry call it? A wallaby tail. Yeah, a fucken wallaby tail. She's a fucken sexy bitch, I tell you. I'm going for GOLD! Here, pressed up against the grey wood of the fence, trying not to nick the head of my cock on the sword grass all around me. It doesn't take long. Happy days.

I wipe my spoof on the fence and get a fucken splinter, so I flick the rest of my future generations screaming onto the scalding sandstone patio. I press the fly of my boardies together and when I turn, Mr fucken Pizzoni is there, just watching.

– I'mfinis, he says.

Fuck off. Did he see me? The cunt looks at the binoculars around my neck, peers over the fence and gives me a sly grin. I can't give him his thirty bucks quick enough.

Later in the arvo, Shamus and my mum get home. I'm on the phone to Scorps organising our weekend. We're going to Paddo's and he's gotta get ID.

– NED!

It's Shamus calling for me, in a tone of voice I don't like to hear. I put my hand over the receiver and shout out to him.

– I'm on the phone.

– Come out here, please.

Fuck. That wog cunt has told them I was wanking over my neighbour.

– I gotta go, I tell Scorps and hang up. When I get to the lounge room, Shamus is on the patio looking furious. Fuck this. I walk outside and see my mum's there too.

– You wanna explain that to me, he says and points at the flowerbeds where the dope plants are. Should be. Were. Now there's just a mass of what looks like grass clippings.

– What happened? I say.

– The gardener's mowed over my dope plants, that's what happened, says my mum, half pissed off, half trying to stop herself laughing.

Yawannamedacudadawedsaswell?

You want me to cut all the weeds as well? That's what the wog cunt was saying.

– I didn't see it, I say. – I promise.

We walk over to the beds and Shamus crouches, sifting through the mulch for something resembling his crop.

– He cut the fucking grass, alright, he says.

CONSTABLE HERBERT

– Leave it there, I dare ya, you haven't got the guts, says Scorps.

I hold on to the tip of my bishop as I look around the board for possible ambushes. His queen is blocked. I'm okay from the right and from the left. What is he going on about? I leave the bishop.

– Mongo.

He fakes to take my bishop but moves his rook down to cover my knight and queen.

– You couldn't even take it, what were you goin' on about? I say.

– I was unnerving you.

He leans back and exhales his Dunhill, a rebellious act, considering we're surrounded by three hundred packets of Marlboro that I sell for a living. Now I have to give up either my queen or the knight.

– Fuck. You know it's illegal to sledge during chess?
– Piss off. Show me a rule book that says I can't.
– It's probably not in the rules.
– Have your move, ya faggot.
– Fuck.

I'm waiting for the ciggie girls to turn up at Kaspar's place for our shift and Scorps has come over to perve. Kaspar, of course, is not ready. I can hear him singing a Beastie Boys song in the shower.

– Getting nervous are we, Neddy? Feeling the pressure, huh? That's understandable, you're not very good.
– Scorps. Can you let me think?
– Is that what that noise is? Go on, move your queen, it's that or your knight.
– Jesus.

I move my queen back to safety and he sweeps in with his bishop from the other side to take it.

– Ahh, what? I'm not thinking.
– That's obvious.
– Shit.
– And now my lowly foot soldiers are having their way with your queen in my dungeons. 'Ned, you've failed me!' she's screaming.

Scorps is monstering my queen on the armchair with three of his pawns.

– Sssssh.
– Help me, they're taking off my dress!!

I look at the board and see the hopelessness of my situation.

– Do you give up?
– No way known, you cunt. I can come back from this.
– In. Your. Dreams.
– You watch.

– Have ya move, ya faggot.

I look at him leant over the board at me; shaved head, eyes glinting with malice, three day growth, and realise these chess games are the only time that Scorps looks in control. He should be, the cunt gets enough practice. He stays up 'til dawn most Friday nights, standing in his kitchen overlooking South Bondi, playing endless games of chess, the microwave just in reach so he can heat up a plate, rackin' line after line with whoever's his new coke buddy.

I asked him once how he can bear it, the drug-fucked night-owling?

– Mate, if I go to bed too early, I swear, it's like I hear this music in my head. It's like 'doof, doof, doof' and I just know there's a party going on somewhere and I'm missing out on it.

– So why don't you go out?

– It comes to me.

We're a great pair. Scorps never wants to go to bed. All I want to do is sleep.

BZZZZZZZ. It's the door.

– Fuck, that scared me.

– Is that the hotties? asks Scorps, hopeful. – Go let 'em in.

– You fuckin' let them in.

– You'll cheat.

– No I won't.

– Bullshit. You've got more to gain. I already have you in check. He leans back, implacable.

BUZZZZZ.

– CAN YOU GET THE DOOR, YOU FUCKWITS? Kaspar screams from the shower.

I stand.

– Fine, I say and walk down the hall, pick up the intercom and buzz the chicks in. I prop open Kaspar's front door and hear the security gate clash inwards downstairs.

– Right, we gotta finish this up, I say.

– Looks pretty finished to me, says Scorps, already scoping the hallway for the girls.

There's heavy footsteps coming up the stairs, a bloke, and just as I wonder about the wisdom of leaving the door open, I look over at Kaspar's coffee table, the mull bowl and then off to the side, the scales, the baggies and other dealing paraphernalia.

Things slow down.

I see the hand holding the badge come through the door, then the blue uniform. The cop is midtwenties and looks angry. I glance at Scorps. His mouth drops open.

– I want you to stay where you are, the cop shouts at us.

I don't say anything. Don't even move. I don't know how much shit Kaspar keeps in his apartment but I know I don't want to be in the same postcode as it, let alone the same room.

– Who else is in the house? asks the cop.

I hesitate, weighing my words.

– Just . . .

– Fuck, Herbie, what are you doing?

The front door slams and Kaspar walks into the room, dripping water. The cop bursts out laughing.

– You should have seen these blokes' faces, says the cop.

– Fuckin' don't come up here like that, mate.

It takes me a second to realise Kaspar knows this cunt and then my heartbeat starts again.

– Sorry, mate, I couldn't resist.

– Whattaya want?

Kaspar and the cop exchange looks.

– Come in here, says Kasp and they disappear into his bedroom.

COOGEE TAVERN

Scorps and I are blind. Again.

We've been on the rocket fuel in the shower and now we're getting dressed to go out with the group. We're both trying to look older than we are, because we're going to the Coogee Tavern and there's always a hassle with the bouncer.

Every week, it's what we work towards. Saturday night at the Tavern. We steal dribs of money from our parents for beers, scab condoms from older brothers that we'll never use, and tick off each member of the group as they swindle their parents with some bullshit they're going to play squash or see *Footloose* in George Street.

It's a military fucken operation and it can all come undone at the entrance to the Tavern where the big blond bouncer with the mullet pulls you up and asks for ID. He knows we're taking the piss, that we're all underage, but if you've got ID and look passable he'll let you in. The bloke who owns the place would go broke if it wasn't for all the baldies sucking West Coast Coolers in the joint.

It goes off at the Tavern, but poor Scorps has never managed to actually get inside. Luckily, the mongo they've got as a doorman has a memory like a goldfish and never seems to recognise us from week to week. So tonight we're dressing the part. I'm wearing one of my mum's white jackets with a white beret, while Scorps has found a yellow and black striped jacket which he thinks looks cool but makes him look like a bumble bee, if you ask me. We're trying to look a bit Peter Stuyvesant, a bit jet set. As soon as we get up to Kingsford Junction, Gitta picks us.

– They're women's clothes.
– No they're not, I say.
– Yes they are, they've got the buttons on the left side.
Fuck. They do too.
– Is there a difference?
– Of course there is. Women's jackets have the buttons on the left. Men's are on the right.
Why do I always find this shit out when it's too late?
The Buccaneer is making that high-pitched cackle of his.
– Have a look at the hommas in their chick's clothes, he says.
– Fuck off, Buchanan, you dreg.

The problem with Scorps is that he looks twelve. The poor cunt's got more attitude than Mussolini in the surf, but he just hasn't developed physically. He's got this pink-cheeked puppy dog face that would have rock spiders reaching for the vasso and he's also a good four inches shorter than the rest of us. He looks like a baby, the little baby scorpion. Scorps.

– Do I have eight legs and claws? he'll scream. He hates his nickname.
– Shut up, you pissant.

When we get to Coogee, we all hang in the park opposite the beach slugging hipflasks of voddie and work out the order of entry. The Buccaneer and Mex will go first because they're ugly cunts and they look the oldest. Then goes Birdy and Larry with some of the chicks; Halftime and Hump and Guru will go next and then me. Last of all is Scorps because the guy is like poison. If you're with him, you're fucked as well.

– Why do I always have to go last? he says.

– Cos you look nine, pissant.

– Why can't someone go with me?

– Cos then we'll get knocked back.

Scorps starts sulking. A sad bumble bee. Larry nods at me.

– Get the white wog to go with you.

– Fuck off.

– Yeah, says Birdy, you're his bum chum, you fucken go with him.

– No way.

Scorps looks at me.

– Please, mate.

– Fuck.

We all hang outside the shop on Arden Street chewin' Juicy Fruit and the groups peel around the corner. Scorps is shitting himself. He's almost as white as my beret. Everyone in front of us gets in, no problem. Then it's our turn. I've got a mate of a cousin of a mate's old learner's permit that says I'm eighteen. There's no pictures on the driver's licence, it's just a piece of well, well, folded paper and the bouncer gives me the benefit of the doubt even though I don't look a day over sixteen. I reckon it's the beret that does it. Scorps tries to scuttle in behind me and the bouncer's arm comes down like a boomgate.

– Can I see some ID?

I wait inside the door as Scorps fumbles for his licence. It belongs to a friend of a friend of a cousin's flatmate's sister. The shit he had to go through to get it. He had to catch a train out west to his cousin's place to borrow it and pay the guy five bucks and he has to go back out there and drop it off tomorrow. And it says his name is Pedro Santopietro. And he's nineteen.

If Scorps is nineteen, then I'm Tommy Carroll pulling in backdoor at Pipe.

– This isn't yours, says the bouncer.
– Yeah it is, says Scorps.
– You live in Greenacre?
– Yeah.
– You been here before?
– Yeah, heaps of times.
– How'd you get here?
– I drove.

The poor cunt's voice sounds like one of those chipmunks that sing the sped-up songs.

– Yeah? What sort of car you got?
– Commodore. VK.
– Six or eight?
– Eight. Four point nine litre. Hundred and six kilowatts.

The little cunt knows his cars, I'll give him that. The bouncer susses him.

– How'd you afford that?
– I saved up, how d'ya reckon?

Scorps is doing well. Only problem is he's standing with his Lightning Bolt surf wallet open, his pink school bus pass visible to the world. I watch in slow motion as the bouncer grabs it.

– Eh!! says Scorps. Poor cunt.
– This you? asks the bouncer, meaning the bus pass.
– Nah, nah, it's me little brother's.
– So you're carrying around your little brother's wallet and his surname is Arnold?

Scorps looks at me.
- He left it in me car.
- Yeah, the twenty thousand dollar VK, Alan Bond?
- What?
- What star sign are you?

Now we practised this shit on the bus on the way here. I'm Aquarius, but on my driver's licence it says I'm born 14 August 1967, so that makes me Leo. Scorps is a Gemini, but on his licence he's a Taurus. And he's drunk. And he's nervous. And he's got no pubes.

- Ge-Gem-Gemin-Taurus.
- Get the fuck away from here, mate, says the bouncer. He folds up Scorps's ID and puts it in his pocket.
- Gimme me licence.
- It's not yours, baldie. I'm giving this to the cops. Whoever gave it to you is in a lot of trouble.

Scorps backs off, then blows himself out of the water.
- Give it back, mate, please give it back, it's not mine.

The bouncer leans forward and bitch slaps Scorps in the ear. He starts to cry.
- Now fuck off, baldie.

I back into the music. It's this new song 'Holiday' by some woggie-looking chick called Madonna.

LIBERTY LUNCH

About midnight, we find ourselves in one of the men's cubicles. We swapped flirty lines at the bar, before I laid the biggest line of all on her: three inches long, white and she can snort it in the bathroom with me.

She crams in, tall, lithe, blonde, as I chop up the shit Kaspar has sold me.

– Isn't that your girlfriend out there?
– Yeah, she's cool. We're just doing a line.
– Are we? she asks as I hand her a rolled-up fifty.
– Sure. You got other ideas, have you?

Sam doesn't answer until she's hoovered her share, in case I don't like her answer, I suppose. She stands watching me, shifting her weight from one high-heeled foot to the other as I bend to the cistern and come up moaning a little. The gear, which has the distinct taste of kerosene, explodes in my sinuses, before dribbling down the back of my throat like a chemical spill.

– Tasty, huh?

I put my hand around her waist and start kissing her, press my cock against her long brown legs. She's into it, until voices sound in the bathroom and she pushes me away. I look through the door crack and see Kaspar. He's wearing an ankle-length blue sheepskin jacket with a white felt hat, doing the Bondi pimp thing. He's talking to a Roosters player, who's racked out of his brain as well. Kasp is nodding his horse head very seriously, like he's actually listening to the bloke and not thinking of the next startling Kaspar Show statistic he can casually reveal.

When I turn around I see Sam sitting on top of the toilet, legs pulled into an aerial crouch, so you can't spot her feet under the door. I can see the bottom half of her white panties, so I reach down and stroke the lower curve of her leg and she pushes my hand away, freaked by the possibility of discovery – that anyone would think she's a slut who'd fuck another girl's boyfriend in the toilet over a line of coke.

Kasp and the rugby league player are talking about drugs; someone has fucked them on a gram and they're trying to tap some coke from one bag into another, to fuck someone else on their gram. I listen, feeling nothing but lust for the new cunt in the cubicle with me.

That's what makes me ill about this scene. Despite its shallowness, its emptiness and pathetic fascination with drugs and money and fucking each other's girlfriends – as soon as I do one line of the Devil's dandruff, I am one of them. I'd fuck Scorps's girl if I had a chance, do it in his bed; I'm just a rank, rutting animal with a hard-on when I get on the rack.

– We sweet? asks the Rooster, nervously eyeing the door as Kasp holds the bag up to the light. He nods and the music barges in the door as they exit. I put my hand on Sam's panties, try to peel the fabric away and hit the starter button, but she's gone off the boil.

– What's up?

– This doesn't feel right with your girlfriend out there.

– I told you she's fine with it, we've got an open relationship.

– Alright, well, if she tells me it's okay to fuck you, I'll do it.

Jesus, talk about cocaine morality.

We go back out into the crowd, me wondering what the fuck I'm gonna do. I see the cop that was up at Kaspar's place, laughing with two suntanned chicks. He looks like he's just done forty push-ups and is wrestling a crocodile behind his lips.

– Cunt-stable Herbert, I say as I walk past, and the chicks frown at him.

Bella is chatting away to some big pork chop she used to date, who had a swing at me last time we were at a party together. I think I'm in love with Bella; shit, we live together now. The thing is, if I do make this formal, get down on one knee like every other sad clown seems to be doing at the moment, all this becomes reality, it's my life, not just some stage I'm going through and I wince, then talk softly to Sam.

– I'll go and tell her the deal and she'll give you the wave, I promise.

Sam, who looks like she needs one good tap on the head to get her undies off, nods at me and I can't believe she's going for it. I walk over and take Bella by the elbow and move her near the entrance. Fifty or so flockers are waiting outside on Campbell Parade to get in to Liberty Lunch so they can crowd into the dunnies and do coke as well.

– What's up, babe? she says and looks at me, barely focused, a glazed, drug-fucked, dead-eyed visage. It's a tight race who's more racked.

– See the chick over there, the blonde?

– Yeah, her name's Samantha.

– Well, I was gonna go and have a line with her in the dunnies and she's worried you'll get pissed off.

– It's fine with me.

– Alright, well, can you just give her a little wave to say so?

Bella turns and gives Sam her nicest hand wave. She could be at the races with Rhett Butler in *Gone With the Wind*. Did they go to the races in that book? That's what getting stoned for your entire high school career gives you. What was I doing? Focus, Ned.

Then I'm back at Sam's side; she's seen Bella's wave.

– See what I mean?

PUBES LIKE STEEL WOOL

We're having a spewing competition outside Kingsford McDonald's because we're idiots and we're bored. The Buccaneer, the fat cunt, starts it after he skols his chocolate thickshake to stop us scabbing off him. The rest of us ate inside but he arrived late and had to get takeaway. When we all started hassling him for some, he shoved the whole of his Big Mac in his mouth, then ripped the lid off his thickshake and downed the lot. Now the fat cunt's got an ice-cream headache that's making him whine in a high pitch.

– Squeal like a piggy, screams Larry as the Buccaneer pushes his fists into his temples. After about a minute of walking, he starts to heave, makes a performance of it, then fountains a spray of minced food and ice cream onto the front window of an auto-parts store on Anzac Parade.

– You fucken grot, Buchanan, yells Halftime.

– How's this bit, says Birdy bending over a chunk of burger. – It hasn't even got teeth marks in it! He gets his face near the spew, pretending he's going to lick it up, then gets a whiff, dry heaves and makes himself spew on top of the Buccaneer's filth.

We try to push Birdy into the vomit but he dances away. I start to make myself heave. I can feel the last of my thickshake in the back of my throat and, as I bring it up, it's still cool. It comes out with a sound like 'GAK' and hits the pavement with an equally satisfactory sound.

— Awwww, he haw haw, laughs Mex. He's got the biggest nose in the form. It pulls his lip out from his teeth and makes him look like a shark in profile. He gets paid out about it a fair bit but he's a pretty good bluer, and can bash me, so I don't give him too much cheek.

Larry's had his fingers down his throat behind a tree and after a few goes he emerges and hurls a long line of liquid at us like some kind of fire-breathing creature. It misses most of us, but a splatter gets Birdy on the jumper.

— You filthy fucken cunt, Lawrence, screams Birdy.

He tries to wipe it on Larry but it gets serious pretty quick.

— Yeah? Try it, Birdy, you fucken pommy cunt.

He shapes up to Birdy, who drops off very quickly. Birdy's not stupid.

As we walk into the guts of Kensington, I tell Larry my news.

— I fingered Justine last night.

— Fair dinkum?

— Yeah, but how's this. She's got pubes like steel wool.

— She's a fucken slap-head, mate, whattaya expect?

Justine is my first serious girlfriend and definitely the first chick to ever let me put my hands down her pants and play with the pink bits. The juices that have gathered in the cleft of my fingers are a rare perfume that will soon be passed around the back seat of the 604 to Charing Cross.

– Smell that, I say to him.

Larry doesn't rear away, he has a good sniff and nods his head.

– That's alright, eh?

I met Justine four weeks ago down the beach. I was sitting with another girl named Pog eating Zooper Doopers, our legs dangling over the edge of the grey concrete promenade at Maroubra, when she dropped it on me.

– You know my friend Justine thinks you're a spunk? she said.

– Fuck off.

– You fuck off.

– Which's one's Justine?

– The blonde one.

This was thrilling news because I wasn't used to anyone finding me cute. But a spunk? That was fucken unreal. Then Justine high-kicked over the pedestrian crossing from the wog shop carrying a white paper bundle of hot chips. She was in tiny, black nylon shorts and a leopard-skin bikini top that barely restrained her two tanned weapons of mass destruction. I don't think I'd ever seen a smaller girl with larger tits. Sold.

Down the beach, Justine is known as the blonde nip because she's one-eighth Japanese and has inherited her grandmother's demure Asian stature. That DNA, however, has been blindsided by a huge dose of Ye Olde English bustiness. Her tits are not meant to be on a girl so tiny. They make her look like she is always in a rush, dragging her toward some point in the future. And they're dragging me into Kensington today.

The reason all the boys are hanging out is because we've just started school holidays, but the chicks at Our Lady of the Sacred Heart don't finish for another two days, so we're gonna go heckle them at lunchtime. Justine and Pog go to OLSH and the Buccaneer's pretty keen on Pog. Mex has been eyeing off

Vanessa and Scorps likes Gitta. Larry, Halftime and Birdy all think they're a chance with Helen Hutchinson, but they've got Buckley's if you ask me.

– Did ya tit fuck her? asks Larry.

– Nah.

But I'd thought about it. It was all I thought about.

Our Lady of the Shit House backs onto a golf course in Kensington and the rear of the school juts onto a large steep hill where most of the chicks sit out on the grass at lunchtime. We've timed it so we get there just after their lunch bell and can go up to the fence and trade obscenities.

Scorps, Larry and me have brought our skaties with us. I have, of course, dressed for the occasion. I've got on my hot-pink hooded tracksuit top with a pale lemon Billabong T-shirt, red trackie pants, white socks and black happy shoes – the kung fu slippers you get in Chinatown. I look hell. I've also been proxing my hair, so it's blond, almost white in spots, and if you grab it at the ends it breaks off in your hands.

The coolest thing you can be at the moment is a surfer. Blond hair, blue eyes and brown skin is what all the chicks are after and most of my mates look the part. Larry's blond, so is Birdy. Scorps is sunbleached in spots and Halftime's hair is white from all the swimming in chlorine he does. A few months ago, I got off the bus at Kingsford and went into the chemist and asked for a bottle of peroxide.

– Yeah, my brother's come off his bike and grazed his thigh, I said to the chick behind the counter.

– You sure you want peroxide? she says.

– Yeah, my mum says that's the best stuff. You've got to dilute it, eh?

When I got home, I locked myself in the bathroom and rubbed it through my hair, leaving it overnight. The next day my mop had an orange tinge to it and started to lighten with each weekend at the beach. I was stoked. Instant surfer credibility. Pity I couldn't do a re-entry to save my life and squatted on my board like I was a Vietnamese peasant.

As we top the rise of Tunstall Avenue, we see the girls on the lawn. They're about halfway down the hill, a mass of blue and white, each chick barely identifiable from the next. They look like one of those documentaries about penguins you see on *The World Around Us*. There must be three hundred of them, all squawking, eating lunch. I'm a fucken killer whale in the shallows. It takes me a few seconds to suss Justine and her group and when I do I whistle and she waves.

– SHE'S GOT PUBES LIKE STEEL WOOL! screams Larry.

– Fucken shut up, I say to him but it's too late. He's already told the Buccaneer and Birdy my story. I'm rooted.

– EW! EEW! SHE'S GOT PUBES LIKE STEEL WOOL! screams the Buccaneer.

– You guys are fucked, I say.

There's nothing I can do except separate myself from the source of the heckles. A diversionary tactic. It's well documented in the wild. I jump on my skateboard and start down the hill. It's probably about a hundred metres to the bottom. I'll fly past the chicks, cover myself in glory and shut these cunts up behind me. By the time I'm a quarter of the way down I realise I'm in trouble. I'm reaching terminal velocity. Halfway down I start to get the death wobbles, I'm going so fast. I shit myself and jump off my board.

In front of me, a Commodore station wagon is parked in a driveway. I've got to be doing about 40 kays when I leap off. The problem is my kung fu shoes have those hard plastic soles on them that grip as well as Lego blocks. I immediately slip, go arse over and backflip into the tow bar of the Commodore. Did I mention there's three hundred schoolgirls watching?

It's a big impact. The air goes out of me and I lie on the road, head pointing downhill, knowing I'm in serious trouble. I look to my left and the chicks are standing, open-mouthed. Not one of them is eating. They're horrified. I look up the hill and the boys are bent over, convulsing. They can barely breathe they're laughing so hard. I'm in agony. My back is on fire. I drag myself to my feet and walk slowly up the hill, trying to draw my first breath since impact.

Larry and the Buccaneer have sat down on the road they're so weak from cacking themselves. A car appears over the rise and they all move out of the way and I remember that I don't have my board. I turn to look down the street and the tone of their laughter changes.

– FUCK OFF, LOOK AT YOUR BACK! screams Birdy.

Scorps has jogged down to grab my skatie but is still laughing as he walks up to me.

– Oh, mate, that's the funniest thing I've seen in my life. Hold on, turn around, you're bleeding.

I try to look over my shoulder but the pain's too much. I drag my trackie top around and see it has a long, blood-soaked slit in it. Now, all the boys are around me, still struggling to keep it together. I pull up my jumper.

– Aw, fuck off, says Larry.
– How's the gash?
– You can see your spine.
– You've got a cunt on your back, says the Buccaneer.
And cunts for friends.

NUMEROLOGY

I go into a newsagent one super-fragrant top of the morning and fill in some mega-draw Lotto coupon with the vital statistics of our relationship. The day we met, Alessandra's age and mine, and other nauseatingly smitten numbers. When the frowning drudge behind the counter runs it through the machine, it makes a squawking sound, smearing ink over the entry, and he has to do it again.

– It's never done that before, says the frown, and I smile, taking it as an omen of the potency of mine and Alex's numerology. I give it to her that night as we eat chilli noodles and lick laksa off each other's chins, and tell her if she wins she has to stage a play called *Us – the Musical*.

When she calls me the next day, she's whispering excitedly that she has something very important to tell me. I swoon and think about the prescient Lotto machine.

– Is it about you or me?

– It's about us. Come over.

Driving there I decide red lights and stop signs are polite suggestions which I have every right to ignore in a situation like this and, fuck it, I can pay any fines with our new found LOTTO FORTUNE!

I handbrake the car into the kerb and leap up the fabled stairs and find her glistening from her run in shorts that are still illegal in some southern US states. She wipes her top lip and kisses me and I have to slow my heart and remind myself that yes, this is happening, I am not standing behind some other lucky fuckin' bastard, watching him melt under her lips.

– Sit down.

– We won, I knew it.

Little curiosity brackets form either side of her face and she pushes both hands on top of my knees.

– I didn't want to tell you in case it didn't come off but I've been called back for a final casting for a children's show I auditioned for two months ago.

– Ah.

– It's down to me and another girl.

– No Lotto?

– This is better than the Lotto.

I remember myself and realise just how wiped out she is about this.

– This is great, Alex.

– Well, there's just one catch.

I fight to keep the smile on my face and my throat clear of fear. Here it comes.

– You okay? What's wrong?

– Nubbin. Telm me.

– If I get the job I'm gonna have to move back home.

– But that's . . .

– I know it's a long way but . . .

– It's a twelve-hour drive.
– I haven't got it yet, it might not happen.

But I know. Things go right in this girl's world. Friction does not exist.

BALDIES ON THE GOON

Justine walks through the bog of sand that is our driveway wearing fishnet stockings, a red smear of a skirt and a platinum wig. I can't believe she is my girlfriend. She looks beautiful. Her tits are so big that, for a moment, they block out every thought in my head except breathing and I can do that when I'm asleep so it doesn't count.

Summer's on its way out, but there's still some heat in the night and all the girls are dressed in that stretchy Lycra shit. I can feel the heat of the sand through my shoes – rubber-soled, white tasselled loafers. On really hot days I used to shake the smaller gum trees out here on the street and Christmas beetles would thud to the ground around me. They'd try to crawl away but I'd collect them and put them in an old pillowcase. Slowly it would fill up, there'd be hundreds of them, clawing over each other, the mini-grappling hooks on their legs poking through the cotton. They'd shit and piss themselves in confusion and it would stain the pillowcase, until I'd pour them out into the hot sand of our driveway and cook them to death. Hundreds of them. Can't remember why I did it.

This is the first party I've held in my life. At school we debated the theme for at least three periods (Religion, General Studies, Geography) before we decided on a P & S Party. Everyone has to come dressed as something starting with either letter. The word went around, my parents relented, now Justine's here in fishnets. Sometimes life works out pretty good.

Justine has come dressed as a Slut which bodes well. Guru has turned up as a Penis and Hump Malone is his Scrotum, which means they have to hang together all night. Larry's come as a Poof, Scorps is a Prostitute and I am just Pissed. For some reason my mother has decided that Shamus should be the chaperone for the evening, while she goes out for dinner with my Uncle Truman who's down from the mountains on a bender since my Aunt Sandra died. My mum has given Shamus strict instructions to limit the amount of grog we drink, but that's like telling a fat kid to make sure no one orders pizza.

By 10 pm there are eighty of us throbbing though the house to Billy Ocean's 'Caribbean Queen'. There are so many pastel colours it looks like Walt Disney's projectile vomited in the lounge room. I've seen at least three ciggie burns in the shag carpet but don't give a fuck because I'm trying to get Justine into my bedroom. I manage to finger her in the bathroom for a while before Birdy (dressed as a Pommy) and Larry shoulder charge their way in, the faggots.

– Get the fuck out, I yell at them.
– I need to brush me hair, says Larry.
– Yeah, I wanna brush me teeth, says Birdy.
They think they're hilarious. Justine straightens her skirt.
– Can youse fuck off!
Birdy smiles at me as Justine pushes past.

– Dregs, she says.

Larry tries to flick the head of my cock through my pants.

– You could crack fleas on that, he says.

– You guys are fucked.

I walk through the dining room to get another beer and see my stepdad has the silver plastic bladder out of a cask of Lindemans Riesling and is free-pouring it into Helen Hutchinson's mouth. Helen (dressed as a Stewardess) is five foot eleven, blonde and has the sort of body that makes you consider the possibility of an intelligent creator. There's no way she was just thrown together. She's magnificent. My stepdad leans her back to receive more wine and he cups her arse.

In the garden I see Suggs vomiting out his nose. He's come as a Paddle Pop by painting himself brown and taping a large stick to his arse so it looks like it's jammed in his ring. He should have come as his nickname, Seagull, because as soon as you start eating he sits down next to you and squawks for food or scabs five cents off you. He's got orange hair and freckles the size of Sultana Bran flakes and his eyelids are lined with blood.

Amazingly, Pog (Sort) is helping the cunt, sitting with him as he vomits.

– What's going on there? I ask Larry, who's followed me outside.

– She was pashing him and he spewed.

– That's sick.

– You get any carrot, Pog? yells Larry.

She smiles.

– Nah, but a bit of hot dog bounced off my tooth, she says.

We laugh. She's a hell chick.

Someone's turned the stereo up full blast, blaring 'Legs' by ZZ Top. It's distorting heavily and I can see the kitchen windows shaking. I turn to go inside, and catch Mex and Maggot standing near the bushes at the far end of the garden. I've got two plants back there, but have found a large wire garbage bin and upended it over them like a sheath.

– Watch those cunts, says Larry.

Mex sees me, starts laughing and pushes Maggot, and they wrestle on the grass. In the lounge room, I see it's Shamus who's put the music up loud. He's on the green divan with Helen and Vanessa, who has even bigger tits than Justine and has come dressed simply as Sex. I love OLSH girls. Helen leans forward on the couch wobbling, her hair covering her face. Shamus is really enjoying the music, his face creased up like he's doing a shit as he shakes his head and passes a joint to Vanessa.

Near them, another girl wearing fishnets has collapsed behind an armchair and the Buccaneer (dressed as a Stud, as if!) is feeling her legs. He rubs the inside of her thigh, smiling at Guru, who reaches over and touches her as well. The Buccaneer sticks his hand deeper up the girl's dress and touches her groin. He looks confused and then the girl sits up, drunk, and I see it's Scorps in his prostitute outfit. On the wall, one of my Uncle Truman's Aboriginal bark paintings is vibrating to 'When Doves Cry'.

My mum's going to be home soon, so time's running out for me to fuck Justine. I have to focus. It's been a heady couple of months. I've gotten my first real girlfriend, I've kissed a chick sober for the first time, I've fingered a pussy and gotten a dozen raging hand jobs. Sex is hovering closer. I can feel it in the wind with Justine, but like the wind, it squirrels past, hot and breathy, impossible to bottle.

The hardest part about having a girlfriend is trying to get some time alone with her. My mum's like a prison guard on patrol every time Justine comes to our house, and Justine's parents make us keep the door open in her room whenever I'm over there. We'll lie on her bed, my back to the door, and she'll grab my cock, stroke me up and then we'll hear footsteps and I have to drag the furniture back indoors. It's like trying to hold a barbecue in the tropics.

I realised pretty quickly the only way to guarantee a result was to do it under her parents' noses. Whenever we watch *The Cosby Show* or *Magnum PI* in the lounge room, we snuggle under the doona and Justine prises the helmet off my little German soldier while her parents sip cups of Bushells. The feeling of a girl – a real live person, other than myself – touching my cock has been a revelation and I sense it will lead to a lifetime of manoeuvring to get my penis back into female palms.

As for sex, it's been tough. It would be fine if I could just back Justine up against a wall in some quiet alley and slip it in, but she's got a fair bit invested in this as well. It's her first time and she wants it to be cinematic. Parties, where there's little parental supervision, tend to be the only option, and there's not much cinematic about having your undies around your ankles and three drunken blokes burst in and try to take photos of you, which happened to Vanessa last month. So the OLSH girls are jumpy.

If I was being honest with myself, this party is just one big elaborate cover story for me to fuck Justine. Tonight has to be the night. Shamus is so pissed he wouldn't know if the house was ablaze. I walk into the bathroom, and Gitta and Pog are very carefully watching him as he gets Helen into the shower in her panties and bra, trying to sober her up.

– She alright? I ask and Helen squelches out another stream of riesling.

– You'll be fine, darling, says Shamus.

– Her mum's gonna be here in forty minutes, says Gitta.

– Get me a towel, says Shamus.

Gitta's watching my stepdad like he's a witch doctor, awed and a little scared but not quite believing what she's seeing.

– Where's Justine? I say.

– I dunno, says Gitta.

Things are getting out of hand. Another chick I don't even know has passed out under the dining room table and there's mashed corn chips all over the lounge room where Larry's wrestling Kaspar. The Hun cunt has finally turned up but he didn't come in fancy dress. Tara, his new girlfriend, is watching horrified as he goes pink (see, that starts with a P, Kasp) in Larry's headlock.

– You give up, Hun?

– Fuck off, Lawrence.

I sit down to watch next to Birdy, who's patting Winston.

– Check out his eyes, I say.

Birdy slowly pulls back the dog's fringe and Winston growls, low and dangerous. Birdy is too drunk to heed it. He yanks the hair further back and Winston's red eyes suddenly glow evil in the light. The dog leaps and snaps at Birdy's face, like one of those werewolves out of the *Howling*. Birdy sways back, just in time.

– Fuck, he says, fingering his face for damage.

I laugh, just as Kasp lashes out with his feet and the bowl of French onion dip lands near the fireplace.

– Settle down, you fucken dickheads, I scream at them and walk into the kitchen to get a cloth. Justine's in there with Joe Gold. My timing isn't perfect, so I don't actually catch either of them doing anything, save a smoothing of clothes and dumb smiles as they try to act all innocent.

– Aaaaay, mate, says Joe Gold, all smiley. He goes back to his Kahlua and milk and by the end of the night I don't have a girlfriend.

SINCERITY

Andrea is making us tea, me, Scorps, Chong, Grumble, and she's laying the martyr act on a little too thick for my liking. Then I remember she is dying and I hate myself for being such a cunt.

– You boys don't come around much any more, she says and I smile and tell her I've been heaps busy at work and I've got a new chick and my car's been playing up and, Jesus, I sound pathetic, while Scorps just says nothing. He doesn't like Andrea and doesn't hide it, while I play the nice guy, pretend I'm interested in her. Mr Sincerity.

Fuck, save us all from the sincere, the worst hypocrites of all, I'm thinking, my face tight as I sip my tea. I don't know why but tea depresses me. It's what people who've given up the piss, or just given up, seem to drink. Tea, endless cups of fuckin' tea. It always reminds me of plastic-covered couches and doilies and lace hanging off withered tits as some old bird pours me my . . . tea. It goes nowhere. No one ever sparked an orgy with a pot of Twinings.

Andrea looks terrible, her skin is drawn, opaque, and her actions slow and painful like she has sand in her joints. I don't wanna ask how long she's got because she's trying not to think in those terms, but the question's breathing in the living room with the rest of us, the unwelcome stranger sitting in the corner. Chong just hangs beside her like he's an Inuit warlord humouring us before he feeds us to his dog team. Fuck knows what's going on in his head. I can see Grumble wants to go outside to have a ciggie, but he feels weird about it, seeing that's what fucked Andrea, the Winnie Blues, and even though he's around here more than any of us and has a great relationship with her, he won't budge. I throw him a bone.

– I'm just gonna make a call, I say and hold up my new mobile phone.

– You can use the phone here, says Andrea, sensing my desire to escape.

– Nah, it's cool, work pays for it, I say, and Grumble stands to join me in the breach. Scorps looks like a South Vietnamese soldier staring up at the last American chopper flying out of Saigon. I crack the balcony door and go down the side that's shielded by the curtains. Grumble looks pissed off.

– This is so fucked, he says.

– She doesn't look too good.

– She's fucked, he says viciously and kicks a succulent in a plastic pot off the balcony. It splatters on the driveway below like an ink blot.

– Fuck, Grumble, settle.

– It's fuckin' fucked, he says again and I see him blink away a tear.

The next day we somehow get our shit together to go for the

early at Maroubra and Scorps gets a pie and chocolate Moove for breakfast and jogs back to the car with the paper.

He throws the *Daily Telegraph* down in front of me.

– Seen this?

The headline says 'IN COLD BLOOD' and shows a group of blue-uniformed coppers standing on Bondi beach, surrounding some fruitloop who's waving a chainsaw. The story says the bloke was a schizo and wouldn't drop the thing, so the coppers shot him. Eight times. Did a good job of it.

– Yeah, I heard about this, I say.

– Have a look at who one of the coppers is.

I read the story. The two police who shot the guy have been suspended pending blood tests. One of them is a sergeant: a beefy guy I've seen around hassling Lebs for being Lebanese. The other guy is Constable Stewart Herbert.

– That's the bloke . . .

– Fuckin' oath, says Scorps.

THE HOUSE THAT TRUMAN BUILT

Well, if you told me you were drowning
I would not lend a hand
I've seen your face before my friend
But I don't know if you know who I am

I don't know how this guy does it, but he's just nailed the way I'm feeling. He's some drum-playing maniac called Phil Collins. He used to be with a band called Genesis. Now he's out on his own and I've found his tape amongst all the Willie Nelson and ZZ Top; all the shit Shamus listens to.

We've got these big double doors in the lounge room wall that you press and they click open. That's where my parents keep the stereos. There's a big reel-to-reel number that I've never seen used and then there's this silver job underneath it. The record player doesn't work any more because my mum threw a whole pineapple at Shamus when he wouldn't turn down the music. Now it only plays tapes. They sit in a huge jumbled pile in the cupboard, which makes it look like we've just been robbed. My sister and I cleaned the pile up once, alphabetised it, but the next time my parents had a party it ended up even worse than it had been – plus, it had bits of smashed pineapple through it.

There's a loud crash out in the lounge room, and I take off my Walkman headphones and strain to hear if it's good violence or bad violence. Then I hear Shamus's laugh. He sounds like a pirate in a movie.

– ARRRR, RARRR, RARRR, he screams, then whoops, like you'd hear from a hillbilly during an anal rape in a burning barn. 'You're so Vain', by Carly Simon comes on. That trembling bass at the beginning always makes me uneasy. It's Sunday night and my parents have been having lunch. Or they were. Now it's just solid boozing. It's raining outside and the leak in my roof seems to have moved to the other side of the room.

I get out of bed and open my doors. They're just louvres, so they let in light, smoke, noise. Thankfully there's another door between me and the party. I twist the knob and the door pops open like it's pressurised and the music and smoke hit me as if I'm walking into Paddo's. There's still about seven people at the table, slouched in different attitudes of drunkenness.

Doug's there, his chin on his chest, smoking a Camel unfiltered. There's red wine over the front of his safari suit and he's motioning in the air like he's conducting an invisible orchestra. His partner, Sherie, has her eyes closed talking to my mum, who's shaking her head a lot, blinking. The table looks like it's been used for an autopsy.

At the other end is Don Simpson. He's leaning forward on his chair, elbow on his knee, like he's Napoleon, talking to my grandmother, who looks the soberest of the lot. As I walk past, she sticks out a hand and grabs me and kisses me.

– Shouldn't you be in bed?
– The music's too loud.
– Abigail.

My mum looks at me and blinks a bit more.
– What's wrong, darling?
– The music's too loud.
– I'll go and turn it down. Shamus! she says and stands up.

Our house was built by my Uncle Truman. One of the more unusual features is a hinged wall that separates the lounge room from the dining room. It takes a grown man to do it, but I can just about move it myself now. You push the wall, and it swings open so the two rooms become one huge sea of dirty white shag carpet. Throw a thirty foot long table in the middle, more piss than should be legal, three days of my mum's cooking, and you have the basic Lancaster Crescent party.

I went up to the grog shop with Shamus this morning to help him load up the Merc. We stacked that many cases of beer in the boot, the car sank 'til the frame rested on the suspension. I know Shamus could not possibly have drunk all the alcohol himself, but he looks like he has at the moment. His curls are glistening with sweat as he crinkles up his face, singing along with Carly in a voice that sounds half asylum patient, half Apache Indian. I'm sure he doesn't think the song is about him, does he? Does he?

– AROOOO, YOWWWW! he screams.

Shamus seems like he enjoys his life. He's just turned forty and his career at Channel Four is taking off. There's talk he's going to move from reading the morning news to the late night bulletin. He doesn't see my mum go to the stereo and twist the knob back from nine to three. Shamus opens his eyes, looking like he's been told marijuana's just been legalised.

– Abigail?
– Don't you turn that back up, the kids have school tomorrow. They're trying to sleep.

– I wouldn't think of doing any such thing.

He sees me in my pyjamas and smiles.

– Sorry, darling.

I walk into the kitchen and my feet stick to the tiles from all the spilled beer. Bob Doubtfire and my Uncle Truman have their heads bowed, holding cans of Fosters, mumbling about something. Bob looks sick but that's because he's a degenerate alcoholic. At Christmas, he woke up in the barn at my uncle's place and reached for the milk bottle he'd filled with water before going to bed. He was down to the last 100 ml when he realised it was the wrong bottle and he'd just drunk half a litre of paint thinners. It was only a couple of hours later he decided hospital would be a wise course of action.

I open the fridge and it's stacked with cans of Reschs silver bullets, Fosters and dry Australian white wines. There's a couple of large wooden bowls of half-finished salads slotted in amongst the disorder. They look like flying saucers that have crash-landed and been abandoned by their occupants. I reach for the milk, hesitate about drinking out of the carton, then do it anyway. I see my Uncle Truman looking at me from the corner of my eye.

– Hello, me darling, he says and grabs me in a bear hug. I can feel his beard on my forehead as he kisses me in the hair. He smells of beer and cigarettes and liverwurst. Truman's like the rough bearded warrior king you see slumped in the throne at the end of a banquet table. It takes Doubtfire a few seconds to focus on me, and when he does he looks like Keith Richards without the money or blood transfusions.

– How you going, kid?

He reaches for my cheek with a fist of nicotine-stained fingers, which I endure patting my face. Then he seems to forget I'm there and I put the milk back in the fridge and wade into the cigarette smoke, stepping on a broken spring onion in the carpet. I reach down to pick it up and glance into the corner of the room, where the untrafficked shag is almost white. Sprouting amongst the tufts of pale wool are three tiny marijuana seedlings. The rain of the last week has leaked under our French doors and germinated the lost seeds in the accumulated dirt of the shag. I think about showing Shamus but head for bed instead.

Back in my room, I can hear the muffled sounds of *Tusk* by Fleetwood Mac. I go to my bookshelf and take down the big *Wordpower* dictionary my stepmother gave me for Christmas and open it. Inside I have cut out the pages to make a hollow, like you see in spy movies. My canister of dope and my little red, alloy hash pipe are in there. I break up a bud and jam it in the cone, open my bedroom window and suck the baby down in three or four big drags. I stick the pipe under my bed, put my Walkman back on and get back into Phil.

And I can feel it, coming in the air tonight, oh lord
I've been waiting for this moment for all my life, oh lord
I can feel it in the air tonight, oh lord, oh lord
And I've been waiting for this moment all my life, oh lord,
  oh lord.

Man, this Phil Collins dude really knows what he's doing, I think as I drift off.

THE BLACKNESS

I'm sitting with my mum in her car in Elizabeth Bay, the geographical low-water mark for Sydney's junkies. Kings Cross, where most of them score, is up the hill. They bang up, then follow the natural slope of the land and end up here. Not a good place to park your Mazda.

My mum's crying.

– Can't you just snap out of it? I say to her.

I'm frustrated. This shit's been going on for a while and I feel helpless. I dread having to call her because even the most tiptoeing small talk ends up in the same bleak forest.

– How you doing? I'll say on the phone.

– Not good. I'm very down.

– Are you getting out? Maybe you should go and see a movie?

– I can't even get out of bed, Ned. It's just crushing me.

I'll hang up the phone and feel like necking myself after ten minutes of that.

My mum's come down to Sydney for the weekend to get away from Shamus and she's rented an apartment in Billyard Avenue, which is kind of fuckin' bizarre, now I come to think about it, because it's literally fifty metres from where her brother, my Uncle Truman, was found dead a few years ago.

After my Aunt Sandra had her heart attack, Truman kind of lost the plot. He wrote a 600,000 word novel about their love and hit the piss constantly. Everyone always says the only reason Shamus isn't dead is because he just drinks beer. Truman was different. He smashed Scotch into himself and could do two, three bottles during a bender.

A few years before he died, Truman went up to my Uncle Matt's holiday house at Forresters Beach and hit it hard. He woke up in the middle of the night and found he was shitting vile black blood, litres of it, because his renal artery, the one going to his kidney, had backed up and exploded from all the alcohol abuse. He called the ambos, but was lucky to make it.

From then on it was downhill. He dragged it out another couple of years, moved into Elizabeth Bay and savaged the bars around the Cross; the Bourbon and Beef, the Kings Cross Rex, the Goldfish Bowl, Hampton Court and the Mansions. His kids, Flynn, Bailey and Sass, couldn't do much about it except neglect their studies and make their own lunches for school. One night, when Truman didn't come home, they went out looking for him.

There's a set of old convict-built stairs that crumble down from Kings Cross to Elizabeth Bay. They must be twenty metres high and let's just say, after that night, Sydney City Council erected a much higher fence around them. Who's to say if it was accidental or intentional, but Truman went off the side and his children found him, cold and crumpled at the bottom, in more of that cursed blood.

The kids have been shell-shocked since. They were ravaged

by the death of their mum, but their dad's death could finish them off. My mother isn't coping with it much better.

– I don't know what to do, Neddy, it's just all around me.

– What about the pills your doctor's giving you?

– I've tried every fucking pill in creation. I can't stand the pills any more.

She's weeping, head in her hands.

I look across the road. There's a famous house called 'Boomerang' there, behind a high white wooden fence. I hear Lachlan Murdoch just bought it for eight million. It's just across the road from the shithole one-bedder my mum's rented. Water finds its own level, eh?

– The blackness, she says and I don't know if she even realises I'm there any more.

HYDRO

– You're mad, says Larry.
– My mum knows, it's sweet.
– Your mum knows?
– Of course she fucken knows, whattaya reckon? I say.

I'm showing Larry the crop I'm growing in the garage. Larry's got his own plants so I know he won't try to rip me off. I think. I'm not the trusting type when it comes to mull, but if the plants disappear, I'll know who it was for sure and I can drive round to Larry's joint and steal his plants to get the cunt back. I throw my schoolbag into a corner of the room. It's like *The Day of the Triffids* in here, dope plants from arsehole to breakfast.

– Just don't say anything to anyone at school, I say to him. – My mum doesn't want anyone to know she knows. She says it makes her look like a bad mother.

After those cunts Mex and Maggot taxed my plants at the

P & S party, I decided it was too risky growing outdoors and put them in pots and dragged them into the garage, kept them under lights when I was at school. It worked pretty well but the plants never did as good as they could, cos of all the sunlight they missed. Dope germinates flowers when the daylight hours shorten, so I was playing havoc with them; they thought winter was coming and they'd flower when they were only a foot tall, which is like your sister getting tits and menstruating when she's five years old. Not a good look.

Since then I've got serious about my smoking and growing. The only guys who can even touch me in our form for mulling up are Foilie, Larry, Joe Gold, Grumble, Mex and maybe Suggs. Suggs is a fiend but he's also a scab and never has any money, so his addiction is hampered. The others are all heavy smokers, but I don't think any of them have access to the mountains of dope I've got growing in my shed. I'm pretty sure I'm the only student at Seaview College whose parents are letting him cultivate a commercial quantity of marijuana in their garage.

It doesn't make much sense for Shamus to go out and be paying two hungie an ozzie when a spastic with a hose and a patch of dirt can grow the stuff. That was my sales pitch to my mum, and she went for it. Call it household budgeting. My mum's been a dope grower for most of her adult life, so she's even given me a few tips on how to get the most out of this crop. Really, it's all a bit hit and miss when you don't know what the seeds are that you're getting. Most of mine came from a friend of Shamus's, who's got a pretty serious crop up the coast on a sugarcane plantation. Shamus has been getting quarter pounds from the dude but the bloke certainly hasn't been giving them away.

– Help us get them out of here, I say to Larry.
– How fucken many is there?

– Twenty-three, I say.

Once I hit sixteen, my parents converted our garage into a granny flat. It's not real warm in winter, and when it rains, water leaks under the door, but it means I don't have to come into the house, so I can basically get home when I want. It's also given me a hell location to pull billies without getting sprung because you can usually hear the front door of the main house open if my mum comes out to the garage. She's cool with me growing but she hates me choofing.

Larry and I drag the big plastic tubs out into the yard and dot them around the garden.

– So they don't look like a dope plantation, was what my mum said. She insisted we spread the plants out instead of cluster them in one spot. The bottom of the pots make a good chunky scraping sound as we haul them over the dirt and eucalyptus pods.

– Where's your mum and Shamus tonight? asks Larry.

– Out. Some party for Channel Four, I think. Show us the gear.

We go back into the garage and Larry sits down on the couch while I reach under the bed for my mull bowl, ready to start chopping up a mix. Despite all the plants, we've had to score because my children aren't ready to go and we don't want to smoke leaf. It's bad enough that Shamus attacks them with scissors every time I turn my back, so I have to give them a bit of breathing space so they can mature.

– How's the smell in here? says Larry.

It's warm in the room and the air's still thick with the reek of resin. Larry rips open the Velcro of his Ocean & Earth surf wallet and digs inside one of the pockets, producing a flattened piece of aluminium foil. He carefully unfolds it, each layer revealing a series of bumps in the silver, until he levers open the final flap and displays the dope for me to see.

– What the fuck is that?

Larry giggles. Inside are four heads the size of broad beans. They're a dark brown colour, which grades into purple the deeper you look into the buds. They're much smaller and more compact than the heads we usually smoke, beaded with what looks like dew but what we'll later discover is supercharged resin. Larry's scored off a bloke named Rufus, who lives in Henrietta Street behind school and used to be a cop. Some of the boys have been talking about Rufus's new gear at school, but this is the first time I've seen it.

– That's sensational.

– Hydro.

– What the fuck's hydro? I say.

– It's like what you're doing here but more technical. It's the same as those hydroponic tomatoes we studied in biology. You just stick the plants in water and you can feed the nutrients straight into the plant.

– Give us it here.

I take one of the buds and start to chop.

– Fucken sticky. Smell that.

I hold the bowel up to Larry's nose and he sniffs like he's a wine poof in the Barossa. I continue to chop, discovering a seed, then another.

– Look at that.

I hold them out on my palm. The seeds are bigger than a match head and dark, almost black, wired with tiny purple veins.

– They look like Frankenstein's eyeballs, says Larry.

I roll one of the seeds on my palm. It's as hard and shiny as a ball-bearing.

– Hang on to them.

About seven, the sun starts going down, the cicadas are tearing up the place and we hear the throb of a V8 outside in the street.

– Who's that?

– Grumble and Chong, I think.

A minute later there's a tap on my door and Grumble, Chong and Scorps appear, already ripped.

– Fuck. Look at youse, says Grumble.

We're all completely coma-ed.

– What the fuck did that guy give us? says Scorps theatrically as he flops into an armchair. He puts a hand to his forehead, a gesture I'm sure he's picked up from his mum. They scored off Rufus as well. Half the school scores off Rufus. He's only got one kidney or something and the dealing is paying for his dialysis.

– We were driving here and we nearly ran over a dog, says Grumble, looking upset.

– That fucken shit is making me trip.

– I'd prefer to run over a kid than a dog.

– I drank a fucken two litre bottle of Coke I was so thirsty.

– You always drink a two litre bottle of Coke, you fat fuck.

– Get fucked.

– I'm serious. I feel like I'm gonna have a heart attack.

– Turn this up.

– Not too loud.

– Turn it up.

Scorps reaches over to the stereo and bumps it, causing the record to jump.

– Fucken handle, Scorps.

– Yeah, I'm just turning it up.

It's 'Have a Cigar' off *Wish You Were Here*. We've been giving Pink Floyd an absolute caning for the last six months. Roger Waters is a genius. Scorps starts playing air guitar to the lead-in. I join him, mouthing the sound of the guitar.

– Chickaboom, moo moo, mow mow moo moo mow, mow moo, moo mow.

Then I switch to electric organ, while he stays on lead. Larry starts playing lead as well. We all nod our heads as if we're actually jamming. Grumble is quicker off the mark, grabbing for the imaginary microphone. He keeps the mic on its stand, but leans it back to his mouth, turns his head sideways, waiting, then gives us the opening.

Come in here, dear boy,
Have a cigar.
You're gonna go far,
You're gonna fly high,
You're never gonna die,
You're gonna make it if you try,
They're gonna love you.

Grumble is a natural showman. A psychopath, but still he's good on the mic. We all join in for the chorus.

And did we tell you the name of the game, BOY,
We call it riding the gravy trainnnnnnnn.

Chong is trying to take over packing duties but I'm too smart for that.
– Fuck off, get out of it.
I pack one for Grumble, who sucks it down like he's an anteater. Scorps is next and, as usual, he makes a production of it, stooping over the bong like he's giving himself a head job. He lights the cone, then powers through, the smoke exploding into the clear plastic of the bong like a genie getting home from work. He lets go of the shottie and it clears in a split second, screaming into his lungs. He exhales with a moan.
– Amen.

*

Then there's a helicopter above us. I'm pressed up against the wood veneer of my bedroom wall, the flap of a *Bird Noises* poster tickling my ear. The fucken thing is above us, its blades thudding, a high winding of the engine. It must be a police chopper. A spotlight breaks through the windows and lights the bodies of the five of us in our school uniforms, corpses in a gas-heavy no-man's-land.

– YOU – YES YOU, says a voice on a megaphone.
– STAND STILL, LADDIE!

I jolt up and look around me. The lights are dim. Grumble and Chong are mumbling to each other. Scorps is asleep with his mouth open. Larry's gone. I look at the stereo. It's a Sanyo combo system with a record player on top, twin cassette on the bottom and AM/FM tuner. They've got *The Wall* on. There's a clamour of bongos and drums then a scream that sounds like a monstrous mechanical eagle plunging for the kill.

We don't need no education,
We don't need no thought control.

Oh, fuck. I stumble out of the door and vomit in the grass. Once, twice, bringing up the pizza pie I had for lunch, the Jupiter bar, the salt and vinegar chips from the Jungo. I look up and the boys are laughing.

HOLD PLEASE

She's at the mirror in a sheer grey evening gown that hugs to her waist like a classroom fantasy and I put my arms around her and draw myself into her arse, smelling her neck like it's the last flower in a muddy WWI battlefield.
 – You look staggering.
As we drive to the Hermitage listening to Nirvana's *Bleach* she holds my hand and we change gears together and, as hokey as it sounds, the fact she doesn't want to let go of me, even to drive, strikes in me so deep I know it'll be there like shrapnel next to my heart when I'm eighty and aching and my grandkids will be shaking their heads wondering why Pop gets so sad listening to that dumb old twentieth century band Nirvana.
Alessandra pulls into the lacquered blackness under a grove of figs and looks at me suspiciously.
 – Not another picnic, is it?

– Keep walking.

We shuffle through the tangy harbourside bush and, just as I've about given up on Scorps, I see the first torch lighting a grove of mad eucalypts. As we walk into the shivering circle of light, we see a pile of rocks topped by some banana leaves on which sits a basin of warm water. I smile and motion Alex to wash her hands. I hand her a towel Scorps has hung over a nearby branch and we continue into the gathering darkness as the sun crawls towards bed overhead.

At the next clearing, Scorps has wedged a silver bucket into the armpit of a tree and two glasses of champagne stand in the melting ice. We smile and sip the champagne, and look over the brush into the harbour where the evening breeze is rocking the boats to sleep.

– We should get down there for sunset.

I take her hand, feeling the twist of her fingers in mine; the wind sculpts her hair away from her profile, and I wonder at the grace of the universe for leaving me this moment and almost simultaneously I'm struck by the humid fear of losing it. As we walk down the curving rock staircase to the smooth malt sand, we see the tiny beach has been lit by half-a-dozen bamboo torches, while Scorps stands sentry in his monkey suit, white napkin hung over his forearm.

– Sir! Madam! Welcome! Can I offer you more champagne?

Alex explodes into smiles, and runs and hugs Scorps, who looks over her shoulder at me with an expression that says, 'See, they can't resist me'. He's laid out the table on the sand under the lazy branches of a snoozing fig – white tablecloth, silverware and glasses with a sputtering torch for company. As we pad into the soft sand, the harbour rolls into view like a scene change on a Broadway stage and I silently thank my city, where everyone's a millionaire, every heart has a view.

*

Scorps is chafing in his tuxedo, sweat coagulating around the shaving rash on his neck as he lugs the last of the food down onto the beach.

– This ain't worth a hungie.

I have to agree it's been a little more trouble than I'd expected.

– I'll give you a hundred and fifths.

– If you can do an extra fifths, you can do another huntz.

– If I give you two huntz, I might as well take her to some cigar chompin' suit joint.

– Look at the personal service you're gettin'.

– One seventy-five.

He does his de Niro smile/frown thing.

– Is a deal.

He retires to the servants' quarters, a bench over the other side of the beach, and the tip of his joint flares every twenty seconds or so as he lies under the stars and mutters to himself about overtime. I look at Alex over the tight expanse of the tablecloth, the second bottle of Krug run aground on the sand, and before my dippy mind can recommend against it, my tongue has gone and spilled the needs.

– I've never felt this way before, I say.

Then:

– I really dig you.

And, of course:

– I think I've fallen for you.

All very reasonable stuff, if it had been three or four months into the relationette, but it's three weeks and though I can't quite hear them, I see the alarm bells ringing in her eyes as they track the teleprompter of her future.

The departure lounge feels like an intensive care waiting room. Alessandra sits with her bag, holding my hand, and I shake my daydreams from my sinuses and look at her and wonder if she's really the one, if it really can be any purer and realer and deeper than what I feel for her. As we drew each other into bed after dinner last night, to the first heartbreaking note of the 'Last Goodbye', she smiled at me and sucked my lips and said, 'Let's make a baby' and I wondered if Dale Carnegie had put this in his book under the chapter heading 'How to break hearts and make someone your eternal slave'.

I've spent a week swinging between the complex despair that I'll lose her forever, and manic activity: helping her prepare scripts, get used to an autocue and checklist all the things that could go wrong at the audition. Somehow it kinda made up for the guilt I felt at praying she wouldn't get the job. If I owned a goat, I'd have cut the fucker's throat under a full moon.

Now, as I watch her catwalk calves slay the other passengers in line for the flight, I wonder how any producer could look past her, and resign myself to life without her canary yellow light. She throws out a little wave as she disappears into the boarding tunnel and I shuffle back through the empty syringe of the airport to count the heartbeats before she's back again.

THIRD RAMP

I'm standing outside Kaspar's place on Campbell Parade, shouting up at his window as the tourists slow to look at the species known as the Bondi boy. Thing is, I've gone to school here and lived here for more than twenty years, but I don't call myself a Bondi boy. Mr Boom is a Bondi boy. Scorps is a Bondi boy. Same with Kasp.

There's plenty of Bondi boys who know my head to nod at, but they also know I wasn't at the beach at third ramp in 1983, hanging with the crew. So I'm no Bondi boy. I just wish the cunts with their straw cowboy hats and white thongs, who moved here from Perth nine minutes ago, would work that out.

I'm in trackies, pissed off I'm even here, but Kaspar's being an arsehole and says he won't pay me unless I come down here and 'talk things through with him'. He hired me last month to do some MC-ing for the rugby league and he's 'less than impressed with my professionalism'.

– We need to talk about this, he said on the phone.
– What's there to talk about, Kaspar? I did you a favour, just give me the fuckin' money.
– Yes. I know that's what you think, but it's not that easy.
– Why? Because you wanna patronise me for a half an hour to make yourself feel better?
– Just come down to my place.
– Get fucked. Just send me the cheque.
– That sort of attitude's not gonna get you paid.
– Fuck you, Kasp, my attitude? I did you a favour.
– I paid you to do a job.
– Which I did.

Which I certainly did. It was just my after-hours performances that have gotten me in strife. Somehow Kaspar has landed the contract to run the rugby league's supporter bus. It visits regional NSW and Queensland towns to make the poor cunts who live in the middle of nowhere feel like people in the city give a shit about them. Local teams send their three worst players along and they pass balls to rural Australia's future car thieves and drug addicts while Kasp keeps the show rolling with witty banter on a microphone.

I suppose it's a well-intentioned promotion. Kids get to pick up diseases off the manhandled Marlboro Premiership Cup, lift it above their heads for photos with their dads. Budding referees can watch contentious plays on a video screen and decide which supporter base they would piss off with their imaginary rulings. Birdy is running the technical side of things so when Kaspar asked me to cover for him it seemed like a four-day lark in the sticks.

Once I did some MC-ing, I had a new appreciation for the Kaspar Show. It's hard work talking shit for three or four hours, especially if you know nothing about rugby league, like me. Kaspar made it seem effortless and, getting right down to it, was quite gifted at making children feel like superstars after some reserve grade meathead had spiral-passed a footy into their face.

Only problem was it conflicted with the snow season, and the Hun, an alpinist from way back, also had a gig doing snow reports from Thredbo. He also has a new, younger girlfriend to impress with his wardrobe of skivvies and a frothing mass of Sydney clients screeching for his gear.

So I took over the MC-ing on the road train while he went to the snow. In fine rugby league tradition, every night we obliterated ourselves in whatever fly speck we'd rolled into that day. It was fun. I got to witness first grade league players' penchant for group sex, avoided several fights with drunken hecklers and saw parts of the State you usually only stop to piss in at petrol stations.

On our final night, in the nation's capital, we all headed off to one of the funkier bars in Canberra and, after several dozen drinks, I took my clothes off and showed the patrons a flaccid Oscar. Again, getting nude is in the greatest of rugby league traditions, but Kaspar didn't appreciate the feedback he'd been receiving.

– He's just pissed off you were more entertaining than he usually is, said Birdy.

Trying to get my cash off the cunt has been going on for ten days and Kaspar has become increasingly unreasonable. I threatened to call his bosses, he threatened to break my legs. My threat was probably a little easier to carry out, but I didn't doubt Kasp had the resources to see his through either.

– So what do you want to do, Kasp? Spank me?

– I'm sure you'd like that, Edward, but I just need to debrief you about certain aspects of your behaviour.

– Get fucked, Kaspar. This is not a career for me. I filled in for you so you could go to the snow with your moll. Don't forget who did who the favour.

– Well, I guess you don't want the money.

I have no recourse. I need the cash and the Hun cunt has me over a barrel. So here I am standing outside his apartment, buzzing the prick and no one's home. I call his mobile and it goes to voicemail.

– I'm here, Kaspar. Where the fuck are you, you cunt?

PADDO'S

Mandy is drunker than me and she's giving me a hand job in the corner of the dance floor at Incognitos. She's a hell glamour, or she is after five Sambucas which are *two bucks* a pop from the bar. How's their fucken form, eh? What a rip-off.

I'm not sure Mandy really knows what she's doing, so I've manoeuvred her into a corner, where's there's a kind of curtained-off legends area. It actually feels like she's trying to drag an eel out from under a rock ledge the way she's grappling away down there. There's a good chance she'll pull my knob out by the roots, but I'm too afraid to say something in case I break the spell.

The DJ is playing 'Wake Me Up Before You Go-Go' for the nine hundredth time tonight and I'm keeping an eye out for either one of Mandy's older brothers, both of whom would love to bash me under normal circumstances. They're both ironmen – run, swim, paddle wankers who walk around like they're carrying watermelons under each arm. I can't even begin to imagine what they'd do to me if they caught Mandy giving me a drunken handie on the dance floor at Paddo's – sorry, Incognitos.

This joint used to be called Paddo's but the owners had some troubles with the licensing police because they were letting so many baldies in and had to close down. They reopened about three weeks later, exactly the same location, same decor, different bouncer, except they were called Incogs. The place is as narrow as a terrace house – I think it used to be a terrace house – and has white gauze curtains and bench seats running down the walls. There's kids everywhere dressed in hot pinks, egg-yolk yellows and apple greens, smoking Alpine ciggies and drinking West Coast Coolers and Swan Lager. I don't want this to ever end.

I'm still coming to terms with the fact that places like Paddo's exist – where there's girls to dance with and you can buy drinks and can carry on like a fucken maniac and no one seems to care. There's heaps of guys and girls from different schools here and there's a definite hierarchy as to who you can try and get on to.

The rich bitches, the Ascham scrags, the SCEGGS sluts, Kambala molls – all tend to go for Cranbrook faggots and Kings and Grammar poofs. The other chicks – St Catherine's, St Clare's, some OLSH and Sydney High chicks are all ours. Seaview Boys are definitely the low-hanging fruit, unless you're Joe Gold who manages to fuck anyone he wants to, including my ex-girlfriend Justine, the cunt.

I don't reckon there's any twelve-year-olds in here tonight but there's definitely at least one thirteen year old and my sister Megan and all her friends (St Catherine's) are here and they've just cracked fourteen. They'll fucken ruin it for all of us, I bet. One of them (Sydney High chick, for sure) will get parra, fall over, crack her head and have to go to hospital and they'll ask, 'Where did you get the alcohol?' and she'll say 'Incogs' and that will be the end of the greatest fucken nightclub in the history of mankind.

— What's wrong? I say to Mandy (St Clare's), who's breathing kinda heavy through her mouth.

— I feel sick.

— You wanna sit down?

— I think I'm gonna spew.

— Don't get it on me.

— I think I'm gonna spew.

— Sit here.

I put her in a chair, and go and find her friends and tell them she's about to chunder. Fuck this. I go looking for Scorps. The DJ's got his shit together finally and is playing 'Once in a Lifetime' by Talking Heads. The Black Rat (Seaview College) dances past me wearing his leather pants, with his hands in the air like he's one of those Spanish flamingo dancers. He's a fucking worry, the Rat.

Same as it ever was . . .
Same as it ever was . . .
Same as it ever was . . .
Same as it ever was . . .

I start jumping up and down doing the crazy David Byrne dance with the Black Rat and Birdy, then Joe Gold gets up on the seats along the wall and some chicks (Ascham and Kambala) start laughing at him until one of the bouncers (Randwick Boys High) appears and drags him down and tells him he'll be punted if he gets up there again. As soon as the bouncer is gone, Joe gets straight back up there. The chicks are loving it.

Joe Gold's going crazy, flicking his peroxided fringe around like Marilyn (the transvestite, not the movie star). He does this for two minutes, and the whole time I'm waiting for the bouncer to reappear. The song finishes and Joe gets down, and no sooner have his feet touched the ground than the bouncer materialises and gives him a look like he knows Joe's been fucken around but can't prove it. He's a charmed fuck, Joe Gold.

– Mandy just gave me a handie on the dance floor, I say to Birdy.

– Better hope her brothers – (Dover Heights Boys High) – don't find out.

– Are they here?

– I saw Damien before.

– Fuck off.

– I'm serious. He was doing tequilas at the bar with Cheyne Horan (Dover Heights).

– Fuck off. Cheyne Horan's here?

– Nah.

– Dickhead.

– I'd be more worried about me own sister if I was you, Neddy.

– Why?

– Look's like Mr Boom might be getting a hand job as well.

He nods in the direction of the back of the club. I crane around a few heads and see Megan grinding with Mr Boom (Vaucluse High) to Blondie's 'Atomic'. He's twirling his hands through her bob, singing along with the song, telling her her hair is beautiful.

– That's not gonna happen, I say to Birdy and walk towards them, only to spot Mandy's brother, Damien, at the table with his sister. Fuck, she's just spewed beside her chair and the bouncer's going over there. As soon as Damien sees me, he pushes through

the crowd, knocking over some dreg (Cranbrook) who's carrying a silver ice bucket with a bottle of wine in it.
   I bolt.

BYE NOW

Uncle Doug has come back from the hospice and they've left him in the living room like a big, noisy piece of furniture. He's yellow now, where the skin draws tight across the face forming the death's-head they all get when they're real close. It's been coming for about three months, but once the nurses saw the big guy in the black hood wandering around Doug's bed, they called Sherie and told her to come get him.

Everyone who was ever close to Doug has come to his house and is taking turns sitting beside him as he breathes like only old people and the dying can: they don't give a fuck how much noise they make, breathing has become a desperate practicality and, even though it sounds like he's sucking the dregs of a thickshake, it's not something that should be done with politeness, by himself, so he doesn't disturb others.

Everyone's trying to be upbeat about the situation but I can smell it in the air.

– You'd like to think he's gonna open his eyes and say, 'I'll be okay', don't you?

– I don't think that's going to happen, Neddy.

I'm sitting with Megan who's come straight from work, looking neat and serious, hating journalism as much as I did. We're taking turns stroking Doug's hand, which is a claw now, the skin so taut and discoloured the poor fuck looks like he's made of rice paper sitting on top of custard. Outside in the tiny courtyard, Shamus and his rat pack of journo mates are smoking a joint, drinking VBs, trying to put some distance between them and the horror story playing out inside. Doug scared a lot of people when he was alive, but he's doing a far better job with this effort. He's the first of Shamus's crew to go, and now all those ciggies and benders are looming like an ugly, unreasonable doorman in a lot of people's future.

Megan's getting teary as she looks into Doug's face and, not for the first time, I wonder how the fuck she got to be so sweet and compassionate and reasonable, while I got to be me. There's some chick who works with Sherie, a meaty blonde I'd definitely fuck on the fifth beer, taking sandwiches around outside, and I'm drifting to her arse between Doug's splutters for life. His eyes are slit open and milky, like dogs get when they're out to it, his breath a chemical stew of the drugs he's pumped full of and the food he can no longer keep down. I take his other hand, and Megan and I both look at him, the wild man, the wanderer, King Kong crushed on the pavement after his fall from the Empire State. His breath is very short now, like he's hyperventilating. We look at each other, Megan so sad and present to the moment she catches me there for a second, then Doug sighs, and a dribble of blood flutters out of one nostril. We look at him like he's a TV in a blackout.

– Has he stopped breathing? I say and lean in.

– Sherie! screams Megan.

I back away from him, knowing he's gone, wondering if he heard everything I was thinking.

THE PLANETS

I arrive at Forresters Beach just before lunch on Christmas Eve with this new chick I'm rooting, Tiffany. I open the flyscreen and see my mum in the kitchen talking to herself, saying, 'Ice, ice,' as she pops cubes out of a tray and into a glass of white wine.

— Aaayyy, I say, using a bit of a spazzo voice.

— Oh they've let you out. Did you get the bus by yourself? says my mum.

— I've got a friend with me, I say, staying in the retard act.

My mum kisses me.

— Did you have correct change, because I know you always have trouble with that?

Tiffany just looks from me to my mum, back to me, smiling kinda stupidly. In reality, I'm the stupid one even bringing her along to Christmas, but her parents live in Malaysia and she doesn't have anyone to spend the day with. I've always had a weakness for Asian women and we are still in Week Two of fucking. It seemed a waste to leave her at home.

My mother asks me and my cousin Alice to set the table.

– When you move it, be careful the legs don't bend in. It'll fall over, she says.

– Nice to see you're still buying quality furnishings, I say.

– That's not fair, says my mum. – The table's old. It's been danced on.

My mum seems pretty chirpy but she is half pissed. The real indicator will be next week when she's driven back up the Mountains, when everyone's gone and she's left with Shamus, sitting on that couch smoking, always smoking.

It's a big crowd this year. All the cousins and uncles and aunties are present, along with some of our closer friends like Massive Thirst, Doug and Sherie. Most of them are already nursing cold cans of VB and look relatively sober. My Uncle Matt and Aunt Anne have been renting this beach house for about fifteen years. In the early days the owners offered to sell it to them for $60,000 but they didn't have the spare cash back then. Now it'd be worth a couple of million. That's pretty much the way it seems to go with my family and money.

Just before lunch, Sass pulls up with Bailey. She's picked him up from the train station at Gosford because he's banned from driving until he's a hundred and seven. Bailey's talking loudly, coming down the hill from the street. Sass rolls her eyes as she walks in.

– He had a little six-pack on the train, she says.

Bailey thumps in through the screen door with an enormous duffle bag we'll later discover is crammed full of Disney character satin boxer shorts, cheap women's perfume and a ten-litre display bottle of French champagne, courtesy of the shoplifting gang he's been working with.

– I'm sorry I'm late, he says. – I had to see eight guys at eight different pubs, and by the time I got to the sixth, I was so pissed I forgot about me train.

Shamus is straight on to Bailey, herding him onto the balcony to see if he's got any dope. I follow along because it's always interesting what Bailey pulls out of his pockets.

– I've got a few pills, he says, bringing out a plastic sandwich bag that was once clear but has gone opaque from so much time in Bailey's jeans. – Three of them are good and three of them are iffy, but I don't know which is which.

– We better take 'em all just to be on the safe side, says Shamus and whacks one straight in his mouth.

– What if I get the shit ones and you get the good ones?

– I'll be sure to write, says Shamus and he laughs his pirate laugh.

Tiffany isn't much chop at conversation during lunch and does a lot of turning to me, staring, waiting for me to explain what someone has just said. As always, there's a tonne of food, with my Uncle Matt and my mum duelling each other in the kitchen to produce the most exotic dishes from scratch. If the recipe requires chicken stock, they have to roast a chicken, boil the carcass, extract the stock that way. Fuckin' foodies. After the tucker is served, Matt stands and thanks everyone for coming and makes our family's traditional toast to dead relatives.

– To absent friends.

– To absent friends, we all intone, and I look at Flynn and Bailey and Sass. The orphans. Sass gives me a small smile. Of the three of them, she seems to have come through the least damaged, maybe because she's the youngest. She's smart and conversation with her is never dull. Her smile means about five different things.

– Can you go outside if you want to smoke, Shamus, says my mother.

– It's just a cigarette.
– We're about to eat.
– I've got to have one as well, Shamus.
– And close the fucking door, you'll let the flies in.
– He's like a bloody incinerator, there's always a cloud of ash around him.
– Did I tell you that? That's what Larry use to call him, the Waterloo Incinerator.
– Derr.
– Fuck, I thought you just made it up.
– Are you going to watch the Sydney to Hobart this year, Alice?
– Nah, Kelly's away this year, so I can't get out on the boat.
– What about Fabbo, do we know what boat he's on this year?
– I think it's called *Spoof*.
– He's racing?
– I think so, I'm pretty sure.
– It's a great excuse to avoid us every year, isn't it?
– Don't say that. That's obnoxious.
– Someone told me that's how the race started. All these rich wankers with yachts wanted an excuse to get away from their wives and families after Christmas, so they started a yacht race.
– Who told you that shit?
– I heard that too.
– DON'T YOU DARE cut the meat that way!
– Anne. Down a few decibels, please.
– Let Matthew do it, PLEASE! That's not how you cut a ham.
– Jesus, how's my eardrums?
– Can someone pass the white down here? No, the white, darling. Where are you from, again?

— St Leonards.

— No, I mean where are your parents from?

— Oh. Malaysia.

— Who brought that?

— I think it's left over from the wedding.

— Oh, for fuck's sake. That's dreadful. Taste that. No wonder.

— Huns of the vine.

— No, it's Rothbury's.

— That's what Dadda calls people who bring bad wine to parties.

— Oh, Jesus. That's tragic, I don't want to swallow it.

— Here, pour it in Shamus's glass, he won't know.

About halfway through lunch, I realise my Aunt Anne's making an awkward attempt to rekindle Bailey's interest in working in the Northern Territory, to get him out of Sydney and away from the drugs. After Truman died, Bailey got a job as a jackaroo on one of the big cattle properties up north and worked his way up to leading hand before he pulled the pin and returned to the rich tapestry of shitheads he associates with in Sydney.

— When I first got up there, they told me you've got to choose a horse, eh? says Bailey. If there's one thing Bailey loves more than a joint, it's telling a story.

— So I go over to the yards and they've all got numbers and I say, 'What about that one? Number 138, what's her name?' One of the blackfellas who looks after them says, 'That's Daisy' and I think to myself, Why not?

As he says this, Bailey put his hands to his chest like he's swearing an oath, then turns his palms over like a Jewish tailor showing us fabric.

— 'Daisy', that sounds like a nice, pleasant horse, I say to myself. Well, the blackfellas, they tried to warn me about Daisy. They said she was mean, and once you'd chosen a horse up there, you can't switch her back halfway through the season.

But I kept saying to myself, Daisy, how bad can a horse be with the name Daisy?

My end of the table's gone quiet listening to Bailey. Up the other end, Shamus and Doug are passing a joint between each other, mumbling with their chins on their chests in a way that tells me their Es have kicked in. Shamus has already made a couple of pingpong ball cracks to Tiffany. Doug even stooped to a 'love you long time' joke but by that stage I'd managed to get her pretty pissed on the Rothbury Estate and I don't think she heard. Or she pretended not to.

Maybe they'll go to sleep soon. I risk going for a piss and when I get back, Bailey's still talking.

– But the thing is, it was a dry camp, says Bailey.

– Are we still getting Bailey's Tall Tales of the Outback? I say.

– Shhhhh. Go on.

– Don't shush me, Anne.

– Whattaya mean, a dry camp?

– There's no drinking. No booze at all. You have to drive into town and that takes almost an hour. So it keeps all the blackfellas and most of the whitefellas going crazy on the drink.

– Isn't that charming?

– And we're only earning like forty bucks a day but everything's laid on, you don't pay for food and you're sleeping under the stars most of the time, so it adds up and then you go into town and get on it.

– What's this got to do with Daisy?

– Hang on, I'm telling you. So every time you come off your horse, or you get thrown while you're mustering, it's ten bucks in the drinking kitty for when you go into town. We use the money to buy a keg and we set it up in the back of the ute and we drink it until it's gone.

– Classy.

– So you're riding through the bush and chasing beasts, there's rabbit holes and logs hidden in the long grass, you want a horse that's not gonna throw you, because it's easy to come off.

'Artificial Flowers' by Bobby Darin comes on the stereo and it suddenly gets cranked to about eight. Shamus is standing by the stereo, kicking one leg like he's trying to get shit off his shoe, while Doug coughs on the joint on the couch.

– Turn that fucking music down, Shamus!

He drops it to about six, so my mum hustles over and twists it down to one.

– You won't see another fucking skerrick of dope if you go near that dial again.

– Abigail! he pines as she walks back to the table.

– I'm going to fuckin' puncture my eardrums with my car keys if you don't finish this story, Bailey.

– Rightio, so I get on Daisy for the first time and froonk, she throws me straightaway.

– Ten dollars.

– Yep. All the blackfellas are laughing, saying 'We told ya', so I get back on. Froonk, I'm on me arse again. Twenty bucks.

– You've learnt to count, Bailey.

– I get on again, she takes off and she runs me under some low-hangin' tree branches, I'm off again. Thirty bucks. And then she does it again. So I've worked for free me first day. She knows if she keeps it up she stays in the pen and does fuck all for the rest of the season. Two hundred bucks that fuckin' horse cost me in a week. Fuckin' Daisy, I called her Useless Cunt, because that's what she was.

I walk into the kitchen later in the afternoon and my mum comes in, waving her hand in front of her face like she's shooing flies, a sure sign she's drunk.

– What's its name again?

– It is called Tiffany, Abigail. That's so fuckin' uncool.

My sister Megan comes in with some plates.

– I'm sorry, I'm sorry, I just get confused, says my mum.

– I don't even remember the names any more, says Megan. – I know they won't be here next month, so why bother?

– It's like the Vietnam War, hisses my mum. – So many innocent faces.

Things slow down. Some of us run across the dunes to have a swim, but Tiffany doesn't want to get her hair wet. Shamus and Doug fall asleep, there's several arguments over Paul Keating's legacy within the Labor Party, and my mother manages to avoid the bedroom where her brother nearly died shitting his own blood.

Sometime close to midnight someone puts Holst's *The Planets* on the stereo. If my Uncle Truman had a signature piece of music it was this. I don't know who put the CD on but they've chosen well, it's the 'Jupiter' movement. It's the sort of music that's so uplifting it makes you think it's possible to build colonies on the moon. If it was in a movie, Indians would be running across the plains to embrace the white man, or a Nazi would be throwing open a railway boxcar's door to free Jews.

I sit down alone in the lounge room and listen as the music flows out of the big glass doors, over the verandah and down the dunes. After a minute, Sass walks in and sits beside me on the couch and I hold her hand. We listen, lost in the music, and then Flynn is beside us, taking his sister's hand as well. It takes a little while longer but finally Bailey almost sleepwalks in, drawn by the notes above the sea spray.

I stand to leave them to themselves. As I exit the room, I look back at the three orphans sitting, listening, looking like shipwreck survivors huddled on a rock.

COOPER PARK

Somehow we've ended up in Cooper Park. All ten of us. Scorps and I are only being tolerated because I've got mull I've stolen from Shamus, and Grumble and Joe Gold are running low. Kaspar has brought along his girlfriend Tara and she's blind. We're all blind but Tara is fucken paralytic. Kasp is going tonguies with her on a bench as we sit around watching.

– Grab her tit, Kasp, says Joe Gold and he does.
– Show us your tits, Tara, go on, says Grumble.

She doesn't, so Grumble walks up to them while they're kissing and hoicks up her top. It's spandex or something, so it hangs up there, exposing the white fabric of her bra. She's too blind to move it back down, but Kaspar makes a fist at them and covers her without taking his mouth off hers. Grumble takes up his challenge.

– Yeah, Kasp? You wanna fucken go, do ya?

He stalks back towards them but Kaspar turns Tara towards

Grumble like a shield. Grumble laughs.

– You fucken homma, he says.

I'm rolling a joint while this is going on. It's one of my few talents. I'm not too good at surfing, fighting or any of the other high masculine arts. In the pantheon of useful teenage skills, reading and writing – my fortes – don't blow up anyone's netball skirt. My joint rolling, however, is second to none. I was apprenticed by Shamus, and this was further refined by Leonard, the ex-junkie who works for my mum.

I have a system. Most blokes use two Tally-Hos or, if they're really cheap, just one. I use three, sticking the first two together at a twenty degree angle so that one end of the joined papers is about one centimetre wider than the other. To this wider end, I then stick the third paper, sideways. This allows you to roll a trumpet. It's not the greatest shape for smoking – it tends to burn a lot of dope uselessly, but we're teenagers and appearances are everything. A monstrous glowing fatty makes us all feel like Bob Marley.

So I roll the joint. A lot of breath has been wasted on the whole do you add tobacco or do you not add tobacco argument. Me, I like to add tobacco. If it's good enough for the Rastafarians, it's good enough for me.

Tonight, I'm adding extra baccy because there's plenty of us and I want to stretch out the thax I've got left. I'm concentrating on my trumpet as Scorps watches on, keeping a sly eye out for a reappearance of tit.

– How blind is Kasp's chick? says Scorps and I nod.
– You got a lighter?
– Nah.
– Fuck. Go get a lighter off Foilie.
– You go get the fucken lighter.
– Fuck. You watch. They'll take it off us.
– Just get a fucken lighter, you homma.

So I go and ask Foilie for a lighter and Grumble hears me and tries to take the joint off me. Somehow I manage to hold him off, spark it up and, after one toke, it's snatched out of my hand, bypassing Scorps altogether.

– That's fucked, he says quietly.

The joint goes around Grumble and Joe Gold and Foilie and Maggot twice but no one says anything because they don't want to get bashed. Grumble is the one who hands it to Tara.

– Here you go, darlin'.

She smiles like a spastic, tokes, coughs and a minute later is spewing next to the picnic table. By the time the joint gets back to me, it's a cardboard roach. Kaspar bends over Tara as she dry heaves. He hugs her and they start kissing again.

– Aww, there'll be fucken chunks in that.

Tara, to her credit, seems to have perked up after the joint. She kisses Kasp with increasing enthusiasm and starts to rub his cock through his pink King Gee Tropicals.

– Go, son, says the Buccaneer, who's watching developments like he's Louis Pasteur in a Parisian laboratory. Everyone goes quiet now for fear of derailing the delicate events unfolding. Tara is lost in her own world as she fumbles with the drawstring of Kaspar's pants and unravels his horse cock into the darkness.

– Have a go at the knob on him, says Foilie reverentially.

– Full on, says Scorps.

We all don't know quite what to do with ourselves as Tara starts stroking the thing. Kasp seems to have forgotten about his audience as well. He's as drunk as ten Abos and has moved his hand down to Tara's crotch where he's rubbing her, being pushed away, then rubbing her again. She's insistent about keeping him clear of her cunt with her left hand, but her right is still choking his turkey neck.

– Fuck off, whispers Scorps.

– She's going for it.

Tara leans down and takes Kaspar's cock into her mouth. Around us, all you can hear is the wind in the bushes, fruit bats gnashing on figs in the big black trees overhead, and the distant noise of traffic as it chortles along Bellevue Road. Kaspar leans back as she takes more of his huge cock in her gob. The Buccaneer is sniggering, kneading his prick via the pocket of his canvas pants, while the rest of us stand around like we're Greenpeace activists watching a dodo chick emerge from its egg.

Grumble is the first to move. He crabs behind Kasp and unzips, taking Tara's hand and placing it on his own erect cock.

– Grumble's got nothing to write home about, I say to Scorps, who looks like I could push him over with my pinkie he's so enthralled. It takes Kasp a few moments to realise what's happening, and when he sees what's going on he breaks away from Tara, who looks around, blinks a few times and smiles stupidly at us. Kaspar tries to throw one at Grumble but Joe Gold jumps in and punches him, then Grumble gets him in a headlock.

– Make her suck us off, says Grumble to Kaspar, who's struggling. Grumble's pants are down around his thighs and his cock and balls are being ground into the dirt. I watch as Maggot moves over to Tara and sits down with her, smiling.

– How you going, Tara? he says and starts to rub her waist. Kasp is choking on the grass. Tara seems oblivious.

– Okay, okay, okay, says Kaspar.

In the time it takes Grumble to let him go, Maggot has already gone to work pashing Tara.

– Aww, that's so suss, says Scorps. I think he's talking about the whole situation.

– He's pashing her after she was giving Kasp a head job. He might as well have sucked him off himself, adds Scorps.

273

Kaspar stands up and sees Maggot and Tara, and folds in on himself in resignation. Now Grumble has moved in and has his geenoss out again. She takes Maggot into her mouth and Kasp sits down. Tears are in his eyes but he doesn't make a sound. I watch as the boys – the Buccaneer, Foilie, Joe Gold, all nine of us start unzipping and form a line. It's more ordered than anything I've ever seen at the bus stop and hierarchical to the extreme. Every guy in front of you can beat you in a fight.

Kaspar just watches, crying softly.

T-REX

I'm back at the airport, inhaling jet fumes and the ghosts of Alessandra's departure, waiting for her amongst a group of meeters and greeters as the mussed hairstyles and crushed suits start to shamble out of the boarding tunnel. Through the crowd, I see a familiar swagger and realise it's one of the Wynn brothers, who cracks a huge smile, slaps me on the back.

– You didn't have to come and pick me up, faggot.
– I'm picking up my girl, dickhead, I say.
– Which one? Have I met this one?
– Dunno, don't think so.
– Mate, you should see the fuckin' chick who was on the plane, he says and he doesn't have to finish the sentence for me to know. I nod down the tunnel and there she is, glowin' in army pants and a crop top, the centre of gravity and light in the zip code.

Alessandra smiles at me as she saunters up the slight incline, and I can feel Mark's disbelief as she slides into my arms and I hold her like an awkward teenager drinking a beer for the first time because she'd called me yesterday and told me she didn't get the job.

The plaster creaks as the young doctor tears into it with his tiny circular saw, sending a white dust-puff premonition into the surgery.
— It tickles, doc, says Alex, and the doctor smiles again at his little nickname.
Alessandra is leaning in her chair, head thrown back, not even glancing at the doctor's handiwork, as he does his best but fails miserably to keep his eyes off the cool olive finery of her thigh. He handles her like she's a Fabergé egg, and as he cuts up to the elbow, the cast falls open like a sarcophagus and where I expect her arm to be pale and crusty with dry flaked skin, it's dusted opaque with plaster like Turkish delight. She stands with a little hop and scans the surgery like a Tyrannosaurus rex with a new set of teeth.
— Thanks, doc!
— Don't put too much strain on it today.
— Okay, doc!
She drops me home because she's got to be at work at the surf shop in a couple of hours, which is plenty of time for us to have lunch or fuck or talk or smile at each other, but she's got stuff to do. I'm trying to work out what has changed, why I feel like a used car parked outside a Ferrari dealership, but that match head won't spark.
I get stoned instead.

ANZAC DAY

— Come on, you head betters! Where are yuzz? You've all packed up and gone home already, have ya? Come and get me money. Come on, up youse come!

Kaspar is holding court up the rear of the Watto Bay, waving a wad of tiger-yellow fifty dollar notes, acting like the punish he is. He's lucky he's six one cos some cunt would have broken that Dudley Do-Right jaw of his a long time ago if he was only five nine. Kasp is a suck but I'll give him this, he has a go and he doesn't back down from most cunts. Which makes him even more unbearable at times like this. The Kaspar Show – commercial free.

— Here you go, you Hun cunt, a hungie a head, I scream at him, and Kaspar steps into the ring, barely acknowledging me, still on the lookout for other punters, the intimation being that a hundred dollars a toss is just a side bet for a prime mover like him. He must do alright out of dealing, the

German cunt, cos he's always throwin' it around like there's no tomorrow.

The Fish and his old man are in the other corner, taking more fifties from Kaspar, laying them down in neat piles at their feet. One hundred, two, three. Fuck, Mr Nazzareno looks like he's goin' hard early cos he's got almost eight hundred on this spin and half of it belongs to the Horse Head Hun.

– Alright, get back, get back, get off the fuckin' tarp, you wombats, screams Kaspar in that half singsong, half whine of his that just makes you wanna bash the cunt every time he opens his mouth.

The spinner is trying to act all nonchalant, but I know he's a detective from Seaview Police Station and I tell a few of the others around me to watch the cunt. He keeps his money in a wad between his ball sack and arsehole and pulls it out at intervals to count – like we need to add his arse juice to the hundreds of other bacteria swarming on the currency.

That's the fucked thing about Aussie money, it's plastic, so some double-thumbed grub can wipe his snot on a twenty in Geraldton and it ain't soaking in, it's just staying there like an egg on a Teflon frypan, 'til it ends up on the other side of the country, smeared all over your hands. Anyway, this mongo with his money down his pants is spinning. He makes a big show of it, making sure the ring is clear. I'm screaming at him like a maniac because it's Anzac Day and it's every Australian's god-given right to act like a lunatic.

– HEAD 'EM UP, OFFICER, SOOOOOOO-EEEEE, I scream like the pig fuckers out of *Deliverance*. Kaspar waits vainly for quiet, then:

– Come in, Spinnah!

And up he goes. It's a nice spin too, I'll give him that, good and high, the pennies twisting in the air like cats that have tumbled out of a window. The punters' eyes lift, following the coins, as if watching an overhead bomber. They land, safe inside the ring, coil around each other like hula hoops and fall.

– TAILS! goes up the cry and I feel sick. I'm already three hundred in the hole and it's barely twelve-thirty, and that's not counting the money I've spent on cabs and piss and the bag I'll have to get later in the night. Fuck it. Kaspar walks over and looks at me for his money. I give him an 'as if' stare. I'm not picking it up for the cunt. He bends down and takes the two hundred.

– Always nice doing business with the white wog, he says, pulling out my high school nickname. – You wanna go again? The cunt's flush now, he's got my hundred and Mr Nazzareno's five, so he's playing with house money. It's a nice position to be in.

– Two hundred, I say.

– Ooooh, says the Hun, look who's all growed up.

He hands me the cash and I put it down at my feet with mine. I feel nauseous. The coins aren't dropping my way. I can just feel it. The Watson's Bay Hotel is always a tails ring, I always get skinned here. They play with three coins instead of two, the tarp's never pulled tight enough, blokes kick the pennies. I'm cataloguing all the reasons I'm not gonna win, and by the time the next spinner is up, I've already kissed the money goodbye. Really, what I'm doing is giving myself no hope, so the universe takes pity on me and gives me a . . .

– FUCKING HEAD 'EM UP, I scream as the spinner, a fat bloke with barbecue sauce stains on his shirt, tosses the coins high and they land.

– TAILS!

– FUCK, I scream.

That's me done. I walk off leaving the fuckin' German cunt to his money and can hear him over my back saying, 'Yeah, yeah, yeah. Any more you head faggots wanna try it on? There's a little space over here where the white wog's just left off.'

I wanna go to the bar but I feel like I'm gonna spew. This is my all-time favourite day of the year, when all the boys are in one spot, but I've hardly said two words to any of them, I've been so concentrated on the ring. I glance up at the balcony and see Scorps drinking a moccachino – coffee, for fuck's sake – with his new missus. He looks down on me patronisingly, like I should know better than to waste my money in such spurious pursuits. Perversely, Scorps chooses not to punt on Anzac Day and won't go near two-up, probably because his losses will be too public. I don't even bother walking up the stairs to him.

The beer garden is absolutely heaving with young stuff in midriffs and muscled tradie superstars in T-shirts and trucker caps trying to pretend they're not looking at each other. One of the Wynn brothers is staggering around with the look of a bloke who has to neck three cold ones before he leaves the house. He's got a broken nose and broken eyes and stinks of trouble, so I'm not surprised when he runs into some poor cunt in an Elwood T-shirt and scatters his tray of drinks on the concrete. Someone calls out 'Taxi!' and I want to execute them for crimes against originality.

It's a beautiful sunny day and you really wouldn't want to be anywhere else. Seafood is streaming out of the restaurant, the beer and mixed drinks are sweating on the metal-topped tables, but I feel like I'm at the centre of a hurricane wondering what the fuck I'm doing here – what the fuck is the point? And just as I'm working myself into a depression worthy of a cab fare home to bed and darkness, Mr Nazzareno wanders up looking like a bloke who stepped off a boat from Italy with nothing but the clothes on his back. He's wearing paint-splattered tracksuit pants and sandals with socks.

– Legetoutahere, finesumenelse, he says.

Tony's retired now but he spent thirty years as a garbo for

Seaview Council, counting up enough dosh to buy himself a huge bit of land in toney Vaucluse. He built the biggest wog palace you've ever seen in your life, complete with a sheep in the backyard to keep the grass down. He's been in the country longer than I've been alive but I still can't understand what the fuck he's saying. Come Anzac Day, it's always the same.

– Cumon, wefineanozagame, he says.

Tony Nazzareno is a head better, I'm a head better and the Watto's ring fucks us every year, so every year we move on, usually to Rose Bay RSL. Tony's too pissed to drive – which is a rarity and shows how far down he is – but he's found some mate of his who's been fishing off the wharf to gives us a lift around the corner in his tinny. By context I can understand what Tony is saying to me.

– Come on, let's get out of here, we'll find something else. Another game.

Puttering along the harbour, water slapping against the aluminium of the boat, I almost feel human again, almost like I'm living my life, until Tony's mate starts in on the Philippines and how he's just come back, bought himself a wife for two months, fucked her in the arse three times a day, then tied her to the bed while he went out to take in the local Easter passion plays.

– Mate, fuckin' realistic, lemme tell ya, he says. – They even nail a Jesus to the cross, through the hands and all. He's a gook of course, but apart from that the only way you'd know it was all an act is the disciples are smoking durries.

We're all cunts, I think. Some of us just try harder.

SKELETOR

The paramedics are loading my sister into the back of the ambulance. She is fifteen years old and weighs thirty-seven kilograms. She has been starving herself for almost eighteen months now for no apparent reason – well, that's what everyone thinks, but I've got a pretty good idea why.

She's crying and so is my mother, who's getting in the back of the ambulance with her. It's just before Christmas and the cicadas are shrieking. Thankfully, we've finally paved our driveway, so the sandpit that used to constitute the entrance to our house has been replaced by a generic slap of concrete.

Megan is being unreasonable. She doesn't want to go to hospital but she's fainted and lost consciousness for more than five minutes. My sister is one of those souls who should have been put on the earth aged thirty. She's just too kind and sensitive and giving to go through the agonies of being a teenager. She'd actually physically injure herself to save another person even the smallest amount of pain, so she's constantly taken aback by the negligence and malice other people have towards her feelings.

Last month she had her Year 10 formal and she looked beautiful, glowing, happy. It wasn't until we got the pictures back from the chemist and saw her standing next to her friends in a strapless dress that the jarring reality of the stranger who'd been living amongst us hit. Megan has been wasting away. We've known it, but we didn't really know it, if that makes any sense. In the pictures of her with her formal date, Mr Boom, her collar bones stood out like door handles and her face was drawn down into the skull – that look cancer patients get when they are going to die.

My mum and Megan have been arguing for the best part of a year about her eating habits but I don't think any of us realised how bad it had gotten until we saw those pictures. She looked like Skeletor from *Masters of the Universe*. She's been going to the toilet after dinner and throwing up her food, so now one of us has to stand outside the bathroom when she's showering to make sure she doesn't chuck.

It can be hard to tell, though – that's why she does it in the shower – so my mum has to smell her breath to see if she's spewed, but Megan brushes her teeth or gargles or eats parsley. It's a lot of fucken effort to starve yourself.

You hear about these weirdo chicks who look like an ironing board yet think they're fat. You see them on *A Current Affair*, pelvises showing through their pants, and you think, Fuck, they're idiots, you'd just sit them down and jam the food into them. You'd make them eat. But it's not that easy. I've talked to Megan a bunch of times about it, but she'll just get upset, tell me it's none of my business and walk off. Then I'll get angry with her – yeah, I'm a patient fuck – and tell her she should think about what it's doing to Abigail (I call my mum

Abigail now because Mummy sounds a bit gay) and that she's being selfish and then that really gets her upset.

Megan's psychiatrist is named Dr Sharon Sax and she's trying to get to the bottom of it all. She's spoken to everyone in the family so far and seems to think it has something to do with my mum being overweight and Megan punishing her for not having a perfect figure and thus not giving her a perfect figure. Shamus went along to see Dr Sax a few weeks ago and got aggressive, told her it was unfair to lay the blame at my mother's feet because she's been such a good mum. Dr Sax said she wasn't blaming anyone, that she's not really sure what's going on with Megan. She says it's a slow process, but she needs to spend some more time with my sister before she can make any accurate judgements.

Dr Sax has spoken to Megan and Abigail and Shamus but not to me. From what I can tell, none of them has told the doctor about the diary. The diary went for about seven months and basically it was a stream of profanities and insults to Megan written in class by my school friends. They'd scribble in it and I'd take it home and Megan would read it and respond. She seemed to relish the arguments and the slagging off, but towards the end it got pretty nasty. The boys would draw pictures of her sucking off dogs or getting raped by various animals. Most of the insults would go something like this:

Dear Megan
You are the dirtiest, fattest, bush pig I have ever seen. I doubt you could even make a dog cum, which is what I hear you do in your spare time you fucken gross slut. When I see your fucken ugly moon head on the bus I want to spew but know you'll just get down on your knees and lap it up like the fucken swamp donkey you are.
Get fucked.

The reason my friends concentrate their insults on Megan's weight is because I told them to. For as long as I can remember, whenever Megan and I would argue, I'd end up calling her a fat bitch or an ugly slut. Hearing me do it, most of my friends who'd come over to our place felt little reason to hold back when slagging her off. The most common insults for my sister over the last few years have been, in no particular order:
– Fat dog.
– Ugly dog.
– Fat bush pig.
– Ugly bush pig.
– Stupid moll.
– Stupid, ugly, fat moll.

And I don't mean that every now and then we'd throw one of these choice phrases at her. This was our everyday communication. Megan's doctor can delve as deeply as she wants to, but I'm pretty sure, if you're looking for a trail of evidence as to why she's doing this to herself, it leads right to my bedroom door.

MOTHERFUCKINGYANKEES

By now I've gotten to the Regis and need another drink. I feel around in my pocket like it's a dark hole in the ground, hoping to find something. I come up with a hundred dollar note and my stomach shoots down the elevator shaft of my body. I walked out of the house this morning with more than six hundred bucks – over a week's wages and now it's in fuckin' Kaspar's pockets.

The two-up ring is calling. They've moved all the chairs and couches out of one side of the main bar and there's hundreds of people standing around the action screaming and calling for bets, notes held aloft like battle ensigns, and there, next to his bemused missus, is Kasp. The game at the Watto closes at sunset and now the cunt has come up here to rub everyone's nose in it. The two of them look like they've already started in on spending his winnings. They could be chewing pieces of ironbark, they're that lined.

– Here ya go, Kasp, I say, waving my last hundred, and take his money to put at my feet. I nod at Penny and go back to my posse over the other side of the ring before she can tell me how good it is to see me and make me feel guilty because I haven't bought her flowers. Kaspar must have ditched the snow bunny and has gone back to the comfortable old shoe. Must be love.

The spinner this time is a skinny, confused-looking fella wearing a Yankees cap – truly the lowest form of life – so I take a deep breath as he throws the coins high, they spin and come down HEADS.

You fuckin' beauty, I think, and Kaspar doesn't even bother to walk over. He knows the money is mine and he's already waving his wad of fifties around looking for further victims. I decide to talk to the spinner.

– How ya feeling, mate?

He looks at me like I'm speaking a different language and I soon realise I am. The cunt's American and says he's never played two-up before.

– Have you had sex lately? I ask.

– Why?

– I'm determining your aura of luck.

– This morning, he sneers.

Fuckin' bet you paid for it, you ugly prick.

– Have you had a speeding ticket lately?

– Not for ten years.

– And you actually like those cocksuckers, the New York Yankees?

I stab a thumb at his cap

– All my life.

I look him over for any other noticeable impairments to good fortune, then take Kaspar on again. For two hungie this time.

I hate the New York Yankees for much the same reason I

despise any other successful, glamorous sporting franchise, be it Manchester United, the Roosters, the Waratahs or the Australian cricket team. They're smug cunts, whose success has bred more success – and because I'm extremely uncomfortable with success, especially other people's, I despise the cunts on principle. But I'm not stupid, and I tend never to bet against these teams, mostly through bitter experience.

I also know that two-up is a strange game, part luck, part intuition, and that some time during the day, probability, strange beast that it is, chooses to abandon almost every two-up ring and a ridiculous run of luck strikes one team of betters. And because this cove is wearing the despised New York Yankees emblazoned on his head, something tells me not to bet against him.

– HEAD 'EM, YOU YANKEE CUNT, I scream, almost putting him off as he tosses and, down they come, HEADS!

Now, I've won back three hundred of my money but I'm still in the hole. I ask the Seppo does he feel up to it, and he just laughs, ignoring me, a typical arrogant Yankees fan but a very good sign for me. I take Kasp on again – for four hundred. A few people are starting to take notice of the size of our betting. The Regis, like most pub rings, is populated with once-a-year punters who'll bet five dollars here, ten there, the embarrassing cunts.

Even Kaspar is paying a little more attention to what's going on, if only so he can shut out his missus, who's tugging at his poloneck pointing at the amount of money he's laid out. The MotherFuckingYankee sets, spins and . . .

– YOU FUCKIN' BEAUTY. HEADS!

Now I'm ahead for the first time all day. It's a beautiful feeling that almost every true gambler knows, when you look back and realise all your drinks, food, cabs, FUN, have been paid for by some other poor bastard's sweat and blood. But every punter also knows it's not enough and, now you're betting with someone else's money, you get cocky. I eyeball Kaspar, who's starting to take real good notice of me, and hold up the lot.

– Eight hundred, Hun?

He curls his lip like he's Billy Idol, then counts out the readies, hands them to me and walks off. Penny gives me a dead-eye stare that counts as the first honest communication we'd had in our lives. Fuck 'em. I pile the cash at my feet as other punters peer over.

– HEAD 'EM UP! I scream.

And up they go. I already know how they're gonna land.

HEADS!

Now Kaspar's starting to look worried. In the space of about seven minutes I've taken fifteen hundred dollars off him, which has to hurt, even for a drug dealer. The wad of fifties he's been waving around the ring is starting to look a little anaemic but I'm hot. The world has tilted on its axis. The probability of spinning four heads in a row is approaching astronomical but I think the MotherFuckingYankee has more cork in his bat.

I walk over to ask him has he been eating well, kicked any black cats lately and been donating to charity? I get a Yes. No. Yes. I'm on this fucker for the duration. I now have sixteen hundred dollars in my pocket and people are really starting to take notice of me. My number one fan, however, is a tall, blond German cunt who once bashed me at school, by the name of Kaspar Körtlang.

– How you travelling, Hun? You got any fuel in the tank or you had enough?

– Just put the money on the ground, Jelli, he says to me and hands me a wad, everything left in his hand, which is just under two thousand. The spinner, the Yankees cap-wearing cocksucker, is also doing extremely well, so his increasing winnings have to be covered by tail betters. The cockatoo comes over to

Kaspar and me, a little pissed off that I'm sucking up all the tails action.

– We have to set the centre first, I need some of that cash for the centre.

Kaspar is adamant.

– I don't wanna bet with the centre, mate. I want this cunt's money or no one's at all.

He stoops to take his cash, but the cockie relents and finally covers the Yank's mound of notes with a pastiche of offerings from other poor misguided tail-betting mongos. There's a real buzz in the ring now as people point at the piles of cash at my feet and in the centre, with more than a few tail betters betraying that just-been-raped expression I've worn so well. I am a fuckin' lunatic.

– HEAD 'EM UP, YANKEE, I'm screaming, and other head betters, equal beneficiaries of the run of luck, join with me, the team of us nearly hoarse as we howl like mongrel dogs trailing red rocket erections into hot summer sand. Kaspar and Penny are having heated words, but I'm almost oblivious, swilling an ice-cold Veebs that someone's shoved into my paw, enjoying the attention of several wide-eyed youngies who've just joined the fray to see what all the palaver is about. As the MotherFuckingYankee spins, I turn away from the action, still not one hundred per cent certain of the outcome, until above the screams, I hear 'FUCK!'

It's Kaspar, shrill testament to the fact that I've just cleaned the cunt out for almost three and a half grand. In the next ten minutes he makes several harried trips to the ATM, working his and his chick's account as I take another five hundred, then six hundred, then a lazy thousand he's managed to borrow off one of his cokie mates during the next three spins.

The MotherFuckingYankee ends up spinning an incredible twelve heads in a row, the probability of which is something just less than a blowfly being able to grow arms and knit a wetsuit out of vermicelli noodles. Kaspar is a broken man. He's done over five grand, while I'm awash in hundreds and fifties, and more than aware I'd better jump straight in a taxi before some cunt decides to get me in the dunnies and make a four knuckle withdrawal.

GUMMY SHARKS

Scorps, Birdy and Kaspar are looking at their watches in between pool shots as I sit on a stool at the front of the Sheaf searching for signs of her in the twilight crowd on the footpath. Scorps is losing patience.

– Call her and tell her we'll meet her there.
– Just a bit longer.
– Mate, if we leave it any longer we'll miss the boat.
– Ten more minutes.
– She's a fuckin' hour late, call the bitch.
– Fuck off, Kasp.

He presses his thumb to his forehead, meaning I'm under the thumb.

– She's pushin' you around, Edward.
– Fuck it, I say. I look at my watch and dig up some coins. I've already called twice but haven't told the boys that. Alessandra said she was drying pants or something. It takes her

six rings to answer and she moans when she hears it's me.
— I'm coming.
— Alex, they're getting pissed off.
— I'm coming, alright? Jesus!

She hangs up on me and I lean my forehead, with its thumbprint, against the payphone and take in air like I've been underwater, trying to work it out.

What has changed?

Twenty minutes later, I'm standing on the sidewalk as Birdy runs around on all fours being led by Kasp to show me the leash I'm on. They both bark like dogs out of the cab window as it accelerates up the street, and then I'm left in the dusk waiting. Alex arrives ten minutes later in the same pants she was wearing that afternoon, with her mate Smiley, aka Michelle, and a sour-looking dude with cheekbones and sore-looking lips. She rolls her eyes when she sees my mood.

— Where are your friends?
— They left, Alex, they got sick of waiting.
— Well, we're here, aren't we?
— Yeah, sorry, bra, they were waiting for me, says Simon, the dude.

When we get to the wharf, there's about a hundred and fifty people in the line. The boys are sitting on pylons and give me a clap when I walk down from the street.

— Congratulations — no, really — well done, says Birdy.
— Nice night for a queue, eh? says Kaspar.

There's only two small speedboats taking people out to the barge, six at a time, so everyone's settled in for a long wait. Alex is whispering to Simon as I plump down next to her.

— This is what we wanted to avoid.

She turns to Simon and they laugh. I look at them like

they've just stolen my car, stand, then walk to the edge of the wharf with Scorps

– Who's the spanker?
– Simon.
– Is he Alex's *friend*?

The way he says friend leaves me in no doubt what he's getting at.

– They used to model together.
– Oh, is that the story?
– Don't start, mate.

We watch another group in dinner suits pile into a speedboat. No one wants to get in the front because of the chop and spray coming over the bow. I push ahead.

– Come on, I say to Scorps.
– 'Scuse us, 'scuse us, pregnant lady comin' through, move aside, there's a sick woman here.

And then we're piling into the underloaded speedboat, giving Birdy and Kasp the finger as we leave the wharf. I catch Alex's eye, and she frowns and puts her hand on Simon's forearm.

An hour later, Kaspar, Birdy, Alessandra, Simon and Michelle arrive out at the barge. Alex is laughing outrageously with Mr Fuckin' Cheekbones and when she sees me she walks past with a snarl and gets herself a vodka.

– At least she gives enough of a shit to be angry, says Scorps.

Alex doesn't come near me for the next hour, instead she races around the barge, looking for other people to talk to, face stiff with determination, like she's a courier carrying the cure for cancer. I ask Scorps for the time and it's eleven-thirty, and I know it's now or never if I'm gonna smooth this out, otherwise I'll be kissing Kasp at midnight and I hear he's all tongue.

– It's like someone's let a vagina bomb off around here, Kasp says to me as I brush past him on the dance floor. Alex

is clapping along with Simon to 'How Bizarre' by that awful fuckin' Kiwi band like she's some kinda free-basing flamenco bitch when I grab her elbow and pull her aside.
– I wanna talk to you.
– You always want to talk.
– What's that mean?
She turns but I grab her.
– Do you want to be with me?
– I'm here, aren't I?
She walks away and I feel like I'm in a *Home and Away* episode.

I sit watching the dark shapes of the trees on the shoreline as the crowd begins to count down to midnight, faces twisted with fun, the great night of forced merriment, as the new year is born into the arms of negligent drunks and people who wouldn't normally open a door for one another swallow each other's saliva. The fireworks scream for attention on the Harbour Bridge and I don't feel any different from how I did an hour ago.

A bass score of bungers sends the barge babes scurrying to the railings, and as the crowd parts a little I see Alex with her arm around Simon, parting from a tad more than a New Year's kiss and my calves turn to lead and I wish I could just slip into the silvered ink below and sink to the silt, close my eyes in the quiet among the empty bottles and green rocks and dumb gummy sharks.

I AM AN ASTRONAUT

Some weeks I reckon I buy five, six, seven packets of cigarettes but never smoke more than about twenty durries. It's an interesting dance. I'll come home about six or seven, filled with terror at the empty night that stretches before me, when friends are washing their kids' arses or settling in to beat the buzzer on *Sale of the Century* or retiring to the den to finish that report for Wednesday's meeting. I have nothing but space.

I am Ned Jelli, astronaut, floating through time and blackness with nothing but my keyboard as witness, and the horror of that realisation grips me – this is where you're meant to grow up, isn't it? This is what dinner parties and art gallery openings and the fuckin' opera are for, no?

This is why you end up at the pub, with a slimy seventh schooner in your hand and some midweek bush pig snuffling around your barstool, because what else do you do with the space? Fortunately, I understand one of the absolutes of space – without your own supply of oxygen, you black out. Which is exactly what I want.

So I search for my cigarettes, the silken Stuyvesants, and then I realise I've thrown them in the bin, with just two smoked. What's more, because I knew I would trawl through the garbage trying to retrieve them, I have squirted them with cockroach spray, soaked them in dishwater then screwed them into a little ball.

Lately, when I get out of bed and shake my head at the sad spectacle that is my addiction, at my refusal to be happy, I will take the full packet (only one ciggie smoked) and hurl it out my window, down the grade into the jungle that fills the back garden of my block of flats. Ten hours later I'll find myself, torch in hand, poking through faded Fanta cans and chip packets, burrowing into bushes, looking for my cigs until I face-plant into a web and nearly inhale a spider the size of a chimpanzee's hand.

So, tonight, I'm stuck. My only ciggies are a mash in the bins outside, soaking in Baygon. It's too far to walk to the shops and I don't have a car, since the HQ threw a piston driving back from Canberra after going to see my sister Megan. I pad downstairs to my neighbour, Hubert, who's always good for a handful of loose tobacco, but even he, pushing fifty-five, seems to have a life tonight and I'm left staring at his unanswered door like a shy Mormon.

I consider trying to sleep without tobacco but the ciggie is more than just a brief moment of headspins, more than a muddying of the waters so that I can sink with the silt to the bottom. It's an exclamation mark at the end of the day. It says FUCK YOUR WORLD and YOUR RULES. I will poison myself in whatever way possible BECAUSE IT WILL ALL END SOON ENOUGH. If I don't smoke, if I don't pull those toxins into me, I'm left to stare at the insides of my eyelids pondering the possibility that life can be good and maybe all that I've been doing is wasting time. Then all the nights I've lost going to sleep at 6 pm swim in front of me and . . . fuck, fuck, I need to smoke tobacco.

Luckily, there's always the dog ends. I search through my kitchen garbage and, yes, there's butts I've thrown out over the last few days. Some are soaked with tuna oil and melted butter, but I pick through the refuse, a homeless man in my own home, until I've accrued a pile from which I can salvage enough tobacco for one cigarette.

I get out a frying pan and break the wet butts into it, to dry out the damp tobacco, and when it's crisp and ready for smoking I confront the problem of rolling papers. I have none, of course, because Crusader Ned, the one who imagines himself jogging on the sand, farting the pure gas of vegetarianism, the one who says he'll never drink again, has thrown out the cigarette papers, knowing full well that Caveman Ned will be looking for them soon enough.

Now I have all this glorious tobacco and only a sliver of paper is keeping me from the smoke, the pretty poisons, so I search my cupboards, pieces of three day old tuna and peanut butter still stuck to my fingers, until I find a bus ticket. Perfect.

I've heard they used newspaper to roll cigarettes during the war. A bus ticket can't be any worse. I roll it up and have to use plenty of slag to glue it together but it seems to work rather well. I spark it and suck it in, the smoke so much stronger, hitting my lungs like buckshot. Lying in bed, I draw away my hatred, step into my tin can and float.

THE MAZE

We're walking along the road that encircles Bronte Cemetery. There's about two hundred of us, a surprising number, though a lot of them seem to be mates of Chong's and Hayley's buddies from school. Scorps said he wasn't going to show because Andrea had been rude to him just before Christmas. I pointed out she *was* dying of breast cancer.

– I'm sure you'd be a little grumpy, too.
– She's still a fuckin' bitch.
– Was a fuckin' bitch.

Scorps is feeling guilty because he never visited Andrea when she got sick. I know I feel a bit guilty, but it's more because of the relief I'm experiencing now she's gone. Now I don't have to feel guilty about not visiting her any more. I know I didn't go around to see her enough, but it was tough pretending I was there for any reason other than for Chong.

He's holding it together pretty well, but then Chong reacts

to most things the same way. He could be getting a blow job or an amputation and it would be hard to tell from the expression on his face. His son, Victor, is only four, so he doesn't seem to have realised what has happened. Hayley, Andrea's daughter by another guy, is fourteen and she's pretty cut up, but all the boys have rallied around her and she's trying to be tough. Poor thing.

I wish I could manufacture some lasting sympathy for Chong but all I can think about is last night and how quickly things are going bad with Alex. How did it get like this? Everything I say to her lately is taken the wrong way; while every molecule in my body wants to smooth and hold and love her, crack her open laughing, every crease on my face is also projecting need, and when she looks at me, I see her wishing I'd just disappear, make it easy for her.

Yesterday we came back from breakfast and she said she wanted to do some laundry, and I couldn't think of anything more exciting than watching her sift through her pastel panties.

– Sweet, I'll just hang, I said.
– I'll drop you home.
– I'll come to your place and just hang while you do it.
– No, I'm gonna drop you home.

I make her park the car and take her to a tiny children's hedge maze that Woollahra Council, strangely, happily maintains in the park next to my parents' new place in Paddington. I sit her down as open as a kid at confession and pour it out on her, tell her I've been a fraction until I met her, an incomplete song, and now that we've found each other I'm beginning to live without the humming dread of loneliness, without the buzz of need and confusion and suspicion that I'm missing the best part, the universal joint that holds life and sanity in place and . . .

She's just blinking at me like a lioness. The sun tracking above us feels like a gun sight. She does her washing alone.

That night, at dinner with Simon and Michelle and some big blond fuckwit she knows who deals coke and drives a ute, I'm pissed off even being there with others, wondering why my company alone is not good enough. Miss Fuckin' Positive Thinking Alex refuses to acknowledge that there's even a bubble in the silk of her life, because to do so would be to let the negativity in and she never does that. And then we're walking to her car and I'm talking, wheedling, hating the sound of my own voice, pushing at the doors in her head, and she keeps blinking, slow, like I'm a fuckin' commercial break and then I'm screaming, furious, letting it rip out of me, hopped on the heat, the brat twisting in his high chair and she's fuckin' blinking, the big cat, unmoved, and I want to fuckin' hit her and share the pain and . . .

Then I see Chong take Victor's hand in the procession and I wonder what sort of friend am I. His wife's dead.

It's a beautiful day for a funeral and, I guess if you were going to get buried anywhere, Bronte Cemetery would be the spot. The real estate in this joint has to be worth billions. It's just acres and acres of graves overlooking the ocean, surrounded by some of Sydney's most expensive property.

– How much do you reckon this joint would be worth, all up? I say to Scorps.

– I reckon you'd get half a bil for it at least.

– And the rest.

– They'd sell it in one lot, you're thinking retail.

– Listen to you. Retail.

Kaspar turns and looks at us, wearily.

– Have some respect, guys.

He says it far louder than we were talking. Several older women I've never met before turn and look at us, ensuring we're seen as heathen, disrespectful arseholes, and Kaspar the keeper of all that is good and wholesome.

YEW

The bell for lunch rings and I walk out into the quadrangle, into the cool shadows near the headmaster's office, wondering if the boys will be going for a re. It looks like there's millions of us out there, all in navy and gold, swarming over benches and stairwells and backpacks like blue-arsed flies. I guess some of us have got a clue, have got a plan, but mine doesn't stretch much further than the next hour.

I run upstairs to my locker and put my books in there. I've got a picture of Gary Elkerton pulling in at Kong's Island. I've drawn a little thought bubble coming out of his mouth that says, 'Yew'. If there is a sound that sums up living around here, it would be that.

Yew. Drawn out so it sounds more like 'Yeeeeew'. It can be cocky, sarcastic, flattering and an all-purpose put-down when some cunt thinks he's top shit.

– Hoo-yeeeew, you say to the dickhead and everyone knows what you mean: too good, you.

It's cold today and I'm wearing my V-necked jumper over my shirt, with my blazer over the top. I've got my jacket collar turned up like I'm the lead singer of the Stray Cats and I'm feeling pretty damn well cocky.

– Hoo-yeeeeew, says a voice and I see it's Kasp hangin' shit on my upturned collar.

– You going for a re? I say.

– That's a possibility, Neddy.

– Where you going?

– I'm not able to disclose that information at present, my friend.

– Who's driving?

He ignores the question.

– We're gonna jig the rest of the day.

– I've got a geography test next period.

– With who?

– Seahag.

– Fuck it off.

– I can't, she's already seen me today.

– Looks like no rehabatchi for you then.

I weigh the possibilities. Seahag is our geography teacher. She has a mane of long red hair, drives a green RX7 and dresses in far too provocative clothing for a woman of a hundred and ninety-eight or however the fuck old she is. Her face is incredibly lined and wrinkled but she's holding on to the sparkling, gossamer thread of youth like there's no tomorrow. One thing above all – you don't fuck around in Seahag's class and you don't jig. If I ditch this test, there's a big possibility it will affect my assessment for the Higher School Certificate. It seems deeply irresponsible to miss the test just to smoke drugs, but then it's equally irresponsible for the NSW Board of Education to expect boys our age to make decisions about the rest of their life when they can't see past the weekend.

Ten minutes later I'm in Grumble's big brown Ford Fairlane, bombing along the narrow terrain of Henrietta Street at ninety kilometres per hour. It's Grumble, Chong, Kaspar, Scorps and me, now firmly bonded by the brotherhood of the bong, the fact we smoke more dope than anyone else in the form. Scorps goes through the glove box looking for tapes, then slams one into the stereo, rewinds it, gets a few bars of Nik Kershaw.

– Fuck it off!
– I like that song, I say.
– FUCK IT OFF!
– Righto.

He rewinds some more and gets the Radiators, in the middle of the song.

– YES! Rewind it.

He takes it back a bit more, hits play and we're on.

You got me steaming at a hundred degrees.
Each time I see you I grow weak in the knees.

It's one of those crystal cold Sydney winter days and the ocean looks like a lake of light, reflecting the distant sun in a million brain-searing glints. As soon as we turn onto Birrell Street, the sunnies come out, Ray-Bans, Oakley frogskins and Kaspar in his Pierre Cardin aviators.

– Youse have gotta throw in, says Scorps.
– Fuck off, cunt, how many times've I blown you out?
– Bullfuck.
– Bullfuck yourself.
– Youse are fucken throwin' in.
– Stop here, stop here, stop here, says Kaspar.

We're at a corner store on Murray Street.

– Me dad threw out the bong, I gotta get an Orchy.
– Wolfram threw out the milk bottle?

– Fucken old cunt.
– How'd he find it?
– Chong left it out.
– Bullshit I did.
– Bullshit you didn't.
– The milk bottle? That's fucked.
– Get me a Jupiter bar.
– Yeah, get me a Coke.
– Give us the money.

But best of all, I love
You give me head
YOU GIVE ME HEAD!

We scream the lyrics through the open windows of the Ford. Kaspar just smiles as he walks into the shop, the wog owner craning over the counter to see who the idiots are outside. We're deliciously amped at the thought of a lunchtime re-ha. Kasp is back in under a minute, laughing to himself as he gets back in the car.

– Go, go, go, he says and as soon as we round the corner he unloads a pocketful of Mint Patties he's rockied. Grumble floors it and the heavy Ford's suspension rocks up the hill past the psych clinic where they've been treating my sister for anorexia. Then we're winding down Bronte Road, sussing the surf at the reef, absolutely brimming with youth and hope and potential and endless shining days.

Kaspar skols the Orchy.
– You got a downie? says Grumble.
– What do you reckon?
He walks into his bedroom and I take in the house, all dark wood and heavy European trinkets, like you'd imagine Sigmund

Freud's den would look. When Kasp returns, he's got a blackened silver downpipe that's coated with about seven hundred sessions worth of resin. He heats up the plastic of the Orchy where the downpipe will go.

– Nah, nah, don't do it that way, says Chong.

– Fuck, I'm sick of you telling me how to make bongs, Chong.

– Then start doing it properly.

– Reckon I might have made one before.

– Then why do you do it that way?

The theories of how to make a bong are as varied as the vessels we use to construct them. Plastic is the material of choice, though desperation has seen Coke cans and chocolate Moove cartons used and, on one occasion, an apple. Coke bottles are possible, though the hard plastic is not as easy to work with as that of the Orchy or the Mr Juicy. In our time, shampoo bottles have also gotten a start, as well as motor oil bottles and cooking oil containers.

Observing these strange contraptions is like viewing the minor space craft you see in a *Star Wars* armada. At first you're struck by the bizarreness of the shape, that anyone would chose such a ridiculous structure for flight. Then you realise that it's necessity that has forced the choice. Once you recognise it gets the job done, you accept it as readily as you do the architecture of an X-wing fighter.

We were all extremely impressed by Kaspar's glass-cutting prowess and the patience that saw him drill through an old 600 ml milk bottle, then add a downpipe.

– I'm spewing about the milk bottle, he says.

We all are. It was the perfect size for a bong. Large enough to cool the smoke, yet not so big that it went stale and rank before it hit your lungs. I'm currently stealing test tubes and condensers from the chemistry lab so I can construct a mega-bong using stands and rubber piping. For now, however, the Orchy will have to do.

– How do you want me to do it?
– Give it here.

Chong puts his lips to the bottle and heats the side of it with a lighter, blowing until a tiny pinhole explodes from the side. Quickly, while the plastic is still warm, he jams the downpipe in and then jiggles the black rubber seal around it so the thing's in there snugly.

– Why'd the walrus go to the Tupperware party? asks Grumble.

We shrug.

– So he could get himself a tight seal.
– Yew, says Kaspar and starts packing.

TOMBSTONING

I'm too lazy to walk to the Bergs this morning to swim, so I drive. The Val hasn't even warmed up, coughing along Sandridge Street and I'm waiting to turn right into Campbell Parade when my mobile rings. It's Birdy.
 – Have you heard about Kasp?
 – No, I say.
 – He's killed himself, mate.
I slip Ivy into neutral and roll back down Sandridge, pull in to the gutter and get out. The swell's southerly, moving in past Boot Bay, glittering like a sword fight. I shiver.
 – How'd he do it?
 – He fuckin' drowned himself, Ned.

We meet at Kaspar's apartment because it seems like the logical centre of mourning. His flatmate, Toby, is some bloke I've never met before. He moved in a few months ago to share the rent when things started going downhill. Now he's been lifted to rockstar status. He is the Last Person to See Him Alive. Toby seems nice enough but looks embarrassed by all the attention. There's so many people in the flat, hung over, blowing noses, wondering if they should cry, shaking their heads.

– I can't believe it.
– He's the last bloke I thought would do this.
– He was like a brother to me.

As the beers go down, Toby's friendship with Kasp grows until he, too, had 'been like a brother' to him. I don't blame Toby. We're all feeling it: Birdy, Chong, Scorps, Grumble – the grand drama of losing a mate in such cinematic circumstances. Our loss, however, is tempered by the cold fact that he's gone – we've lost one of us. The others, the dozens of new best friends that have appeared out of the Bondi sand to scream and cry or strum guitars on the grass in front of Kaspar's flat have nothing to hold them back. Their sorrow has no boundaries. Wannabe models and promo girls are wailing like Palestinian widows when, at most, they've racked up with Kasp a few times in his lounge room, scored off him, sucked his horse cock.

Every now and then, an authentic Bondi boy enters and walks around the flat, studying the faces, until they see Chong and hug him.

– Fuckin' stupid bastard, what was he thinking, Chong?
– I don't know, mate.

– Who the fuck's that cunt? asks Scorps as we stand around one of the benches on the grass opposite Hall Street, sharing VBs from a ripped case. The bloke's singing a song he's written for Kaspar, as two hippie-looking chicks dance shoeless in front of him; an audience of people none of us has ever seen before watches cross-legged on the grass.

– I dunno, says Birdy, but I bet Kasp was like a brother to him.

– Lot of fuckin' brothers here, says Grumble, and I can see it building in him.

People ask me how I know Kasp and everything that comes out of my mouth sounds like bullshit, like I too had known him for five seconds and am trying to talk up our friendship. The fact is, my last interactions with the cunt had been our ugliest. I'd told people he was losing it. In my head, I knew I'd wiped him as a friend after that argument. Part of me is surprised, part of me smug, because I'd sensed all along how insecure he was.

So many new best friends – and isn't that always a sign of trouble with people, when they've got millions of mates who've only known them a year, who haven't been around long enough to push through the first disagreement? Some tall Israeli clown has gotten hold of one of Kaspar's Indo guns and is doing the rounds of the crowd getting them to sign it with a black permanent marker. He approaches us, looking like he's lost his family in Belsen.

– We're getting friends of Kaspar to sign his board. Did you know him, guys?

The five of us, Birdy, Grumble, Chong, Scorps and me, hold our beers to our chests. None of us has seen the guy in our life, not even Chong who actually is the closest thing Kaspar had to a brother. Grumble looks like he's gonna punch the guy. He steps forward, in that way he does, taking centre stage.

– Nah, mate, not the bloke you're talking about.

Then he spins, walks away and throws his full beer at a bush.

DRY-ROOTING IN ADELAIDE

I'm standing with Larry on the corner of some park, near some church, when a bus hauls by with Shamus's face on it. His head's five foot tall, nose pores the size of ten-cent pieces, and he's grinning at us benignly, like he's just baked some cookies. Channel Four would have you believe the cookies are oatmeal, but we know better.

We've come down here to visit because Shamus has got a new job as the hotshot evening newsreader and my mum's been commuting, enjoying her husband's competence for three minutes and no doubt keeping an eye on extracurricular activities.

Adelaide's not gonna win any awards for excitement, lemme tell you. Larry and I have been wandering, paying the joint out for two hours and we've pretty much done the city. Shamus told us not to expect Carnivale: 'It's Yass with poofters,' he said.

– That's classic, says Larry of the bus.
– If only they knew, I say.

It's always been a source of amusement for my mates to come around and punch bongs with Shamus on a Saturday before we go into battle on the football field. The soaring violins of Barry White and the Love Unlimited Orchestra's 'Love's Theme' would introduce Donnie Sutherland and his music show *Sounds*. Shamus would crank up the television nice and loud, do a couple of high-pitched farts and blame the dog.

– Winston.
– Fuck, I'd say and swerve around the stench.
– Someone's been eating dead Chinamen, he'd say.

My mum would be out of the house, taking Megan to her shrink so she could relearn peristalsis, and I'd be eating Weet-Bix. Birdy or Larry would be clanking around the kitchen in their footy gear waiting for a lift to Queens Park so we could ruck out some Cranbrook faggots.

– Won't be long, boys, Shamus would say.

A newsbreak would come on and there would be a pre-recorded segment with Shamus telling the world about AIDS statistics, suit immaculate, hair curry-combed into a heraldic beak, while the real deal sat in his underpants, breaking open roaches from the night before.

Before he got the gig in Adelaide, Shamus won CNN's Best International Report of the Year. Bungee jumping had just been invented and people still considered it a shortcut to the grave. Your intrepid reporter Shamus Kinsella strapped a handy cam to his chest and leapt into space, his shrieks and curses amusingly bleeped out as he plunged towards the ground. His trophy was a twelve inch silver-plated dish that is now black from its new career as a mull bowl. Shamus had all sorts of trouble getting it through the airport metal detectors coming down here.

Anyway, tomorrow is the first Adelaide Grand Prix and that's how Larry's managed to convince his mum to give him two days off school and fly over with us. Tonight is the big launch, where Shamus gets to meet the boss of the network and everyone slaps him on the back and tells him he's a legend until his ratings drop. Larry and I just want to score some Adelaide buds.

We go and watch the F1 cars doing practice laps and nearly lose all hearing because we're too cheap to buy those squishy little earplugs they sell. The machines scream by, almost too fast to follow, and after about six minutes of whiplash I add car racing to the list of completely useless fucken sports I don't care about.

The argument between my mum and Shamus starts the next morning.

– You're just a fucking child, I hear her say.
– Abi-gail.
– What did you think was going to happen?
– I thought he could take a fucking joke. He used to be a journo.
– You're pathetic.

It takes a day for us kids to get the full story.

Shamus and Uncle Doug, choppered in as a special envoy of havoc, smoked more dope than was advisable before the big event. Stoned as they were, they decided to go into the gardens of the Mirage Hotel where the launch was being held and blow another number before the speeches started. Thanks to South Australia's progressive attitude in decriminalising marijuana, the denizens of Adelaide have been growing particularly good pot for some years now, of which Shamus and Doug were immediate beneficiaries. In fact, the dope they'd scored was so good, the two of them got lost in the hotel's newly planted tropical garden and were still stumbling around when Shamus's presence was required on the podium.

Shamus and Doug finally found an exterior wall of the hotel and followed it, hacking through the undergrowth, two crazed, Great White Hunter S. Thompsons, until BOOM! they ran into a floor-to-ceiling window. Behind the glass was the grand ballroom. The host of network dignitaries turned to see their newest acquisition sniggering with his mate in the bushes.

Things go downhill from there.

Shamus, realising his fuck-up, starts on spirits, which is never a good idea, and becomes progressively more adventurous on the dance floor after dinner. When the network boss's platinum-blonde wife is momentarily without a polka partner, Shamus steps into the breach, gives her a few rock 'n' roll twirls, and over they keel onto the polished marble floor where my stepfather proceeds to dry-root her in front of the guests.

The network boss, rumoured to have a long-standing affection for underage males, is forced to hoick his newsreader off his wife, then orders Shamus upstairs to the company suite without dessert.

Shamus replies: 'Why don't *you* go upstairs and fuck some little boys.'

The announcement comes out in the Adelaide papers on Monday.

'Shamus Kinsella has resigned as the Four network's newsreader citing personal reasons.'

I'd always wondered what 'personal reasons' meant in news stories. Now I know.

ADOLF HITLER'S KNEE

Birdy, Scorps and I go up to see Kaspar's dad, Wolfram, later in the day. He opens the door, an ogre with yellowing grey hair and a mouth full of teeth that look like crumbling stock cubes.

– What sort of coward is my son? he says to us, then turns and stalks back inside, leaving the door open. Standard Wolfram.

We walk in and mumble some apologies to him but he's one of those people who always seem to be reading from a script. It isn't that he doesn't listen to what other people are saying – he doesn't even seem to hear them. As long as I've known him he's been playing the wounded father. Nothing Kaspar did was ever good enough, he was a disappointment and now he's gone and proved it in the most spectacular way possible.

– What sort of coward is he to do this to his father? I ask you?

He's close to hysterical, but as the urge to comfort him rises up in me, I remind myself this is pretty much his standard state of being.

– Why would he do it? *Why? Why? Why?* he says, pounding the floor with his walking stick.

I look around the place: the layer of grime on everything, a piece of fruit stuffed under a cushion on the couch, papers cluttered on windowsills. A madman's house.

– Because of you, you crazy old cunt, I want to say but throw out another line instead.

– He was obviously in a lot of pain, Mr –

– What about my pain? Does he care about my pain?

We sit outside in the weedy backyard and he sighs and moans. I want to punch him, but keep reminding myself his only child has just killed himself. Scorps is doing his best to remind him that Kaspar was his son, not some fantasy he can remake now he's gone.

– He never treated me with any respect, he never acted like a son should.

– Ahhh, Mr Körtlang, he always talked about you, he always said how much he loved you. I think you're being a bit hard on him.

– Then why is he not here, now? Who will mow my lawns? Tell me, will you mow the lawns for me, or you?

He looks at me. His eyes are diseased, speckled with brown, like a dog you know will bite you if you go too close.

– Mr Körtlang, I've got my own parent's lawns to mow. You can hire people to help you.

– And where will I get the money? The Jews, they will bleed me dry. They will try to steal from me if they come to mow my lawns.

Here we go. We've all been waiting for the Führer to appear and it has only taken three minutes. Kasp used to tell us how Wolfram had sat on Hitler's knee when he was a child. It had apparently made an impression.

– There's non-Jewish lawn mowing services, Mr Körtlang.

– You watch, the Jews will try and take this house off me now that Kaspar is gone, you watch them.

– Mr Körtlang, that's not possible . . .

– Not possible? You do not know Jews like I know Jews.

After about half an hour, a friend of Wolfram's arrives. His name is Hans and he looks like a middle-aged European playboy fallen on hard times. He's wearing a scarf and carrying a bottle of Chivas, which he cracks open and pours neat for us. I lean back in my chair and squint into the brightness because I've forgotten my sunnies.

On the floor of the garden shed, thrown here and there, I can see about a dozen boards waiting to be repaired – Kasp's sideline before the MC-ing took off. He did a good job too, but, fuck, he was slow. There'd been a change in government while he last fixed my 7' 2". The door of the shed would usually be padlocked, so it looks like Wolfram's been in there creating mayhem. I nod at them.

– Yeah, I know, says Birdy.

– Glad I got my board off him.

– My gun's in there somewhere, I'm scared to look.

– He was always smoking the marijuana, says Wolfram.

– Yeah, that's true, Mr Körtlang, says Scorps. – But I don't know if that's why he kill– why he did what he did.

Cos we all know how hard Kasp had been hitting the rack.

– The question is, why was he doing so much of the stuff? Hans says a little later as we walk around the backyard.

– It's not hard once you're on the escalator, I say.

– I don't think we should tell Wolfram this, he says.

– Nah, probably not a good idea.

– But you say he was snorting a lot of cocaine?

– He was a charger, he loved it. It has to have had some effect.

We look back at Wolfram, who's leaning in, hand on Birdy's leg. Birdy looks like he's just about to have a Band-Aid ripped off his knee.

– I don't know what he will do, Hans says.

CRANBROOK FAGGOTS

We've been warned.

Anyone found off school grounds during school hours will be suspended. Anyone caught damaging school property will be expelled. Anyone caught throwing eggs or attacking students from other schools will have their Higher School Certificate revoked.

Like we give a shit.

It's muck-up day and I've managed to convince the olds to lend me the Moke because it has no sides on it and is far easier to hurl eggs and flour bombs out of. We're smart enough to keep away from St Catherine's and St Clare's because they'll be expecting us, so we head to Double Bay to find some Ascham sluts.

Our attempts at disguise amount to rubber Easter Show masks (I'm Australian cricket captain, Allan Border) and taking off our ties, so we could be from any number of schools who dress in navy pants and blue shirts. If anyone grabs us, we'll tell them we're from Marcellan. Grumble's driving his Falcon and Joe Gold's got his Subaru. It's just before 7 am and all I've had for breakfast is three Anticol cough lollies. Scorps, Birdy and Larry are in my car.

– I wish a cyclone would hit Sydney, says Birdy.
– What?
– I wish a cyclone would hit Sydney.
– WHAT?

I've got the Oils on, *Head Injuries,* and without a roof on the Moke it's fully windy and hard to hear what anyone is saying. Larry's dancing in his seat, singing 'Stand in Line' tone and word perfect; lyrics I'm not really sure he entirely understands.

We stop at the lights at Double Bay and some rich fucks look us up and down. Larry points at an old bitch wearing a baby tiger fur, screaming the chorus, even issuing Peter Garrett's grunts flawlessly.

– Ah, huh, huh, huh, haaa, shudders Larry, head sideways, eyes like a mental case as he 'performs'.

Scorps and Birdy are still talking in the back.
– I WISH A CYCLONE WOULD HIT SYDNEY.
– Fuck, I thought you said a psycho.
– Me too.
– Why do you want a psycho to hit you?
– Nah, a cyclone, a tornado or some shit like that to hit Sydney. Two hundred kilometre an hour winds.
– Why?
– So the surf would get fucken huge, eh?
– Mate, you wouldn't even be able to stand up if there was a cyclone.
– Bullfuck.
– You'd get blown over.

– You'd get cut in half by a coathanger blown out of someone's house, I say.

– Fuck off, I could handle it.

I don't know why Birdy bothers having these conversations. He picks some circumstance that we'll never encounter and tells us how well he'd handle it. Mountainous surf, poisonous snakes, supermodels, life on the battlefield – Birdy would take them all in his stride.

– It'd be hell, says Birdy.

Behind me, I see Grumble pull up. He gets as close to the Moke as he can, then touches bumpers and starts to nudge me into the intersection.

– Fuck off! I motion back at him.

Kaspar, Suggs and Chong are making obscene gestures out of the windows. I grab a couple of one and two cent pieces out of the Moke's centre console and toss them back over my head onto Grumble's windscreen. They make a nasty stinging sound as the lights turn green. I accelerate, and Birdy and Scorps hoick gollies at them.

I careen up the Rose Bay esses, a winding stretch of road that'd be challenging for Enzo Ferrari but is verging on suicide for P-platers, like us, to take at speed. We fang it nonetheless, jockeying, cutting each other off, braking, trying to overtake, until we reach Neilsen Park.

Joe Gold's heard that some Ascham sluts are having a champagne breakfast down here to celebrate their leaving, so we pull up at the far end of the car park and wait so we don't tip them off. Joe's about a minute behind us, in the Subaru, and when he pulls up he's got 'Broken Wings' by Mr Mister playing softly on his stereo. That's Joe for you. He's also got a life-sized ceramic leopard in his bedroom.

– Are they down there?

– Dunno.

– Someone go suss it.
– You suss it.
– I can't, they know me, they'll put us in if they see me, says Joe.

No one else has this problem but Joe Gold. He seems to be fucking or have fucked a girl from every major private school in the Eastern Suburbs. His current, Lexy, is so indescribably hot, my face twitches when I think about her naked.

– I'll go, says Birdy and he runs off, crouching, darting behind Moreton Bay figs like he's avoiding enemy fire.

When we planned this, Joe Gold suggested we just egg them, then Larry brought up the water pistols filled with piss. Then I mentioned shit bombs.

– Now, there's a suggestion, said Larry.

Yesterday I baked a good fourteen inch loggie right through school, clinching it into myself until I got home and could unravel it into a sandwich bag. It felt like a hot sausage as I hefted it in my hand, then double-bagged it for safety.

Most of us have wangled those super-soaker water pistols from cousins, younger brothers, neighbours – it doesn't matter. Larry stole one from the day care centre down the road from him. Grumble has one of those backpack numbers, where you have a five litre tub hooked over your shoulders. He's spent days filling it with piss, sneaking into his bedroom when nature called. Now it's sloshing around as we stand around the Moke, listening to *10,9,8,7,6,5,4,3,2,1*.

Larry has his Hulk Hogan mask pulled over the top of his head so he looks bald, the hand is out, five fingers stretched maniacally, doing more of his Garrett impersonation as we pass around a hipflask of voddie. I pull out my shit bomb, giggling.

– Fuck, you're a grot, says Kaspar.
– Where's yours?

I look around and see the same smiles. I'm the only cunt who's shit in a bag.

– Well, fuck youse, then.

I get out a Stanley knife and start slashing the plastic bag so, when it impacts, it'll split and get shit everywhere.

– That's fucken wrong, says Grumble.

– You've got fifty litres of piss on your back, mate.

'US Forces' is cranking now. We all lean our heads back to scream about Superboy and plutonium wives and nuclear bombs that worry us far less than the size of our cocks.

Then Birdy's back.

– They're down there, there's about forty of them. Chicks and guys.

– Who are the guys?

– Cranbrook, I think.

– Fucken Cranbrook faggots.

This is exceptional news. Cranbrook is one of our rival boy schools, although the rivalry is more a product of tradition than anything personal. I don't know any Cranbrook boys and the only time I've met one has been on the football field or pushing in at the bar at Paddo's. Fees at the school are approximately triple what you pay to go to Seaview, thus the cream of Eastern Suburbs money send their sons there. Cranbrook boys are therefore pilloried for being faggots. There's even a song:

Tiddlywink young man, catch a girl if you can
If you can't catch a girl, catch a Cranbrook man

For as long as I can remember, this has been an accepted fact. If you go to Cranbrook, you are a faggot. You suck cocks. You take it up the date. As we sneak along through the car park, we see there's at least a dozen BMWs, new model Commodores and Volvos adorned with the usual surf stickers. I can't help wonder if our faggot hatred has got something to do with the fact Cranbrook boys are rich.

A minute later we emerge from the trees and see them gathered around a group of three picnic tables. They've laid out linen, with fresh fruit and ice buckets full of French champagne. It's a crisp morning, not a snort of wind, and a ferry is churning by in the harbour. For a moment we're all stilled by the perfect beauty of the scene: dozens of teenage girls and boys, holders of privilege and youth, supping from flutes, eating croissants and strawberries, laughing. A group of about ten are gathered around a ghetto-blaster singing along to 'That's What Friends Are For'.

– I fucken hate this song, I say to Larry.

Our group of invaders pauses as the breakfasters slowly register our presence. Before us are the daughters of CEOs, Federal MPs and investment bankers. They're the sons of television moguls, business leaders. They're not just rich, they're old money and they will never have to worry about what comes next in their lives.

Some of the girls turn to us and a few manage smiles, as if, perhaps, we've brought our own pastries and Veuve Clicquot to join them. The ferry's foghorn sounds out in the harbour, a couple of gulls chirp mournfully and the tiny breakers lap onto the creamy sand.

Woh-oh-oh, keep smilin', keep shinin'
Knowin' you can always count on me, for sure
That's what friends are for-or-or-or

I watch the egg arc above us. I'm not sure who throws the first one. It streaks through the blue sky, twisting like a torpedo punt, hanging, dipping, then exploding on the table in front of the daughter of one of Sydney's most prominent Queen's

Counsels. She looks down at her splattered uniform like a stupid gut-shot soldier.

– Oh my God, she says.

Then it's on. The first volley of eggs has them, girl and boy alike, turning their backs on us and sprinting in the opposite direction. Egg yolk cascades off shoulders and mats hair, fills shoes and darkens the pale blue of the Cranbrook faggots' shirts. Grumble is going feral strafing the closest of them with his piss machine. Some of the chicks even laugh until the stream hits them in the mouth and they realise it's urine. Then they're screaming, climbing over each other to get away.

Unfortunately for them, we've arrived from higher ground and the only place to run is onto the beach. One gangly boy, the son of a mining executive who recently laid off fifteen hundred workers, grips the ghetto-blaster to his chest, still piping Dionne Warwick, loping along as we hit him in the back with five eggs.

For good times and bad times
I'll be on your side forever more-ore-ore-ore-ore
That's what friends are for-or-or-or-or

We turn our attention to a petite, olive-skinned girl, whose mother married an extremely successful cosmetic surgeon, as she tries to hide behind a garbage bin. It's carnage and thankfully we've had the foresight to bring many, many eggs. Like barbarians sweeping down from the north into civilised Rome, we grab the bottles of champagne and drink as we continue to hurl eggs at the group, now huddled on the sand.

Strangely, none of the Cranbrook faggots tries to marshal a counterattack. Several throw overhand clumps of wet sand, but most of them are too busy shielding their eyes. Still the eggs come and, from the short distance we're throwing them, I gather the impact hurts. The girls are screaming, the boys not doing much better. They have no choice but to back into the water to get some distance between us.

Slowly we drive them into the ocean, eggs still exploding around them like mortars. The son of the mining exec holds his stereo above his head, until a well-aimed shot from Scorps strikes him in the hand and the ghetto-blaster plonks into the water, silencing Dionne for good.

We're cacking laughing, hooting, when I realise I still have the shit bomb in my left hand, dribbling bits. There's now a crowd of mainly girls standing in the shallows, howling, carrying on. I do an underarm flick of the shit bomb, lobbing it high into the air, hoping for the best.

We make our escape and I watch Birdy drinking from a bottle – surely his first taste of French champagne – as Larry knots a stolen Cranbrook tie around his scone as a headband.

THE ZOO

Chicks seem to think they're going to the Blue Room or up to Hugo's for a night out. Guys in cowboy hats and white suits and thongs are having ciggies out the front of St Francis's church. Two hotties I've never seen before but wanted to meet all my life are crying near a bush and being comforted by the Israeli kook who wanted us to sign Kaspar's board. He gives me a nod as I pass, like he's the bouncer at a club he's just let me into. I see one hundred strangers before, deep in the church, I find faces I know.

– Who are these people? I ask Birdy and Scorps.
– Some of the ITN boys are here and their chicks.
– It's a massive turnout.
– Where's Chong?
– He's giving a reading, he's up there.

Chong's rooted near the altar, Wolfram snapping at him, pushing him this way and that. He's as animated as a stuffed toy. Nearby, I can see Grumble sitting in a pew, head bowed, his dangling wet ponytail darkening the collar of his shirt as he prays to whatever god inhabits his firmament.

– You seen Penny? I ask.

– Yeah, she's up the back. She doesn't want to see Wolfram till later.

– Probably a good move.

The priest opens proceedings talking about God for ten minutes and Kaspar for one. Chong stands to say something, then changes his mind and sits. Instead, Grumble walks to the pulpit looking like he's going to bash the priest.

– The only bloke who should be up here talking about Kaspar is that guy sitting there.

He points at Chong.

– Gary Chong was his best mate, but Chong can't talk today and I understand that so I'll just say this. I don't know why this happened. Kaspar was one of the best blokes I know and I know plenty. So I hope you can hear this, mate, I love you and we're all gonna miss ya.

Then he steps down and sits next to Chong. I wasn't expecting the *Four Weddings and a Funeral* speech, but W. H. Auden it's not. Now some chick I've seen in clubs from time to time gets up. Her defining characteristic on each occasion I've met her has been she's always fucked off her face. She's crying and seems sincere but I can't hear what she's saying, it's been reduced to static.

Is this how it ends, Kasp? is all I can think. Is this what it's been reduced to, when your funeral becomes an invite, your death a delicious reminiscence for wankers?

WHO THE FUCK ARE YOU? I wanna scream, but I don't, just listen to this chick sob into the microphone about Kaspar's two gram spirituality, his golden heart, his tender nature and the angel we'll all have looking over us from now on.

*

We've got our boards in Birdy's car, so we walk to the beach to get them. It's a convoy of everything Bondi: there are surfers wearing T-shirts and skatie shoes and personal trainers in short sleeves with haircuts that cost more than my rent. There's drug dealers and coke sluts a-plenty, a used-car salesman, property developers, musicians, and three professional rugby league players. There's plumbers, chippies, shapers, disgraced coppers, boat brokers, stockbrokers and brokeback mountaineers, their boyfriends, their girlfriends, their skin-cankered parents and the guy that used to work in the milk bar on Hall Street before they turned it into a fuckin' shoe shop for Brazilian tourists.

The nightclub black stands in for funereal, the high heels on the Mitchell Street concrete are Kaspar's dirge as the procession winds up Warners, across Campbell Parade, then onto Ramsgate where the spectators start to mass on the point: dozens, then a hundred, until there's not enough room to swing a manbag.

Chong's got the ashes from Wolfram and he's been driven down by a group of the Bondi boys. His place as Best Mate has finally been acknowledged, albeit awkwardly by the flockers, the unknowns, the two-minute noodles Kasp seems to have gathered around him for his final attempt at neural obliteration. I stand with Scorps on the sand, holding my board, looking fat and white, Scorps looking fatter and whiter, staring up at the hundreds of balconies overlooking the beach that never seem to get used because the owners work seventy hour weeks in advertising, film, fashion. Bondi's empty eyes.

We wait about twenty minutes until all the crew has arrived; fifty, sixty, then a hundred of us, all with boards, some with noses snapped off, twinnies, single fins, cola-brown mals that look like they've been exhumed from under houses. Chong goes first, the ashes balanced on the end of Kasp's longboard.

We give him time, then the lot of us scream like we're going over the top at Gallipoli and charge the shorey, churning foam like the beginning of a triathlon.

I'm not sure what the hurry is, but every one of us is feeling it. The water's cold, but the sun's cranking January on us. As we paddle, we pass straight over the spot where the South African tourist – a Jew no less, Wolfram – saw Kaspar's board tombstoning and paddled over. The tourist followed the leg rope, tight as a girder, down to the green depths where he found Kaspar, chilling like a leg of lamb, rocking on the sand in the current, bracelets of diving weights holding him down.

Once we're out the back, we join hands and form a circle – just like *Play School*. Chong's in the middle of the ring, bobbing on the mal, looking like a ceramic statue. I've lost Scorps and Birdy and Grumble in the paddle and end up holding hands with a hairy blond Bra boy who's on half a snapped Coolite. His mate, a skinny yellow wog, balances on the other half and looks like he's never been in salt water before.

– You right? I ask him.

– Sweet, mate.

We hold hands. The links join around the circle, the nonsurfers in the group struggling to stay upright until, one by one, it's complete and the *Baywatch* histrionics of the whole ritual disappear for seconds of silence. Chong holds the urn with Kaspar's ashes above his head, not a lick of emotion crossing his black Korean eyes.

– ARGGGGGGHHHHH, he yells, then upends the urn, dumping the ashes on his head, streaking his face and body grey, a screaming primitive.

THE VB TIDE

She's kept me waiting again, and when she tootles over the hill in her little blue car I can see Simon filling the passenger seat like a damn exclamation mark. We walk into the club and the door ape waves them through, like naturally they'd be together, then lowers a thick dick of a forearm in front of me. Alex has to come back and explain to 'Aaron' that I'm her 'friend' and I walk in seething.

    I stand in the crowd and wonder how the fuck I ended back here amongst all this joyless celebration and watch her dancing with Simon and Michelle and I have to leave. I go to the Judgement Bar at the end of the block and drink until the cold hate in my gut has dissolved on the VB tide, then I'm back on the edge of the whirlpool and Alex asks me to dance but I feel stiff as old chewing gum and retreat to a corner with my safety beer and scribble ugly notes on a coaster.

    I'm tired of her indifference. I close my eyes for long moments and ask myself do I really want to do this and the beer answers YES!!! Then I'm at the dance floor, dragging her out of the bar, telling her I can't take this any more and have to end it and she says, 'If that's what you want'.

I rage out of the club and down the long flight of stairs to Oxford Street, all the time listening for the sound of her heels coming after me but hear nothing except the bass of fuckin' 'Professional Widow' for the ninth time that night and, feeling myself fill with the poisonous realisation she's not following, I let it lift me back to the dance floor where I watch from behind a pillar as she gyrates with Simon.

Ten minutes later we stand on the street and she's like a puppy that's been held on a leash by a cruel child. I systematically break the night down for her and tell her why she should have done this or said that and why it's not happening for me, all the while waiting for her to break in with 'Don't talk like that, baby, we can make it alright' but she's already regressed from 'If that's what you really want' to 'I think it's better this way' and I can feel it slipping out from underneath me.

I drag her to her car, further from the fun, sealing her inside with me. She's worn out by my expostulating and unsolicited character advice and somehow I've managed to reposition what is essentially two people hanging out together and fucking into some kind of physical, emotional and moral endurance test where she's being judged on every remark, eyebrow movement and outfit.

She's tired.

She has to go now.

I can feel the wind calling up behind me like a scene out of Kurosawa's *Throne of Blood*. I see the dangerous shapes through the mist and the menace all around me; I'm losing her, and no matter what I say, it's wrong, it's bad, it's needy, and behind the cold I can feel the heat.

The anger that she's doing this to me.

To me.

This has never happened. I'm in control here, I own this plotline, you can't tell me I can't have this.

She goes silent, so I snap open the door like a fat brat harumphing out of his cricket coach's Tarago. I look at her and feel the night air ease in the open door and she just stares through the windscreen, holding the steering wheel like it's the head of a poisonous snake.

I know I shouldn't do this but I've already done so many things wrong and now I'm like a drunk at a piano, pounding my fists into the keys and thinking just because it feels good it sounds like music to everyone else. I look at her and know she's not even in the car any more, she's opening her front door and slumping on the couch and thinking, Thank fuck that's over. She just wants to leave but I'm holding her there, insisting on peeling off one more layer. I stand at the open door bending down to show her my shame, tears on my face, nose loosening with snot.

– I can't believe you're doing this to me.

– You're doing it to yourself.

– So it's over?

She whispers her answer.

I slam the door and run up the street like mad dogs are chasing me and anyone watching would be hard-pressed to see a thirteen year old boy let alone a twenty-six year old man but I'm running until I see a cloud of dark leaves and I hurl myself into the shrubbery and crouch and cry and cry that I'm so weak, that I've let this girl in so deep and she doesn't even give a shit.

I hear the soft whir of her engine and peer under the branches to see the wheels of her car. I part the bushes like some pathetic feral child raised on Hollywood fictions.

– Leave me alone, I scream at her, but mean exactly the opposite and she's already nauseated by this wretched display and takes me at my word, drives off down the hill and leaves me to my mosquito bites and expectations.

ANGA

We all smell a bit and are unshaved, wearing trackies and ugg boots but that's the way it goes when you're up the coast. It's a bit of a treat for Birdy because he has a wife and that requires a modicum of personal hygiene, but Chong and Grumble seem to have adopted it as their new uniform since they moved up here, to Angourie.

— You know it's not long till you start fuckin' relatives, I say to Grumble.

— Who says I haven't already?

— So that's why you and your sister always look so disgusted with each other, eh?

We've been surfing at backbeach for the early and while it hasn't been epic, it's been empty, which is the next best thing. Grumble and Birdy rode mals while the rest of us stayed on shortboards, Scorps swearing like a crazy man every time he missed a wave because he had his 6' 3", not his 6' 8", which he'd lent to me.

– Mate, you're a hundred and ten kilos and you're riding the same board you were when you were seventeen, says Birdy. I just keep paddling wishing he'd shut the fuck up.

– Yeah, well, if Ned'd give me me other fuckin' board, I'd be fine.

I sit up on my – well, Scorps's – board and check the horizon for bumps.

– Mate, what do you want me to do? I say to him – You said, 'Don't bring a board, I'll lend you mine', and now the conditions aren't to your liking, you wanna swap.

Scorps paddles for a smaller, inside one. He looks like an Indonesian boat person on a piece of corrugated iron. His head is almost poking over the nose of his board as he labours away, bitch tits bursting out of his wettie. Chong starts laughing and paddles inside of him, sliding effortlessly into the wave.

– FUCK! screams Scorps, frustrated.

We go back to Chong's for breakfast and it feels like I'm camping. Somehow he's lucked into a caretaker's job at a surfer's guesthouse just outside of town and the owners have let him set up shop in the garage. It's a bit better than a garage, more of a modern barn, two storeys, with a kitchen and bathroom out back and all the tools and vehicles parked in front. Chong doesn't pay rent, just has to keep an eye on the place and fix anything that breaks. The place looked like a blacks' camp when we arrived. It's the same feeling I got every time I went up to the Blue Mountains to visit my Uncle Truman and my cousins. Barely controlled chaos. I dunno how his son can even find a spot to do his homework.

Victor is calling out for attention from his dad, but Chong's just one of those guys who is stiff, unemotional, or at least that's the way he is around us. You feel like saying something to the guy, but then he's brought up two kids, lost his wife to breast cancer and is making a life in a new town, so what do I know? My biggest challenge for the last twenty years has been trying not to get a beer gut.

Chong and Grumble are straight into it. The bong appears, there's already a mix in the bowl and they're punching them by 8 am on the verandah. I don't know how they can do it. I used to be able to, now I just shake my head. Birdy is the same as me; we start looking for cereal bowls.

– Where's your fuckin' spoons, Chong?

Chong's hooking his second cone into himself. He exhales the smoke with a low gasp of pain like someone's standing on his chest.

– Over there, dickhead.

We hear the clatter of Victor's school shoes as he comes down the unfinished staircase.

– Good morning, Vic, we all say and he goes about opening cupboards looking for breakfast.

– The spoons are here, he says to Birdy. The kid hears everything that goes on in the barn. It makes me wonder what else he hears. Chong's sitting outside on a log where we had an open fire last night. He leans so he can see in the door.

– What do you want? he says, in the tone of voice parents use for their kids.

– Mohinga, says Victor.

– Get a bowl.

Chong finally stands and it's not hard to picture him in a barley field in Chonju or bolting a steering column onto a Kia in a plant in Pukpyongdong. He shuffles into the kitchen and snaps on the electric jug.

– Is Karen picking you up? he says.

Victor just nods his head. He's cute as shit and clearly enjoys having all his big brothers around to tell him stupid jokes. He sits on a stool, his legs a good foot from the ground. I notice his left sock has a smudge of dirt on it and wonder if it's from this morning or Chong's just forgotten to do the laundry. His legs are long for his body and it's clear he's going to be a tall, striking drink of water in a few years. A six-one Eurasian teen boy in a small country town. I hope he likes condoms more than his dad did. Chong's gonna have to switch on if he doesn't want that going pear-shaped.

Chong's fussing in the cupboard with something that looks like a packet of Cup-a-Soup but with Korean writing. He tears it open and pours it into Victor's bowl, then adds the boiling water.

– Wait, he says to Victor and he just sits there, swinging his legs, watching Scorps and Birdy as they bicker over the milk, captivated. I'm sitting down to Vegemite and toast as the smell of garlic and chilli wafts off Victor's soup. Fuckin' Chong and his gook food. The kid must reek of it. Maybe he won't have to worry too much about condoms after all.

We head back to backbeach around ten-thirty and it's picked up to about four foot but there's only two guys out. We can see them looking up at us on the hill praying 'Don't stop here, you cunts' but it's too good. The wind's swung offshore and it's walling up inside.

– If this was Bondi, there would be eighty blokes out there, I say.

– And the rest, says Scorps. – When's the last time you saw a wave like that at south end?

– Gonna be hard to paddle into them on a six three, says Birdy and I shake my head.

– I'm riding my six eight, says Scorps as we walk back to the car.

– Fuck off, Scorps, I say and we're into it again.

Chong and Grumble laugh as they dig through the icy cold

wetsuits, still grimed with sand and bits of grass from our early.
— You fuckin' hommas, says Grumble.
— That's my rashie.
— Bullshit that's yours, mine's the Peak.
— Whose is that, then?
— Chong, you're wearing my fuckin' rashie.
— Just wear that one.
— Fuck off, Chong, give us my rashie.
— Don't worry, just use that one.
— Fuck.

Scorps is still trying to squeeze into his wettie, which is two sizes too small for him, when I grab the 6' 8" and grind a bit of wax onto it.
— Nuh.

We exchange words, he gets sulky and I end up on Grumble's mal. Paddling out, I'm struck by the uselessness of surfing. If you were going to create the perfect sport for the egotist, this would be it. Paddle out, catch a wave, do some manoeuvres, flick off. It's all about you. No rules, no team-mates and, if the surf's not huge, no consequences. It's total sensual indulgence. It's all about having . . . fun. That's it, fun, and I realise how long it's been since I just had fun, stopped thinking for half a fuckin' minute.

I sit up on my board and look at the point, the wind-scrambled vegetation, the soft, honeycombed rocks, and it's as perfect as it probably was a thousand years ago.
— You don't get to see this stuff kickin' a football, I say to myself.

We surf for a couple more hours, then have a late lunch, crack open a few beers, and before we know it we've followed the thread into the Bowlo. Chong's the only Asian face I've seen for three days and it's safe to say he's the only gook who drinks at the Bowlo. Grumble says the first time Chong walked into Angourie Bowling Club, it was like the music stopped in the saloon and all the heads turned as one to look at the stranger in town.

Then Mr Chong took over. Gradually, the cement-spattered tradies and purple-faced pissheads realised Chong was in the TAB more than any of them. Every time they'd look up at Sky Channel to watch the seventh at Warrnambool, there would be the gook cunt with his schooner, laying the whip into his imaginary mount. When it came in at 11 to 1, they'd scream for joy and realise they were both on the same horse and smile at each other, because, fuck, we both just won four hundred on that fuckin' thing.

Chong would come in some days and they'd nod their heads, just to be polite, and maybe ask him what he was on, just to see what the slap-head would be backing. Every now and then they'd mention the weather and he'd say something about the surf being good at Spookies and they'd wonder how the fuck he knew about that spot and that it worked best on a north-east swell. Then maybe fishing would come up and Chong would tell them about the bream he caught at Pippi Beach or the bush buds he got off this tiler in Yamba and, fuck, it's hard to dislike a bloke who likes fishing and mulling and surfing and a beer and a punt.

I go to the bar for the shout with Grumble, and the barmaid gives him a smile like he's had several cracks at her and she doesn't want to give him too much encouragement.

– Hello, darling, he says, as enthusiastic as I've seen him all day, and leans over the taps to give her a kiss.

– David.

I get the shout and see Scorps has joined Chong in the TAB, the two of them staring up at a tote screen like it's the Star of

Bethlehem. I don't know why Scorps's gambling bothers me so much more than Chong's. Chong has always been a punter and seems to know what he's doing, even if it has pretty much the same result. Scorps's plunges are mindless, on horses because they've got the same name as a chick he used to root in Hawaii whose cousin loved bourbon and he just switched to Jim Beam in the shout and that's gotta be a sign, eh?

Scorps's gambling just seems to be another wall to keep the real world out, like a dam of pillows that you see around those hugely obese people who give TV interviews. They pile cushions around themselves to give them support and think, Maybe, just maybe, people won't see how pathetic I am. Scorps's gambling takes him away from the group, isolates him in whatever corner the TAB is, gives him some kind of *Rain Man* collection of figures and events to keep running through his mind – so what? So he doesn't have to talk to us? So we don't see how little he has to say? So we don't see how scared he is? I'm scared too, mate.

I put Birdy's beer in front of him.

– What's up with that? I say to him, nodding at Scorps.

– They're both pathetic.

An hour later we're blind.

I check my phone to see if my new girlfriend has left a message but I've got barely any reception and I'm not in love with her so I don't give a fuck. I won't be climbing any mountains for better coverage. A group of local guys has streamed into the bistro and are ordering dinner. They're a mix of young and old, fat and fit, the younger blokes easing into schooners while the ageing pissheads have got themselves bottles of white wine to do the job properly. They all dress the same and talk the same and for a minute I wonder what they see when they look at our group, slouched around a table, barely talking because we're so slow with VB and sunburn and red meat.

I go to the bathroom and piss the hot clear piss of beer.

You're not missing much, Kaspar, I think to myself, and get that shudder you do sometimes when you're doing a massive leak.

When I get back, the boys are draining their glasses.

– We gotta go, Chong's gotta get home to Victor, says Birdy.

I look at the clock, it's nearly 10 pm.

– He's been at home by himself all this time?

– He's got his own keys, he just lets himself in after school, says Grumble.

We pile in Birdy's car and I'm glad it's not me behind the wheel.

– You alright to drive? I ask him.

– You want to?

– Not really.

– Anyone want to drive?

– Scorps should drive, you don't need your licence.

– I don't need a thousand dollar fine either.

– Come on, Scorps, I drove last night.

– Alright.

Scorps takes it easy out of town until we leave the bitumen and get onto the dirt.

– Fuckin' slow down, Scorps.

– I am.

– You're drivin' like a fuckin' idiot.

Scorps fancies himself a bit of a driver. He bends over the wheel, steering with one hand, constantly making subtle adjustments. I don't trust his reflexes tonight.

– Who's this coming up?

There's headlights in front of us and the silhouette of something on the roof of the car. It could be roof-racks, or a ranger's siren.

– It's the fuckin' cops, put your belts on, says Birdy.

Mine's already on. Has been since the moment Scorps got behind the wheel. Grumble reaches for his and Chong just leans back, hiding his beer at his feet.

– Just relax, he says.

Scorps slows right down. The cop car's headlights flare and jiggle on the corrugations of the road, then they blast past us in an eddy of opaque dust.

– Don't look back, says Birdy, and Scorps watches them in the rearview.

– They're fuckin' off, he says and everyone pulls out their beers. I drop one and everyone starts groaning, winding down their windows.

– You're a fuckin' pig.

– That reeks, you cunt.

Grumble just laughs, then rips one off himself. Scorps floors it to clear the air in the car and a minute later we're pulling in to Chong's place. We bump up the driveway and the headlights pick up Victor, sitting on the front step of the barn, arms wrapped around himself.

– What's he doing? says Birdy as we stop. He's the only other one of us with a kid and his parenting instincts are a little sharper. Chong opens his door.

– Why are you out here? he snaps at him as we get out of the car.

– I couldn't find the keys, Dad.

– They're under the pot.

– No they're not.

– Then they're round the back.

– They're not.

Victor's shivering in just his school shirt and shorts.

– Why didn't you ring me?

– My phone ran out of batteries, he says.

Chong opens the front door and lets him in.
– Has he been out here since three-thirty? I ask Birdy.
– Fuck, Chong, says Scorps, shaking his head.
In the kitchen I hear Grumble open the cupboard where Chong keeps the bong.

THE CONQUEST OF GAUL

We sit in the quadrangle like recruits at a draft waiting for our names to be shouted out, to be called up for service in the battle called Life. I don't know what I expect. I can't see much further than the piss-up we're all having at the Pigs tonight and spending the two hundred bucks I have in my pocket that Leonard has slipped me as a graduation present.

My mum and Shamus have taken a month off to go to New York, so I'm being babysat by my grandmother and Leonard. It's been a strange few weeks. I'd score a fifty off Leonard, then get grounded by my nan when she found my hash pipe. Ahh, the conflicting messages of youth.

The teachers hand out a bunch of prizes and everyone claps like it matters, like anyone is going to give a shit in ten years' time that I won the Biology and English prizes at Seaview College. You hear about kids and they win awards and are on the swimming and football teams and take retards to the park on the weekends and *fundraise* and I just wonder, Where'd you find the time? How'd you know to even do that stuff?

They were *planning ahead,* they were *thinking of their future.* What does that mean? I'm thinking of where I'm going to score for tonight. I'm thinking if Leonard can get any of those ounces that his mate in Hillsdale used to hook us up with.

When I was in second grade, I wanted to impress the kids at news the next day, so with the last film in our new Polaroid camera I took some pictures of Winston, our dog, dressed in a red sloppy joe. I can remember crying for hours when my mum wouldn't let me take that picture into school. It just didn't make sense. Why was she being so cruel?

I came across the photo a while ago. Winston looks distressed in the red sloppy joe, his two front paws pushed through the arms, and there, in the background, are about thirty marijuana plants sticking out of empty chlorine buckets.

In the same pile of pictures, I found my mum and Shamus's wedding photos. I stared at my mother's corsage for a full minute before I realised what it was she had in her hands – a sticky bud of sinsemilla the size of your fist.

Maybe that's why I never thought of planning ahead? Because no one I knew ever planned ahead – they were too busy growing dope, smoking it or buying it to worry about the future, and once they were stoned, well, fuck, Caesar didn't plan the conquest of Gaul after a few cones of hydro, I'm pretty sure.

I wish I could say I'm filled with something – joy, anticipation, a sense of fulfilment – during my graduation, but I'm just really stoned. Leonard rolled a fat one before the assembly and he blew Larry, Birdy and me out in his Cortina. The whole occasion floats by. I can't even be sure it's happening. How do I know I'm not just some drug overdose lying in a hospital somewhere with tubes up my arse, dreaming the whole thing?

When each member of our form stands to get their graduation

certificate, the headmaster, Brother Wayne Kerr (say it fast a few times), reads out what we intend to do in later life. This has been heavily policed. Many of us had our first, second and third options kyboshed by the teachers, who found professions such as bauxite miner, professional swordsman or fluffer instructor strained credulity. Somehow mine got through.

– Ned Jelli has been with the college six years, says Brother Kerr. – And as you saw earlier, he won both the English and the Biology prizes. He says he's still not sure what he'll do with his life, but is leaning towards a career as a professional hitman.

People laugh. I'm just stoned. I get my certificate and get the fuck out of there.

CHARCOAL TABLETS

My flatmate just doesn't get the whole take-a-message-when-someone-phones protocol. She's a legal-aid lawyer, pretty overweight and kind of pissed off with life. She's on antidepressants at the moment and it leaves her in a funk. She'll forget her handbag on the roof of her car, leave the keys dangling overnight in the front door, even forget to flush and leave a chunky shit greasing up the bottom of the toilet, a halo of caramel around it where it's dissolving from eight hours in the water.

– How come there's no dunny paper covering it? asks Scorps.

– That's the thing, it's sitting in the water all by itself.

– So she doesn't wipe her arse?

– She obviously squirts it out and then gets in the shower.

– Oh, man, I don't want to think about that.

– *You* don't? I gotta use the same soap.

I've been out with Scorps and Birdy, just pounding beers at

the Icebergs, making bungled attempts at the female population of Bondi. It's my thirty-sixth birthday in four days and I'm tossing up whether to have a party. Nothing fancy, just invite the people I want and get on it. That's what I'm telling myself anyway. I have a morbid fear of throwing parties in case no one turns up. It seems much safer not to have them.

– To the Forty Club, says Scorps as we sink our first downstairs in the public bar.

– The Forty Club, I say.

Since we were twenty-one, we've been celebrating each milestone in similar fashion – every five years we've stayed single and carefree is a bonus. The Twenty-Five Club was a cinch. The Thirty Club's required a little more ducking and weaving on both our parts. The Thirty-Five Club was stretching the joke.

– We're getting old, he says to me.

– Speak for yourself, you fat cunt, I've never felt better, I'm a sensation.

I lift up my shirt to give him a peek at my abs. I've been running a bit lately.

– Put it away, mate, says Birdy.

– You're gone, you can't partake in this discussion, I say to him.

– Whattaya mean?

– You and Laney, you're married.

– So what?

– So you're gonna divorce her?

– No.

– There you go.

– What? That makes no sense. I just don't want to see your cock.

– I wasn't showing you my cock.

– This time.

*

The phone's ringing when I get home. It's about midnight and I can't be fucked. It's probably just Scorps telling me how much he loves me or how much he hates himself – hard to pick when he's drunk. I let it go to the answering machine and slide into bed. Then the phone rings again, gets the machine, hangs up and starts ringing again. I'm about to get up but I hear my flatmate thump out of bed onto the cold concrete floor and trundle into the lounge room.

– Hello?
Then:
– Do you know what time it is? she says to whoever's on the phone.

I know that tone. It's for me.
– NED!
Fuck. I get out of bed.
– Tell your fuckin' friends not to call so late, she says and slams her bedroom door behind her.

I pick up the phone. It's my Uncle Matt.
– Your mother's tried to kill herself. She's fine. I'm at the hospital now.
– How?
– She took an overdose of pills.

I drive up to the Blue Mountains once I've sobered up a little and get to Katoomba Hospital after dawn. My uncle briefs me before I go in. I feel like I'm in a bad movie of the week.
– She called me and told me she'd taken the pills and I called Triple O, he says.
– What time was that? I ask.
– About midnight.

It's a two-hour drive from Sydney to the Blue Mountains where my mum and Shamus now live.
– And the ambos broke into the house?

– They knocked on the door and when they didn't get any answer, they went in, the door was open and they found her unconscious in the bedroom.

– She's fuckin' lucky.

My mum's propped up in bed looking pretty clear-eyed considering she tried to top herself six hours before. Her mouth and tongue are black from all the charcoal tablets the doctor has fed her to soak up the poisons in her system.

– You look like you've been sucking off Satan, I say to her and give her a kiss. She chortles. She's always been my greatest fan. I'm always the funniest person in the room when she's around.

– I just couldn't take it any more, Neddy, she says.

– Why didn't you call me, tell me you were crashing?

– I did try to call you, she says and the tears come.

I hold my mum, my mummy, and I squeeze and wish there was something I could do.

– I left a message with your flatmate for you to call me, she says.

My mum gets out of hospital the next day and comes home to Mount Piddington. It's not exactly a festive vibe but we all try to stay chirpy, and after a day she's up and moving. She looks like she's wading through mud when she walks, her speech is slow and it's as much as I can do not to run from the house screaming.

On her second day back, Shamus disappears for most of the afternoon and doesn't reappear until well after dark. Sometimes it's like trying to keep a dog in the yard. He's been living with the pressure of her depression for months and months now, so I guess he needs to clear his head. When he finally gets home it's obvious he's charging on something. He doesn't want to eat and starts hooking into the red wine.

There's a short argument between him and my mum. There's tears and he retreats to the couch and his CNN mull bowl, watching the History Channel, surrounded by a cloud of ciggie ash and self-loathing.

– Do you know where he's been? I ask my mum in her bedroom.

– He's been down the road with Bash.

– Who the fuck is Bash?

– Some trucker he drinks with at the pub.

– He's been at the pub?

– No, he's at Bash's house snorting fucking speed.

– You've got to be joking?

My mum starts to cry and rolls over in bed. My head is a soup. I walk out to Shamus. His jaw is grinding as he watches TV, smoking, just waiting to counterattack.

– Mate, what are you thinking? I say to him.

– It's none of your business, Ned.

– I'm sorry, Shamus, but it is my business.

– Don't push it, Ned.

Shamus is closing in on sixty now. I'm half his age, but I wouldn't underestimate him. He's still quick and he'd be nasty in a stink, especially against me. In all those years living with him, he only hit me once, an open-hander across the face when I called my mum a bitch. Still, I'm scared of him, scared of tilting the world my way, having to take up the lonely wail of the alpha dog in our family.

– I'm trying to talk to you, Shamus. Your wife just tried to kill herself and she needs you more than ever and you're down the road snorting speed.

Shamus's head rips around to look at me and he lifts off the couch. I can see his heavy silver bracelet jumping through the black hairs on his wrist. His voice starts to keen.

– I will not be spoken to like this, Ned.

In the bedroom, I can hear my mum's crying escalate.

– Then how do you want to do this, Shamus? I can't let you keep doing this. Abigail needs you.

– Don't you dare question my love for your mother, he yells.

I can hear my mum calling for me, so can Shamus.

– You're upsetting your mother, he says to me, disgusted.

– *I'm* upsetting her?

I laugh and he stands and turns towards me, shaking with chemicals and whatever poisons feed his heart.

– Don't you laugh at me, Ned.

I don't want a part of those eyes. There's no truth in them, you can't make them understand. They've spent a lifetime running away from truth.

Or maybe they've seen it clearer than I know.

ALWAYS

Of course we go and get drunk after graduation and, of course, the venue is Billy the Pig's. I should be over the moon, but it's just a blur. I drink Heinekens and have zammy shots and we pull sly cones out in the lane, near where they stack the kegs and the trucks unload for David Jones. We're all happy it's over, can't believe we never have to go to school again, that this is the beginning of our lives. Some of us have jobs lined up in the money market or advertising, some of us are planning to go to uni.

Me? I end up stumbling along William Street down to a hundred and twenty bucks after the Heinies and sambucas and the twenty dollar foilie, I bought off Foilie. Ever since Flo and the raging rajah, I've had an absurd interest in prostitutes. During our final exams, Joe Gold, Foilie and I used to cruise around after midnight to break up the monotony of study. Joe would come by in his Subaru station wagon and pick us up and we'd burn up and down William Street checking out the streetwalkers. We'd pull up beside them and wind down our windows.

– How much, love? one of us would ask.

– I'm not getting in there with all of you.

– Just tell us how much, you fucken moll.

The pro would lash out at whoever was nearest, try to spit in his face, kick the door of the car. I was like an infant given a set of shiny house keys; I couldn't stop staring.

I love whores. I love their slutty clothes and their fishnets and cheap skyscraper high heels. With the good ones, the ones the gear and the street haven't worn down too much, I love the curve of their synthetic shorts around their arses and the way the fabric dives into their cunts. They're like outrageous orchids: their hair, their clothes, their facial expressions, all markings on flower petals, directing the eye, the bees, to one point, the pistil of their cunt.

Most of all, however, I love the fact that if you have enough money you can walk up to any of them, even the most aloof and untouchable, the iciest blonde with the weariest eye and she will take off her clothes and fuck you, suck your cock, let you suck her tits and knead her arse. Not maybe or sometimes or perhaps. Always.

I'm without a car or a cab, the lowest of kerb crawlers, drunk as only a teenager can be, walking between outposts, checking out the talent, weighing up each one's good points and bad. I must do three laps of the street, up and back, up and back, until I settle on a dark girl, an Islander, wearing what looks like a white one-piece swimsuit, zebra-skin ankle boots and white woollen leg warmers.

– How much?

– How old are you, darling?

– I'm eighteen, I lie.

– Oh, aren't you a little sweetie?

– Come on, how much?

– Full strip a hundred.

Which means she'll do me the courtesy of taking off all her clothes. Some girls just roll up their skirt and make you fuck them like they've stopped to pee.

– What about a head job?

– Another twenty, darling.

– Fuck, I mutter, disappointed. Another twenty knocks me out of contention, cheap as it is. I have to get home and there won't be buses running until about 5 am. Still, twenty is cheap for headdies. Grumble once asked a whore what he'd get for twenty dollars.

– I'll take off my shoe, she said.

It's academic, I decide. I'm more interested in penetrative sex than blow jobs. I know I'm getting rorted and she's charging me overs because she thinks I'm just a kid but I am only a kid. And, man, she looks like a South Pacific Jane Fonda workout wet-dream in that one-piece. I already have a semi and it's lolling around in my undies (electric blue Bonds) like a soggy spring roll.

– Okay.

She walks and I follow. Her arse is perfect. Not a trace of cellulite and her thigh muscles flex under the sheen of her pantyhose like a boa constrictor crushing an Amazonian child. A familiar feeling dribbles into my arms and legs – the one I get before a fight, football or making a phone call to a girl I really like. Was I really going to have sex with this woman? The spring roll starts to stiffen.

– Where've you been tonight? she asks me, happy to be entertaining someone who isn't five stone overweight and covered in greasy black hair.

– I was out with some friends.

– What's the occasion? You look pretty dressed up for a Tuesday.

And she's right. I have on my paisley shirt and black jeans and pair of winkle-pickers that are half patent leather, half suede. I look hell.

– We graduated today, I say, shaking my head as soon as I say it.

– Aww, but I thought you were eighteen?

– Yeah, I just graduated from TAFE. I'm a carpenter.

She smiles at me but the truth is sitting there between us, plain as my scruffy little hard-on.

– I might have to give you something extra to celebrate.

She leads me up some narrow stairs to a terrace just off Bourke Street, into a one-room flat. I give her the hundred, then hide the rest of my cash in my shoe. She tells me to shower and by the time I get out she's stripped off completely. Her breasts are smallish and defeated-looking and her vagina's kind of engorged and purple, like a face that's been seven rounds then copped a head clash. I want to eat her out, but she won't have any of it.

– No, no. No you don't, she says, grabbing me under the chin like a grandma shucking a ten year old, steering me away from her cunt.

She won't let me kiss her either. What a fucken gyp. She lies down, ready to accept me, and I hop on. She seems to be getting a thrill out of my body and is rubbing my hips and chest, then my thighs, working my cock and balls.

– You're an eager thing, aren't you?

I'm stiff as a six-day-old baguette. I've spent weeks, months, trying to get girls to even touch my cock, and this woman, this stranger, is treating it like an old friend.

– Come up here, she says and for the briefest second she looks like a Samoan bloke who used to play with Larry in the second row for South Eastern. Just for a second, then she's back to being the Islander sex kitten between my legs. As I move up, she shimmies down and takes my cock in her mouth.

You fucken beauty, I think. Something extra, alright.

It takes me about ten seconds to realise that, somehow, she's put a condom on my cock. On the way down, she's slipped the thing in her mouth, and rolled it on with her lips and tongue. I'm impressed and have to reach down and pull my todger out of her mouth to stop myself from spurting my surprise. She may as well be an anthropologist watching a mountain gorilla fountain diarrhoea after eating too many green bananas. She knows exactly what's going on.

– Don't get too excited, now.

I let Oscar hang out there in the cool for a second, before she pops him back in her gob. Watching a beautiful woman put your penis in her mouth has to rank up there with a public execution or a street fight for things you can't stop looking at. As for the enjoyment – well, the condom makes it feel like getting a foot massage while you're wearing ski-boots.

– I want to fuck you now.

– Okay.

As I shift down to get our bodies aligned, she reaches over to her bedside table and grabs a half-used tube of K-Y jelly.

– Got to get myself ready for you.

I've never seen a woman use lubricant before. She squeezes out a ten cent piece of the clear gel then strokes it onto my penis like it's getting sunburnt and she's being friendly with the sunscreen.

I wake up the next morning about six, the sound of traffic excruciatingly loud.

MY GOD, are those fucken cars driving through my head?

Close enough. I'm hugging a telegraph pole, my skull about six inches from the metal screams hauling down William Street. I smell piss. Not my piss, just the piss I've been asleep in, the piss on the pole. I blink a lot before I work out I'm just up the road from the brothel. It must have been some root. I've staggered out and collapsed on the pavement. Nice of her to see me to a cab.

I feel in my pockets for my cash and find none, and wonder if the bitch robbed me. I start to walk and remember I've put my money in my shoe. I unlace my winkle-picker and there's my last twenty.

I take it back, you're not a bitch.

THE LAST SUPPER

And then it's 2 am and you're leaning against another bar, in another club and you know what you want, like a damn aching amputee and it's never going to be in this place but you've laid out a couple of hundred on chemicals and grog and cover charges and cabs and the tight maul of cold gold shame that's there every morning has finally loosened for a few sweet minutes and you'll be fucked if you're gonna go home without something warm on your arm or at least a close call to masturbate over.

You've watched the fresh generation of lurking, pseudo Casanovas and latex playgirls and you're trying to master the plaster of your face, paint it with a likeably indifferent smile and mould your posture into a confident slouch but the question is pounding through you like a migraine. What's the point?

You tell yourself that one day you'll be sad and saggy and look at pictures of yourself from now and wish you'd gone out a few more hundred times and utilised your comparable beauty, lived life to the fullest, fucked it like a gaffer-taped guinea pig, not wasted a chance.

But now it's a sweaty new morning and the clubbers are walking around with billboards of need hung around their necks announcing 'I hate myself and I just want sex' or 'I dress this way for attention but don't think about talking to me!' and the pheromones in the air are almost choking you. The charge of sex and violence is making you wanna puke up the beer and Thai food and coke (which was mostly speed) but you keep it down because it stops you thinking about her, about the last time you saw her.

Braking down the hill, the pads of her car were worn, grinding against the discs, a horrible sound matching the energy inside her Barina.

– You should get those fixed, you'll gouge the discs, I say.
– Yeah.

We come to a stop at the traffic lights. Left is my place. Right is the way to Alessandra's. Her hand hangs over the steering wheel as she sighs and winds down the window.

– It's worth fighting for, Alex.
– I'm tired.
– Tired of what?
– Everything.

She's staring through her windscreen at the numberplate of the car in front, which is pouring out some bad R&B song. It reads 2REAL4U. Alex's snarl has returned. The space between our seats seems biblical. I can see the traffic on the cross-street slowing for its orange light. Her hand hangs above the indicator switch.

– I'm going to Queensland on Monday.
– I thought it was Friday?
– I moved it up.

– I don't want to feel like this, Alex.

– You choose your feelings.

I close my eyes and rest my neck against the moulded gunk of the seat. If she turns right, I'm staying at her place. If she turns left, that's it, she's dropping me home and it's dead. Like a round being slid into its chamber I hear the plastic clunk of the indicator as she moves the lever. I hold my eyes closed and listen to the blinker's ticking, my heartbeat speeding up to overtake its rhythm as I wait for the roll of the car to tell me her decision.

Later, when I lie in bed alone, my breath leaves me like notes from a lost opera and I know that when I turn under the Glad-Wrap sheets all I'd find is old smells from our last supper.

THE BONDI TRIANGLE

Some bloke comes back from the dunnies and sits down opposite me and Scorps, and hands Scorps a tiny baggie. Scorps doesn't even look at it, just leans up off his stool so he can wedge it into the top pocket of his jeans. The guy, Scorps's latest coke buddy, is wearing a Paul Frank hooded top, exactly like one I have at home. Two ex-girlfriends have told me it's a piece of shit and looks terrible, but I like it, so I've held on to it. And here's this cunt wearing the same thing. I get that shiver you do when you see a homeless guy wearing the same shoes as you, or chicks get when they see some trashy boiler has 'their' handbag.

We are one.

It's State of Origin and we're sitting in the Lung, the smoking section of the Icebergs. Usually we'd be watching the game with the Wynn brothers at their place, because they're Queenslanders. There's nothing quite as enjoyable as winning a football match when the enemy is next to you and you can scream abuse at them, question their sexuality and tackle them into furniture. Now, however, the Wynns are surfing in Indo, Grumble and Chong are back up the coast, Kasp is dead and Birdy's watching the game with his family. That leaves just me and Scorps and the cast of freaks, alcos and degenerate gamblers who populate the Lung.

– So what have you been up to? I ask Scorps.
– I just been hanging, cruising.
– What's goin' on with that? I say and tap my nose.
– It's all good. I'm doin' fuck all.
– It's a Wednesday night, mate.
– It's sweet.

I laugh.

– You're fuckin' kidding yourself.

Scorps's alco mate in the Paul Frank hoody looks uncomfortable and heads to the bar. He doesn't ask me what I'm drinking.

– Fuck, Neddy, says Scorps, meaning ease up.

Is it because Scorps's weaknesses are so apparent that I feel mine so keenly when I'm around him? Everything that comes out of his mouth lately seems to edge against me like a serration. He talks so much crap – but maybe that's my problem too? I talk so much crap as well.

– Neddy, I feel like I'm turning a corner. Things are going really well for me, he says.
– Then how come every time I see you you're rackin' up?
– Mate, it's sweet, I swear. I'm feeling good.

He looks at me, coke sincerity pumping out of his sad eyes.

– It's been a tough year for me, but I'm turning the corner, I can feel it.

It's always a tough year for Scorps. This one just folded on top of the rest. Over New Year, one of Scorps's banker mates asked him to water his plants and feed his dogs while he was away in Barbados or Monaco or wherever the fuck bankers spend their vacation. Bizarrely, the dude let Scorps drive his hundred thousand dollar Porsche as part of the deal. So Scorps does his usual five-day binge over New Year's and about 3 January remembers there's two pedigree beagles starving to death in Paddington. He's with Mr Boom, blind, hasn't slept, and decides he's gonna drive to Paddo to feed the dogs. Even Boom knew it was a bad idea.

– Maaate, I reckon you should wait until tomorrow, eh? he says to Scorps.

– I'm sweet, I'm sweet, says Scorps and somehow backs the Porsche out of his garage, navigates Campbell Parade, then floors it down Jacques Avenue, gets airborne and takes out five parked cars. Mr Boom is out of the passenger door immediately and does the bolt, but Scorps just walks around the wrecks in a daze until the cops arrive. Somehow he avoids jail time, probably because they didn't blood test him for rack and pills, and he ends up getting three hundred hours community service.

– I'm just living a weird life at the moment, he says to me.

I can't remember the last time I went surfing with Scorps, or had a feed or even did something other than drink piss. I can't even remember being outside of Bondi's Bermuda Triangle with him in the last five years. The Bergs, the Regis, the Rats. Three points on the map but blokes get lost in there for years and when they emerge they look like this cunt walking towards me in his hoody.

Pauly Frank's back with two beers and doesn't meet my eyes as he pushes one in front of Scorps, ignoring my empty glass. I've never met half these blokes Scorps is hanging with now, the new crew of pissheads who don't get up him about his punting and coking and grogging. Sadness cries out to sadness, I guess. Scorps is just a slightly weaker me, what I would have become if I'd had ten hours less love from my mother aged five.

The game is pretty tight: 16-10, New South Wales's way. Scorps keeps looking in the other direction to the TAB where the greyhounds and trots are being shown on a half-dozen smaller TV screens. This place should be packed tonight, but there's less than thirty people up here, all guys over the age of thirty, all going to fat, drinking to forget how fuckin' tiny their lives have become, how they missed the gravy train when it passed and now they're stuck with man boobs and mortgages wondering how the fun ended so quickly.

Halftime's talking to a table of older drunks, all accidental millionaires thanks to the property boom, embittered, scheming how to keep their money away from their wives now they've traded up to younger women and gotten caught.

– Here comes Neddy, says Halftime. – We don't see you for months and then back you come, return to the mother ship.

– Don't take it personally, mate.

Halftime's as drunk as I've ever seen him, maybe because his marriage is on the rocks and he's sleeping in his car.

– When we're all wearing kaftans, Neddy, you'll have someone to drink with.

– I'd prefer a muumuu, I say and turn back to the TV as some pudgy Queensland faggot starts jumping up and down as the Maroons make a break.

– OH HO HO HO! YES!! he screams as the winger goes over in the corner to even the scores. He does a little arse wiggle in front of the television for the benefit of the only two chicks in the joint. They've got boyfriends but this red-headed cunt thinks he's a chance, or enjoys being the 'zany' one in the group. He's never been bashed in his life and needs it. I fight the urge to king-hit the fuckwit and walk to the toilets instead.

This place, the Bergs, it exists so about two hundred blokes will have somewhere to get fucked up. Its unspoken motto: here, you can get as drunk as you want and no one will tell you

you've had enough. Here, you can turn up every night and get slaughtered and no one will tell you you have a problem.

I urinate and take out my pen. There's a noticeboard above the trough and I've graffitied it before I even realise what I'm doing.

I write: *THE BERGS WILL SINK US ALL.*

Then I leave, not knowing the score.

EPIPHANY

Larry's mum is giving us a lift to the train station. There's me and Larry, the Maroubra crew, and we've just picked up Scorps and Chong from Bondi. Mrs Lawrence has taken a right and gone the long way down Queen Street instead of heading along Oxford and Moore Park Road towards Central.

– You get on the drink last night, Maisie? I say to her, using what I estimate is a witch's voice to tease her. Mrs Lawrence is a good sport, she enjoys the banter.

– Shut up, you little wog bastard, or you'll walk to the station.

– Yeah, shut up, you little wog, says Chong.

– Fuck off, Chong, you pig dick.

We're all laughing, enjoying the fact that Mrs Lawrence doesn't give a shit what we say as long as we don't use the C word. It's heading towards evening and we're booked on the overnight train to Byron Bay, where we then have to change for Brisbane, then we get a bus to the Gold Coast for schoolies. We've come through the Kings Cross tunnel and onto William Street when Scorps takes it too far.

– Slow down, Mrs Lawrence, we'll look at the whores, he says.

– Watch your mouth, she says and shakes her head. She's never liked Scorps.

The traffic's heavy and we move slowly past the spot where I picked up my Islander friend a few weeks ago. I can't see her tonight, but there's plenty of others dressed like they're about to go on stage in the Eurovision Song Contest. The mood in the car is a bit tense, so Mrs Lawrence lets Scorps off the hook.

– I don't know why you'd bother anyhow, there'll all blokes, she says.

I go cold.

– Whattaya mean? I say.

– That's where all the transsexuals stand, says Mrs Lawrence.

– So what? They sleep with men?

– If you pick up someone from that side of William Street, I'd say that's what you're looking for.

– Aww, that's filthy, says Chong.

Larry turns around and sees my horror.

– Look at Ned, he's been wanking about the chicks on the wrong side of the street.

GRAND FINAL DAY

I walk up the driveway to Nudge's place and think to myself it would be nice to live like this. The streets of Bellevue Hill are quiet and damp and leafy and safe and all the houses have views of the harbour and it all seems right. People don't bash their wives or fuck their kids around here, surely.

Nudge has somehow managed to luck into living in a disused mansion. It looks like the Brady Bunch house – groovy fifties architecture, a weird angled roof, lots of slate and river stones stuck in the walls. Guru is already there, stacking piss into tubs of ice, when I mount the stairs.

– Jeez, this is a shit spot, I say and Guru laughs like he does when he thinks something's not that funny but wants to be polite.

– Grab a cold one and go in and sign the book, Neddy, I'll look after your beers, he says.

Guru is working on the world's most besieged widow's peak.

At school, I remember being envious of his natural curls, the way his hair would tuft up and sweep back over his ears, while my brown mop just fell down my face like a grass skirt. Now his is gone.

I walk in the house and am hit by the smell of mildew. The carpets were once expensive but are now stained. In one corner, the roof has opened up and what looks like ferns are poking through the plaster that's shrouded in grey mould. A big screen TV sits in the middle of the room, hemmed in by battered couches that would look at home in a shooting gallery.

– Neddy, says Nudge as he walks in the room with a couple of can handbags. He hands me one that says *Beauty is in the eye of the beer holder*. I stretch it over my Extra Dry.

– Still on the poof beers, are you mate?

– Well, I'm a poof, aren't I?

– That you are, Neddy.

– How the fuck did you score this joint, mate?

Nudge laughs, looking pleased with himself.

– Let me give you the tour.

He walks me through the kitchen, which is as big as my apartment, then out a side door to what used to be a grass tennis court. It has sweeping views of Sydney Harbour, the Bridge, the Opera House. The land the court is on must be worth three million alone.

– The bloke who owns it comes down the Bergs and he needed someone to look after the place before he knocks it down, says Nudge.

– They're gonna knock it down? That's a shame.

– It's falling apart.

– What's he going to do with the land?

By now we've circled around the back of the house. Nudge points up the garden.

– Hothouses.

– Jesus fuckin' Christ, this is enormous.

The grass is unkempt but, as we reach a low brick fence, the lawn on the other side stretches perfectly. It's flat, manicured, arcing towards a beautifully kept, three storey Federation-style mansion. Nudge steps over the fence.

– Where you going?
– This is his other place.
– What?
– This is where he lives. He bought this other one so he can knock it down, spruce up the tennis court and have some grounds.
– I don't know anybody who has grounds.
– You do now.
– Does he have a daughter?

We walk out onto the lawn, past the house. I peer in through the windows and see rooms crowded with heavily polished antique furniture.

– What's this cunt do?
– I think he cans tomatoes or peaches or something.
– Anyone home?
– Nah, he's in the States on business.

We walk to the front of the house. The driveway sweeps down to Victoria Road. The view is the same as the tennis court, only better. The harbour sits in front of us, all the big-money landmarks spaced out tastefully, so you don't miss a thing.

– So this is how they live?
– Magnificent, isn't it?

An hour later, the girls turn up and go to the bathroom to get changed. We don't get much of a look at them, just a glimpse of blonde hair and skin under their top coats. There's about twenty of us now, all drinking beers on the deck, sipping the view, talking shit about the Grand Final and how the Roosters are gonna smash the New Zealand Warriors. It's a pond of red, white and blue, all the boys being diehard Roosters fans.

– Who you backin', Neddy?
– The Warriors, mate.
– You've got to be joking?
– I'm a Souths fan, brother.
– So, there you go, we're neighbours. You can't actually want the fuckin' Kiwis to win the Grand Final? We'd never hear the end of it.
– Mate, better them than the Rooters.

I'm facing the view, but it's not hard to tell the girls have arrived behind me. The boys stand straighter, beers pulled into their chests like teddy bears. One of the girls is in her late twenties and shouldn't be wearing a G-string. Her name is Petra and she's very ordinary. Her legs are dimpled and bruised in spots, though she does have enormous pale breasts which sway as she bends to the ice to retrieve her first beer.

The next girl, however, makes up for Petra. She is Kasia and she's about twenty, with acres of taut skin that leave the pads of my fingers aching to touch. She's topless as well, wearing a tiny white G-string that adheres to her vagina lips like bubble gum over a tongue. I don't know where to put my hands, so I walk over for another beer and Nudge calls me off.

– Neddy. That's what the girls are for. Kasia, a beer for Ned, please.
– Of course, she smiles at me, then stilts over to one of the tubs in her white stripper heels and bends over for all twenty of us to see. A soft moan escapes Foilie.
– Magnificent, says Nudge. – Magnificent.

I try not to stare at Kasia but most of the other guys are not so discerning with their ogling. I only know about half of them, but the half I do might as well be strangers to me. Their necks are thickening and there's a hunger in their eyes when they look at Kasia that I understand but somehow feel uncomfortable unveiling in public.

I've decided to spend the day with a different group, well, let's be honest, a richer group – the blokes I know who actually seem to be getting on with life, having kids, carving out careers, paying off mortgages. They all look so tired. They've got cold beer and white bread and bitch tits but they're so terrified of not having a house and a Range Rover and superannuation that all they have time for is work and reality TV and grog shits on Friday morning after a few too many on a Thursday night.

These are your options, Jelli, I think to myself as the dildo show starts.

A RESULT

The teachers take three months to mark our HSC exams and then we're given a score out of 500. Geniuses – like the Asian kids who don't come up for air for two years – get around 480. I get 411. Grumble – 260. Larry – 310. Scorps – 330. Birdy – 303. Kaspar – 354. And Chong – 380. It's like a concentration camp serial number tattooed on your arm. Everyone wants to know.

– What'd ya get, what'd ya get? we all ask each other.

Chong is the only Asian in our form not to get over 400.

– You're the dumbest gook I know, Chong, says Grumble as we have rollcall up at the Pigs. There's about a hundred and fifty of us in the bottom bar all looking suntanned and primed to explode into the world. Halftime, our school captain, looks so bronzed and white-haired, he could be a photo negative. He reads the roll of students and we answer 'Here' then skol a schooner. They say it's a Seaview College tradition but it seems like just another excuse to get pissed.

It's January, so we've already been on holidays for a few months and the separations are beginning. Blokes you thought you were good mates with, well, when you see them up the Pigs that night you realise you haven't caught up with them all summer. And then there are the guys you've been hanging out with ever since the last day of school and you end up talking to them the whole night.

School was the glue that kept us all together and as it dissolves so are a lot of our friendships. But tonight we're all still reaching for the esprit de corps that had fizzed around us in those final days of study, when it suddenly dawned on us all that it was over – the drudgery of books and exams did finally end and sooner rather than later we'd be saying goodbye. It was like a slice of chocolate cake we were trying to savour, the portion getting tinier with each bite, so we'd take a proportionately smaller nick away with us, enjoy it more deeply than the last.

It's chaos at the bar. Dumb cunts are pushing their marks a little higher, some of the brainy guys are dropping theirs so as not to appear too dorky. Me, I'm just drunk. Every time I finish a schooner I smash it at my feet; the bouncer can't find me in the heaving crowd at first, but when he does, he throws me down the front stairs.

I go around the back of the pub, to where the kegs are stacked, and it's almost as packed as upstairs. There's a group of the boys and some St Clare's chicks drinking twist-tops. As ever, Larry is wrestling someone on the pavement, while Foilie and Kaspar are pulling a quiet few in the long grass of a driveway of the house next to the pub. Suggs stands over them staring.

– Give us a cone, he says.
– Fuck off, Suggs, you scab.

I step in and plead my case for a billy and, surprisingly, Foilie relents, sprinkling some grains into the cone like they're truffles. I've blown him out before. At least he remembers.

– Fill it up, I say.

– Get rooted, that's all you're getting.

I pull it anyway and exhale. Suggs watches me like I'm fucking his sister.

– What? I say.

Suggs just giggles and walks away.

– Fucken spinner, says Foilie.

I swap clothes with Scorps to throw off the bouncer and sneak up the back stairs. An hour before closing, I'm on a table, my pants around my feet singing.

– I've been SUCKED, I've been FUCKED and I'm HAPPY.

Two are true.

THE CONVERSATION

I haven't been up to visit my parents for more than a year. I dunno where the time goes, but it does and then all of a sudden my mum's on the phone upset because I haven't made the effort to drive the two hours.

– Was I that bad a mother? she says and I wish I knew what to say. I blame them for everything that's gone wrong in my life and take credit for all the good. So here we are at the Valhalla in Mount Piddington. It's the kind of old-school retro pub, filled with local pissheads and a coal fire, that you'd find charming if you were dropping in with a cute chick for a quick glass of red after bushwalking. When it's your only option for socialising with your parents it makes you want to open a vein in the dunnies.

Despite the cold we sit out on the verandah so Shamus can smoke. There's a few other tables of people huddled around those tall gas heaters that look like the Tin Man's erection.

Shamus gets the first round, and I gulp mine down and go in for the second. I walk to the bar, weaving through a dining room filled with middle-aged couples staring over each other's shoulders, out for a Saturday lunch. You'd think it was a nursing home. All you can hear is the twink of cutlery and the hiss of traffic out on the highway in the cold rain.

In the main bar, the levels of conversation aren't much better. The drunks are stooled, hung over the taps like farm animals at a trough. Another group stare bleakly up at the TAB screens hoping that's gonna change their lives. I triangle the drinks and wander back through the diners in the above-ground cemetery.

As I shoulder open the door to the verandah a gust of laughter, a little too loud for the atmosphere, greets me. My mum and Shamus are chatting away up the end of the balcony, about fuck knows what. I stand there watching them for a solid two minutes and they keep at it, chortling and whispering while the other couples mutely poke cubes of steak into their mouths.

I stand at the doors, watching. They both go silent and look out down the valley at the wet gum trees and the mist. Shamus says something out of the side of his mouth and my mum laughs again and has to put down her wine because it's gone up her nose.

WONDERLAND

The promenade is an oily current of rollerbladers and wogs in mesh singlets and sandpiper jogger girls whose kneecaps are the thickest part on their bodies and who look like they could fall down a crack in the sidewalk. Every person who passes me is like a frequency on the FM band, scraping by my awareness, eyes pleading ignorance or judgement or guilt as they take in the nice man pushing his grandmother around in her wheelchair.

The heat's frightening, so I've got my shirt off, clutching paper napkins to wipe Grandma's chin as she struggles with her chocolate ice-cream cone.

– You right with that?
– Yes, yes.
– You want a hat?
– Yes, please.

I take off my baseball cap and put it on her backwards.

– You wanna be a homegirl or go traditional?

– I'm a traditional kind of girl.

I turn it around for her as she watches the water like an old photograph.

– You know we have the most beautiful beaches in the world, she says.

– Yeah, they're up there, I'll give you that.

A pudgy girl with a belly ring and a nose stud futzes past.

– Whattaya think of those piercings, Grandma?

– They look silly.

– It's all the rage now. Here, I say, and give her another serviette to mop up a vein of chocolate trickling down her wrist.

– So were hula hoops but you still looked silly walking around with one of those all day, she says.

– Hula hoops, I wonder when they're gonna come back.

– I don't think they will, you have too many other distractions nowadays.

We sure do, I think. We all drink from the same river, always have. It's on every person's face as they walk along the beach, safe faces but inwardly aching with their own cowardice. How much courage does it take to live in Tamarama and work in advertising and fuck your best friend's wife on the side? Where does bravery even enter the equation? The smart ones at least feel disgust. The others, they just wish they had three bedrooms instead of two, a 2007 beamer instead of an 04. They aren't even in the game.

Two blokes jog past on the soft sand with creepy-brown-guy suntans, red Speedos, talking on their mobile phones as they run.

Imagine explaining jogging to some starving Somali?

– Yeah, well, it's like this. I eat so much, I have to run so's I don't get fat, eh?

We all drink from the same river here. We all want the same things. We look the same and sound the same and wear the same boardshorts and belts and shoes and trucker caps. We read the same books and magazines and watch the same television. Scariest of all, we even dream the same. We all want to look like TV stars and have our backyards blitzed and cocktails with a twist because to go outside what's spooned up to us by the big boys requires effort and effort, that's really not what Wonderland is about.

Wonderland is a perfect tan and seafood barbecues and not having to fuss with finding a goddamn parking spot. It's about getting the exact right flavour drink *immediately* when you feel thirsty. It's about not having to fuck the same woman when you get sick of her. It's plotting to root your neighbour's wife to inject it all with some kind of drama, some kind of zing, because we're all hollow inside, drinking from the same shit stream.

The Icebergs, the Astra, the Pavilion, Mermaid Rock, Hobbit's takeaway, Forrest Knoll. They're coordinates on some map of a mythical land, a Tolkien topography. It's the dreamland here. It's a VB glow at sunset and a joint to make us think kooky but don't rock the boat, baby. We're full of prawns and fresh bread and cold beer so why even wonder what else could be? Why even think different when this is almost perfect? We're almost perfect? We're all on the edge of sleep, so fat and happy, the prawns are coming out of our arses intact, gleaming, untouched, because we're so full of fresh food, we don't need to digest it any more.

Grandma and I have reached the end of the promenade by now and out of habit I look for Kaspar's mural – the memorial that some of the boys organised to have spray-painted on the wall near the skatie ramp at south. I search for it and can't see anything but rap tags and big R.I.P. cartoons for wogs and car thieves who've had three swims at Bondi in their short lives.

I walk back and check the spot again to make certain.

– Fuck, I say to myself and pull out my phone, dial Scorps.
– Whattup?
– They've painted over Kasp's mural on the promenade.
– You sure?
– I'm standing in front of it, it's gone. There's some zigzag shit here for a bloke named Rio.
– That's fucked.
That's Bondi.

GONESKI

– Have you spoken to Suggs? Larry says to me.
 – Where is he?
 – Over at the table talking to himself, the fucken psycho. He's lost the plot.
 We're at the top bar of the Pigs and I'm sucking on a Heineken, sunburnt as a cunt. I look over at our table. Birdy, Scorps, Grumble, Chong and Kaspar are sitting in a half-moon around one side of it, sipping schooners. Suggs is perched on the other side, empty chairs around him, his hands clasped between his knees, staring at his feet.
 – What the fuck's he wearing? A ski parka?
 – He smells like a homeless man.
 – It's forty degrees outside.
 – He's fucken lost it. He's a tripper.
 – What's he saying?
 – The usual shit.

– He draws you in, doesn't he?
– Don't encourage the cunt, says Larry but I'm already wandering over towards Suggs. He looks up at me like he's squinting into the sun and giggles. I sit down next to him.
– Got any mull? says Suggs.
– Nah, mate, sorry.
A giggle.
– Listen, listen, listen, the cat's pissin'.
Suggs talks in a low whisper, just on the edge of audibility.
– Sorry, mate, what was that?
– You should know, you made it go.
He giggles some more and tries to grab Birdy's beer off the table.
– No you don't, mate.
I look up at Larry, who's already sick of him.
– Fuck him off, Ned.
– Fuck him off, says Suggs and giggles some more.
I try to ignore him and catch Kaspar's eye.
– Hey, Edward.
– Hey, Kasp, how you been?
– Yeah, good mate, just working with Triple M doing traffic reports. Whatabout you? What are you doing with yourself now?
– I'm working at the newspaper.
– Doing what?
– I'm doing a cadetship.
– What's that?
– It's like an apprenticeship. To be a reporter.
– Reporting on what?
– Did you see that story today about the standover man, Roy Thurgar?
– The guy who got murdered at Randwick?
– Yeah.

– I did that story.

I'm trying to feign humility but I'm feeling pretty pleased with myself. It's my first front page and it's actually quite surprising I've taken half an hour to slip it into conversation tonight.

– Got the splash, says Suggs next to me.

– What'd you say?

– So busy reporting on other people's achievements you'll never achieve anything yourself.

– What?

– Always the messenger, never the message.

I look at the cunt. He's off his face. He gives me a vicious little glance.

FUCKIN' SCREWS

My cousins Sass and Alice and I have decided to drive down to visit Bailey in jail. He's been in six months, but because they've stuck him on the NSW border, none of the family have seen him. On the phone he sounded chirpy enough.

– I reckon it's the best thing coulda happened to me, he'd said the week before.

– You might meet the love of your life, Bailey.

– Aw, nah, mate, don't be like that. I mean it's gotten me off the piss and I can't touch the drugs in here so, I feel like me head's the clearest it's been for ages.

– That's good to hear, Bailey, I'm glad.

– What about you then, Neddy? I hear you quit your job.

– Yeah, mate.

– What are you going to do?

– I dunno, mate, I think I'm gonna get out of here.

– Overseas?

– Yeah.

– Wish I could do that. But no cunt will let you in their country once you've got a record.

– Anyways, what can we bring you down? What are we allowed to bring with us?

– Well, I'd love youse to bring a slab with you, but I don't think you'll get it past the screws.

– Alright, mate, no beers.

It's a long drive down to the NSW–Victorian border. The three of us take it in shifts and by seven in the morning we're at Goulburn, eating the traditional meal of McDonald's required for any trip over two hours' duration. We walk into Maccas and there's an enormous couple perched on some wrought-iron chairs near the door.

– Guarding the exits in case anyone tries to leave with the food, I say.

There's six more grossly overweight people at the counter, waiting to order.

– Jesus, I know where all the fat people in Goulburn hang out, says Alice.

– Go easy on the fat jokes, says Sass and sucks in her stretch-marked stomach. – I've had three people in the last week ask me if I'm pregnant again.

– Awww. What do you tell them?

– No. I am just fat. But thanks for noticing.

By ten, we've reached Batlow, a tiny apple-growing town at the edge of the Snowy Mountains.

– You remember coming down here when we were kids? asks Sass.

– Ye-ah, I say, my voice rising the half an octave at the end of the sentence that marks the Australian way of speaking.

We both start to sing.

Oh I'd love to live in Batlow
As much as I'd like to live
In a great big tree
With a couple of dags
And a wombat.

– What the fuck is that? asks Alice.
– Don't you remember that song?
– We didn't come on that trip.
– That's right.
– We went skiing at Tumut or some other dud resort that gets about six inches of snow but that year they had the most snow in like, fifty years. It was fantastic.
– We stayed in Batlow and we made up that song.
– It must be a happy memory, says Alice, sarky as ever.
– It was cool. That was the first time we ever saw snow.
It was fun. Abigail and Shamus and Megan, Uncle Truman and Aunt Sandra. We were a family. We had snowball fights. It was the scene in the movie before the parents die in the car crash.
– I remember Bailey skiing. There was this quarry, that you weren't meant to ski in, but Bailey kept going it, hurtling down this slope that was almost vertical.
– He's a mad bugger.
– He was eight or something like that. He'd stand at the top of the hill and all these older skiers would stop to watch him and away he'd go. He did it so many times that other people tried to have a go, and they'd dig in a ski, crash, fuck their knees and hobble off to the ski patrol.
Sass is smiling at the thought of her brother.
– He's a mad bugger.

*

We get to Tumbarumba just after 11 am, buy some fresh bread then push through to the hills, over a ridge and then, in a gash in the pine forest, we see the prison.

– Top spot, says Alice.

– Yeah, I reckon. Worse places to be in jail.

We wind down the hill until we reach a grey stone ceremonial-looking gate that says *Massif Correctional Facility* with a huge sign telling us all the things we can't do and bring inside the prison. Alice pulls the car into the parking lot, trampling over a pair of muddy runners and underpants.

– It was a quick escape, I say.

As we're unloading the car, two overweight prison officers with braiding on their shoulders stroll up the road holding two-way radios. I jog over and they look at me like I'm an insect.

– Excuse me, gentlemen, can I ask you a question?

– Of course.

– We're here to see my cousin and we've brought him some books to read . . .

– You can't bring those in.

– Well, he said he'd signed all the paperwork and that it had been approved.

The older of the two, whose shirt looks like it belonged to a drunk admiral, flares his nostrils and shakes his head emphatically.

– Who would have done that?

– I don't know.

– That's impossible.

– He said it was all approved.

– Well, I'm the one who would have approved it, and I haven't, so I don't know who would have.

– So we should leave the books in the car?

– Don't bring 'em with you.

I walk back to the car.

– We can't bring the books.
– Why not?
– I dunno.
– Fuckin' screws.
– Yeah, fuckin' screws.
– Listen to us.

The processing unit for visitors is a square building split by a pane of safety glass to separate the screws from the visitors. There's a fat chick and guy with nightclub-ready hair, both in uniform, waiting. As soon as the male screw sees Alice, he comes out through a door and gives us a smile.

– Hi. How you doing?

We explain who we're here to see and the screw chuckles.

– Ah, Bailey Black. He doesn't like getting out of bed in the morning.

We laugh as well. None of us has visited a relative in prison before. We don't want them soaking Bailey with the fire hose because we've been rude.

– So what have we got here? he says, examining our goody bags.

We've stuck to the rules scrupulously. All the food items we've brought are store-sealed in plastic, there's no seafood, no marinades or sauces or any dressing for the salads.

– You never know what people put in them, jokes the screw. He's mid twenties, with a deep, even tan that suggests nudist beach. He can't take his eyes off Alice.

– Ah, I don't know about those, he says and points at the handful of salt and pepper sachets we knocked off from Maccas.

– What's wrong with them?

– The salt's fine, but the pepper, they use it to throw the sniffer dogs off.

– Really? says Alice.

The screw wants us to know he's the man. He scoops them back into our carry bag.

– I won't say anything if you don't, he says, then opens my plastic bag.

– What's this, then?

– Cheese, I say.

– One, two, three . . . five different types?

– Bailey likes cheese.

The screw is bewildered.

– Cheese? Very fancy. We've never had anyone bring in cheese before.

– That's our family for you, says Alice. – Very fancy.

It's a bit creepy how well these two are getting on and for a moment I consider the possibility that Alice may find love in a minimum-security prison at the foot of the Snowy Mountains. It seems like a good moment to mention the books again.

– Excuse me, mate. We brought some books down for Bailey that we've got in the car and I was wondering how we go about giving them to him.

The guy's got a screw's nose for rorting and senses I'm trying to work an angle.

– Books? I never seen Bailey Black pick up a book.

– Well, he asked us to bring them with us.

– There's a million books in the library.

There's a shimmer of hostility to the way he says it, like the faint pong in a dunny an hour after someone's done a nasty shit. His face hardens and for a second I see him with his baton, after lock-up, taking pleasure harassing my cousin.

Bailey doesn't get his books.

The visiting area looks like it could be in any suburban school or hospital. There's a few posters on the walls, tables and chairs and huddled families talking to pissed-off-looking men with goatees, wearing green shirts and pants. We wait in the picnic area, which is shaded with trees and has a BBQ in the centre. The cage around the gas bottles would be more difficult to break out of than the fence surrounding the prison.

– Wouldn't be hard to get out of here, would it?
– I guess most of the blokes inside don't want to get out.

We sweep some blossoms off a table and wait for Bailey. When we see him emerge through the waiting room, Sass hides behind a tree. He opens the door, looking clear-eyed and huge across the shoulders.

– Hello, mate, I say and hug him, then he grabs Alice.

A moment later, Sass appears and he laughs his billygoat cackle at her ruse.

– Sass, ahhh, I didn't know you were coming. Look at youse.

We sit down to the cheese and Bailey starts telling us about his mates.

– Me cellie's a good bloke. They're all good blokes in here. There's no real hard cases.

– So what'd your cell mate do?
– He stabbed a bloke eight times. But the bloke deserved it.
– Of course he did, Bailey, says Sass.

We're all leaning in like perves at a public pool, listening for Bailey's next revelation. The screw with the good hair walks into the yard to do a lap and make sure no one's building a nuclear device with chicken chips, sausages and plastic egg flippers. Bailey drops his voice as he watches him.

– He's a cunt, that Brett, says Bailey.
– Is he? He seemed alright to me, I say and Alice makes a face.
– He's a creep, he was making my skin crawl.
– He waxes his legs. I gave him shit about it and now the cunt won't leave me alone.

– He took a shine to Alice.

– Fuck, that's how observant I am. I thought it was love between you two.

– I was just being nice so he wouldn't rape Bailey in his cell with a broom handle.

Bailey laughs.

– There's none of that in here. Or none I know about. They keep it pretty dark.

– Maybe you're just not pretty enough?

Bailey considers it with an arched eyebrow.

– Could be, there's some good-looking blokes in here.

– See, there you go, you're developing an eye for cock already.

– Can you stop it, Ned.

None of us is trying to be pushy, but we're all circling the subject of What Bailey Will Do When He Gets Out. I buy some Cokes and ginger beers, and Bailey gets around to the subject himself. He holds up his can.

– This is the closest I've come to the piss for six months.

– Ginger beer?

– Yeah.

– Don't they use shoe polish and potato peels and make moonshine under the beds?

– Nah, mate. Bit too much hassle, though I've had a few smokes.

– Dope?

– Yeah, they get it in. Me old cellie had a mate who was burying a bag for him out in the pine forest for when we go out to work and he was selling it.

– For how much?

– A lot fuckin' more than what I paid outside, laughs Bailey.

– As long as you're not paying in sexual favours, sweetheart, says Sass and pats his arm.

– I don't really miss it, eh, or the piss. Though sometimes when you get back from workin' all day, you wouldn't mind a cold one.

– Or seven, I say.

Bailey nods. He's tasting them in his head.

– But as soon as I get out, I'm straight to the Tumby pub and then I'm gonna fuckin' get on it for about a week before I settle down and work out what I'm gonna do.

There's a bit of sly glancing around the table.

– Got anything else in mind?

– I've got another mate in here, Wongie, and he's keen to see me stop doin' crime so he's said he'll hook me up with a job selling real estate.

– Real estate?

– Investment properties. He said he made four million before he went in. All I got to do is sell one property a week and I'll be making about a hundred and fifty thousand a year, he says.

– And this Wongie? What's he in for?

– It's either heroin or speed. He got done with it in his car, but the car was parked and they couldn't prove it was his and they did some kind of deal with him.

– What? He's an informant? I say.

– I don't think he's a dog, or else he'd be in the bonehouse at Goulburn, not here, but he worked something out.

– What's his name?

– Wong.

– So he's Asian?

– Yeah, Chinese.

– He wouldn't happen to be mixed up with the Triads, would he?

Bailey frowns and rubs the side of his face.

– Yeah, I'm pretty sure he is.

395

We're struggling to hide our expressions.

– But he's a good bloke and it's not like he's a killer.

After a few hours, we run out of things to talk about and Bailey cracks the door for us.

– Youse can go when you want. I don't mind.

– It's okay.

– Nah, all the boys are waiting for me to train with them, so I don't mind.

So we start to collect our shit, bag everything, and I watch as Bailey scoops the sachets of pepper, gives me a wink, a hug and then he's gone.

Driving back up the mountain, it strikes me clear. After all the years we've been trying to turn Bailey onto the straight and narrow, find him real jobs, get him away from the drugs, all the deep and meaningfuls at family gatherings – we might as well have been trying to convince a Labrador to eat a rocket salad or Papa Giuseppe to give up making linguine.

– Bailey likes it, I say. – It's his identity, he likes being able to tell us that they send all the dogs to Goulburn, and that you don't fuck with the Lebs out at Parklea, it's his thing.

Sass sits in the back seat staring out the window and does a little belch.

THE LOST BOYS

We could probably make the drive back to Sydney, but Alice and Sass seem keen to stay overnight somewhere and get on the drink.

– You can't beat a Chinese meal in the country, says Alice, but I think she senses Sass wants the night off from her kids and since she's not expected back, she's getting on it. We decide on Yass, because it's about halfway back to Sydney and it looks like there's a few pubs for us to stumble between.

The first pub we stop at doesn't have rooms, or the second, despite both having huge signs on their roofs that say *Accommodation* and *Sleep with us tonight*. The third pub, the Commercial, doesn't have a sign, but it does have rooms.

– That makes plenty of bloody sense, doesn't it? says Alice as we lug our bags upstairs. The girls have scored a double room outside the men's dunnies and their door looks like it's been recently repaired after being kicked in.

– You have to pay extra for that, I say.
– Nice touch.
– I'm only down the hall. I'll probably wake up by the time the sixth bloke's going through you.
– You're a sweetheart.

We prop downstairs at the public bar and the bushies give us the once-over but seem placated when all three of us order middies of New.

– No fancy fuckin' sheila's drinks tonight, says Alice.
– Up your skirt.

It's a pretty sad old crew in the pub, except for the barmaid, who's remarkably attractive and quick witted. The beer's painfully cold and the Porky Bits Sass insists on eating are going down well. There's an avalanche of afternoon sun pouring in through the far window, cutting through the smoke, so we wangle a table next to a gibberer in a green singlet who's got the body of a thirty year old and the grey-beard head of a sixty-plus bikie.

– You can't fuckin' trust no cunt, specially those Americans, he says to me and winks.

He wanders off back to his table to continue monstering a bloke in a dirty VB shirt and the tarted-up town beauty of twenty years ago who now looks like a rugby union international wearing his ex-wife's dress.

At the next table there's a group of hardened bushies who're all on schooners, smoking durries. One of the guys is wearing blue Stubbies with work boots and Parramatta socks and has remarkable tanned thighs. I keep looking at them flex as he steps on and off his footrest telling a young bloke next to him a story.

This dude is the youngest guy in the pub, at about twenty-three, twenty-four years of age. He's got gel in his hair and he's wearing a Quiksilver shirt that was fashionable for about three weeks in Strathfield four years ago, but he sets the standard for happening in Yass. He's looking at Thigh Man likes he's a god. Fuck me.

– I feel like I'm in a museum for blokes who don't want to go home to their wives, I say.

– Well, there's at least one wife who doesn't want to go home either, says Sass.

We can't find a Chinese restaurant and have to settle for the new Australian national cuisine.

– Thai restaurants, I thought we'd escape them in Yass, says Alice.

The food's actually pretty good and laughably cheap, and after a bottle of white we stumble out and head to one of the three town pubs we've not had a drink in. We walk in and there's six guys at the bar, none of them talking to each other. They're all sitting on beers or bourbons, staring up at TVs showing either a rugby league game or the Adelaide trots.

– All happening here, says Alice.

It takes a minute or so for the blokes to realise there's actual women in the bar and that one of them is a great sort. Then the head-turning starts and it's not discreet. I quieten down the part of me that's offended – these blokes don't know the chicks are my cousins. They've obviously sized me up and thought, Fuck it, if it gets ugly, I can take him.

One of the guys, seated directly in front of us, is wearing a cheap nylon football jumper from one of the local teams, the Binalong Warriors. Once he twigs to Alice being behind him, he cranes around every twenty seconds in a manner that has me worrying he's going to tear a neck muscle.

– Must have Binalong time between roots, I say to Alice.

– Someone had to say it first, says Sass.

Old mate Binalong is drunker than Poland. After his fourth

gawk back at the girls, he almost falls off his stool, rights himself, then goes over anyway, spilling his can of Jack Daniel's and Coke all over the pale blue of his jumper.

– You alright there, champ? says Alice, whose attention far outweighs the four bucks he's done on a spilled drink.

– It was almost gone, he says.

At first I can't work out if the guy is extremely drunk or has a speech impediment. Then I realise it's both.

– Yoozefromass? (Youse from Yass?)

– Nah, mate, we're from Sydney.

– Yoozeavinadreenk? (Youse having a drink?)

– Yeah, we got one right here, mate.

As the guy talks, I get glimpses of inside his mouth. It looks like he has enough teeth for two people, with dual sets of molars running next to each other.

– You play footy? asks Alice.

– Nah, but we had a good team, eh? But they've moved it into the Canberra comp because we ran out of players.

When he nearly knocks over our table staggering, the girls finish their drinks and we move on.

– Did you see that fuckin' guy's teeth? I ask them.

We walk along the main street and there's a group of teenage kids sitting on pushbikes, staring enraptured through one of the side windows of the Criterion Hotel. We slow as we pass, thinking there might be a stink going on inside, but it's just three guys with beer guts playing pool.

– Ahh, see what they've got to look forward to, says Alice.

We decide to head back to our own pub and sit on high stools to have a final few coldies. We're drinking for fifteen or twenty minutes when our mate in the Binalong footy jumper staggers in, props at the bar and, amazingly, is served. He stares blindly around the pub three or four times before he sees us and shuffles over with his can of Jack Daniel's.

— Heydoyuzmemberme? (Hey, do you remember me?)

— Yes, mate, we only saw you twenty minutes ago.

— I was looking around and didn't recognise youse, eh?

I realise we're not going to get rid of the guy, so I engage him.

— What's that on your face, mate?

He blinks at me.

— What's that on your face? You cut?

There's a large brown slash on one cheek. The guy finally wipes at it and looks at his hand.

— It's only rum, eh?

— How long you been on the drink for, fella?

— Since Friday, eh?

— That's a nice session.

— I came into town Friday arvo after work and then I lost the boys and I slept at this bloke's house, so I just started in again this morning.

It's painful to watch Binalong talk. He looks like he has marbles in his mouth. It's not hard to imagine he's the town clown.

— Whattaya do for work, mate?

— Farmhand, eh.

— What's that entail?

He looks at me.

— What do you have to do as a farmhand?

— Whatever. Fix fences, dig ditches. Whatever they want.

— Pay alright?

— Keeps me in these ones, eh? he says and holds up his rum.

There's a loneliness and sadness vapouring off the guy that I can't even penetrate. It's not that he doesn't want to be happy – he wouldn't even know how.

– This is all a bit grim, isn't it? I say to the girls as Binalong goes for another can.

– I don't think that boy's had too many hugs in his life, says Alice.

A big shaven-head guy, wearing a white shirt open at the chest, walks in and looks us up and down. He obviously knows Binalong but isn't too keen to chat until he sees him join the girls and me, so he wanders over.

– Eh.

I see through his open shirt he's got a spray of tattoos across his chest and shoulders.

– Nice cartoons, mate, I say and he looks like he might hit me.

– What?

– Nice ink there, I say and point at his tatts.

– Oh. Yeah. It's me life story, he says and opens his shirt to show us one side of his chest and arm are covered in screaming skulls.

– Pretty scary life story.

– It's what it was like growing up on the meat trucks, he says.

– Whattaya do now?

– Drive a meat truck.

The dude's name is Shane and he promptly announces he's been diagnosed with manic depression and isn't allowed to drink.

– This is the only pub in town that hasn't barred me, he says.

– What's that then? says Sass, pointing at his red-coloured mixed drink.

– It's a fire engine. It's cordial.

I imagine these two wandering the streets of Yass like wraiths after closing. Neither has a girlfriend. When Shane announces

that he's feeling angry and he just wants to smash something, we bid them both goodnight.
 – Youse don't have to go, says Binalong.
 – Yeah, we do, mate.

POT PLANTS

Scorps and I are sitting on the grass at middle watching the sunrise. We've spent the night drinking with the boys at the Hotel Bondi to celebrate Scorps moving to Hawaii to go to university. About midnight, Birdy pulled out some trips and we leapt on him like a litter of hungry puppies, licking him happily in our enthusiasm. We dropped and an hour later decided it would be a good idea to dress in some of my girl-friend's clothes. My skirt's too small, Scorps's dress has a split up the side.

– I feel like this is the last day of my youth, I say.

– I dunno about that, mate, but it's the end of something.

– We have to grow up now, we have to get serious about our jobs and be someone.

– I love it here, he says and he pulls out a handful of grass then flicks at the bleeding blades. – I just feel like there's something more out there for me, like if I stay here too much longer my roots will grow too used to a small pot and I'll never be able to have the big life I want.

We're kids but we both know just about everything worth knowing. We're almost right.

Walking down the street in our skirts and floppy women's hats we know this is life as it is meant to be: not too serious, a free-form adventure. As we sit on the edge of the grass and feel the cool air turn luke, the garbage trucks grumble by and the sun winks above the surf. We lie back in the frosty vapours of the acid, pulling strands of meaning out of the staggering seagulls and the joggers, and the cocked foreheads when they see the two boys in dresses chuckling exhausted to themselves.

ONE LAST CIGGIE

And then it's morning again and I listen to the rain outside, thankful that it removes the option of running, the beach, of unveiling myself to the world. Unveiling myself. I get up unsteadily and walk into the lounge room and look out the windows at the ocean, at the view I'm paying so much money for and never seem to use. There's joggers on the Bronte to Bondi walking path, just smudges of colour in the grey morning but colour nonetheless.

In the shower I think about Shane and his tattoos and the boy from Binalong and his eight hundred teeth. I start to cry, for them, for me, because we're all so fucking clueless how to make it work. The shower curtain touches cold onto my back and I thrash around, tearing it off its plastic rings, taking it as further evidence life will never roll my way. I watch the water spatter unobstructed onto my discarded boxers.

The towel is still damp from yesterday, because it's been in a ball in my room. I dry myself while I walk towards my dark computer.

Unveil myself. I don't even bother to get dressed, just sit at the keyboard, the grain of the towel biting into my arse as I type.

ACKNOWLEDGEMENTS

I'd like to thank Adam Gibson, who first planted the idea of *The Lost Boys* all those years ago at North Bondi, as well as Kinga Burza, for resuscitating the concept in Paris and Craig Henderson for being the first person to read it and say, 'It fuckin' rocks'.

I also want to thank my mother, Julie, for telling me to just write the pieces and let the puzzle solve itself and my stepfather, Sean, for his unconditional love and support. Neither of you understands how huge your input was.

Thanks also to Robyn Townsend for listening and Giles Clarke for stating the obvious. Ro Markson was also instrumental in encouraging this work.

I want to thank my agent, Sophie Hamley, for getting back to me four hours after I emailed the book, telling her it was the 'greatest thing written in Australia this year'. You didn't know me from a bar of soap and you were an instant fan.

I also want to thank my publisher, Alex Craig, for

championing the novel and seeing the heart of the story beyond the 'fucks' and 'cunts' (and for using both words so freely during our first dinner).

Thanks also to Sarina Rowell, my editor, for recognising import in Elle Macpherson's shit, and Julia Stiles for seeing that the Zeitgeist need not look like a *Hello* magazine shoot. Also, Jeremy Nicholson for his beautiful cover design (it takes a surfer to know the feeling) and Uge 'Spiro' Tan for the cover photo.

Lastly, I want to thank Kym Ellery for giving me a safe, loving place to write this novel and, most of all, Paul Andreacchio, my muse and my mate, whose ideas, generosity, patience and plain goodness made this work possible. I always thought muses were meant to be beautiful and female, but you'll do me, Pablo.

'Time'
Roger Waters/Nicholas Mason/David Gilmour/Rick Wright
© 1973 (Renewed) Hampshire House Publishing Corp
For Australia & New Zealand
Alfred Publishing (Australia) Pty Ltd
All Rights Reserved   Used By Permission

'In The Air Tonight'
© 1981 Philip Collins Ltd
For Australia and New Zealand: EMI Music Publishing Australia Pty Limited (ABN 83 000 040 951) PO Box 35, Pyrmont, NSW 2009, Australia
International copyright secured. All rights reserved. Used by permission.

'Have A Cigar'
Roger Waters
© 1975 (Renewed) Roger Waters Overseas Ltd
For Australia & New Zealand
Alfred Publishing (Australia) Pty Ltd
All Rights Reserved   Used By Permission

'Another Brick In The Wall'
Roger Waters
©1979 Roger Waters Overseas Ltd
For Australia & New Zealand
Alfred Publishing (Australia) Pty Ltd
All Rights Reserved   Used By Permission

'Once In A Lifetime'
David Byrne/Chris Frantz/Tina Weymouth
©1980 WB Music Corp, Index Music Inc & E.G. Music Ltd
All rights on behalf of itself & Index Music Inc administered by
WB Music Group.
For Australia & New Zealand
Alfred Publishing (Australia) Pty Ltd
All Rights Reserved   Used By Permission

'Gimme Head'
Words and music by Geoffrey Turner
(c) Rondor Music Australia Pty Ltd.
All rights reserved. International copyright secured.
Reprinted with permission.

'That's What Friends Are For'
Burt Bacharach/Carole Bayer Sager
©1985 WB Music Corp, New Hidden Valley Music Company,
Warner-Tamerlane Publishing Corp & Carole Bayer Sager
Music Inc
For Australia & New Zealand
Alfred Publishing (Australia) Pty Ltd
All Rights Reserved   Used By Permission